THE
SCATTERED

Richard Holledge

COPYRIGHT © 2012

Richard Holledge
All rights reserved.

Disclaimer

ISBN-13: 978-1477457672

ISBN-10: 1477457674

AUTHOR'S NOTE

I first heard of the Acadians when on a journalistic assignment for The Times of London to write about Louisiana's signature pepper sauce, Tabasco.

There was a mention in my guide book about the expulsion of these French-speaking people by the British from Acadia (or Nova Scotia as they called it) at the start of the Seven Years War in 1755. The guide book mentioned their slow and difficult exodus to the southern state.

A few years later, by chance, I was reading *Crucible of War,* an account of the battle for power in North America between France and Britain by historian Fred Anderson, who described the expulsion as "chillingly reminiscent of modern 'ethnic cleansing' operations...executed with a coldness and calculation rarely seen in other wartime operations."

What my guide book did not explain was that most of the expelled Acadians were sent to the British colonies in North America—and treated shamefully—and that one group was prevented from landing in Virginia and shipped to concentration camps in Britain.

After six painful years they were condemned to dismal exile in France with many compelled to take painful detours to tropical hell holes in Haiti and Guyana and even the bleak outpost of the Falkland Islands.

This struck me as an extraordinary story with many resonances to the way unwanted and dispossessed people are treated by powerful countries today. Furthermore, though the facts are known by many in the Acadian community, this is a saga that has yet to be told in a way that captures the anguish, the sheer fortitude, and the will to survive of this small band of 'cousins' as they called each other.

There was a Jambo LeBlanc, the victim—and hero—of this book. He was 26 when the British seized him, his wife, and two children from their home in the village of Grand Pré. That was on October 27, 1755. Thirty years later on June 29, 1785 LeBlanc landed in New Orleans and settled nearby.

I have visited New Orleans several times since Hurricane Katrina on writing assignments and met LeBlancs, Terriots, Richards and Heberts—all names shared by those who endured the Great Expulsion. Now, of course, they are called Cajuns.

ACKNOWLEDGMENTS

Carolyn Cavele who inspired the idea.

Leslie Holledge who made the book possible.

INSPIRATIONS

"Waste are those pleasant farms, and the farmers forever

departed!

Scattered like dust and leaves, when the mighty blasts of October

Seize them, and whirl them aloft, and sprinkle them far over the

ocean.

Naught but tradition remains of the beautiful village of Grand

Pre...

–from **Evangeline** by Henry Longfellow

"Stuff happens."

–Donald Rumsfeld, US Secretary of State, 2003

Book One

ONE

Grand-Pré, Acadia

September 5, 1755. 3 p.m.

Men and Lads of Ten

"Don't go," she said, fixing him with those odd eyes of hers.

"I have to."

"Come on!" shouted a soldier. "Keep moving. Name?"

"LeBlanc."

"Le what?"

"LeBlanc. Jambo LeBlanc."

"Spell it."

"L-E..."

"Never mind. Get in there." The soldier shoved him, catching him sharply on the elbow with his musket butt, and sent him sprawling over the step into the church. "Next."

Marguerite had hung on to him when he turned to go. She had hoisted the baby on to her hip and briefly let go of the boy's hand to hold her husband's arm with a grip as tight as a tourniquet, but he shook his head resignedly, kissed her and pulled away. Then he turned and kissed her again. He stroked little Osite's cheek and tousled Jean-Baptiste's hair before pushing his way through the crowd gathered outside the palisade that the British had built around the church. Who would be foolhardy enough to ignore a summons that threatened '*pain of forfeiting goods and chattels in default*'?

"Wait here," he said to her. "I'll be back in a minute."

The order was to be in St. Charles by 3 p.m.—just the men and *lads of ten*—and right on time they started to shuffle through the corridor of soldiers, shoulder welded to shoulder like a wall of red, staring straight to the front, blank-eyed. As they reached the church door they were jostled up against the wall and searched, arms held high.

"What are you looking for?" asked Jambo.

"Guns, knives, anything you might use against us."

"We don't use weapons against people," said Jambo. "That is not our way."

"And we certainly don't bring them into church," said Pierre Richard, the trapper.

"We can't take chances," said the lieutenant who was taking a register of their names. He seemed to be in charge, but he looked absurdly young— *about twelve,* scoffed brother Charles. What little authority he had was undermined by the way he stood—as if he was balancing awkwardly on the sloping deck of a ship in a gale. It was only when he came close that Jambo realized the Englishman had a wooden leg.

"That's the lot!" shouted the precarious officer to his commander, who was watching from the doorway of the abbot's house. A Union flag had hung outside it since the troops had arrived, and judging by the restless guards outside, the meetings and the to-ing and fro-ing of messengers, it had been taken over as their makeshift headquarters. Jambo reckoned that was why Father Chaulvreux had been arrested a few weeks before and dragged out of his home, leaving it free for the British Colonel.

"I make it 418, including the youngsters," said the lieutenant.

"Get them in order," replied his chief, "and be quick."

Inside, the villagers milled around, waiting to discover why they had been summoned. *As nervy as sheep when they have been rounded up for slaughter,* thought Jambo, but he immediately pushed the image out of his mind. There was a low hubbub as the men made jokes to hide their apprehension—a febrile jocularity emphasized by sudden spikes of loud, forced, laughter. Only the fathers, grim-faced, wrapping protective arms around their fearful sons, stayed silent. The boys reminded Jambo of the young deer he had startled in a forest glade the week before—timid, wide-eyed and poised for flight.

What can they possibly want with these children? he wondered. *They're scared stiff. How can they be so heartless to frighten them so?*

There was a flurry at the door and the one-legged lieutenant shouted, "Attention!"

The soldiers straightened up, guns and bayonets at the ready. In an instant they were transformed from slouching bystanders into a threatening force. An enemy.

The British colonel paused at the door. Jambo had seen him only from a distance. Some of the time he would perch calmly on an ammunition box outside the abbot's house, sipping tea, or perhaps something stronger, while he listened to his officers, then he would leap to his feet, his mood swinging to fraught and furious, giving orders, dictating message, and impatiently grabbing letters delivered by the rangers who galloped into the village and set the dogs barking. In the evening when things were quieter, he scribbled intensely in what looked to be a journal.

In that late summer heat, his face was almost as crimson as his military frock coat. Hardly surprising given that the heavy uniform, which stretched to cover his solid frame, looked as if it weighed a ton, and the tricorn hat perched on his head was so tight that his wig was forced out comically, almost at right angles, to his fleshy, perspiring cheeks.

Rather than stride commandingly to the centre of the church, the colonel slipped, rather self-effacingly, through the crowd to take his place behind the oak table that served as the altar. He made a gesture as if he was patting the air to bring his reluctant audience to silence.

"Gentlemen..."

TWO

The Village Green

September 2, 1755. Three days earlier.

Noises Off

It had been three days since the notice demanding their attendance had been nailed to the door of a barn next to the green.

The villagers had gathered around as Rene LeBlanc, the notary, adjusted his horn-rimmed spectacles and read a notice addressed to the '*Inhabitants of the district of Grand-Pré etc.*

'*I order and strictly enjoin all the inhabitants as both old men and young men, as well as the lads of ten years of age, to attend the church in Grand-Pré the fifth instant that we may impart what we are ordered to communicate to them.*'

"What time?" asked someone at the back of the crowd.

"Three of the clock."

Rene had run his fingers though yellowing hair.

'*No excuse will be admitted on any pretence whatsoever.*'

"They don't usually order us around like this, do they," said Jambo.

"Why not just whistle us up like they normally do?" wondered Pierre, his bulk blocking the view of many in the small crowd.

"All amounts to the same bloody thing," said Francois. "Give us your harvest, hand over your sheep and cattle. The bastards."

During the years of occupation the villagers had become resigned to troops marching in, setting up camp, and commandeering supplies for the months ahead—the best of the harvest, the pick of the cattle. They never paid, but the transaction guaranteed the villagers would be left alone for the rest of the year. Everyone grumbled but it was all quite cordial. The soldiers would strut around, make sure their wishes were met, and then enjoy themselves partridge shooting, even enlisting the local lads to act as beaters. But this was the third time in less than a year that they had come visiting.

To the villagers' consternation, instead of arriving over land as usual in a noisy flurry of dust and a retinue of high spirited boys and girls—even Jambo could remember as a lad how a cheery soldier had let him carry his musket—they had arrived silently by sea at dawn and beached on Boudrot Point before marching along the levees, bayonets bristling, and up the hill into Grand-Pré. There were no cheery soldiers this time. The children were brushed aside.

"Maybe they just want to get to know us b-b-better," joked Charles.

The soldiers had pitched their tents on the green, and within days had churned it into a muddy mess, littered with rubbish and wasted food. Their smoldering fires spread a pall of smoke that hung miserably over the village smelling of grease and half-cooked cabbage. And as if to show their contempt for the well-ordered existence into which they had intruded, they dumped their slops and left-overs—sheep heads, pigs' carcasses, gnawed bones—outside the encampment in rotting piles.

"Right by the gate to the graveyard," grumbled his mother Jeanne indignantly. She was so hard working, so meticulous in her care of home and children, that she regarded any assault on the fabric of the village as a personal affront.

"That's the British for you," said his father. "Think they own the place."

"No manners," said Marguerite.

Contempt at their uncouth guests turned to outrage when the soldiers broke into the church.

"Come quick," urged Marguerite who had raced to them in the fields with the news. "They are smashing down the door."

"Looks like they are using it as a storeroom for their provisions and ammunition," said mother as the men arrived, breathless, to witness the last of the soldiers straining to shift a crate of ordnance.

"Perhaps if they had not imprisoned Father Chaulvreux for teaching the true faith they might have been able to use the key," said Jambo. "It would have saved a lot of bother."

Yes, their behavior had been more hostile than usual and this summons was distinctly peremptory, even threatening, yet, even then, as they clustered round the notice, he assumed that it was just a matter of the British stepping up their demands for the food they had worked so hard to cultivate and the livestock they had so carefully nurtured.

"Every time they come it means less for us," said Oliver Terriot, the cobbler, hopping with vexation. Years of repairing the villagers' footwear had made him short-sighted, and he wore glasses that were so thick that he looked positively shifty. And worse, for such a little fellow, the hours hunched over his work had made one shoulder slightly higher than the other, which made him comically lopsided.

"Reminds me of a rather sprightly question m-m-mark," joked Charles.

"It's always the same," went on the cobbler. "I'll spend my time repairing their boots and then they will march off without paying a sou."

"They're sh-sh-shameless," said Charles. "They work up a thirst shooting our p-p-partridges and drink my b-b-beer without paying a cent."

"It's bad enough that they force us to slaughter our hogs for them," said Jambo. "But they actually expect us to round up the cattle and sheep, and then drive them across to Chedbuctou, or Halifax, as they insist on calling their new capital."

"Oliver's right, they never pay," said Landry. "The number of times I have translated for them. Not a penny."

"Perhaps you should try to sell them the flour from your mill," joked Oliver. "Your bread is better than your English."

"They're pests," said Francois. "Greedy swine."

"Oh Francois, don't get so angry," said Marguerite, who was one of the few villagers who could charm the plowman out of his frequent rages. No easy matter. He was a turbulent fellow, as beefy as a prize bull with hands as big as serving dishes, coarsened into leather from years whacking the backsides of his oxen and heaving at his plow.

"It makes you so red in the face and that's most unfetching, dear Francois," she said sweetly. "I used to think it was because you spend all day in the fields pushing and shoving that plow of yours but now I'm not so sure. Maybe it's because you try to cool down by drinking so much spruce beer that you're always losing your temper and looking for a fight."

"I'm sorry," mumbled Francois, chastened. "I'll watch my tongue."

"And your fists," she said. "They always land you in trouble."

She and Jambo had once asked him about the ragged, white scar, which ran like a snake from behind his right ear to his neck bone and he had looked sheepish and muttered: "I tripped over and cut myself on the plow blade."

They were teasing him. Everyone knew he had been in a fearsome set-to with a tavern owner in Annapolis who had refused to serve him more drink.

"Poor Francois," said Marguerite. "That's the problem; he can't find a wife so he settles for the bottle."

But now they were all listening intently to what the notary had to say.

"I think demands for a few ears of corn and a cow or two more will be the least of it," said Rene, puffing on his clay pipe. "Don't forget, we have a new governor now, this fellow Charles Lawrence. This will be about the oath. He will want to make his mark, and the best way for him to impress his chiefs in London is to force us to swear allegiance to the crown."

"That ass King George," said Francois.

They all paid attention to Rene. As befitted his importance as notary, he was one of the few who could read and write and had a sharp tongue that cut many adversaries down to size. He was more than a thinker and a lawyer, he was also a shrewd businessman who traded with the British, the French, and even the Mi'kmaq Indians who still skulked around the peninsular, and ferreted out deals, driving a hard bargain with anyone who had the money for the sheep, cattle, and furs he had to sell.

Jambo had seen him buy a horse at one end of the market and sell it half an hour later for a profit at the other. But, perhaps what impressed the villagers more than his money or his learning was that at 71, he had been widowed twice and fathered 20 children.

"The old man's still got it," they would leer admiringly, but for Jambo he was a revered uncle, a man whose wisdom, good sense, and sound faith made him the example he followed more than any other.

"If it really is about swearing allegiance to the British, it's no problem for me," said Jambo. "King George or King Louis, who cares. After all, the reason our forefathers left France was because its rulers showed no justice or loyalty to its people. We might speak French, but we owe them nothing."

"We don't owe anyone a thing," said the cobbler.

"The British don't see it like that," said Rene. "This time I fear they might have decided to put extra pressure on us to toe the line."

"But why?" asked Charles. "How often do we have to p-p-put up with this charade?"

"We seem to have the same argument every year," said Oliver.

"Since '13," said Jambo's father. "The year the French were forced to hand us over to this mob. Treaty of Utrecht, it was."

The group looked at him with surprise at this unexpected display of knowledge. He was better known for whiling away his hours in the tavern playing dice and getting drunk than for his knowledge of history.

But Jambo had heard it many times before. Father's little joke.

The older man nodded, pleased with himself. "It was the year our Marie was born, that's how I know. Daughters, such a trouble for a father." And he cackled.

"Quite right brother—about the date anyway—but the problem

throughout these forty years, as you all know, or should by now, "said Rene patiently," is that we have refused to agree with the clause in the oath that insists we take up arms on their behalf. That's what really enrages the British."

"But, why should we?" asked Pierre.

"Let them fight their own battles," said Oliver.

"We are neutral," said Jambo. "We fight for no one."

"How many times do we have to t-t-tell them?" asked Charles.

"Everything is changing, and changing fast," said Rene. "Just think of all the fighting that has been going on across America between the French and British. It's reaching a climax, I tell you. Look what happened only last month when the British laid siege to Beausejour."

"Who would have thought the French battalion would surrender the fort so easily," said Pierre.

"Less than two weeks. How could they be so f-f-feeble?" asked Charles.

"Then a contingent comes here," continued Rene, gesturing at the encampment. "Did we not stand on this spot only a month ago and watch the British sail up the bay toward Beausejour, only a day's sail away? Forty ships was it? Two thousand men? Well, these troops despoiling our green are the victors of the siege.

"This is not the usual mercenary crew who can't wait to get home, but highly trained soldiers from Boston with a year to run on their commission, and their colonel—that's his signature on the notice—is one of the colonies' most professional officers. Lawrence will want to keep him and his men busy, and it's an obvious move to station them in Grand Pré on their way home."

"He is the devil," said Francois.

"He is certainly dangerous," said the notary. "He is imperious, resolute, and ruthless, and he hates us. That's a dangerous combination. Taking the fort is not just a feather in the cap for him, no, what has delighted him as much as routing the French is that he discovered that there were 300 of our cousins in the fort, and many were carrying weapons."

"What is that to do with us?" asked Pierre. "Beausejour is in New France not Acadia."

"It's on the border, so it's all the same to the British. I'm afraid our men have played into his hands. Now Lawrence can tell his masters in London that he was right—that we refuse to carry arms on their behalf, but are happy to fight for the French. It is proof that we are the Papist traitors he likes to call us."

"I heard that those cousins of ours in the fort were threatened by the French commander with having their cattle and canoes confiscated, even jail, if they did not stay and help," said Oliver, wiping his leather-stained hands on his apron. "They had no choice."

"D-d-damned either way," said Charles.

"That's right," said Jambo. "It is the British who have been treacherous. I was told that their colonel said he understood our people's predicament; he realized that they had been forced under threat of death to side with the French. '*It is not your fault,*' he said. '*Have no fears. Go in peace to your farms*'."

"He arrested them a few d-d-days later, and forced them and their families to watch their homes being b-b-burnt to the ground," said Charles.

"He tricked them," said Francois. "What else would you expect of the bastard British?"

"It's barbaric, I agree," said Rene. "But—maybe you haven't heard—two days ago some of those prisoners escaped, joined forces with the Mi'kmaq Indians and ambushed the British at Sheperday. Twenty soldiers and seven officers were killed."

"Never," said Pierre. "I cannot believe our cousins would attack like that. It must have been the Indians."

"Who? Why? None of that matters," said the old man wearily. "It happened. First Beausejour, then Sheperday. Lawrence can argue that he is justified in doing what he likes to us. Look what happened to our elders who went to Halifax to present a petition begging that he drop this demand about fighting for them—arrested and thrown into prison."

Francois said, "I was there. Our delegation went in peace and they were treated like dogs. Lawrence threatened to hang our men from the battlements. How I cursed the bastards. They pinned me against a wall at knifepoint but I said, Strike, sir, if you dare. I shall be the first martyr of Acadia. You can kill my body, but you shall not kill my soul."

Some of the listeners smiled at the account; others tutted impatiently. They had heard it before and most knew he was exaggerating. After all, what would he have been doing in such an important delegation? He had spent too much time in the tavern stoking his imagination.

He was not to be stopped. "When Lawrence asked if the rest of us felt the same way, we all shouted, '*Yes sir, yes sir!*' He was apop…apoc…foaming at the mouth."

"That's all very heroic, Francois," interrupted Rene, "and we're very grateful to hear your account. Again."

Even the choleric plowman was abashed by the notary's disdain. The old man went on, "It is intemperate behavior like that which gave Lawrence the excuse to treat our elders—one hundred of our most respected councillors, mind—like criminals.

"He already has a dossier drawn up by his inspectors which, he claims, proves that we are supplying the French with arms, and he has notified London that we have allied with the Indians to cause mischief in their eastern settlements—that includes Acadia."

"A dossier! Anyone can draw up a dossier," said Jambo. "And anyone of fair mind would know it to be false."

"Of course it is, but who can gainsay him? He also claims we have been overcharging for the supplies we sell him."

"Overcharge! They just-t-t-take it," spluttered Charles.

"He told his council that we are indolent and idle. There is no doubt that he wants to punish us for our treachery whether it is true or not."

"So you think these troops have been ordered here to teach us a lesson?" asked Pierre.

"I fear they might be," said Rene. "What I do know is that there is nothing Lawrence and the British will stop at in their determination to conquer all of America, and that means driving out the French. We know there is fighting on the borders with New France—all the way from Beausejour to Quebec and south to Ohio—and there is threat of conflict in Europe, in the West Indies, and a place far to the east called India. They were prepared to tolerate us but now everything is coming to a head, and we stand in their way."

"Little us," said Terriot. "Who would have thought us so important?"

"Well, there is n-n-nothing we can do today," said Charles. "Instead of standing around here, let's discuss this over a d-d-rink. At the rate the British are going through my spruce beer, there will soon be n-n-none left."

"Not me," said the notary. "I have to see Benedict Bellefontaine at his farm to arrange his daughter Evangeline's dowry. The wedding with her blacksmith, young Gabriel Lajeunesse, is set for October."

"Or me," said Michel Comeau, one of Pierre Landry's mill workers. "I'm not hanging around here. I'm getting out before things turn nasty."

The rest gathered in the smoky comfort of the tavern where they supped the strong, black brew, and devoured wild game cooked in bear oil, soaking up the delicious mess with chunks of bread.

Charles, with typical insouciance, seemed more preoccupied with the news that the Bishop of Quebec had denounced them from the altar for holding parties after dark, though his noisy defiance might have been one of his ploys to lighten the mood.

"Have you heard? He actually stood in the altar two S-s-sundays ago and accused us of singing *chansons lascives.* What a pious f-f-fool. Surely he understands that night is the time for parties, and the morning for r-r-repentance. Come Jambo, where's your lute? Let's play."

They did not play together again for many years.

THREE

Grand-Pré

September 4, 1755. 6 p.m.

The Last Day

"I love this time of year," Jambo said to Marguerite two evenings after the impromptu sing-song. They had strolled from the levee, along the track up to their cottage, beside the green where the British had made their camp. She paused by the door, holding Osite, their eleven-month-old baby girl, while he went limping after three-year-old Jean-Baptiste and Poutu, their ancient dog, who had both wandered off the way they had just come.

Below them, the evening mist was creeping in from the sea. It sidled around the hanging branches of the willows that lined the red mud banks of the river, and skimmed knee high across the fields, a checker board of arable green and the tawny yellow of uncut corn.

There were a few still working, and one or two fishing boats drifted out in the bay, casting long shadows over the water, but the spirals of smoke eddying from the cottage chimneys signaled that the day's endeavors were coming to an end, and the villagers were settling down to their evening meals.

Autumn was usually the busiest of times for the villagers. As well as gathering the harvest and making sure the mills were kept creaking all day, the last of the apples and pears had to be picked, fish had to be salted and laid down for the winter alongside the slaughtered hogs and sides of beef.

As one of the community's most skilled carpenters Jambo spent every hour repairing fences to keep the cattle in and the wolves out, mending barn doors, and strengthening stable roofs.

"The sluice in the levee is fixed now," he said. "I thought I'd seen off that family of beavers last month, but obviously not judging by the way the way they chewed through the wood again. The tide has swept away a yard of the bank and the lower meadows have been flooded with salt water. I'll set another trap for them tomorrow. It just proves how the British will always have a need for us."

He took Osite from her mother's arms and hurled the gurgling infant into the air. "They don't understand how the levees work. They are too busy fighting to grow crops and have no idea how to lay traps. That's why we will always be safe despite their threats and all this talk of the oath. I know Uncle Rene fears the worst, but as long as they need to eat, we will stay untouchable."

"I just wish they would let us get on with our lives," she said. "After all, we were here before them. It is our country."

He put his arms round her. "Don't fret. It will be nothing, I'm sure. Just a lot of noise. If I were you, I would look forward to the bonnet we can make out of the beaver fur."

"I'm rather hoping for a coat," she said, with a skittish moue of pretend disappointment, and gave him a peck on the cheek. She held him close and kissed him again, urgently, as if to reassure herself that he was real, that he was still there. He was momentarily taken aback by her ardor, but then, she was always surprising him.

They were interrupted by the young lieutenant with the wooden leg who came stomping up to the door. He seemed more embarrassed at chancing on their embrace than they were.

"Good evening. My name is, er, Brooke Watson. Er, Lieutenant," he muttered.

With his pink face—scarcely in need of a shave—bright eyes and curly fair hair, even the uniform could not hide the fact that he was younger than Jambo.

"We are making a check on all the people living in the village. Is this your house?

"It is."

"Very nice. I need, er, to make an inventory of the cattle, the number of sheep, pigs and chickens. I shall have to examine the stores of corn and wheat. All your supplies and possessions, in fact."

"Why do you need to know?" asked Marguerite.

"Just routine," he was surprised to be asked such a direct question by a woman. "Makes it more efficient to, er…" He tailed off. "Your names?"

"Jambo LeBlanc, and my wife Marguerite."

"Jambo?" He looked quizzical.

"My given name is Joseph, but there are many of us called that in my family so they call me Jambo—Joseph 'dit Jambo' LeBlanc—that's how it goes."

"Ah. LeBlanc. The White family." He gave a bark of a laugh. "Jambo White." He poked around the house, listing their clothes, his tools, the wine they had stored, and the food they had laid down for the winter. "This is such a rich country," he said as he made his list. "You are very, er, lucky. I have heard a sheep can be bought for five shillings, and a bushel of wheat for eighteen pence. I envy you."

"Our luck would appear to be yours too," said Marguerite. She looked at him steadily with her unmatched eyes and gave the merest of contemptuous shrugs.

"Yes, yes, of course." He was discomfited by her tone of voice, and fussed about until, inventory completed, he said with incongruous politeness, "Well, Mister and Missus White, I have to instruct you to be in your houses by six o'clock from now on. Make sure your doors are shut, but not locked, if you don't mind. I am afraid we can't let you wander around unchecked as if you, er, owned the place."

He barked again as if he had made a joke, and limped off awkwardly, pausing to call over his shoulder. "Don't forget the meeting in the church tomorrow. Three o'clock."

"What a curious character," said Marguerite.

"Makes you wonder what the British army has come to with funny little fellows like that," said Jambo, but he was surprised by the shiver of apprehension that trembled through him.

"Did you notice he did not answer me?" asked Marguerite.

Jambo did not answer her either. Maybe Rene was right after all. Perhaps the British were planning to arrest them. Maybe they would make an example of some by throwing them into the new prison they had built in the bay off Halifax and force the rest to work the fields.

They could hear the lieutenant shouting orders as he went, and minutes later soldiers filed out of the encampment and took up positions on the ridge, along the levee and as far down to the shore as the jetty at Boudrot Point.

"There must be fifty of them," he said. "And they've all got their muskets with them."

"What are they doing?" asked Marguerite, holding on to his arm.

"They just want to frighten us," he said dismissively, determined not to show his alarm. "Show us who is in charge."

"Hard to be frightened when the man giving the orders is a one-legged lad," scoffed Marguerite, regaining her equanimity. "His limp is worse than yours."

"I hope he doesn't think I am making fun of him," said Jambo. His leg didn't hurt much anymore, but it was a constant reminder of the savage January night seven years before when he had been caught in a bear trap. He had snared a couple of rabbits and was looking forward to getting to the warmth of home and to mother making a stew of his catch, but the snow had been tumbling down for two days, driven into drifts by the wind, and burying paths he thought he knew so well that he could walk them blindfold.

Deep in the forest, up to his thighs in snow, he tripped and *snap* he was caught fast, the steel jaws holding him. Blasts of the icy blizzard whipped through the trees forcing him to burrow into the snow to protect himself from the chill and wait for dawn, unless the wolves got to him first. As night set in they had begun to circle, driven to a snarling frenzy by the smell of fear, and the taste of his blood that had spilt on to the snow. He threw them the rabbits, which the ravenous beasts leapt on and devoured within seconds. They wanted more. They wanted him. They crept closer as they sensed his growing weakness. He was sliding into unconsciousness when Pierre, the trapper and his closest friend, almost fell over him in the dark.

"I was about to give up," he said as he cut the delirious carpenter loose and carried him home. "I've been looking for hours, but if it hadn't been for that dog of yours yapping away I'd never have found you. Mind you, I couldn't have gone home without you and faced your mother. She had us all searching—your brothers, even your father. She forced him out into the gale to check the traps in the spinney."

Pierre was big as a bear, but as reliable and gentle as a pup. A good man to have by you if you were in trouble. But there was nothing he could do about the snare which had ripped apart the muscles in Jambo's calf and left it so weakened that he was never able to put his full weight on his right leg again.

FOUR

St Charles Church, Grand Pre

September 5, 1755. 3.35 p.m.

The Final Resolution

"Gentlemen ..."

The collar of the Colonel's tunic was so soaked with perspiration it was black. He pulled at it to ease its clammy grip on his neck.

"My name is Winslow," said the Englishman. "Colonel John Winslow. I am in command of this regiment."

How disconcerting it was to be in the church being addressed by this strange apparition and not the abbot. They had not been allowed in since the day the soldiers had broken down the door. *It would have taken more than a few loutish soldiers to despoil it,* he thought, as he rubbed his elbow which was sore from the musket blow that had propelled him through the door.

It was still the same house of God where he had worshipped since he was a boy, squirming restlessly on the hard pews while the abbot preached, what seemed to a youngster, his interminable sermons. It remained the heart and soul of the community, a haven of calm certainty with its unadorned white walls, oak ceiling, and narrow windows through which the afternoon sun shimmered in dusty shafts of light.

Apart from the soldiers who had been lounging along the sides like mercenaries sullenly waiting for their rum allowance,

Apart from the over-heated Colonel, who commanded their attention, a parchment in his hand.

Alongside Jambo were uncle Rene, the notary, and his father, another Rene. Why did so many LeBlancs share the same given name? There were at least five other Joseph LeBlancs in Grand Pre alone. Across the aisle were his brothers—all older than him—huddled together, who before Winslow arrived, had been talking hectically in an unavailing attempt to disguise their anxiety. What a brood of them there were. Thirteen children his long-suffering mother had given birth to—nine sons and four girls—a typically prodigious Grand-Pré family. How had she coped? Especially as father, who was as feckless as she was steadfast, paid so little heed to them? *Whatever will be* was his motto, happier to be in the snug of the tavern and gossiping than working to provide for his wife and children.

"Haven't we found a husband for you yet?" he would tease whichever girl was still awake when he wandered tipsily home at night. "Time you were married and left me in peace. Which one are you by the way?"

It was his idea of a joke and the girls would shrug and laugh, but mother was always offended by his crassness. Sometimes, she would line them up—oldest to the right—and reprovingly *introduce* them. "Claire, Marie, Marguerite, meet your father. Father, your daughters. And in case you have forgotten, there's also Madeleine. Remember her? She's the one who got herself married."

"Oh yes, to that nice young farmer. What's-his-name. Has he got brothers? Surely the rest of you can find a man." Then he would doze off in front of the fire.

Now, however, he was sitting bolt upright as the Colonel started to read from the parchment in a high pitched, clipped, English accent that the Acadians found both hard to understand and somewhat comical, even after 40-odd years of British rule

He got as far as, "I have received from his Excellency..." when, late as usual, Jambo's eldest brother Charles slipped in beside Jambo on the pew.

"Almost missed the f-f-fun," he stammered.

The Colonel stopped, glaring at Charles.

"Does anyone speak English? It is important that you all understand this."

For a moment Jambo was surprised that his Uncle Rene did not volunteer. Not only was he more fluent than any of his countrymen, his legal skills would have been ideal if the British had trickery in mind but then he remembered the old man's warnings when they stood around the notice three days before. Yes, he had a shrewd idea that he would have been the spokesman for disagreeable news.

Instead, Pierre Landry, the mill owner, nervously raised his hand.

"Very good, merci," said Winslow—he pronounced it *mercy*. "Stand here next to me, please."

Landry stepped to the front and stood by the officer, gulping like a river herring caught in the shallows.

"As you know," he continued, "my regiment has been bivouacked here in Grand-Pré for the two weeks past. We are grateful for your hospitality."

"And my spruce b-b-beer," muttered Charles. At first he had been more than happy to welcome the thirsty troops, but his easy-going nature had been tested by the visitors' reluctance to pay for a single drink.

The colonel cleared his throat and fiddled with the paper in his hands.

He's nervous, thought Jambo. *But why?*

"Gentlemen, I have received from his Excellency, Governor Lawrence, the King's Commission, which I have in my hand, and by whose orders you are conveyed together, to manifest to you His Majesty's final resolution to the French inhabitants of this his Province of Nova Scotia."

"Acadia to you," muttered Charles. "That's the name of our c-c-country."

He went on to say something about how the king had granted them '*more indulgence than any of his subjects in any part of his dominions,*' but Jambo fixed on the two words: *final resolution.* His stomach gave a lurch, like the first time he had come face to face with a bear in the forest. Every instinct had been to turn and run, but he knew he had to stay as still as a tree. The beast had looked at him and raised a huge paw, but turned and crashed away into the undergrowth, leaving him with a heart that was pounding so hard he could almost hear it.

Winslow went on, "The part of duty I am now upon is, though necessary, very disagreeable to my natural make and temper, as I know it must be grievous to you who are of the same species."

"Species. What are we, animals?" That was Francois. A soldier took half a step forward. The trapper stayed silent.

The Colonel wiped the sweat from his face with a large handkerchief. "Without hesitation I shall deliver you his Majesty's orders and instructions— that your land and tenements, cattle of all kinds, and livestock of all sorts, are forfeited to the Crown with all other your effects, savings, your money, and household goods—"

There was an immediate racket of indignation from the men. They were bemused; angry; fearful.

"My God. How can that be?" Jambo saw Pierre half stand in protest but remembering his boy was next to him, blinking in fear, sat back and gripped his arm.

Some pushed forward. One man at the back stood on a pew to shout "Thieves." Another yelled, "Cowardly robbers." While another was struck in the side with the butt of a rifle when he stepped into the aisle, yelling, "Bloody British Brigands."

"Swindling swine," shouted Francois, his face a fearsome grimace of loathing.

"N-n-nothing new about that," said Charles. "You are always taking our supplies."

"Have you no shame?" asked Oliver Terriot, the cobbler, blinking resentfully behind his spectacles.

Their babble almost drowned out the rest of the colonel's sentence. "And you yourselves to be removed from this province."

Removed? Jambo was mesmerized by Landry's face, grey with anguish as he gabbled out the translation. It was if the hapless miller felt he himself was responsible for the terrible judgment. But no. No, it could not be. He must have misunderstood.

Winslow took a deep breath and pulled himself upright. A button popped from his tunic and rolled toward Jambo who instinctively stooped to retrieve it, but drew back as the young lieutenant hobbled obediently forward to spare his master the embarrassment of an undone uniform. For a second they came eye to eye. It was odd, the British officer actually looked sorry for him.

"Thus, it is peremptorily his Majesty's orders that the whole French inhabitants of these districts be removed."

An involuntary no, no, no rose from the men, which swelled in anger, but as the soldiers lifted their muskets, faded to a rallentando of frightened moans that were more like a collective sob.

Winslow raised his voice, reading fast now from the document with Landry struggling to keep up. Jambo was too horrified to concentrate. There was something about *through his Majesty's goodness* that they would be allowed to take sufficient money and household goods—*as many as you can without discommoding the vessels you go in*—and a promise that families would be kept together and travel in the same ships. But what did that mean?

"I am sensible that this must give you a great deal of trouble," said Winslow, raising his eyes from the paper and surveying his audience. "I hope whatever part of the world you may fall, you may be faithful subjects—" He faltered. "— a peaceable and happy people."

They stared back, aghast at this fat, sweaty little man with his message of damnation. Landry stood facing the crowd with unseeing eyes.

Tears coursed down his cheeks.

The colonel folded the parchment and focused at some imaginary object above the heads of the crowd. He seemed as upset as the men before him. No one stirred.

Almost as an afterthought, he cleared his throat. "I must also inform you that it is his Majesty's pleasure that you remain in security under the inspection and direction of the troops that I have the honor to command."

It had taken a minute. The edict whirled around Jambo's head as he tried to make sense of it. *Happy and peaceable. Happy! Faithful subjects. Disagreeable. Grievous. Remove, remove. Remove.*

One minute. He had told Marguerite he would only be a minute. How could they have expected this? At three o'clock they had been free men living in a country that their ancestors had hewn from forests and marshes, building levees to forestall the racing tides of the Bay of Fundy, plowing fields and planting orchards, fishing and hunting. His great grandfather had sailed here more than 100 years before to escape the tyranny of imperial France, to find a new life in a land of equals, where the title *messieurs*—so important to the status of the gentlemen class—was unknown. Where poverty was a distant memory and where they helped each other create a prosperous, self-sufficient, and peace-loving community. Now they were to be taken from the land they called Acadia. They were to be *removed.*

Silence. Not a cough. Not a murmur. Not even a snuffle from the boys.

Jambo held his breath as if he had a stag in his sights and was about to squeeze the trigger. It was so quiet he could hear the high-pitched whine of a mosquito. He tried to see where it was to divert his attention from the panic that was surging through him. He tried to breathe rhythmically to clear the pressure that was building in his chest and to stop his shaking hands.

In truth, the silence lasted only a few seconds. Then a boy, it might have been Pierre Richard's lad—he was only 14 years old—gave a whimper. Jambo expected an outburst of anger from the crowd and braced himself for violence. The soldiers obviously felt the same, because he could see them tense and ready to pounce. Instead there were a few shouts of '*Rot in hell*', and '*Damn you,*' and another said '*May God forgive you,*' but most stood in dazed bewilderment—after all, what could they do? One move, and they would be mown down by British muskets.

His father slumped onto the pew, his uncle Rene held his head in his hands, and Charles wrapped his arms around his chest as if trying to comfort himself.

Then Jambo, who prided himself on his self discipline, surprised himself—Marguerite was always teasing him for his lack of spontaneity, and true, he refused to take any action without thinking twice—but now, pushing the thick black hair off his forehead he stepped into the aisle.

He meant to be calm, but he blurted out, "What? What are you doing to us? Why? This cannot be."

The soldiers took one stride forward from their positions against the church wall. The rays of the sun caught the raised tips of their bayonets.

"We have no quarrel with you." Jambo was back to his steady self. "I cannot understand what you have against us that makes you behave in such a way. Remove us? Can you not leave us in peace in this land of ours? We have no fight with you."

The men cheered, but Winslow stared at him, more in pity than anger. He gave a jerk of his chin and a twitch of his shoulders as if he was trying to shake off the burden of what he proposed to do. Then he recovered himself, folded the parchment, and almost ran for the door. He was going at such a pace that he stumbled and caught his unruly wig on one of the doorjambs that had been splintered when the church had been broken into.

If the villagers had not been so distraught it would have been laughable to see him fumbling to replace it.

As the colonel struggled to free himself, Jambo pushed through the throng until he found himself face to face with him. He was so close he could smell his breath and was shocked that it smelled of port, but before he could speak again the soldiers were between them, bundling the young LeBlanc and the protestors to the sides of the church, knocking over the pews and the altar table in their violent haste to restore order.

If he had seemed apologetic before, the indignity of having to replace his wig in front of the jeering crowd had enraged the colonel and driven away the scruples that had appeared to beset him.

He spoke with quiet fury. "You shall be locked up here. There is nothing you can do. It is best you face your fate with calm and dignity, because there is no way of escaping it. You will be looked after fairly. I shall arrange for food to be delivered."

In an urgent aside, which Jambo was near enough to hear, he said to the lieutenant, "Set the guards. Barricade the church as arranged. None must escape."

He slipped through the door leaving the lieutenant to face the Acadians.

"Restez ici!" he shouted. "Escape is impossible."

"Restay eecee," mimicked Charles, but the Englishman had gone. The door was slammed shut, and within seconds they could hear timbers being nailed across the door and see soldiers appearing at the windows, their outlines black as crows against the light.

They nailed timbers across the frames, first horizontally, then vertically. Within minutes, the church had become a prison with wooden bars that were silhouetted like huge crosses against the setting sun.

"A c-c-crucifixion," said Charles.

"Our Calvary," said his uncle.

"Or just two bits of wood nailed up to stop us escaping," said the carpenter, calm now, determined to keep his consternation under control.

FIVE

St Charles Church, Grand Pré

September 5, 1755. 4 p.m.

Too late

The moment the last nail was hammered home, it was Francois who tried to galvanize the trapped men out of the cowed acceptance of their plight. He leapt on a pew roaring like some Old Testament prophet, holding out his huge, calloused, hands in angry entreaty.

"Come cousins, we must fight. Don't let them get away with this. We outnumber the bastards. We can destroy them."

He was puce with rage, his scar seemed whiter than ever against his flaming skin. "We can overwhelm these potato heads and flee to the forests. They will never find us there. We can be in Quebec within days and the French will protect us."

There was a chorus of '*ayes*' and '*kill the tyrants.*'

Jambo said, "Francois, my friend. Hush. Think for a moment. What can we do? There may be more of us than them, but we have no guns, no weapons at all."

"You're so, so, *sensible,*" retorted the plowman as if it was the most insulting thing he could say. "We have fists. We cannot surrender meekly as if we had no pride, as if we didn't care."

Oliver the cobbler said, "Jambo is right." His spectacles were clamped so close to his head that his magnified eyes seemed to peer around their rims, making him look both surprised and suspicious. "Our best hope is to talk. To negotiate. I'm sure we can do a deal."

"I'm getting married in two months," said Gabriel Lajeunesse. "I don't want any trouble."

"That is so typical of people like you!" bawled Francois. "Cowards! You grovel at their feet," he said to Oliver. "You're happy to repair their boots and scuttle off clutching their money. And as for you, Lajeunesse, the only difference is that you are under the backsides of their horses. Well, I hope they shit on you. Do you really think the British will wait for your wedding day to the lovely Evangeline? If we don't do something we shall be scattered God knows where, or we'll be dead, murdered right here. There'll be no marriage."

For a second Jambo feared the blacksmith would hit the frenzied plowman, but Pierre came between them, and no one argued with the powerful trapper.

He said, "That's not fair, Francois. We all have to do the best we can to protect ourselves and our families, and yes, make a living."

"There is no point falling out," said Jambo. "We are in this together. We have to be united if we are to have a chance of surviving."

"Listen to Jambo, Francois, what you say is madness," said Uncle Rene, pulling himself upright by the arm of the pew. "If the British want to expel us—remove us—they won't care about killing a score or two if we make a run for it, let alone attack."

"The more dead Acadians, the easier it will be for them to get rid of the ones left behind," said Jambo. "And don't forget we have our women and families outside."

"We have to bide our time to see if we can reason with the British," continued Rene. He gestured at the church. "This is our fate. For now. Maybe if we consider—and quietly, Francois, if you can manage that—what our options are, we will figure a way out of this predicament. Meanwhile, all we can do is make petitions and remonstrances to Winslow in the hope that he will intercede with Governor Lawrence."

"It makes me so, so, angry," said Francois, banging his head with his fists in frustration.

"Indeed," said Rene dryly. "We have to understand that Lawrence has no liking for us, but we can pray he has a conscience. He has been in the job for only six months. Perhaps he will realize that what he is about to commit is nothing more or less than the destruction of a people, may God save his soul."

"I'd rather He s-s-saves our bodies," said Charles.

"Surely it is impossible to clear us away," said Jambo, still grappling with the enormity of the British threat. "Are they planning to take us by sea?"

"They don't have the ships," said Oliver.

"All they have in the bay are those three merchantmen that sailed in last week," said Pierre.

"But," said Jambo, "there are almost 2,000 living in Grand-Pré alone, and thousands across Acadia. They need many more than that."

"Exactly. And where will they r-r-remove us to?" asked Charles. "Prince Edward Island? Quebec?"

"They won't send us to a territory owned by France," said Rene. "Most likely to Massachusetts or Maine. One of their colonies. Who knows?"

"If only we had made our escape when that n-n-notice went up," said Charles. "Think how far away we could be by n-n-now.

Jambo said: "But we didn't."

They were all trying to cope in their different ways. Uncle Rene sat talking to father as if they were passing the time on the bench outside his front door. Oliver, who loved playing card games for money, had magicked a pack of cards from his jerkin and was playing with Charles and Lajeunesse with a cheery mix of bravado and defiance. Francois paced up and down, kicking at the pews and glowering at the darkening windows until Rene calmed him down by giving him a full pipe of tobacco he had smuggled past the guards.

Pierre was sitting quietly, comforting his fearful son. Jambo could not hear what he was saying but no doubt it would be plans for some hunting expedition.

Yes, a good man to have by you in when you were in trouble.

Pierre and Jambo had been friends as long as he could remember and they became closer than brothers when Pierre married his older sister, Marie.

There was no one better to spend the long nights with, setting traps and stalking deer in the forest. He was at one with the wild, his bulk flitting through the trees like a ghost, as if he knew the habits of every animal that lived in his domain. *'Tonight,'* he would say, *'I'll catch that stag that is hiding from me on the ridge toward Blomidon. He knows I am after him but I will have him.'* And he would, returning at dawn with the beast, which he would skin, salt, and save for the winter, though not without saving the best cuts for an impromptu feast.

He must have been the fittest man in the village, all knotty muscle, lithe from stalking, creeping, running and carrying home his prey across his shoulders. Francois liked to boast he could beat him at arm wrestling but Pierre would just shrug. A shy man, he was slow to speak, perhaps because he was not as confident in his learning as he was with his knowledge of the outdoors. Instead of rushing in with a statement, he would instead, scratch his red beard, narrow his steady blue eyes, and ask a question—but one that required a reply that made sense and one, reckoned Jambo, to which he already knew the answer.

However happy he was setting his traps and tracking game, his greatest joy was to be at home with Marie and his ever-growing family. "Seven children," he would say with an air of rueful surprise. "In fifteen years. Where did they come from?"

SIX

St. Charles Church, Grand Pré

September 6, 1755. Dawn.

Of Love and Loss

Jambo watched the trapper, envying his apparent calm as he talked reassuringly to his lad. *Yes, the main thing is to appear as unruffled as Pierre,* he told himself. *Not to let the British think we have any fear.*

Even when he was a boy he had tried to keep his emotions under control. He tried not to cry when big brother Charles pushed him in the nettles, he bit his tongue when his sisters teased him about girls, or his brothers scoffed at the way he kept his carpenter's tools clean and ordered in the family work shop. Even his mother would gently mock him as the steady one of the family—the thinker, and yes, the worrier—though her pride in the serious young man knew no bounds, though it remained unspoken.

He learnt how to hide his doubts and insecurities, and by doing so he did become controlled and rational. He realized that if he appeared to be strong, he was, in effect, strong in the eyes of others, and that earned him the respect of all in the village. Why else would he have been on the village council at age 22?

Only once had he failed to hide his feelings, and that was in the early days of his pursuit of Marguerite. She had mortified him so much by flirting with another lad at the weekly dance that he took to melancholy evenings alone playing his lute.

Which, of course, amused his sisters hugely and delighted Marguerite, who admitted later that she had been playing games with him, but had realized she wanted him even more because he had let his emotions show. Now he had to call on all his reserves of self control, because for the first time since their wedding day five years before, he was separated from her and he was terrified that they would be torn apart forever. He could not guess what was going to happen to them, and he hated not being able to rationalize the situation. He fought the panic. Whatever happened—to him, to Marguerite, the children— he would not surrender to fear, he would not show any weakness. As he leaned against the pew he resolved that the British would never see him weep. Never—whatever malevolent fate Winslow had prepared for them.

It would be hard. The scarcely suppressed hysteria of the prisoners was contagious. They were beset with anxiety, irresolutely sitting one moment, pacing around the next, hardly talking to each other. Even his brothers had stopped their chatter, keeping an eye on the door in case the British relented and let them go or, more like, marched them off into the night.

Long after the doors had been slammed shut, the women kept up a chorus outside the church that was both lament and protest, calling out the names of their men, making each prisoner start up eagerly in recognition, only to slump back hopelessly. What could they do?

He picked out Marguerite's voice echoing eerily out of the dark, and a woman arguing with the soldiers. "Let us see our men. How dare you lock them away!" Yes, it was mother. He shouted out, "Marguerite! Mother!" but stopped, embarrassed, and like the others gave a shrug of resignation. It was pointless. They could not hear him.

"Be quiet out here!" the soldiers yelled at the women. "Get to your beds."

Gradually the noise stilled until all they could hear in the church was the murmur of the soldiers, their occasional soft laughter, the soft pad of boots as they patrolled around the building, and the clinks as rifle butts were rested on stony ground.

The notary said, "We should try to sleep, but first we must pray."

They fell to their knees in silent supplication, and then, miserably, stretched out on the hard dirt floor. He slept for less than an hour and woke, drained and listless. He lay where he was until dawn, with his head awkwardly propped against the end of a pew until his neck ached and he got to his feet with the others, stretching and grumbling as the sun filtered through the windows, casting its wavering crosses on the opposite wall.

He had been dreaming he was on a ship, pitching through the waves, trying to grab Marguerite to stop her falling overboard, but every time the ship lurched she slipped further from his outstretched hand. All he could hear was her disembodied voice calling for help, and as he awoke he realized it was her voice that rose above the pleadings of the women.

To discover what was happening he hauled himself up by clinging to a window sill where he could just see that the women were being contained behind the palisade, barging and shoving as they begged the soldiers to let them in with baskets of food. There was Marguerite, berating the soldiers who stood in her way. He burst out laughing at the astonished expressions on their faces at such a tirade—from a *woman* of all things He shouted and waved, but lost his hold and fell to the floor, winding himself and banging his bruised elbow so painfully that he decided to sit and draw breath while the prisoners muttered and grumbled around him, impatiently waiting for the door to open and their women come in with bread and bowls of syrup.

It had been in this very church a little over six years before as the abbot was droning his way through mass that he had met her gaze, just fleetingly, and knew she was to be his wife. He was amazed. More than that— thunder struck. There, across the aisle, was a girl he had known all his life, but a *woman* he had never seen before—Marguerite Trahan, who used to play with his younger sisters, ice-skating and playing bouton or blind man's bluff. Now her face was a zestful flush of pink framed by the hooded cape, which struggled to contain her thick hair, fairer than most in Grand-Pré. It was as if the brim, pulled low, and her ankle length woolen frock and cotton blouse were designed to hide her newfound womanhood, but not from Jambo. He found he was blushing.

Marguerite seemed to be concentrating on the monotonous cadences of the abbot, but then she stared at him again through the cusp of her praying hands with eyes that were full of mischief and challenge before demurely taking her place on her knees before the priest. How strange that he had never noticed that her left eye was a fathomless green while the other was blue—a slightly steely blue at that. What guilt he felt mouthing '*Lamb of God, you take away the sins of the world: have mercy on us,*' when his own feelings were in such a turmoil of youthful yearning. It was delicious and shocking.

But after that sweet jolt of realization, all they did for months was stare at each other ardently across the aisle and talk awkwardly at the weekly dances.

She played games—how she played games—pretending to concentrate on her weaving as if she hadn't seen him walking past her door, or worse, laughing noisily when she was with her friends as if he was the butt of some girlish joke. And then—what utter mortification—she had taunted him by flirting with one of the Granger boys.

What anguish that had been, and then what frustration. When they did have a moment together, her younger brother Joseph was under instruction from her father to hang around and play the chaperone, something she later admitted irritated her as much as him. But Jambo did not give up—he knew what he wanted and his persistence paid off.

When she was 18, his parents had a meeting with her widowed father and over cider and cakes it was agreed he would be allowed to propose, and as custom dictated, embark on the year-long courtship.

They met every day. She used to call by when he was working in his carpenter's yard or out in the fields fixing a fence or a gate. She loved his sturdy body, hardened by constant physical effort. She would watch his big, roughened hands, dirt under short nails, as he worked. She would color with excited anticipation at the thought of being held by him.

She smelt the salty freshness of the sea on his clothes after he had been fishing, or caught the earthy warmth of his body—a lingering loaminess from the forest—when he had been laying traps.

As for the carpenter, wherever he was going he would make a detour past her cottage to watch her making clothes, cooking for her father or brewing spruce beer, delighting in her skills at all the things he expected a young woman to do. Sometimes, he would dawdle just out of sight to watch her picking apples in the orchard or scything the corn at harvest time, her body moving under the coarse flax shift, breathless with effort, her face flushed, eyes dancing.

In the evenings they would meet under the willows by the river. She would gaze into his dark, almost black eyes, which glowed below strong eyebrows which almost joined together. She had been told this signified a passionate nature, so she naughtily put the theory to the test as often as possible by holding his face with its crooked chin and kissing him ardently. Jambo, the shy lad, was rather taken aback by her boldness.

She confessed that she had noticed him blushing that day in church, and she too had decided at that moment that she would marry him.

The church door was flung open and the prisoners started up. Would they be allowed out to be reunited with their families? At least, surely, the women would be ushered in with food and water. But no, to a chorus of jeers, a platoon of soldiers took up their positions along the walls, guns at the ready, while their comrades brought in the provisions.

Even Francois, who had pushed himself to the front of the prisoners ready to fight his way out, recognized the futility of violence and contented himself with a few expletives at the stone-faced enemy. As they ate, the young lieutenant appeared at the door, his lopsided figure outlined in the morning sunshine.

"I hope you slept as well as possible," he said. "I realize these, er, quarters are not ideal."

"You should be ashamed to treat us like this," said Jambo.

"Ah, Mr. White, good morning. We have already met, but I must introduce myself to your friends. I am Lieutenant Brooke Watson, and er, we have a proposal for all of you, a scheme, er, for your own good. It is essential that the last of the harvest is stored, and the smallholdings are in good order. The cattle, pigs, and sheep need to be tended. That is best for all our sakes."

Francois gave a derisive snort. "For *your* sakes, rather."

Jambo held him by the elbow in case he was about to launch himself at the Englishman.

Watson flushed, but went on. "We will be sending twenty of you at a time to work in the fields while some remain here to be answerable for their return. As for the rest, well, we are a magnanimous people. We do not want you to suffer unnecessarily, that is not our aim. You cannot all stay here in the church, it is much too crowded, so what we intend to do is bivouac some of you on the ships. There are now five in the bay."

"Five," whispered Jambo to Pierre. "More must have arrived overnight."

"They can easily hold fifty men a piece. Just until—"

No one paid attention to the unfinished sentence, or noticed the unspoken threat, because they were too busy clamoring for answers.

"What about our families?"

"And the harvest?"

"Our cattle?"

"Isn't this prison enough without jailing us on a ship?"

Watson, who seemed as ill at ease as his colonel the day before, raised his voice above the barrage of questions that were flung at him from all corners of the church. "We will make a selection of who will go and who will stay behind to work with the women. It will make living more comfortable for you all.

"The ones I choose to go on the ships can take the belongings they need. The ships are well equipped, and once a day your wives and mothers will be allowed to deliver necessary supplies."

Jambo pushed his way to the front. He spoke quietly, cutting through the hubbub. "You do not need to do any of this. It can be made so much easier.

You want us out of the way. Here is a suggestion; we will leave Acadia, go quietly with a few possessions, and just enough food to last us a week. You already have our harvest, we will leave the sheep and cattle behind if that's what you want. Even our horses. You can have everything."

"Yes. Yes," said Oliver excitedly. "It will cost you nothing."

"What else can you do?" demanded Pierre. "Do you intend to murder us all or drown us in the bay?"

"Do you want blood on your hands?" asked Francois, looking as though he would happily slay any British soldier who stood in his way.

Charles said, "You do not have the m-m-means to remove us anyway."

Watson looked away from the carpenter's steady gaze and pursed his lips. Before he could say anything, Jambo continued. "We can be in Quebec or Prince Edward Island within a few days. All of us. You will never see us again. Take this country of ours—take it—but give us our freedom."

"It is too late for that," replied Watson. "All you will do is join your fellow countrymen in New France and take up arms against us—just like you did at Beausejour. That is, er, an eventuality we cannot allow."

Before he could speak again, Jambo was thrust aside from behind. It was Francois, and this time he was impossible to restrain. He stuck his face close to the British officer.

"My God, you potato head, let us have our freedom!" He made violent chopping gestures with his hand as if he was butchering a hog with a cleaver. "We have lived here in peace for 150 years. We are Acadians. Neutrals. But if it's a fight you want, you can have one!"

He made more chopping arcs with his hand, spitting with rage and loathing, but the soldiers just laughed and started back in mock terror, making jeering ooh-ing sounds as if they were afraid of him. Then, joke over, one put the point of his bayonet to his throat and drew a spot of blood, as if to prove they could have done away with him then and there if they had chosen to. Two others seized him and manhandled the protesting plowman out of the church.

"Our first volunteer for a stay on the ships," said Watson, giving his peculiar bark of a laugh as if embarrassed by the plowman's futile outburst. "Now, I shall select the other men to join him."

He went round the chapel, picking out the youngest and fittest of them by tapping them on the chest with the handle of his sword. "You, you and you. Outside."

Within minutes 250 of the prime of Grand-Pré was lined up in two ranks on the green, the boys on one side, face to face with the older men. One tried to run into his father's arms, but he was pulled away by a soldier and manhandled back in line, his face was stained with tears that were as much to do with his shame at seeming so childish in front of the other lads as they were to do with his fear.

Of course, get the strong ones out of the way and it becomes easier to handle the rest, thought Jambo bitterly as he limped forward to join them.

Watson put out an arm and stopped him. "No, you stay. We shall need some young blood to do the heavy work."

He stood irresolutely by his father, who had, in an instant, become a ghost of sorrow as it dawned on him that his sons were to be taken from him. Jambo put his hand on the older man's arm in a gesture of comforting reassurance as one by one his sons said their farewells.

"He held them close and recited their names as if he was frightened he might forget them— Jean-Baptiste, Claude, Jean, Charles, Pierre, Rene and Oliviar. They made light of their fate, joking about not being able to swim, or always wanting to be a sailor. No one laughed, but it was better than letting the British soldiers enjoy their distress.

As for Jambo, they clapped him on the back as if congratulating him on his lucky escape. Charles, serious now, said to him, "L-l-look after Anne for me. And the children."

His plump face under his mop of unruly hair was crumpled with fear, his brown eyes, so often alive with mischief, were screwed tight as if he could not bear to see the future. He took after their father, lazily confident that all would turn out well without having to raise a finger. He was softened by his sedentary life, sitting in the snug, pipe in hand, flagon of beer topped up, gossiping idly, but he always found something to joke about and he made everyone smile. It hadn't always been the case. Everyone used to tease him when he was a lad because of his stutter, and he had grown up withdrawn and defensive until he had met his Anne and fallen in love. It was as if a light had been switched on.

"Who c-c-cares if I s-s-stutter," he would say, acting up. "I've got the p-p-prettiest girl in the village."

The marriage gave him the confidence he had lacked before, but it didn't give him any more of an appetite for the hard work of the fields or the sea that filled the days of the other LeBlanc brothers.

"Running the tavern is p-p-perfect for me," he said. "I get the wife to do all the heavy work, and I sit around d-d-drinking and singing." He was careful not to say that to her face though.

Then they were gone, prodded and jostled by musket-wielding soldiers who shouted to their prisoners. "Come on you Frenchies, get moving! Down to the landing with you!"

Jambo stood uncertainly as they were marched off. He was relieved he had been spared incarceration on the ships, but felt guilty that he had been chosen to stay behind with the older men. He should be sharing the prisoners' plight. They were men he had grown up with—his cousins, as they called each other in Acadia—but more, they were true friends who had done everything together.

What japes they had enjoyed skipping school, learning how to set traps, and blushing with the embarrassment of their first village dances. Pierre had shown him how to catch the herring that teemed close to shore. Francois had led him astray in all the local taverns, and Oliver had tried to teach him how to cheat at cards, but gave up because the carpenter's face was *too honest*.

There was Charles, swiftly back to his normal self, cheering up their brothers, laughing and joking as if he was going for a stroll with the family.

Pierre was stoic as ever with his arm around his boy. One group, with Francois at its head, was singing traditional songs about freedom, their fists held high in a salute of defiance. He caught a glimpse of Pierre Landry, his face pinched with distress, and others like Marguerite's brother, Joseph, who was weeping unashamedly, but most were staring ahead blankly as if they did not comprehend what was happening to them.

As they went, the women lined the path, and a noise like the howl of wolves caught in a trap rose on either side. In a ragged chorus they begged God to intercede and Winslow for mercy.

Some held up crucifixes as if they were weapons and cursed the soldiers, while anguished mothers held their babies high—maybe as a reproach to the villainy of the British, but more in terror that father and child might never see each other again.

He could see Marguerite and his mother a short way down the path, separated from him by a line of soldiers, and he tried to wriggle through to them.

Poor mother, the very bedrock of her existence was being stolen from her. She had looked after her boys for every minute of their lives, from their first faltering steps, picking them up when they bruised their knees, cuffing them round the head when they were naughty, even mending their broken hearts when a girl rebuffed them.

He had never seen her show any emotion, she always hid her passion for her family with matter-of-fact briskness, but now she was a desolate figure. Her bonnet had fallen off and her hair was a wild halo around her face, down which the tears streamed.

He could see, rather than hear, her cry. "My sons. My sons."

"Let me through," he begged the guards, but they butted him away with their muskets.

From the edge of the green he watched the heart-breaking procession winding down to the shore, a pall of dust marking its reluctant progress through the meadows and along the levee to Boudrot Point where the skiffs were moored. In the bay the five ships lay in wait.

"You lot. Get in the church."

Again the door was slammed shut. Again the timbers were nailed into place.

"Will we see them again?" wondered Jambo.

"Only God knows," said Rene. "But I fear the British rule here, not God."

SEVEN

Grand-Pré

October 6, 1755.

Waiting

Every day, as soon as the tide was in, a melancholy file of women would take baskets of food to the shore where skiffs waited to carry them to their men imprisoned in the ships.

Usually, in those weeks between the busy last days of harvest and the onset of winter, the villagers would be in high spirits. Once the early morning frisson of frost had been melted by the autumn sun and the mist had floated away over the ridge to reveal scarlet maples, startling against the funereal conifers, the women would bring picnics to the men in the fields and they would have impromptu parties, drinking beer, larking about and singing as Jambo and Charles played their lutes.

But this October, the ones left behind were consumed by the fear of their impending fate, a lurking trepidation made worse by not knowing what was to happen next. Every shout from a soldier made their nerves jangle, every twitch of a ship's sail made their hearts lurch. When a messenger galloped in from Halifax with a missive for Winslow they would anxiously ask each other, '*Is it now? Are we to be cast out today?*'

The elderly, like father and uncle Rene, were allowed to stay behind near the church, while Jambo and the rag-tag work force of youngsters and women were ordered into the fields to do odd jobs like raking up the chaff for cattle feed and loading the last few bags of flour and winter crops on to carts for their transport to the warehouses of Halifax. Really, they were just going through the motions. There was so little to keep them busy that they spent most of the days leaning on their pitchforks talking until a soldier came near, at which point they made a great to-do of trimming and stacking. Eventually there could be no pretence. The wheels of Landry's granary stopped grinding and the buzz of the saw in the Melancon brothers' timber yard fell silent. There was nothing to do.

Jambo was so restless without the balm of his daily routine, that one evening before curfew he took his tools and strolled down to the levee to see if his latest repairs were still withstanding the pesky beavers. He was annoyed to see the telltale teeth marks on the sluice and instinctively cast around for replacement timbers before stopping himself.

"What is the point?" he asked his dog, who had picked up the scent of a hare and was itching to chase after it. "We might not be here next week. I am not going to do their work for them." To the silent riverbank he said, "Enjoy yourselves, my beaver friends. Maybe you can flood the land and take revenge for us against these devils."

A soldier materialized out of the dusk.

"What are you doing here?" he jerked his rifle at the carpenter. "No one is allowed here this late. Home with you."

"I felt a fool," he said to Marguerite when he and the dog had tramped back up the hill to their front door. She was sitting on the bench darning a smock as the sun began to slip away behind the cliffs of Blomidon.

"But then, I feel foolish most of the time. If only there was something I could do. I feel so restless. It is depressing enough, working away to feed the very men who are determined to destroy us, but it's made much worse doing it alongside women, and then being locked away in the church with old men."

"There is nothing wrong being seen with us women," she said, her unmatched eyes flared in their extraordinary way. It was a signal that he knew well and he swiftly retreated.

"No, no, I don't mean that," he said, hastily. "It's that I feel *guilty*. "I should be on the ships like the others. There's only me and Oliver who are under thirty left on shore, and at least he can get on with his trade—even if they are British boots he is repairing and he doesn't often get paid."

"Maybe we should do something about it," she said, putting down her work and linking her arm through his.

"Such as?"

"Escape," she said. "Make a run for it."

He thought she was being mischievous until he caught the look in her eye. "Escape is impossible," he said impatiently.

"Is it though? What if just one person, or a group, got away and made it to the border?"

"And?"

"They could try to persuade France to come to our rescue or negotiate our freedom," she said.

"But who could go?" he said. "Every family has a man either imprisoned in the church or trapped on the ships. That's why the British have been so clever. Would you be prepared to risk the life of your brother or father in an escape attempt? I think not. The British reprisals would be bloody. No, we are all hostages now. Anyway, France is not interested in us. What are we to them? They gave up on us forty years ago."

She was undeterred. "If we could make contact with some of the other villages we might be able to start a sort of resistance movement. Work undercover, sabotage their wagon trains, pick the soldiers off one by one." She was leaning forward, breathless with anticipation at such daring. "Look at that character Beausoleil Broussard and his freedom fighters. They are creating mayhem among the British."

"I know some people think he is a hero, but as far as I am concerned Broussard is a nuisance," he said. "He is just the kind of person that uncle talks about who is making matters worse for us. He was mixed up with the Beausejour disaster, and escaped only in the nick of time. He and his men ambushed and killed some British soldiers a few weeks ago. That is hardly going to endear us to this lot.

"Be realistic, we don't have the men for a resistance movement. Who would join? Me, Oliver, your father? No, it's all too late—to escape, to fight. We are trapped."

The late autumn rays of the setting sun deepened the red slopes of Blomidon into a rusty blood and the reflected glow lit Marguerite's face. She looked as if she was about to say something, but frowned and shivered, maybe at the cool of the evening or the chill of the menace that hung over them. He put his arms around her and held her close to him, as much for his comfort as hers. His hand slipped inside her smock and she kissed him urgently, kindling the reckless rush of lust that she so easily roused in him.

"Where is mother?"

"She has taken the children to see Marie and feed the chickens," she whispered, her voice husky. She held his face and kissed him again.

"How long?"

"She'll be 20 minutes." She took him by the hand, just as she used to in the early days of marriage when she would interrupt him at work and draw him to her in some woodland corner, and for a few rushed minutes they surrendered to the thrill of sweet, loving abandonment.

They emerged from the dark intimacy of the bedroom just as mother returned. They must have looked flushed and happy—perhaps she noticed Marguerite's chemise was awry—because she asked suspiciously, "What have you got to be cheerful about?" She glowered at them. "What about them?" She gesticulated out to the bay. "What about your brothers? How can you be happy while they are trapped like rats?"

There was no answer. The dog and Jean-Baptiste played in the dust while his mother took and held Osite and sat still as a stone, gazing out to sea at the ships that held her sons.

"So little has changed," she said suddenly. "It was 100 years ago that your great forefather, Daniel, sailed from France. Just imagine if he was sitting here now. He'd recognize it. There are more of us, many more houses and barns, but that's the only difference. They had nothing when they arrived. Life had been so hard for them in the old country. He would tell us how he and his parents had to beg for food on the streets while the rich rode past in their carriages, splashing them with muddy puddles. But when they got here they worked, God how they worked, and they made Acadia a land where now we have plenty and where we are equal and free. Well, we *used* to be free."

She broke into pitiable sobs. It was a familiar tale, but now it had become a lament to a lost world, as if clinging to the past would ease the fears of the present. Jambo could barely bring himself to look at his mother's pale, gaunt face. All her energy, the joy in her small world, all gone.

"Don't worry," said Marguerite. "We shall soon be together again. Those lads of yours will be playing merry hell with the British sailors."

"They'll be regretting ever meeting them, let alone jailing them," said Marie, who herself was fretting over the imprisonment of Pierre and her oldest son.

"It will all turn out well," said Jambo, though he did not believe it himself. "We can build a new home wherever the British decide to take us. Isn't that just what Daniel did?"

Nothing they said could give her hope. She was not listening, just staring out to sea as if trying to catch a sight of her sons in their waterborne prison.

She said, "You know, when he first landed in this country of ours, everyone rallied round. They helped him build a house, lent him farm tools and a horse and a cow. That's how it was—everyone helped each other. If someone was sick, the women would call at the house with medicines. If a man was injured, others would help plow his fields and tend to the livestock. We shared our woes and our joys. We stood together, and that made us self reliant and strong."

He did know. All the LeBlancs had been brought up on the story of Daniel—*Grand Père* as he was called.

When he arrived in 1648 there were a few hundred settlers living in Acadia, but by the time the young Jambo married in 1750 the population had risen to almost 18,000, scattered along the inlets and bays of what had become a small, independently-minded country. By that day in August, when the soldiers came, Grand-Pré had grown to be the biggest community, and the LeBlancs were one of the most prolific families. Charles and his wife Anne already had two children. His sister Madeleine had just married Paul Benoit, a farmer from neighboring Canard, and he never ceased to delight at Marie's match with Pierre, which if their seven children were any proof, was the happiest marriage of all.

The view, the sounds, the smell of the rich earth, and the tang of the livestock were just the way the young carpenter remembered them since his boyhood when he used to come running up the hill to meet his father and grandfather who, like old Daniel, would stop under the trees to survey their domain.

The houses that nestled into the hillside were still made of stone and roofed with thatch in the way that that Daniel would have used, though mother said, "He would find these modern clapboard walls and smooth clay plastering an extravagance. You young people have such comfortable lives."

She dabbed at her eyes. "You and your grandfather would sit and talk forever. You more than the other boys. I don't know why."

"I liked the stories," he said, putting his arm around her. "I wanted to know what it meant to be Acadian."

Marguerite gasped and gripped his arm. She pointed over his shoulder to the bay. "Look."

British ships were sailing into view from behind the cliffs—seven of them. From the ridge, they could see the splash of the anchors as they hit the sea, and the sailors as they busied themselves on deck, but from that distance they could hear nothing, just an eerie silence. There were now 12 vessels in the bay.

"No military flags," muttered Jambo. "Cargo ships."

"What do they want?" she clung to him.

"Us, I think," said Jambo. "They are the ships that will be taking us away."

Uncle Rene and his father came running up as fast as their aged legs would carry them, and as they caught their breath, Marguerite turned to him in challenge, eyes alight with bravado. "We must act. This is the last chance we'll have to escape. I know we've talked about it before, but now we have to try. We have nothing to lose."

Not for the first time, Jambo's sound instincts were swept aside by his wife's fervor.

"Rene, father, maybe we should. If only a few get away that would be better than nothing. We could start a new Acadia far, far, from English rule."

The notary seemed tired and depressed, resigned to their fate. "It's too late," he said. "Some might be lucky and escape, but what about the old people here and the children? And the men on the ships, what of them?"

Father stirred. "I have eight sons out there. And you Jambo, you have eight brothers."

Mother said, "How can you even think that?" Her eyes were blazing, her face contorted with the terror that anyone might agree with the young couple. "I haven't lived this long to abandon my own children."

"But listen to me," Marguerite persisted. "This is our moment. Tomorrow ..."

She was going to say more, but stopped because soldiers came running up with Watson, peg-legging behind them.

"Time that you, er, get to your homes. And you men. It has gone curfew time. Into the church."

EIGHT

The green, Grand Pré

October 13, 1755.

No Escape

Within a week there were twenty ships crowding the waters of Minas Basin—schooners, goelettes and sloops—so many that from the shore their masts were like a forest almost hiding the cliffs that framed the foreboding tableau.

"Where have they all come from?" Jambo wondered.

"More important, where are they going?" asked Oliver.

They were on the green outside the church waiting for the work details to be sent out into the fields.

"God knows, but surely even now there aren't enough to take us away," said Jambo. "There just would not be enough room below decks."

"Time to get moving," said a soldier, but as the men reached reluctantly for their pitchforks gunfire rang out. It came from the shore somewhere near Boudrot Point.

"They've started the slaughter," moaned Oliver, crouching down as if a gun would be turned on him.

"They're going to kill us," said father. "May God have mercy."

"More shooting," Jambo cupped his hands over his eyes to keep out the sun and squinted down to the shore. "By the jetty."

Oliver grabbed him by the arm. "Look over there—on the levee."

It was the most astonishing sight the carpenter had ever seen "What in God's name?"

For a second it looked as though women—about a score of them—had somehow commandeered the skiffs, landed at the jetty, and were now escaping. Along the banks of the River Canard they ran, some took the paths to the forest, others high-tailed it along the levee. As they fled the women shed their garments. In a surreal trail, skirts and bonnets, shawls and petticoats, were scattered across the fields, some left hanging off branches, others abandoned on fences, one length of ribbon somehow found itself draped on the horn of a cow.

"It's our lads!" cried Jambo. "They're dressed in women's clothes. What on earth!"

"They're making a run for it," said Oliver.

The sight filled Jambo with a kind of exaltation and Marguerite wrapped her arms around him as if to stop him racing after them.

Brooke Watson came hobbling from his bivouac. "Get back to your homes, into the church." He looked around helplessly as they stayed where they were, and after dithering for a few seconds, shrugged and dashed off in a helter-skelter of hops and one-legged jumps to muster his men and send them in pursuit of the runaways.

"How did they get those women's clothes?" wondered Rene as they watched the fantastical scene being played out.

"They're crazy," said Jambo, but Marguerite was cheering them on with such enthusiasm that he joined in, even though—maybe *because*—he knew the escape was doomed to failure.

"Go, go!"

"Faster!"

For a second, it was like a game. As if they were children again, playing tag between the hen houses and the pig sties, skipping over excited dogs and hiding in the barns, all the time shouting instructions at their playmates.

"Turn left!"

"Right!"

"This way."

"Over there."

"Why aren't they heading for the forest?" cried Oliver.

"Look," said Jambo. "By the levee that leads to Habitant—two of them together. I'm sure one is Francois."

"And over by the Thibodeau place, among the willows by the river, there are four more," said Uncle Rene. Jambo had never seen him so animated.

"They'll be after the canoes," said Jambo. "They can paddle along the bay and get away if they keep close in to the shore."

In their ones, and twos, and groups of three or more, the fugitives were running doubled-up along the fringes of the meadows, ducking behind barns, and sneaking along culverts. From their vantage point the onlookers could see that the soldiers were already lurking in wait for the men heading for the canoes, and others were racing across the open fields to cut off the paths to the cover of the forest.

The game was up.

"Not that way," muttered Jambo.

"No. No!" shouted the onlookers.

It seemed as if one runaway was deliberately leading the soldiers away from a group who were making a dash across open country toward the cover of a copse. He was standing in the middle of a field, waving and shouting. Was it in defiance or despair? The deed of an heroic decoy? Jambo looked on appalled. It was as if he wanted to be caught. Or be killed.

"Dear God. They've shot him," said father, almost in a whimper.

"And another. See, by the river." Jambo, blinking hard and holding his head in his hands.

The body of the reckless decoy lay, a contorted heap, in the middle of the meadow. The other had fallen head down on the riverbank, his blood deepening its red water. Now, wherever they looked men were surrendering. There were three standing up to their waists in the river, arms raised. A group were held against the wall of the saw mill while others stumbled out from ditches and hedgerows to give themselves up.

It had been a bold, lunatic ruse. It was over.

Marguerite was distraught, her arms still wrapped around him. "I'm sorry. We were sworn to secrecy. I was going to tell you last night when we were with Rene and your father. That's why I was urging us to escape. Every day, when the women made their daily delivery of food to the ships, they varied the numbers on each skiff—sometimes as many as eight or ten, sometimes only two or three. The British had become lazy and stopped checking so they never knew how many they were expecting. What no one knew was that each time the women rowed out, they were wearing a change of clothes under their own. When they were on board they slipped them off and our lads hid them.

"This morning the skiffs arrived earlier than usual. It was still dark and most the guards were still in their hammocks while a couple of them kept watch on deck. They're a dozy lot and didn't notice that many more women were leaving the ship than those that had arrived."

She pulled away, looking embarrassed.

"Believe it or not, Francois Hebert had the idea and persuaded his sister and mother to help. All the women gave something, including your sisters. I donated an old dress and a bonnet."

"My God. I can understand Francois doing almost anything, but I would not have thought he would have the brains to think up something as crazy as this," said Jambo. "But my sisters. I'm proud of them. And *you*, my darling." He kissed her.

"Round up these traitors." It was Winslow, no longer the apologetic figure he had seemed before. His crimson jowls quivered. He was splenetic with fury. "March them to the Hebert house."

They stood in a ragged crowd while Winslow fulminated at the stupidity of the escape attempt.

"I must remind you that I promised you would be treated fairly and honorably. I expected to be rewarded with your own sense of fair play. Instead, because of your stupidity, two of your men have been shot and killed.

"I grieve for the widows and children, but what did they expect—a pat on the back and a pint of rum?" He was getting increasingly animated, striking his thigh with his riding crop as he paced up and down in front of them. "Listen to me. There are still some fools on the run. Maybe they are hiding in your barns or even in your houses. I will give you 24 hours to encourage them to hand themselves in. If they do not surrender in two days, I should serve all their friends in the same way as I am about to do now."

He pointed at them with the whip.

"You, you, you. I don't care who it is. I will make an example of one of you every day until the missing men report to me."

This was not the embarrassed figure that had told them their fate in the church. This was an angry British colonel. He was in charge.

"Now, this is what you can expect. I know the women were involved in this enterprise, but it is not the British way to punish females. It is, however, our way to exact chastisement on troublemakers. Hebert."

Francois, who had his hands tied behind him and his legs in ropes to stop him running away, was pushed in front of the colonel. A scrap of torn chemise hung incongruously from his left shoulder.

"This is your house, I believe," said Winslow.

"It is."

"And this is your family?"

His sister and his elderly parents stood together in a wretched huddle.

"They are."

"It is bad enough that you risked your own necks by this disloyal action, but it brings shame on you that you were prepared to put the lives of your family in jeopardy," said Winslow. "I must teach you and the rest of you, a lesson. Our will must be obeyed as long as you are still in this country."

A contingent of soldiers went inside the house with bales of straw. Smoke leaked from the windows and curled around the open doorway like an evil phantom. A flame flickered through the roof, and another, and then the thatch was ablaze, sending showers of sparks shooting into the evening sky.

What had been for years a small and happy home was, within

minutes, a smoldering ruin. His mother and father were wracked with weeping, but Francois, who remained uncharacteristically self-controlled, held his head high and refused to show any emotion. Only the jut of his chin and the pulsing of his neck muscles betrayed his anger and hatred.

As he was marched back to his on-board prison, two soldiers kicked aside the embers and pulled out two pigs which had been salted and stored to be ready for winter, but which were now as charred as if they had been cooked on a spit. Incongruously, the smell of warm meat wafted over the small crowd.

"Dinner," said one of the soldiers, slinging the remains over his shoulder. "And we won't even have to cook it."

The next morning two groups of prisoners were sent out under guard to pick up the dead men, load them in carts, and bring them to the graveyard.

The first was young Francois Boudrot, only 17, who still lay face down in the river. Yesterday he would have been full of derring-do, excited at the prospect of such a spectacular exploit. Now he was a sodden corpse, covered in mud, and streaked with smears of blood.

The body of the runaway, who had seemed to invite death, belonged to Pierre Landry. At first Jambo did not recognize the mill owner. Half his face had been blown away by a musket ball and his teeth stood out in a ghastly grimace. Yesterday he was an astute businessman, prosperous enough to provide for a growing family. Now he was an ugly mess of gore and bone.

"He won't be doing no more translating for you Papist rebels," said a soldier. "Chuck him on the cart."

Jambo stared at him. He wanted to lash out and hit the smirking soldier in the face. But no. To lose control would be a defeat. It would give them the justification to inflict more violence on them. Instead he lifted the body carefully, stretched it out in the cart, and covered it under a length of tarpaulin. It was not a sight for his widow.

"What was in his mind?" he wondered as the cart bumped its way to the graveyard. The last time he had seen him was in the church, weeping as he passed on Winslow's dreadful diktat, and then sitting miserably by himself as if he felt he was somehow implicated in the crime he had announced.

"He must have gone mad with the hopelessness of it all," he said to Marguerite.

"He was a hero," he said to Pierre's widow. "He saved many lives by his action." But, in truth, he felt Landry had been selfish. If it was a sacrifice, it was also a betrayal of his family who now were left to face an uncertain future by themselves.

"What pleasure it would be to take revenge on Winslow and that ludicrous lieutenant," he said to Marguerite as they gathered around the graves.

"I would humiliate them and tear them to pieces like poor Pierre," she said, her eyes hard.

He put his arm through hers. There was no use pretending there was any action they could take. They were powerless.

"All we can do is to show no sign of weakness," he said. "It is our only weapon."

As they stood in stony dejection the wind changed and carried the rattle of the riggings of the ships in the bay around the silent graveyard. From that moment, the fear of death was always with them, lurking in dark corners, watching over them. Waiting.

NINE

Boudrot Point, Grand Pré

October 27, 1755. 5 a.m.

Removed

It was the day that the villagers were meant to be celebrating the wedding of Gabriel the blacksmith to his sweetheart Evangeline. Instead, the community had been put under lock and key. The men were battened down on the ships or shut away in the church, and the women were closely watched in their homes.

The soldiers were edgy now. There was no backchat, no turning of a blind eye as there had been before if the wives brought extra food to the church, or tried to stay and talk to their men. No, this morning the church door was hurled open so ferociously that it was torn off its top hinges and left hanging askew like a drunk at a wake.

Six armed soldiers burst in shouting, cussing and prodding the prisoners with their muskets.

"Up!"

"Come on you lazy bastards."

"On your feet, Froggie traitors."

As the prisoners unwillingly stood, the old men creaking and trembling, the youngsters sullenly defiant, Winslow entered. This time he was confident, in command. He did not prevaricate.

"This is the end for you in Nova Scotia," he announced.

"Acadia," said Jambo quietly. "Our country is called Acadia."

Winslow flushed, but ignored him. "Go to your houses, get what you need—just the essentials, mind—and wait with your families outside your doors. You have ten minutes, then we will escort you to the ships that will take you away. I do not want families to be split up, so try to stay together. Be calm. Soon you will be in another place where I am sure all will be well for you."

"We will not go," said Jambo. He stood on a pew staring steadily at the colonel, his black eyes filled with the anger that had been simmering since the death of Landry. He could not shake off the image of the miller's blasted face.

"It is better to be killed here. To die in our own country, the land we love."

Winslow looked at him almost sorrowfully. "I do not understand *no* in the face of the King's command," he said. A soldier cocked his musket and pointed it at the carpenter, but Winslow pushed the barrel away.

"Get down, young man," he said. "You can achieve nothing. The decision has been taken. There can be no parleys or delays. This land must be cleansed of foreign peoples."

The carpenter stayed where he was for a few seconds, took in the sight of the prisoners waiting for his lead, took in the soldiers with their guns, and stepped down. Yes, the decision had been taken. He was powerless.

He was escorted to the house where Marguerite had already made a pile of clothes and put aside some food, which they bundled into sacks. They held each other as they took one last look at the home they had made together as if to store a picture for the future—their home no more.

How hard they had worked to improve their simple cottage, lining the ceiling with cane, sawing and planing timber to make the cupboards, the chairs, and the big, solid oak table that they would gather round for meals, family meetings and games with the children. Their bed, boxed in and cozy, was covered in clothes they would not be taking. He checked the little space in the attic where the children slept to see if they had left anything they needed, and in the storeroom at the side of the house he grabbed a handful of apples that had been neatly arrayed with the pears. No doubt, the British would enjoy the two hogs he had salted and the haunch of deer that Pierre had given them not to mention the bottles of wine and casks of beer. The walls were hung with his hunting rifles and fishing rods and the tools of his trade were laid out tidily. There would be no more use for them. He held them regretfully, weighing each one in his hand, as if relinquishing the skills that had made him what he was. He jabbed the short, sharp knife he used for carving angrily into the work surface and turned to go, only to reach back and tuck it into his jerkin.

In the little furnace room at the back of the house the remains of a stew swung over the dying fire, and the warm aroma of that morning's new bread hung in the air.

"I didn't know," she said helplessly. "I just baked as usual."

"I think I will let the horse go free," he said. "I cannot bear the thought of a British backside on her."

Instead, they waited in the doorway as the rain dripped off the lintel onto their heads and watched as the dim figures of their oppressors moved eerily in the dark dawn until, as the sun rose, he could see them clearly, working methodically through the village, clearing the families from their homes, searching each building to make sure no one was hiding, and crashing open the doors if the occupants did not appear immediately.

"You. Next."

There was no time to set free the horse. He carried Jean-Baptiste and their two sacks of belongings while Marguerite held the baby and a basket of still-warm bread and salted meat. He picked up a wooden bear he had carved for Jean-Baptiste's birthday and a doll he had made for Osite that the little girl loved. They went silently, joining the others who were flowing like a tributary toward the sea—the old and the sick carried in carts, as bewildered by their plight as the children. Some skipped along as if it was an outing to a picnic, while others snivelled woefully, hanging on to their mothers' hands. The dog dashed in and out of their legs, sniffing for rabbits and barking at the soldiers. Jambo noticed that a gate had slipped from its hinges and needed fixing. *Who will repair that?* he wondered. *Most likely it will be left to rot away and the cattle allowed to roam and be eaten by wolves.*

Their path took them through the orchards. It was as if they were being mocked by the autumnal lushness of the red, ripe apples and succulent pears that would never be picked. Past the Hebert house, which was now a few blackened beams and wisps of singed thatch, a plow, its shaft half destroyed by the fire, lay where it had fallen. The smoky smell of the ruins briefly overwhelmed the familiar damp perfume of October in Grand-Pré—the cut grass, the piles of hay, the slightly musty smell of the fruit trees, the last faltering trails of honeysuckle.

"Keep moving," grunted a soldier.

Along the levee they straggled, toward the landing stage at the Point where they stood patiently in the rain like cattle in a storm. Osite snuggled into her mother's breast, oblivious. Jean-Baptiste, who was jumping on and off the cart with some of the other boys, thought it was a great game, but he quieted when he saw the grim faces of his parents.

By noon the beach was crowded with villagers. The soldiers divided them into groups and went through their belongings, littering the shoreline with food, pots, pans, clothing, and toys.

"You won't be needing this," said one as he took the lovingly carved bear from a bundle and threw it on the mud. "You have too much stuff." He rummaged in the sacks and removed one of Jambo's heavy coats and breeches, and lace-trimmings of Marguerite's she had optimistically tucked away for some future, hard to imagine, celebration. A splash of red cloth reminded him of the body left lying by the river, its blood congealing in the mud.

"There's hardly enough room for you on board, let alone your precious belongings."

At first, the British did try to keep the families together as Winslow had promised. To his surprise, LeBlanc saw that the men who had been imprisoned on board had been brought back to the shore and were waiting to be reassigned to a ship with their wives and children. Charles and his brothers were there, but he could not reach them through the melee. He shouted, but they did not hear.

Brooke Watson was shouting out names, "Joseph Blanchard and family here. Simon Aucoin, Paul Babin, Simon Granger, Pierre Richard...over there."

"Pierre," Jambo yelled "Pierre, wait for us." But no sooner had the trapper embraced Marie and his children with the frantic joy of being together again, they were hustled onto a boat and taken away into the misty bay.

It was impossible to keep order. The rain poured remorselessly on the screaming, panic-stricken throng, which was slipping and falling on the muddy foreshore, jostling to stay upright and clinging to the nearest person to prevent being pulled down under the waves, trampling on each other in their panic. No one pretended to be brave now.

He heard his father's name being called out, but he could not see him or mother. Amidst the chaos he was transfixed by the sight of his aunt, Marguerite-Marie. Her dripping wet clothes clung to her legs as if she was a mermaid and she was striking an astonished soldier with her sack of possessions. He picked her up by the waist and flung her, skirts flying, into a skiff. Her belongings were scattered and stamped underfoot.

He caught a glimpse of Evangeline, a forlorn figure with the red ribbons saved for her wedding day, snaking in the wet tendrils of her hair, standing on the shore crying out, "Gabriel, my love, where are you?"

Was it rain or tears that coursed down her cheeks? It was of no concern to the soldiers who no longer made any attempt to keep families united, but ruthlessly shepherded their victims toward the waiting flotilla, searching them yet again, taking the names of the men and manhandling them into the boats.

He caught a glimpse of Winslow on a knoll that raised him above the confusion. He was waving and pointing, exhorting his men to speed up the loading before the tide turned. For a second, Jambo was puzzled at the way he stood out so clearly, outlined by a bright light that shone on the hillside behind him.

"Flames. My God, they are torching the village."

"You. Here." A soldier shoved him forward so that the water came over the top of his boots. He turned to pick up Jean-Baptiste and grab Marguerite's hand, but she wasn't looking, she was reaching into the mud to rescue the doll Osite had dropped.

In the second of her hesitation a soldier came from behind and hit him hard between the shoulders with a rifle while another, grabbing him by his arm, half-lifted, half-shoved him into a boat.

"Bon voyage." He laughed.

The families already on board helped him get his balance as the sailors pulled on their oars.

He could hear, "Jambo. Jambo! Wait. That's my husband. Don't go without us." But he was gone. Lost in the mist.

The last thing he heard above the shouts of the soldiers, and the cries of the villagers, was the howl of the dog.

TEN

The prison ships

October 27, 1755, 5 p.m.

The Sarah and Molly

"Get down and stay down."

Jambo was pushed back into the hold, banging his head against the bolt of the hatch door as he fell. He was winded, gasping for breath, and disorientated by the dark. He tried to pull himself to his feet, but his right hand hung limply, bones sticking through the skin. How did that happen? He had scrambled up the ladder and had reached out to wrench himself back on deck but then the pain had been so great he had blacked out for a second and crashed down. One of Winslow's men must have stamped on it or shattered it with the blow of a rifle butt.

What was this? From the shore it had looked like just another merchant ship, the sloop Sarah and Molly. It had caught his eye when it dropped anchor a few weeks' before. *A friendly, unthreatening, name,* he thought. Named after the skipper's wife and daughter, perhaps. Maybe a mistress or two.

But there was nothing friendly about this. Pencil thin shafts of light glimmered through the hatch to reveal a sight that was like the pictures of Hades the abbot used to show the children in class to scare them into learning their catechism.

"See these damned souls here, naked and screaming," he would say, pointing sternly at the half human forms squirming in their dread of the flames below. "That will be you. Look at these scaly gremlins and horned demons— they will pursue you to hell with whips and burning brands if you do not know every word by heart."

From where he lay at the foot of the ladder, bilge water lapping around his soaked body, faces came in and out of focus like those spectral figures of the abbot, but these seemed to be floating in space, one on top of the other. *What was this?* There were shelves of wooden boxes, no, they were more like chicken coops, stacked on top of each other. In them, row after row of prisoners fluttering hopelessly.

Their hair was lank with the wet, mouths distorted in anger, grief, and terror. Their fists bunched in futile fury, or reaching out for help they knew they would not be given. They wept and cursed. They wept at God's abandonment of them and they cursed the English for such barbarity.

He could hear one voice rising hysterically above the clamor.

"Marguerite! Where are you? Marguerite?"

For a second he wondered who it could be calling out for her with such convulsive passion. He realized with a start; it was him.

There was no reply.

His head was whirling with the chaos of it all. *More like coffins,* he thought, *than coops. No, maybe like the wooden boxes they used to take the joints of pig to market. Coffins, coops, boxes...* what he could make out was that the villagers were packed together like cargo in an excruciating confusion of bodies, legs, and elbows, in spaces that were only about four feet high and barely six feet long. There seemed to be four to a box, some jammed shoulder to shoulder, others head to toe. They couldn't all stretch out and if they sat up their heads touched the floor of the box above, forcing them to crouch over their drawn-up knees.

Already the hold was filled with the rank smell of terror, the fug of wet clothes, and bizarrely, a sickly aroma like molasses that caught at the back of the throat. Some had already been sick, and children had soiled themselves, creating a stench that mingled horribly with the stale water that washed around the narrow gangway.

Better to be angry, he told himself. *If you're angry you can't be afraid.* The ship lurched in the swell of the turning tide and he tried to grab an upright to steady himself, but could not grip with his damaged hand. He used the back of it to dab at his soaking face and realized as it ran into his mouth that it was not just water that trickled down his face, but blood.

A sailor materialized, as if out of nowhere, lit by a flickering lantern.

"In there." He pushed him toward a box, pushing his head down to force him in. "And shut up."

"Jambo, my friend. Welcome aboard."

It was Pierre, bent double with Marie and the oldest of their boys, Joseph-Ignace. He could only just make out their faces in the dark.

"Pierre. Who else is on board?" he asked. "Have you seen Marguerite and the children?"

"No, I fear I have not."

He shouted, "It's Joseph LeBlanc here. Jambo. Has anyone seen my family?"

"I thought I saw Marguerite on a skiff behind us," said a voice nearby that sounded like Oliver.

"I think your folks were taken to another ship." A muffled shout, but he did not recognize who it was.

"It's Francois here, Jambo, but I saw nothing."

No Marguerite. No children.

"Mother, father, what of them?"

"I saw them being carried from Boudrot. Charles too." It sounded like Pierre Aucoin. "Maybe your Marguerite has been put with them by mistake. You know how many of you LeBlancs there are."

He bowed his aching head on his knees and prayed while Pierre tried clumsily to cheer him, his arms around the younger man's shoulders like a comforting bolster.

"It will be all right," he said. "When we get to this new land the British have in mind for us, we will all be reunited. It will be fine."

"The liar Winslow said we would not be separated. She was just behind me. And the children. We cannot trust these British. Francois was right to want to knock their blocks off. And this ship…what kind of hell is? It's like a crypt for the living."

"Or the dying. I don't know how long we will be able to survive this," said Pierre. "Remember in the church before they split us up how they said they were humane people and how well-equipped the ships were? They are equipped, all right, but there's nothing humane about it. You won't believe what they have done. We're in a merchantman that has been ripped apart to get as many of us in as possible. Every square inch has been turned into these boxes, and every box holds four of us."

"A prison ship. And we never really believed they meant us any harm. This is fiendish. Uncle Rene was right—they mean to put an end to us."

Disorientated and despairing, the prisoners fell into a night of restlessness and sullen foreboding. So densely packed were they that every move caused excruciating cramps, which made them start with the pain and bang involuntarily against each other or the rough sides of their boxes. He must have slipped into an exhausted minute or two of sleep, head lolling against Pierre's beefy shoulder, for he awoke with a start.

"We're moving!" shouted Oliver.

The anchor was being pulled up, rattling and banging and they could hear the water gurgling against the hull and the creaking of the masts as the wind filled the sails.

It was as if the noisy cheerfulness—the snatches of songs and volleys of curses from the men on deck above them—were intended to mock them in their terrifying predicament. Soon they would glide past the cliffs of Blomidon into the Bay of Fundy before heading out into the Atlantic. In his mind's eye, he could imagine the coastline with the smoke rising from the smoldering village and the homes, the sheds, the byres, and the barns that he had known for his 26 years, all reduced to rubble.

"That's it," said Pierre.

"Yes. That's it," said Jambo.

But then, what horror. For a second it was as if he was at home in their cozy front room where Marguerite was frying pork for a fricot, his favorite stew of potatoes, carrots and dumplings. What was that smell?

It's like burning flesh, he thought and then, *My God, the animals.*

After destroying their homes, the British must have continued by slaughtering their pigs, cattle and sheep, perhaps even their horses. The horses. *If only I had let the old girl run free she might have escaped,* he thought. *And the dog. She was too decrepit to go far, and no soldier would adopt her as a hunting hound.*

But there was worse. A fine dust crept through the hatch and the closed porthole covers and settled on their clothes, clogging their nostrils and silting into their eyes and throats.

It was the ash from the ghastly pyres of dead carcasses that by now must lie blackened and horrible in the fields of their lost land. He gagged, a dry, stomach-heaving retch that made his guts sore.

If only he could see what was happening. In his mind's eye he could witness the destruction of his village, see the houses disintegrate in flames, look on as the livestock was rounded up, shot, and immolated. The soldiers cheering their 'victory.'

They'll celebrate by drinking our beer and cider, he reckoned to himself, peering toward the portholes as if he wanted to catch a last, terrible, glimpse.

But could I really bear to see it? He was befuddled. *The sparks rushing into the dark sky; the screams of the animals; the smell. Would I be strong enough to look on that?* He felt he was fading in and out as if he had drunk too much. *But I can see it. I can see it all in my mind. There's no escape.*

He thought he might be having some sort of mental collapse—not that Acadians were afflicted by such things, he rebuked himself woozily—but when his heart started hammering and his head became as light as a torn bag of feathers, he panicked, coughing and gasping for breath.

Pierre asked, "Are you all right?"

"Perfect." He managed a terse laugh.

"No, I meant…I don't know about you, but I feel as I am going to faint," said the trapper, shifting his bulk uneasily in the coop.

"Me too," said Jambo, trying to prop him up but slumping back, drained of strength.

He had often been told by some of the old hunters who spent weeks in the wilds, living cheek by jowl in huts throughout the winter months, how the enclosed, dark, spaces made them paranoid and frustrated, irrationally distrustful of their companions. They would develop an urge to go outside, even though they knew they would die in such freezing conditions. Indeed, as he contorted himself to fit into his box, he found himself dreaming of leaping overboard, craving the rush of air that would hit him and the invigorating shock of the water as he plunged in.

What did it matter if he was swept to his death? At least he would be out of the hold, free of the confines which were unbearable to a people who spent their time outdoors, their boundaries restricted only by the horizons.

It was bad enough to have the water sloshing around their feet and condensation drizzling down the walls, but utterly terrifying to know that they were trapped below the level of the sea itself. Within a few hours they found themselves sweating, and like Jambo, clutching at their pounding chests and shaking uncontrollably, gasping for breath in the stale air.

But it was nothing, just a minor discomfort, instantly forgotten, the moment the ship reached the Atlantic. The sloop was rolling along steadily when it was hit side on by a wave, which spilled him into the gangway. Then another. Then wave after wave. They made a terrifying cracking sound as they hit, buffeting the ship from port to starboard, and from fore to aft, as it pitched and lurched with the violence of a tavern brawl. The screams of the hysterical prisoners went unheard as the wind wailed though the ship's rigging and rain hit the deck with a *rat-a-tat* like the drums in a Mi'kmaq tribal dance. The sea crashed ceaselessly onto the ship, sending gallons of water surging into the hold with such force that they were spilled out of the boxes and into the filthy gangway.

"Help with the pumps!" shouted a sailor, emerging like one of the abbot's demons from the gloom. "Take the buckets and clear the bilges. All of you—or we'll go down together."

Jambo staggered to his feet and hooked his damaged hand around a stanchion, and with Pierre in front and Francois behind they formed a ragged chain passing buckets of water to sailors who reached down through the hatch. He could barely hold himself upright and was thrust against the side time and again, powerless to stop himself falling and unable to get back to his feet without a sturdy yank from Francois.

After two days, the storm quieted and they were left, stunned by the turmoil, cut and bruised, soaked through and weary to the bone. By then, the prisoners had abandoned all shreds of dignity.

They were lying in their own urine and excrement, while some who had been pitched into the gangway preferred to lie there in the filthy water rather than clamber back into their tiny, cramped prisons, only to be catapulted back out, cracking their heads or breaking a limb. Even then, in calmer waters, they were kept below deck with an erratic supply of food—a mouthful of cabbage stew or just salty, damp bread—which was lowered down in buckets by the sailors.

"Surely, they can't keep us locked away forever," said Pierre.

"Why not?" asked Jambo. "Out of sight, out of mind."

"They don't give a damn," said Francois.

One morning—four or five days out, they had lost count—the hatch was flung open. "Come on up," a voice shouted. "Ten at a time." A pugnacious little man with an eye patch greeted them. "Now listen to me," he said to the prisoners as they shivered unsteadily on the heaving deck. "My name is Purreton. Captain James Purreton." His good eye flicked from man to man suspiciously, as if he feared someone might attack him on his blind side.

"On this ship you do as I say. Here, I have more power than any governor. More even than King George."

"Is this ship of yours able to go anywhere?" demanded Jambo as he surveyed the destruction left by the storms. One mast had been snapped in half, lying athwart the deck, its sail torn and ragged—that explained the crack, like a ricocheting musket shot they had heard below at the height of the storm—ropes weaved across the decks as if trying to escape from their moorings. The barrels that had contained fresh water had been split open and the door to the store for their provisions hung off its hinges, creaking in the wind.

"Not far, unless we get this shambles fixed," said the captain. "We'll have to call into a port for repairs."

"Where will we go?" he asked.

"Wait and see."

The sailors were under orders not to tell the prisoners where they were bound, but they picked up the occasional half-finished sentence and Oliver with his easy-going, gossipy nature soon got the first mate talking. When the ship wasn't pitching too heavily, he played cards with him and let him win.

"We are heading for Boston," said the mate. "That's where the ships are registered. They were commissioned for this little enterprise by Governor Lawrence in August."

Before the soldiers arrived, realized Jambo.

"He put the job out for tender and our owners, merchants from the city called Apthorp and Hancock, won the contract. He demanded that as many people as possible were to be carried off in the ships. He promised to reward them by paying for every person transported. Old man Apthorp couldn't believe his good fortune. It was a simple calculation: the more bodies he packed in, the more money he earned.

"Mind you, it had to be done in a mighty rush. The bulkheads were stripped out and the ballast stones removed to add about 12 feet to the length. Then the floor timbers were removed giving, I'd say, another 15 feet to the height of the holds. All the portholes were covered over, and all but one of the hatches were blocked up."

"So, we're the ballast."

"You could say that." He laughed.

"It must have been worth the while," said Jambo, wryly.

"Sure will be," said the mate. "We normally carry timber or molasses."

"Yes, I'd noticed that disgusting smell," said Jambo.

"I don't know how you can stand it," sympathized the mate. "But it's a small price to pay for us. The charter works out as 44 pounds and 54 pennies a head and that's a lot more than we'd get with a hold full of molasses. Means a nice bonus."

"Well, in that case, you can afford to give us more food and water. Don't you feel any pity for the children and the sick?" Jambo asked.

"Look at this." He pulled aside the broken store door and waved dismissively at half-empty shelves. "The governor said that there should be food for 30 days, but there's barely enough for seven here because all he actually supplied was five pounds of flour for each person, a couple of pounds of bread, and even less beef. And some of that was washed away."

He shrugged. "But listen, try to understand. The Sarah and Molly is only a 70 tonner. We should carry no more than a hundred or so on board, but there are more than 150 below decks and then there's the crew. That's not safe, especially the state the lifeboats are in, so we need to get to land as quickly as possible.

"But more grub? Forget it. The beef is already going off, the bread and flour was soaked when we were loading it, and although Winslow added some turnips, potatoes, and apples, they have all been nicely salted by the sea. I'm sorry, my French friend, it's going to be a hungry voyage."

They tried to keep the hold clean by sluicing it with sea water, and for the sake of decency made a crude privy at the prow shielded as best they could by a sheet of canvas. It was soon swept away by a gust of wind, leaving the prisoners—men, women and mortified children alike—to perch in full view of the jeering crew as they vented into the void.

All the time for Jambo, dazed with the suffocating closeness of the hold, battered by the storm, hungry, weak and depressed, there were questions to which there were no answers. What were the British going to do with them? Where were the others? Where was his Marguerite?

Maybe she and the children had been kept behind in Grand-Pré? Maybe they had been kidnapped by the troops, and Marguerite raped and murdered? What if their ship had sunk in the high winds of Cape Fourchu? It didn't bear thinking of, yet it consumed his every moment.

He would talk to himself, murmuring like the blind beggar he used to see at the town gates to Halifax who sought alms in a low, despairing monotone all day long.

How he missed Charles, who he knew would have kept up his spirits or done his damnedest to, and how he worried about his mother who had, almost overnight, lost her spirit and become reliant on the only son she knew for sure was still alive. As for father, where would he find the strength of will to resist the disintegration of his easy-going life?

All the fears, all the uncertainty—he thought they would overwhelm him and as if he understood, Pierre would dig him gently in the ribs and bring him back to his senses by talking about their last trapping expedition, or the salmon they had caught only a few weeks before. Then he would remember the pledge he had made to himself on the floor of the church: *he would not surrender to fear, he would not show any weakness.*

Daylight helped. The burst of sky that shone through the hatch when it was opened made their hearts flutter with hope that they may yet survive the ordeal and the few occasions they were allowed on deck helped them grow in resilience.

They stretched their limbs and gulped in the bracing air before splashing buckets of salt water over themselves to wash away the stink of the hold and clean their vile, soiled, clothes.

And always to the starboard, the sight of land on the horizon was some sort of reassurance.

"I bet we could swim that far," said Pierre.

"You couldn't even swim across the Canard," said Jambo with a laugh.

There was a shriek so sharp, so fierce, that it seemed to have been borne out of the wind that wailed through the rigging. So pure was the anguish that the prisoners froze, as if some demon was about to strike them dead.

"My baby, Pierre. Fallen over board! In the sea!"

They rushed to the side of the sloop, but there was nothing to see but the spume-flecked waters stretching behind them into the grey distance.

Still the screams. It was Madeleine Daigre, arms flailing like a wild animal caught in a trap, leaning over the stern of the ship as if about to jump in after her son.

"He fell in! My boy."

The women gathered around, pulling her back.

"We must stop the ship," said Jambo.

He shouted to Purreton, "Child overboard! Turn around. Put out the lifeboat."

"Happens all the time," said a sailor. He shook his head dismissively. "Nothing we can do."

"We'll never find him," said Purreton. "Just say your prayers. Keep full sail, bosun."

The mother was incoherent. "He's gone. In a second. Standing there. Next to me. Let go of my hand, just for a second. That's all. A second. Thought he'd seen a whale. The ship gave a lurch and then he was gone. Drowned. Gone. As if he had never existed."

Her husband, Jean, held her and their other child so tightly he might have stopped them breathing. The villagers stood, stunned, gazing back over the wake of the ship as if hoping for some miracle, reluctant to admit the boy had really drowned. That night when the hatches were battened down, all that disturbed a horrified silence was the weeping of the mother and her surviving son, and the murmur of her stricken husband as he and her sister Francoise tried to comfort her.

They all wanted to understand how they could be afflicted by something that was so sudden, arbitrary, and cruel, but all it proved was that they had no control over their fate, over the British, over the elements, over God. They were all against them.

What if. What if the same fate had befallen Jean-Baptiste? He was always wriggling free from his parents' restraining hands to play with the dog or throw stones at the chickens. God forbid Marguerite was on a ship somewhere in the Atlantic grieving at the loss of their children without him to comfort her.

ELEVEN

Boston Harbor

November 5, 1755.

Betrayed

On the morning of the tenth day they awoke to the sensation of the ship moving gently through calmer waters. There was the splash of the anchor, followed by a bump.

"We must have reached land," said Jambo struggling out of the enclosing coop.

"Thank the Lord. But where?" said Pierre.

The hatch was thrown open. "Welcome to Boston!" shouted Purreton. "Your new home."

The ship was tied up to the wharf in a bay with more ships at anchor than he had ever seen in one place before.

"My God, so many people," said Pierre.

"Must be twice the size of Halifax," he said.

"Much bigger," said Oliver, sounding quite cheerful. "Just think of the shoes that need repairing."

"How powerful the British are," said Jambo in wonder. "What chance did we have?" The ships jostled for space in the harbor where there was a constant to-ing and fro-ing of skiffs carrying men on shore leave, others in uniform returning to service, lighters ferrying customs officers and soldiers, and ocean-going vessels heading for the West Indies or arriving from Liverpool. Beyond their masts they could glimpse rows of houses that stretched up a hillside while on the quay, stevedores and navvies wheeled carts, manhandled sacks, loaded crates of rum and stacked timber, yelling to each other as if they were deaf. He and Pierre scanned the port for the prison ships that had been in Minas Bay, but he could see none of them in the melee.

Jambo slunk back into the hold and wedged himself in his box. He fought off the tears of disappointment by holding so tightly to the prison's ragged wooden uprights with his good hand that its splinters drew blood. He shut his eyes and wished the time away.

The next morning they woke to a great thumping and scraping on the side of the ship. It was so abrupt that children were spilled out of their boxes and some of the frailer prisoners, who had been stretching their legs in the gangway, were sent sprawling. Once he and Pierre had disentangled themselves, Jambo said, "It must be another ship."

"Lousy sailor, then."

"But it must be from Grand-Pré. Otherwise, why tie up so close? They would want to keep us together. *Marguerite.*"

Jambo burst through the hatch and before sailors could stop him was on deck and by the railings. Yes, there was the Neptune, there was the Endeavour and three others and on the decks were scores of familiar faces. Everyone was calling out the names of a missing son or a lost mother, aching for a sight of a daughter, an uncle, a father. For some, there were whoops of happiness and relief as they were re-united, for others the silence of dashed hopes.

"Where are the rest of the transports?" he asked Purreton. "There were more than 20 when we left our homeland. What has become of our families?"

"I have no idea," said Purreton. "I only sail this one." He spat, shrugged, and shouted at the crewmen to tighten the hawsers. "They could be anywhere. Philadelphia, New York. Maybe sunk. You name it."

Jambo stared at him, his eyes bloodshot from nights of anguish, and for a second he started forward as if to strike the skipper for his indifference.

"Jambo? Here! J-j-ambo!" It was Charles, waving at him from the deck of The Neptune. With him were Anne and the two children.

"Marguerite? Is she there?"

"Not with you?" asked Anne.

"No."

Charles clambered over the railings and put his arms around his shoulders. "D-d-don't you worry. We shall all be together again soon enough. She will be on the next ship."

But she wasn't. And she wasn't on any of the ships that arrived in the following 24 hours.

She must be drowned, or taken to another of the cursed colonies. He should accept the inevitable—that he would never see her again, or play hide and seek with his little boy, or cuddle Osite. He had lost his family.

"Dear Lord, help me to be strong," he prayed in the silent litany, which he repeated time and again. "I must keep going."

As the only surviving member of the Grand Pré council on the ships, the villagers turned to Jambo for leadership and elected him, Pierre, and Charles to be their spokesmen. Their first duty was to arrange a service for the Daigre boy, and for two others who had succumbed in the storms.

"Is that all?" asked Purreton. "You've been lucky."

The bodies were wrapped in tarpaulins, and the prisoners gathered on deck to mumble the funeral mass while the sailors, used to the routine of such sea-going tragedy, carried on working around them before the dead were taken ashore in lighters to be buried in a paupers' graveyard.

"Will anyone ever visit the graves?" wondered Pierre.

"We shall make it our duty when we are released," said Jambo.

"If," said Francois.

The three were soon called upon to show their mettle when a customs official came on board to inspect the piteous cargo.

Before the official could speak, Jambo stepped forward. "Monsieur. Sir. I am Joseph 'dit Jambo' LeBlanc. I have been asked to represent the citizens on these ships, and we demand to know what is happening to us. Why are we being treated like slaves? What is to become of us?"

The customs officer blinked at the onslaught from this young man, who was as pale with sickness as all his comrades seemed to be.

"The truth is, we know little of this situation," the official said. "We did not know you were coming until a few days ago when a messenger came overland from Governor Lawrence. He did not tell us how many to expect or what he wanted of us. It's very tricky. All we know from the Governor is that you are enemies of His Majesty."

"It is not the case," said Jambo. "We are enemies to no one."

"So why are you here?" The customs officer looked genuinely puzzled.

"We are innocent bystanders in your war with France, but we have been made scapegoats, and as you see, expelled from our homeland. But we have rights. We are not prisoners of war, we are not like the savages you trade in," he gestured at a group of slaves hobbling along the wharf in chains.

"Look," said Francois. "Look if you think you can bear to see how we suffer." He lifted the hatch and the officer peered down, flinching at the stench that hit him in the face.

Purreton said, "They have had to lie in their own piss and shit. There was nothing we could do."

The sailors who heard this laughed, holding their noses in a caricature of disgust.

"Silence." The customs inspector was embarrassed by their crudeness. "I agree. I do. There is no reason for us to treat you like vermin. We British run our colonies with justice and compassion."

"I have little seen evidence of that," said Jambo. "Our people are dying because we do not have proper food and clean water. We are crammed into boxes as if we are being sent to the abattoir for slaughter, except you would not treat your cattle like this. We demand to be treated with respect."

"I shall do what I can," said the inspector. "First I must investigate all the ships to see how many of you there are and the conditions you are in."

"Be quick!" shouted Jambo as the officer and his retinue teetered back down the gangplank. "Or there will be other deaths on your hands."

Later that same day a cauldron was set up on deck—"I put in a word with the council," said Purreton—and the prisoners made a stew out of fresh potatoes and cabbage.

"There is even some rum for you," said the skipper, and he winked with his good eye.

"Better than one of my f-f-feasts at a *bal de danse*," said Charles in a vain attempt to cheer them up.

The next morning the customs man reappeared, clutching papers and looking fussily important, as if he now understood what was going on and was in command of the situation.

"I have done an inventory of all you people and the provisions you have left," he said. "I have told the council that the allowance of provisions is short and that what little you have has been spoiled by salt water. From what I have seen on the other ships, I acknowledge that many of you prisoners are sickly and overcrowded. Some of you will have to leave."

"Some? To go where and to do what?"

"Isn't this were we are to be '*happy and peaceable*,' as Colonel Winslow put it so eloquently," said Jambo.

The inspector fiddled with his papers. It was clear that, despite his earlier show of confidence, he was discomfited by their lack of subservience, made more discomforting by the fact that he was caught up in something he did not fully comprehend. "Let us take this in stages," he said. "There may be work for you here."

"For us all?"

"We had a special council meeting last night to set up overseers of the poor, and as a start it will be possible for some young men to be hired out as indentured workers."

"I knew it," said Francois. "Slavery."

Purreton interrupted, "He is trying to do his best to help. You have already heard that Lawrence made no provision for you here."

"Thank you, Mr. Purreton," said the inspector. "I shall have to move some of you from The Sarah and Molly—eleven by my calculations—and there are 40 more who are ill and have been laid out on the deck of The Dolphin. I cannot allow that, especially in this inclement weather, and I am sure you do not want it either, so I shall put them on land. There will have to be another 12 taken off from the other ships."

"I don't understand," said Jambo, trying to keep the alarm out of his voice. "Surely we are all going to settle here."

"Isn't that why we were exp-p-elled?" asked Charles.

"To be 'removed' to another place," said Pierre.

"He is lying to us," said Francois. "All the time, these potato heads lie to us."

"It is no good you yapping," retorted the official rounding on the plowman. "We are not to blame. This plan, at least, gives some of you a chance to start a new life immediately. I shall return tomorrow, by which time you will have chosen who will be the first to go."

The LeBlanc brothers called for a meeting on deck and found no shortage of volunteers wanting to leave.

"You have to realize that the British are not saying we can go home," he warned. "Not to Grand-Pré. All they are doing is offering work here in Boston."

"And how can we know how reliable that undertaking is?" asked Pierre.

"Will there be somewhere to live?" wondered Oliver.

"I do not know," admitted Jambo. "I don't think they know either."

"What choice do we have?" said Pierre.

"Not much if the customs fellow is anything to go by," said Oliver. "He doesn't appear to have a clue."

"Whatever we choose, we'll be the ones to go hang," said Francois. "That is a certainty."

Jambo said, "It might be the best hope for some families with older children to let them be apprenticed to a merchant here, rather than stay as prisoners on this stinking hulk. It gives them a chance to earn some money, though it will be a pittance I'm sure, and there must also be work for the men, however menial."

"Anything is better than being on this ship," said Jean Melancon. "I can't stand another day of it. I want to find out what has happened to my family, and I won't do that by staying here."

"Me too," said his brother, Phillipe. "Once on land we can escape and make our way home by foot if necessary."

"We've got a saw mill that isn't cutting timber," continued Jean. "We need to get it working."

Jambo started to interrupt, but let it go. They all had to find hope where they could, he understood that, but he feared the best they would find was a new, but hazardous, life of prejudice and exploitation somewhere in the colonies. Not, he felt certain, back in the devastated meadows of Grand-Pré.

With Jambo, Charles, and Pierre sitting in judgment on the freezing deck, they decided to let either single men or families with children of working age be the first to leave; Pierre Alpin because he had no relatives to care for' the Boudrots, who used to have a farm on the north side of the bay, were prepared to have their children indentured and the two Melancon brothers had already stuffed their sacks with the few damp clothes they owned.

As they bickered over who should make up the numbers, Purreton and the inspector came on board. This time he was brusque, as if he wanted the matter off his hands as quickly as possible. "We cannot delay any longer," he said. "We have taken off the sick from the other vessels, so now I will choose the final volunteers. I need a total of thirty."

"The sooner they get on shore the better for everyone," said Purreton as the volunteers were lined up and lowered over the side to the waiting skiffs.

As they were rowed through the slow swell of the bay, snow started to fall, settling on them and the ones left behind who stood on the quarter deck and watched until they were lost to sight in the maze of ships and disappeared into the dark.

"I wonder if we will ever s-s-see them again," said Charles.

"Who knows," said Francois, "but I would not trust these Englishmen to do what they have undertaken."

"Tomorrow, maybe in a week or so, we too should be off these damned transports and on land," said Jambo, trying to keep their spirits up. "We can start anew. It will be hard, but we can do it. It was tougher for our ancestors, don't ever forget that."

As the sun dipped behind the noble houses that lined the hills above the harbor, the crew ushered the families below.

"It's curfew time. Down to your lodgings, my French *amis.*"

The hatch was slammed shut, and as usual, the captives fidgeted around to make themselves as comfortable as possible, soothing the children by telling them their favorite stories and talking in a soft babble of voices.

They were interrupted by a great commotion on deck. The captain was yelling orders, the sailors were rushing about, and the anchor was wheezing and straining as it was wound from the harbor floor. The ship lurched as the sails filled with wind and the current carried it out to sea.

"What is going on?" Jambo scrambled out of his cell. Within seconds the men below were beating at the hatch.

"Where are you taking us?"

"We were meant to stay here."

"Bastards, *têtes caurees,* liars."

But there was no answer. The villagers were once more left forsaken in the darkness of their floating prison.

TWELVE

Williamsburg, Virginia

November 13, 1755.

Never Such Love

"We should have fought when they first came marching into the village" said Francois. "We should have caved their heads in. But we just gave up. Let them drive us from our homeland. Useless, damned cockchafers that we were."

More than most, he had been driven close to madness by the claustrophobia of the hold, and when the ship made its sudden run from Boston, he had led the men trying to tear apart the prison boxes. Even Pierre lent his bulk to the hatch in an attempt to push it open.

Jambo swiftly gave up the futile outburst and retreated to their coop, pulling Pierre back with him.

"What would we do if we did break out on to deck," he said "Overpower the crew and sail to freedom?"

The British soon proved his point. They appeared to ignore the chaos below decks until, deciding the demonstration had gone on long enough, opened the hatch and fired a volley into the hold.

One man screamed as he was hit in the arm, but miraculously no one else was injured.

"Stop it! Stop!" shouted LeBlanc. "It's pointless. They don't mind how many of us they kill. All we have done is make things worse for ourselves," he went on, surveying the wreckage they had wrought. "There is nothing we can achieve while we are at sea."

The next morning, when they were well clear of land, the hatch was flung open. "You can come on deck now. Ten at a time as usual. You'll have to behave yourselves from now on," said Purreton. He seemed more amused than angry. "The next time might be more painful."

"You said we were to stay in Boston," said Jambo. He clenched the fist of his good hand so hard to keep his angry frustration under control that his nails cut into the palm.

"We thought that was where we were to s-s-start our new lives," added Charles.

"You lousy lickfingers betrayed us," said Francois.

"No one actually ever said anything of the sort," said the skipper, dismissively, spitting in his familiar way. "No one wanted you there. You must face it, mon braves, you are not wanted anywhere. Maybe another country will let you land and settle, but this is beyond my control, you must understand that. Orders are given, and I have to obey them."

"Where are you taking us?" demanded Pierre.

"What about the food that we were promised?" asked Jambo

"First things first," said Purreton. "Look, I've done the best I can. The cauldron is already warming. We have fresh bread and clean water. Get your people up here and they can eat."

"And then, where are we going?"

"To Virginia. Lovely place. Warm. Palm trees right to the shore, orange groves, sugar plantations, and as much tobacco as you can stick in your pipe. You'll be happy there, though I'm told it's a bit dangerous—the Virginia Rangers are having problems on the border with the Indians as well as you Frenchies."

One week later, the ship swung to starboard, sailed up an estuary lined with low, wooded, hills and glimpses of well-tilled fields, and dropped anchor.

"Williamsburg—the finest city in the colonies," announced the skipper, his one good eye gleaming with pleasure. "Hard to see from here, but it's full of noble houses and a fine church. For the *true* faith, of course.

"You'll be impressed when you see the Governor's palace—three stories high with a ball room as big as a prairie, though I don't suppose you'll be invited there very often. It belongs to the Right Hon. Robert Dinwiddie. He'll be pleased to see you." He laughed as if he had told a great joke.

"Look," said Charles. "Over there, ships from G-g-rand Pré."

"Yes, thank God," said Jambo. "There's the Endeavour and The Neptune, which was moored alongside us in Boston."

Once again that hope, that faint hope, which had sustained him flickered again. Marguerite and the children might be waiting for him, waving from the deck of another prison ship. But even as he hoped, he expected the worst. For too long now, for every night for a month, he had woken from his cramped sleep sweating in terror at the nightmare that kept recurring—that her ship had foundered, taking her and the children to their deaths.

"What are the ones moored behind?" he asked.

"The Mary, The Prosperous, and The Industry," said a sailor.

"They were in Minas Bay the day they we were expelled," said Jambo, in a voice like a prayer, "Please God, my Marguerite is here."

"Captain, my wife and children might be on board one of the ships. My parents too. Can I go with the lighter to see if I can find them?"

A spit and shrug. Jambo felt sure he was going to refuse him. The skipper stared with his one-eye at the supplicant.

You," he said to a midshipman. "Take this man with you. If he can find his wife and ankle snappers, let them come on board. But only *them,* mind, we can't have *everyone* on the good ship Sarah and Molly, it's not a pleasure boat on the Thames."

They rowed to the Neptune and scraped past the bow of the Prosperous. So many familiar faces—Pierre Landry's family, the Robichauds, and that joker Germain Thibodeaux. And wait—there was Marguerite's younger brother Joseph.

His heart leapt and he shouted, "Joseph! You're safe, thank God. But Marguerite, is she with you?"

"I haven't seen her since we left," he shouted. "Have you tried all the ships?"

"We must go back," said the sailor.

Jambo begged, "Just one more. Please. Over there — that one —The Industry. It was not in Boston."

And there she was. Standing at the railing with the baby in her arms and Jean-Baptise at her side, looking out for him on the decks of the other ships.

"Marguerite." He hardly raised his voice, but she heard instantly, turning to him with a look that was almost rueful in its relief and tenderness.

He could just reach her fingertips from the boat. She was pale and tremulous, but she joked, "So you tried to make off without us? Leave us on the shore. Still, you obviously can't cope without me—you look a fright with that beard and your hair all dirty and unkempt—what a mess. Like a hermit. I hardly recognized you. But your hand, what happened?"

The baby smiled at him and Jean-Baptiste jumped on to a pile of rope so that his chin reached the top of the railing.

"Papa!"

"My brave sailor," said Jambo, the tears rising. And there were mother and father, both spectral with anxiety. "We're all alive," he said and laughed with sheer joy.

"Come on now," said the midshipman, eyeing him as if he were a lunatic. "Let's get you lot back."

The LeBlancs were together again, able to hold each other, dazed with the turmoil of their reunion, and ecstatic that the anguish of being apart was over. Their words tumbled together.

"I dreaded—"

"So did I. When you disappeared on the skiff…you were gone within seconds."

"I didn't realize you weren't in the next boat until it was too late."

"God, how much I have missed you." He put his hand on her cheek and drew her even closer.

"How could I live without you?"

"And me," piped up Jean-Baptiste from his father's knee.

"And you." He kissed the two children, hugging them close as if he could not bear to let them go.

He kept stroking her face and stared hard at her as if his black eyes could bore into her soul and imprint his feelings forever. "There never was such love," he said. No, it was more of an incoherent groan that mixed fervor with thankfulness that the ache had been healed. "Never."

He and Marguerite sat with their arms around each other, lips together, not caring what onlookers might think, talking in ecstatic murmurs while the children happily climbed over them, demanding their share of attention.

"I've been haunted by the vision of your face in my dreams," she said. "Every night I saw it as if you were lit by the moon, standing at the prow of a ship. You were grieving, as if you knew I was dead."

"I thought you were. That storm." He held her, almost suffocating the baby who let out a little squawk of protest. He kissed her but the scrape of his stubbly chin made her whimper more.

"If we can survive that, we can survive anything," he said, comforting the child. "It's as if all our afflictions have been remedied. Everything is clear again."

She burst into tears. "I was so selfish. I thought when the storms hit us that I would drown and that you would find another. Marry. Have a new family."

"How could that be? How could I live without my Marguerite, my compass, my lover? How could you doubt my constancy? I could never be with anyone else."

"It's as if we were young before but now time and fear has made us old."

"But now, together, now we have nothing to fear."

She kissed his damaged hand and then his mouth.

He kissed her back urgently, but she pulled back. Her eyes were clouded, and she laughed. "Behave yourself, you're not at home."

She changed the subject. "Thank the Lord, brother Joseph has been spared," she said. "But have you seen my father?"

"I fear not. Nor is there word of Uncle Rene."

"Evangeline? What of her? To think I had just finished her wedding dress. You should have seen what a glorious outfit we had made for her."

He said, "We can only hope they are still alive in one of the other ports."

"The crew said that the captains had instructions to deliver us to as many colonies as possible, so that we would be scattered and no threat to them," said Marguerite. "But I don't think they knew much more than we did. Our skipper thought at first that he had been ordered to Maryland."

"And we heard talk of Carolina and New York. Georgia."

"Papa," said Jean-Baptiste who had been swinging perilously on the ship's rails. "Uncle Charles is calling you."

"Come on you two, that's enough of all that c-c-canoodling!" yelled Charles from the quarterdeck. "You ought to see this. They are p-p-putting on quite a show for us."

On the quayside, Purreton was being subjected to a tirade from a grand fellow who had arrived on the quayside in a coach and four. He had the complexion of lard with a lumpy nose like a small boulder that stood out from his heavy jowls and drooping eyelids. When he spoke, his thin lips scarcely moved. They watched as the captain, the undisputed ruler of his ocean-going kingdom, was reduced to little more than a foot servant.

"It's the governor," said Charles. "Everyone seems t-t-terrified of him."

Dinwiddie, who spoke with a dangerous sibilance, hissed at the hapless skipper—though he kept his distance, carefully standing on the step of the coach in case his shiny buckled shoes were spoiled by the mud, "Who the deuce are they? Why are they here? By whose orders?"

Purreton, bowed and handed over a document which the Governor read aloud in a voice that alternated from incredulity to incandescence. *'From Colonel John Winslow, for his Majesty's especial service. To the Honourable Robert Dinwiddie, Esquire, Lieutenant Governor and Commander in Chief of His Majesty's Colony and Dominion of Virginia or to the said Governor of the colony for the time being.'* For the time being, what does the man mean? Who is this Winslow?"

"One of Governor Lawrence's officers in Nova Scotia," said Purreton.

"Lawrence! Jumped up..." For a moment he was at loss for words but gathered himself and read. *'It is hereby certified to all whom it may concern that there hath been here landed French persons from Nova Scotia with the baggage and other effects to them belonging. And it doth not appear to me that the said Mr. James Purreton'*—Purreton? Is that you?—*hath in any particular failed of his duty toward them during their voyage and the said is this day discharged agreeable to charter party. Given under my hand and seal...'* Agreeable!" Now he was beside himself with indignation. "This missive was written months ago, without me knowing anything about it, without any consultation."

He tore the letter into shreds, scattering them into the puddles.

"Lawrence." The contempt was palpable. "Only been governor for a year or so. How dare he?" He jabbed the skipper's chest. "Come near. Do not think for one moment that you are discharged. It is *not* agreeable to me. I do not want these foreigners here. In case you, or indeed Mister Lawrence, have not realized, there is a war on.

"We are fighting the French along every mile of the border. Why in God's name would we want more of them in our country?" For the first time, he deigned to look at the Acadians lining the deck who were watching the performance with both bafflement and amusement.

"Send me down the leaders. I must talk to them, I suppose."

Mortified by his humiliation Purreton stalked up the gangplank. "LeBlanc, you seem to be spokesman here. That's the governor, in case you hadn't realized. He wants to meet you. Take two comrades, if you choose."

Jambo and Pierre made their way on shore, their legs wobbling as they stepped on land for the first time in weeks.

Francois made to follow, but Marguerite said, "Not you, Francois, you'll only lose your temper and cause an upset. This needs a woman."

Up close, their reluctant host seemed rather more peevish than grand. He waved a silk handkerchief under his nose with ostentatious contempt at the scruffy, unwashed refugees. When he realized that Marguerite was one of the delegation, he was taken aback and gestured her away.

"She is on our council," said Pierre. "In our country, women have equal rights."

"She can have equal rights here, too," hissed the governor. "Same as the rest of you. None."

His entourage laughed uproariously at their chief's witticism.

"I am Robert Dinwiddie," he said. "I am governor of this state of Virginia. This is my aide, Colonel Washington." He gestured to an unsmiling young man in the blue and red uniform of the local militia, the Virginia Rangers. "This is a disgrace. I cannot understand why Governor Lawrence felt entitled to send you *here* of all places. Indeed, all I know about you is from this letter." He waved at the paper he had torn up and thrown into the puddles.

He stared angrily at them. "You do indeed look to me to be a dangerous and pernicious gang—well, that's what he calls you. No wonder he wanted rid of you, but here, damn it, why not back to France? Can you imagine how very disagreeable it will be to my citizens when they find out you French agitators have been imported among us."

"Sir, I have to object," said Jambo. "We are not French. We are Acadian. We owe no allegiance to France. We have always been Neutral. We have done nothing to hurt the British, but we have been expelled from our homes and from the country which has been ours for generations."

Pierre said, "Can you understand that all we ask is to be taken off these ships, and to be reunited with our families, so that we may return to our homeland together?"

"There is no chance of that," Washington declared. "And be sure that we cannot waste our exchequer on you when we have to protect our border with Ohio against French and Indians. We cannot feed you, and we certainly have no clothes or medicine."

"This is not of our doing," said Marguerite. "We are sick, hungry, and despairing. Scores have died already. Is it such a waste to save innocent lives?"

A flap of the handkerchief. Dinwiddie was speechless.

Jambo thought she had never looked more beautiful. Despite her pallor after the weeks of incarceration, her eyes were alight with the passion that she had brought to the daring days of their courtship.

"We deserve to be treated as British citizens," said Jambo. "For that is what we are."

"Pah! You can barely speak English," drawled the colonel.

"In that case, what are we?" demanded Jambo. "Are we subjects, prisoners, slaves, or freemen? Let us know so that we can act accordingly."

"And be treated as such," added Pierre.

Again the handkerchief, while his aide wrinkled his noise contemptuously and threw back his head in exaggerated disbelief at such effrontery.

"We are prepared to earn our keep," said Marguerite. "To serve as the good citizens we have always been."

Dinwiddie was nonplussed "Will you take the oath of allegiance to King George?" he demanded.

"We have said many times that we are happy to acknowledge British rule," said Jambo.

"We always have," said Pierre.

"And to fight. Will you fight for the British?"

"We take up arms for no one," said Pierre. "We are neutral in that matter."

"In that case, you have no rights here," said Washington. He turned to

Purreton, "For God's sake, as well as ours, take these people back on board and anchor your ships as far out in the bay as possible. I am sure they are a breeding ground for all manner of diseases, and we cannot have the contagion of their sickness or their treacherous beliefs infecting our peaceable residents."

To the surprise of the Acadians and the irritation of Dinwiddie, the skipper spoke up, "Sir, many of these wretches are likely to perish. I beseech you to give them leave to land."

Dinwiddie recovered himself. "I think not captain. But we are not cruel for the sake of it. I will arrange for one pound of rice to be supplied to last each person ten days. Think yourself lucky," he said as he eased himself back into his coach.

"Meanwhile, I need to think what to do with you."

THIRTEEN

The Bay, Virginia

Winter 1755—1756.

Japes and Jail Fever

"It will soon be Christmas," said Marguerite. "We cannot let it pass without a celebration."

"You're right. If nothing else it will show the British that they have not broken our spirit," said Jambo.

"I was thinking more about the children," she said. "They have so little joy in their lives, wouldn't it be nice to give them a treat? At this time of year, I always make them sweet dumplings and apple pie. They so love them."

"I want cinnamon rolls," said Jean-Baptiste.

"But what can we do?" asked Pierre's Marie. "There must be about 40 little ones on The Sarah and Molly alone."

"I don't suppose the British will be rowing across with boatloads of food for us," said Jambo.

"And we don't have anything that tastes much like a sweet dumpling," said Marguerite.

"Cinnamon rolls. Cinnamon rolls," chanted Jean-Baptiste.

"Leave it to me," said Oliver, his eyes goggling behind his spectacles with anticipation at the challenge. "I have a thought."

The next morning, he said, "Pierre, Francois, Charles, come and play cards. "Francois, when I give the signal, pretend to lose your temper."

"Shouldn't be too d-d-difficult," said Charles.

Even Francois managed a smile.

They set up their game on a plank on the quarterdeck, and soon a crowd of curious sailors were looking on. Suddenly, Francois appeared to fly into a rage and hurled the cards across the deck.

"You damned cheat," he shouted at Oliver, and made to grab him round the neck.

Sailors wrestled him to the ground and frog marched him into a cabin under the poop deck.

"That'll calm him down," said the first mate. "Must a good game if it's worth fighting over."

"It's called loo," said Oliver. "It's a game from France, so you might not be familiar with it. The idea is that a pool is formed and each player is dealt three or five cards. Once you've had a look at your hand you can abandon it, or choose to play. You have to try to win at least one trick for one third or one fifth of the pool.

"If you fail to do so, you are *looed*, and you have to add an amount to the pool, which is carried forward and increased again. There can be quite a nice little pot in the end."

"Looks easy," said a sailor.

"Oh it is," said Oliver guilelessly. "Do you want a try just to see how it goes?"

After a couple of turns which the English sailors won, Oliver said, "Tell you what, I don't have any money with me—I must have left it at home—but if you win again, I shall repair your shoes in lieu of payment." He chuckled at his own jokes, but the sailors looked at him blankly.

"If I win, well, I am sure we can come to an arrangement—you being such gentlemen."

The soldiers did understand that and laughed at his nerve.

"All right then, our soles are full of holes."

"And I can make your clothes as good as new," said Marguerite. "That's worth many a penny."

"Yes, we'll get those waistcoats smartened up for when you go ashore and have to impress the ladies," said Marie.

"It's a deal."

The sailors' winning streak continued.

"How many shoes is that?" lamented the cobbler. "It will take me a week to pay you."

But then, surprise, surprise, the tide turned and Oliver won a game. Then another.

"You owe me ten pennies," he said, scooping up the IOUs the soldiers had scattered on the table.

"Well, it was good sport," said the first mate. He fumbled in his pocket for the money.

Oliver looked thoughtful. "Money's not much use to me at the moment. Can you pay in kind?"

"Maybe some food," said Jambo.

"What we would really like," said Marguerite, with her most winning smile, "are treats for Christmas. For the children."

"We'll see what we can do," said a sailor, melting at her flirtatious appeal.

"And rum," said Charles.

"And rum."

They lived up to their promise. Four hogs were delivered to the ship with sacks of rice and corn and a small barrel of rum.

The prisoners did what they could to celebrate. The women did make dumplings and cinnamon rolls, and the men roasted the hogs on a shaky spit on deck before gathering to hear Jambo lead a short service of thanksgiving.

"Not much to be thankful about," grumbled Francois, who was still nursing a sore head from his treatment over the card fight. Oliver had *come across* some razors, which the men used to shave and trim their hair, while the women had washed what clothes they weren't wearing and shared out the few inches of lace they had between them. Then they had a party, which, for a few hours, put a smile on the faces of the children.

Oliver did his card tricks and Charles sang and told stories of adventure and derring-do while the children raced around the ship as if it was a playground.

"It's the first time I've heard laughter for many weeks," said Marguerite. She stooped to pick up one of the Richard boys who had tripped on a rope and grazed his knee. She looked around the crowded deck for his parents.

"Where are Pierre and Marie?"

Jambo smiled, rather sheepishly.

"What does that smirk mean?"

"While everyone is on deck, they are, er below. Both of them."

She looked startled. "You mean—"

"Yes. What do you think? Maybe—"

"I think it's very good idea." She grasped his good hand and held it surreptitiously to her breast.

"We'll have to wait for our turn."

"Turn?"

"Yes. Charles and Anne are there, too."

"How shocking," she said with a smile. "Why didn't you tell me?"

"I wasn't sure how you would react."

"Not sure. After all this time? Remember those evenings in the forest?"

He did. "I think this calls for another mug of rum."

Pierre and Marie emerged on deck looking happy, if embarrassed.

"Come," she said.

"Keep watch," said Jambo to Pierre, and they clattered down the ladder into the hold.

They made love fast and urgently, crammed against the rough wood of the prison boxes, nervous of being discovered, but overwhelmed with hunger for each other.

"God we're like animals," said Jambo.

"It's been so long," said Marguerite. Her face was flushed with drops of perspiration starting from her upper lip, and a rill of sweat slipping down toward her breasts. Her odd eyes were strangely unfocused with the thrill of their risk taking and the passionate rawness of the moment.

"I had almost forgotten," she breathed as she kept him there for a few spasmodic moments and then as sense reasserted itself, held him close for a moment more before pulling down her skirts and climbing back to the bright, chill of the day.

The thrill of their wanton interlude soon passed to be replaced by drab monotony as the days spent anchored offshore turned into weeks and months and as their hopes of freedom receded, they became increasingly edgy and cast down, reacting to their imprisonment in different ways.

Many, especially the single men, grew depressed. They fought each other over trivial matters—who was sitting where, why one had more space than another. There were arguments over whose turn it was to use the wash pump, or who had eaten the last crust of bread. Francois grew increasingly morose, flying into rages without cause, sometimes banging his head against the bulwark with the sheer impotence of it all, but adversity made Charles more determined to be cheerful, spouting a constant stream of jokes and snatches of songs. Pierre seemed to stay unaffected, though even he would sometimes spend hours staring emptily as if trying to escape reality by reliving the nights spent hunting, silently poised in the forest waiting for a deer to trot into his sights.

Even Marguerite would sometimes slip into a withdrawn melancholy, so Jambo would buoy her with the dream of returning to Acadia, maybe that summer, perhaps in autumn, when they would smell the sweet air and pick the ripe apples off the trees.

Jean-Baptise would ask anxiously, "When are we going home?" And they would answer, "Soon." And when he awoke from a nightmare—"I thought I was drowning. The waves came right over the ship, I couldn't breathe"—Marguerite would rock him back to sleep with happy stories from the old days, or sing the child's favorite lullaby *Dors, dors, le p'tit bibi*.

It was the children who suffered most. Some were still too frightened to sleep, others would withdraw into themselves, sucking their thumbs, rocking backward and forward in the boxes, whimpering for hours on end. With so little space, the two year olds who should by then have been happily toddling, had not been able to grow strong enough to stand properly, let alone walk.

"Poor Osite, how will she learn?" worried Marguerite as she rescued the toddler, crawling through the dirty water of the hold.

The older ones, with nowhere to play and run, were always fighting each other or refusing to obey their parents when they were told to stop.

"What can we do?" asked Pierre. "We always did what we were told, but some of these lads cannot be reined in."

"You'd go crazy if you were a 15 year old cooped up in conditions like this," said Marie.

"But this is not our way," said Jambo. "It's not how we bring up children in Acadia."

"Unfortunately," said Marguerite dryly, "We are in the country of Sarah and Molly. Different rules apply here."

Oliver, however, flourished. Easy going, chatty, he had always had an eye for a bargain, and the glib tongue to pull off a deal. In some way known only to him he was always able to *come by* things.

"I used to watch your Uncle Rene in action," he told Jambo. "A deal here, a trade-off there. Brilliant."

He persuaded the sailors to let him on shore to pick up provisions—*to save you the trouble*—and became friendly with the port's landlords and the shop owners, from whom he would wheedle extra supplies. He even managed to get some taffy, a curly string of molasses that was an old favorite from home, for Jean-Baptiste's fourth birthday that March.

"Where did that come from?" wondered Marguerite.

"Don't ask," said Oliver. "There are ways."

But these were brief respites from the grinding cycle of eking out an existence, which, day by day, week by week, gnawed at their will to stay alive.

"We have to be disciplined," said Jambo. "We have to make the British think we are invincible—at least in spirit. We must never show fear or anger—that means you, Francois—and we must convince ourselves that we will rise above this and return to Acadia."

They made sure each day had a rhythm and a reason. They started with prayers every morning, their hymns ringing out around the bay.

"Make sure they can hear us in the governor's palace," he exhorted. "They must not think they can break our spirit."

The few women who knew how to read held scripture lessons for the children, while the rest cooked whatever little food was at hand, salty pork, maize, or rice, and stitched and darned their ragged clothes.

"We, of course, get the d-d-dirty jobs," said Charles, but he laughed and joked as the men emptied the bilges, scrubbed the rancid gangway and cleaned the privies in a constant battle against the flies, maggots, and sickness that bred in the filth.

There was no escape from the constant round of ailments that were bred and nurtured in the clammy confines of that sea-borne world. Sore throats, coughs, and headaches were the norm, draining their energy and morale. One morning Charles's, Anne, woke with a rash that began on her chest and spread to the rest of her body. Soon, most of the prisoners were languishing from chills, searing headaches, and muscle spasms. Many became delirious with high temperatures.

"This is worse than usual," said Jambo.

"I think it's typhus," said Oliver.

"Better known as jail fever," grumbled Purreton, who immediately cut back on the time they were allowed on deck in case they infected his men.

Few of them knew what typhus was. At home, the Acadians had lived such healthy lives that epidemics and disease were strangers to them. Some said they were so robust because they breast fed their children until they were more than two years old. Most put it down to the outdoor life, the uncomplicated diet, and the healing cycle of the seasons. They were no match for the fever that spread with insidious inevitability, propagated by their closeness to each other, unavoidably sharing the sweat of their bodies and germ-laden breath.

First one of Marguerite's nephews, Jean Trahan, died, then old Annie Robichaud. Heartbroken Jean Daigre, who had never recovered from the drowning of his boy, slipped away, leaving his widow insensible with grief. Francoise Gautrot, who had married young Pierre, a farmhand from Gaspereau, only one month before the expulsion, went whimpering, clutching her throat as she gasped for air, while her new husband could only hold her hand, stricken with desolation.

"We need to do something about the bodies," said LeBlanc.

Purreton said: "I know. I have talked to Washington. They are short of men for a task like that."

"Then we shall do it," said LeBlanc. "They cannot be left here. Quite apart from respect for the dead, the corpses will spread disease."

"I'll ask," said the skipper, who next day summoned Jambo to tell him that Washington had agreed.

"But only one of you from each family. Wives and children will be kept here in case, you know, you decide you like the country too well and don't come back."

They were marched to a spot on the hillside overlooking the bay and for the first few days a detail of bored soldiers kept watch but it was obvious the prisoners would not try to escape and they were left alone to carry out their melancholy task.

"I know I shouldn't s-s-say this," said Charles as they prepared to leave the burial ground, shovels over their shoulders, six graves neatly dug, "But you have to admit it's beautiful here. Look at those orange g-g-groves, and the maize—it's only May and it is already a foot tall. This is rich land."

"True," said Oliver. "And the air is so soft and balmy."

"Shame on you both," said Pierre. "Have you forgotten who you are and what you are?"

"And where you come from? No, this is not for me," said Jambo. "I have missed those clear frosty mornings of home where every day starts clean and fresh. I would give anything to be waking up to the nip of a fine spring morning, rather than this steamy heat. Look at us, pouring sweat."

"The mosquitoes are worse than home, too," said Oliver.

"It's like August all year round," said Pierre.

"I'm just s-s-saying that if I had to, I could live here," said Charles, with his nose for comfort—so like his father. "We have to m-m-make the best of things and this is the b-b-best we have."

"We might have no choice," said Jambo. his brother.

"Well, anything is better than being sh-sh-shut away in the ships," said his brother.

"They must let us off eventually," said Oliver. "Surely they cannot mean to keep us on board forever."

"Why? There are fewer of us every day," Jambo gestured at the newly dug graves, scooped from the soft earth for the victims who had not survived the journey. "It would suit the British if we just faded away."

"True enough," said Oliver. "If we're dead, we're no trouble to them."

They paused to sit and smoke their pipes on a bank overlooking the bay where the prison ships were moored, and beyond to the straits that led to the Atlantic. Below them was the little port of Jamestown and the pretty red brick houses of Williamsburg, the elegant capital of Virginia, and behind the sugar cane plantations stretching to the low hills in the distance, dark against the blue sky.

"This tobacco is g-g-good though, isn't it," said Charles and the four men sat and inhaled deeply.

"The governor hasn't said what occupation he'll find for us," said Pierre. "Other than digging graves."

"He'll want to treat us like these pathetic bastards, no doubt," said

Oliver as a gang of slaves, manacled together by hand and foot, staggered along, exhausted by a day in the cotton fields.

"I can't get over how many of them there are," said Pierre.

"I was told by one of the sailors that there are almost 300,000 slaves in Virginia alone," said Oliver, who had quickly become a source of information about their new surroundings.

"That must be almost half the number of British based here," said Jambo.

"Makes me think there won't be enough work for us when we are set free," said Pierre.

"Exactly," snorted Francois. "Why pay when you can get everything done for nothing?"

"It's inhumane, isn't it, the way they trade in the blacks?" said Jambo. He massaged his right hand, which was mending slowly, but was setting so that two fingers pointed inwards like a claw.

"And the British keep telling us how civilized and f-f-fair-minded they are," said Charles.

"That's what they would like to do with us," said Francois.

"They might yet do it," said Pierre. "Make us work for a greedy landlord."

"For a pittance," said Oliver.

"For nothing," grumbled Francois.

"I don't trust the governor," said Oliver.

"He's a rum one, that's for sure," said Jambo.

Oliver joked, "Dinwiddie. *Dim-wittie*, more like."

"Not so stupid, I fear," said Pierre

"And no friend," said Jambo. "Think of all the people who have died since we arrived without him showing a flicker of concern."

"Like the sad souls waiting to come here," said Pierre.

"We'd better get back and tell the families the graves are ready," said Jambo. "They will be wanting to say their farewells."

"God rest them," said Charles. "That's the third time we have been on b-b-burial duty this fortnight."

"Will there ever be an end?" asked Pierre.

Oliver said, "At least, if we are allowed off the ships to live on shore then we can get to know the town and the people. There will be opportunities here."

Jambo frowned disapprovingly at the cobbler's enthusiasm at the prospect of cutting deals amid their misfortune.

"We shall have to make the most of what comes our way but not at the expense of our values. Our Acadian way of life," he said, as the five men finished their pipes and stood up to make their way back to the shore. "As long as we have breath we must be masters of our own fate. Not cutting deals here and there."

Oliver affected not to notice Jambo's reproach and started to say something about *our mutual advantage* when Pierre halted, holding his fingers to his lip and signalled to them to duck down. "What's that?"

Jambo stopped stock-still, alarmed at the trapper's urgency. "Where?" "Someone behind that hedge, just down in the dip," Pierre was whispering now.

"Oh God," said Oliver, trying to hide behind the slender trunk of a young olive tree.

"Might be a runaway slave," said Pierre.

"Or a B-b-ritish spy," said Charles crouching down beside the cobbler.

"I'll get 'em," said Francois, gripping his shovel.

"Keep your voices down," said Jambo, making quietening gestures with his hand.

He signaled to Charles and Oliver to stay where they were – something for which they needed no encouragement since they neither had the appetite for a violent encounter.

"Francois," he hissed. "That way. Pierre with me."

There were three of them — tramps, they thought at first— crouching, more pathetically than threateningly, in the gully of a dried stream. They started to run, but came face to face with Francois, shovel raised above his head like a broadsword.

"Stop there, you bastards."

They froze – hunter and hunted alike.

Then Jambo laughed: "Francois. Don't strike. It's Jean Melancon."

He peered at the tramps as if he could not believe his eyes.

"Yes, Jean, it is you. And Phillipe."

Two of the 'tramps' were the Melancon brothers who had set off with such determination from Boston harbor, and with them, so heavily bearded and dishevelled that he was almost unrecognizable, Gabriel Lajeunesse.

"What are you doing here?" asked Francois.

"You look t-t-terrible," said Charles, bravely joining the group. "No offence!"

"Where have you been?" demanded Oliver as if he had been expecting them hourly.

"I thought you were heading to Grand-Pré," said Pierre.

Jambo said, "I reckoned you'd gone forever when the skiff took you off in Boston. Never thought we'd see any of you again."

They shook hands and then hugged each other.

The three were frantic with hunger. "Have you got any bread?" begged Jean. "We haven't eaten for days." They gave them scraps and they tore at the food like starving dogs.

God, thought Jambo as he watched them. They smelt of sweat and dirt, their hair was straggling around their necks, and their beards were like mats. *I hope we don't look as bad as that,* he thought.

"Well," said Jean, stuffing his mouth with the stale bread. "After we left the ship we tried to get home, but every road out of the place and into the country to the north was crawling with soldiers. We kept travelling through the forests and stuck to ice-bound rivers instead of trails, until we reached a point near Fort St. Croix, you know, across the bay from Grand-Pré. The Indians told us that our village was still in British hands, but we couldn't see any signs of life."

"It was hard to tell if it was smoke we saw coming from the chimneys, or just the winter mist."

"They won't have rebuilt it yet," said Jambo.

"Maybe they will just leave the place a ruin," said Pierre.

"There was no point hanging around so Phillipe suggested we head south."

"All the way back we went, steering well clear of Boston, until we were caught trying to steal eggs from a farm near Philadelphia and thrown into prison," said Phillipe. "It was chaos. Can you believe it, there was an earthquake."

"An earthquake!" Pierre looked skeptical.

"I know. Incredible. The first in living memory," said Jean, not to be deterred from a good story.

"That and the snow," added Phillipe. "What a delight it was."

"Luckily," said Jean, "The guards were more worried about the French raids on the border than us so they pretty much forgot about us prisoners which made it easier to escape."

"That's where we met," said Gabriel. "I slipped away from Philadelphia when some of us were taken on shore in a working party. I was lucky. Most were left behind locked up in the ships, and I have heard since that 250 of our cousins died. The British actually left their bodies on the decks for a week in the freezing cold."

"The shame," snorted Francois, banging his shovel on the ground.

"And the rest, they dispersed them as far apart from each other as possible, splitting up families and friends," said Gabriel. "They gave them a few pennies a week in welfare, but they soon stopped paying out."

"Bastards." Francois was beside himself. "Bastards." This time, he hit the ground so hard with his shovel that he broke its handle. "Bastards."

The blacksmith was febrile, jumpy, close to tears. "When they did let our people take the bodies off the ships, they were buried in a mass grave in the cemetery for the poor while some of the survivors were lodged in what the British call neutral huts."

"That's a laugh isn't it?" asked Jambo with a sigh. "They actually call them neutral while at the same time saying we are enemies of the state."

Phillipe said, "The ones who did not die were taken on as free labor by the landowners."

"More like slavery," said Gabriel. "It was typical British trickery. Luckily, when it came to Christmas time, the guards were more interested in carousing than keeping an eye us. We broke out through a window and travelled by night, sleeping in barns and under hedgerows during the day. God, it was cold. We'd steal food from farms, snare rabbits if we could, or break the ice and coax fish out of rivers. Some things you don't forget, eh Pierre."

"We came across other cousins doing the same thing, hiding and creeping around like hunted deer, all terrified of being caught," said Jean. "Most of them had had their shoes confiscated to stop them escaping, but they kept going. Bleeding feet and frostbite could not stop them, because the alternative was worse—to be seized by the militia and forced to work in the plantations alongside the coloreds."

"Nothing against them, of course," said Gabriel. "We are all God's creatures but it wouldn't be right, considering we are free men. Or supposed to be."

"Remember the Boudrots who left the ships when we did in Boston?" asked Phillipe. "They had been told by that customs fellow that they would get their boys indentured."

"Ha." He gave a terse laugh. "They were taken to some God-forsaken corner of Massachusetts and their children forced to work picking potatoes. Then guess what? The landlord took the money he paid the children back in rent from the parents.

Jean said, "If anyone wants to travel more than 10 miles from his home to look for work, he has to get a passport from the local justice of the peace. If you're caught travelling without a passport it's five days in jail."

"But you can't get a passport without a job," said Lajeunesse miserably. "It's hopeless."

Jambo said, "So much for Winslow and his promises. Look at the way we have been scattered and how so many of our cousins have disappeared. Have you heard anything about my brothers? Any of our old friends?"

Jean said, "We did hear a rumor that your brothers were on the Swallow which docked in Massachusetts. I don't know if any of them were put on shore safely though."

"There was a sighting of your Uncle Rene," said Phillipe.

"Is he alive?" his nephew asked, fearing the answer.

"The last we were told he was in New York, in the mountains with his wife and two of his children, but he has lost contact with the rest of his family."

"And my sisters, anything of them?

"Only your sister Madeleine. She and husband Paul are somewhere in Pennsylvania."

"Thank the Lord for that. It will be some small consolation for mother."

Lajeunesse asked, "Evangeline?" It was as if he could not bear to frame the question. "Have you word of her?"

"Nothing, my friend, I am sorry," said Jambo. He sought awkwardly for the words. "We have to face the fact that many are lost."

"Or dead," said Francois, and then realizing he had been unnecessarily brutal, held up his hands in an apologetic shrug.

Lajeunesse was in tears, his face ugly in its grief. "I shall have to keep searching for her," he said. "I won't give up."

"You will find her, I'm sure," said Jambo, but he was just saying it to cheer the miserable fellow.

"We don't know what to do for the best," said Phillipe. "We keep meeting runaways who are still trying to get home, but we tell them it's hopeless. Others think that if they can get to Prince Edward Island they will be safe there, because it is still in French hands, but I think that is too risky. There are more British troops arriving every month and I am sure they will attack the island and send our people packing once more."

Jean said, "What's made it worse for us is that the bloody man Lawrence did not tell the governors he was sending us to their colonies. They are almost as angry with him as they are with us—that's why we are treated with such callousness. We heard that at least two governors took one look at our cousins, all of them sick and hungry, and said, '*Here are boats and food—go wherever you want. Just get out of our sight.*'

"They only gave them enough supplies for a few days, and anyway, the timbers in the boats were rotten and most of them sank," said Phillipe. "Many of our cousins were drowned."

"I cannot bear to think of it," said Jean. "Some of us have kept walking south, and I have even heard rumor that others have sailed down the Mississippi, because France is still in control there—at least, we think so, it is so hard to discover the truth."

"It's our only hope," said Phillipe.

Jean said, "Come with us. We can make a new home there."

"Will they really welcome us?" asked Jambo. "Can we trust the French? They have done nothing to help us so far."

"How will be able to get away from here?" asked Pierre. "We would not even make the shore without being mown down by Washington's men. They're itching to use us for target practice."

"There are too many of us with families on the ships," said Jambo. "It is impossible."

FOURTEEN

On shore, Virginia

Spring and Summer, 1756.

A Throw of the Dice

"Let us off the ships," begged Jambo after he had come back from heaping earth onto another batch of graves. "We could rid ourselves of our sickness if we were allowed on shore for just a few weeks of fresh air."

"On the contrary," said the laconic Washington. "This is the best reason for keeping you as far out in the bay as we can."

"How many of us have to die before you relent, or at least give us the food and medicine we need?" asked Pierre. "There must have been 200 lost and dead since we were taken from our country. Is that not enough?"

Washington pursed his lips but showed no sympathy, "200? I think not. Not yet."

They had regular meetings with their reluctant hosts, though Dinwiddie rarely attended and delegated the unsmiling Colonel to listen to their grievances. He made it clear he was there on sufferance, and would rather be in action against the French and their Indian allies, who were proving a nuisance on the Ohio frontier.

"We are civilized people," Washington said. "Of course, we do not want you to suffer unduly. But don't forget there is a war on, and your countrymen are the enemy."

Jambo tried to interrupt, but the soldier was not listening. "No one knows more about the situation than me. I was the one who trapped the French at the Ohio River Fork '53. '*Surrender*', I said. They refused. Foolish of them.

"We sent a round or two into their tents, and that was it. That's how this war started. We set the world on fire. I was only 21." He smiled at the memory, revealing a mouth with only two or three stubby grey teeth held together by wire.

So that's why he always keeps his lips tight together, realized Jambo. *I feel almost sorry for him.*

When he told Marguerite she shuddered: *'Poor Mrs Washington. Fancy being kissed by that'*

Washington said, "We have to be on the alert day and night. Last month, scores of our backwoodsmen were slaughtered by your people, and even now hundreds of settlers are heading for the safety of Williamsburg. They are terrified of being scalped by the Indians. More friends of yours."

"Your troops have been defeated since you set the world on fire, haven't they?" asked Francois, ignoring Jambo's admonitory glance. "Couple of years back, wasn't it? Bit of a problem at Fort Necessity we were told."

He ignored the plowman's jibe, true though it was.

"If that was the case, we would be even less well disposed to you than we are. We now know, thanks to further communications from Governor Lawrence, that the garrison at Beausejour was armed to the teeth with you *so-called* Neutrals. *Intestine enemies*, Governor Lawrence called you, and so you are. No wonder you were expelled."

Despairing as they already were, the news from the Melancon brothers had discouraged the exiles more than they cared to admit. It confirmed every morsel of gossip and breath of rumor they had gleaned since their arrival six months before. Their pessimism was made worse by the malice of the sailors passing through on shore leave, or the hangers-on at the governor's palace who took delight in mocking them with the latest updates on the refugees' fate—though the Acadians could never be sure what was true and what was a cruel invention.

"We've just had a message that one of the transports went down off Fourchu Point," said a sailor. "Is that in your so-called country?" he asked, knowing full well that it was.

He added, with succinct pleasure, "They were all drowned."

One of his mates who was a regular on the Cuba run was determined to cap that, "Another ship went so far off course it had ended up in Antigua, miles to the south. It's an island somewhere in the West Indies. Grim. Full of disease. They'll all be dead."

Not be outdone, a soldier who had just returned from action in the north, chipped in, "There was a ship called the Edward Cornwallis which had 417 nicely tucked up in the hold when it set sail, but only 207 were alive when it reached Carolina four weeks later."

"The prisoners on one ship mutinied, killing some of the crew," Dinwiddie seethed. "And you ask us for more medicine? You dare demand to be allowed to live on shore? You know my answer to that. Never." spit gathered in the corners of his mouth. "How many stories do I have to hear about your treachery? Why should I put up with you at all? The governor of New Jersey thinks you French traitors should be delivered to your allies in Old France, because you are such a threat to the peace and security of his state."

"The council has voted to send you away," said one of his aides a few days later.

"Yes, £5,000 has been raised by the Assembly to pay for ships to take you to England."

"You will enjoy it there."

"England or France," said LeBlanc with a calmness he did not feel. "Can they be worse than here?"

Dinwiddie was outraged by his insubordination. "Purreton," he hissed at the skipper. "Get them back on board. I'm sick of the sight of them."

"He gets a bit fraught, you know," said the skipper. "Things are not good on the border with the French, and the Indians are uppity. He thinks you are part of the conspiracy. He doesn't understand you the way I do."

It was true. The skipper had become, if not a friend, an ally. He sympathized with their plight and had come to believe that they were the Neutrals they insisted they were, and no threat to him or anyone else. It was he who had sanctioned the sailors to deliver the treats for Christmas, and he had even slipped in an extra cask of rum at his own expense.

"And, I shouldn't be telling you this, but he is mightily exercised by the arrival of two boatloads of your people just down the coast at Hampton."

"You mean…"

The skipper was being tantalizingly casual. "Yes, they have drifted in from Carolina. Apparently the governor there did not want anything to do with them when they were dumped on him by Lawrence, and he sent them on their way. He gave them food and water, a passport, and these old vessels. I think the governor of Georgia did much the same. He refused to talk to them—not even a '*hello*' like Lord Dinwiddie. To be fair, some survived and actually reached Boston. Trouble is, they were arrested the moment they set foot in the place. As for the rest, I'm afraid some of the boats were not as sound as they might have been."

"They sank, you mean."

"I fear some of your people perished."

"Yes, of course, they did," he said bitterly. But what about these refugees? They had survived. So far. The thought that there were cousins still alive and so near both cheered and dismayed him. Hampton was a small port on the peninsular some 30 or 40 miles south from their bay, but locked away on the ships and surrounded by soldiers as they were, it could have been on the moon.

"How many of them are there in Hampton?" asked Jambo casually.

"About 50, I think. But don't you be getting any ideas about trying to reach them. The road is being patrolled night and day."

As if to reinforce his warning, Virginia Rangers were detailed to stand guard on the ships.

"That proves there is something af-f-foot," said Charles.

"We must try to make contact," said Francois.

"But how?" asked Pierre, gesturing to a Ranger who lounged with a rifle across his lap, watching their every move.

"The best hope is during grave-digging duty," said Charles. "One of us could slip away."

"We would be caught within half a mile," said Pierre.

"And anyway," said Jambo, "I cannot see how we could get to Hampton and back in one day. We would never make it in time for evening roll call."

Unexpectedly, Pierre Gautrot spoke up. "I'll go. I'll take a message. I can swim to shore and sneak through the woods. No one will miss me."

Gautrot had scarcely uttered a sentence since his new wife had died during the typhus outbreak. He had become a solitary figure, lost in the private world of his mourning, but now he seemed full of purpose—*Though,* realized LeBlanc, *maybe it is because he has given up. He doesn't care what happens to him.*

"I will be all right," said the widower. "Remember how, as children, we used to play that game swimming in the bay using a hollow stick so that we could stay under water? I reckon a bamboo will work here just as well. It's not far to the shore, and if I go at high tide I shall be able to get right up close to the rocks, and only have to crawl the last few yards. Then I can make a dash into the woods. It's only a few steps."

That Sunday's service was conducted with so much noise and enthusiasm that the guards kept closer watch than usual on the congregation to see what tricks they were up to. With their attention held, Gautrot slipped down a rope at the aft of the ship.

Over the heads of the worshippers, Jambo could just pick out the spike of his bamboo shoot and his vague outline as he swam steadily to land. The psalm died on his lips. There, marching along the road from Williamsburg toward Hampton, was a platoon of soldiers in their bright red uniforms.

The congregation, sensing Jambo's perturbation, faltered, but he recovered, almost shouting to make it seem nothing was out of the ordinary.

What happened next seemed to be in harrowing slow motion. The soldiers marched along the shore. Gautrot reached the shallows. The water was not deep enough for him to crawl as he had planned, and he was forced to start wading, up to his knees, some twenty yards out. He still had a chance. An outcrop of rock hid him from the troops—if he could reach it in time he might be able to hide behind it.

The soldiers came nearer. He waded with agonizing slowness, almost as if he was paddling for his own pleasure. He had no inkling of the danger, and there was nothing Jambo could do to warn him.

Gautrot reached the stony shore precisely as the soldiers rounded the rock. For a split second they all turned to stone. The soldiers were more astonished than Gautrot, who dropped his bamboo shoot as if in surrender, gave a shrug, and half turned to the onlookers on the ship. It looked as if he was going to raise a hand in a gesture of farewell, but before he could the soldiers recovered from their surprise, fumbled for their rifles and took aim. Shot after shot tore into his half-naked body and he toppled into the water, his blood washed away by the gentle waves.

Jambo was summoned by Dinwiddie. "This attempt was both pathetic and pointless." His jowls shook with indignation, a bubble of snot hung from his lardy nose. "Did you really think you would be reunited with your fellow renegades? You were too late, anyway. I ordered them away days ago.

"Can you imagine how alarmed my people have been to be invaded by more of *your* type? It might not have been so bad if the ships from Carolina were the only interlopers, but there are 300 more from Georgia coasting the shore in canoes, and they will certainly land, rob our homes, and I fear, murder the unguarded and unwary people here."

He thrust his large, bulbous head toward them like some angry battering ram.

"To make matters worse, the farmers fleeing the fighting on the border will be here any day now. What can I say to our loyal countrymen when they find you are still here and being looked after so well? They will think it is *you* who are our friends and allies, not them. I am not sure I can control them, so watch out—they are a wild lot, our men from the backwoods"

His entourage laughed knowingly.

"On reflection, maybe I should do the same as my fellow governors—give you boats to sail away to wherever the wind and tide takes you. It would be a chance to win your freedom. A throw of the dice."

"Indeed," said Jambo levelly. "Freedom or death. We would welcome the opportunity."

"At least you would be off my hands," said Dinwiddie, his leaky nose questing the air as if sniffing out a solution. "Yes, maybe I'll do that. Or I'll keep you on the ships like the governor of Pennsylvania until—"

Jambo finished the sentence, "Until there is no one left alive to bury the dead."

A day or two later Oliver, paused in the repairs he was doing on a pair of ancient boots and said, "I was thinking about our cousins."

They all were. They were tormented by the knowledge that they had been so close to being reunited with a missing parent, with a brother, a sister, perhaps even a lost love. There would certainly have been friends who might have been able to tell them about villagers they had not seen since the day of their expulsion. They would never know. Surely now they were gone forever.

And they were haunted by the useless sacrifice of young Gautrot.

"He had lost the will," said Marguerite.

"Well, we must not," said Jambo.

"Maybe we should take him up on the offer?" said Oliver, polishing his glasses, pursuing his own line of thought.

"Who? What offer?" asked Francois.

"The revered Lord Dim-wittie," said Oliver. "To let us sail away. A throw of the dice."

"I don't think he was actually making an offer," said Pierre.

"R-r-idiculing us more like," said Charles

"And even if he was serious, I wouldn't trust him to supply us with boats that would actually stay afloat," said Jambo.

"But." the cobbler paused for effect, "We could try ourselves."

"Overwhelm this lot and take c-c-control of The Sarah and Molly?" said Charles sarcastically.

"No, not that," said the cobbler busily hammering in a nail.

"So you say we seize some boats and sail way?" asked Pierre.

"And drown within minutes of reaching open sea," said Francois.

"If we get that far," said Pierre. "Haven't you seen those alligators?"

"If we stay here, we know death will claim many more of us," said the cobbler with uncharacteristic feeling. "How many have to die before we *do* something about it?"

"It's a world of difference between taking a fishing boat into Minas Bay and sailing off in one on the Atlantic," said Jambo.

"That's just it." Oliver lowered his voice theatrically, "There's a sloop."

His comrades looked at him blankly.

He burnished his glasses with even greater energy, "It has been moored in a cove just around the headland, between here and the straits that lead to Hampton and the open sea. It should be taking a consignment of tobacco to England, but that delivery has been delayed for another month so it is unused, just sitting there, waiting for someone to raise the sails and float away to the wide blue yonder."

"How do you know about it?" asked Jambo.

"The blacks told me," said the cobbler. "And I had it confirmed by one of the British malingerers I play cards with."

"The blacks!" Jambo was astonished. None of them had ever had dealings with slaves.

"You have become friendly with the slaves?" asked Francois. He spat prodigiously over the ship's railing into the sea. "Slaves!"

"Indeed, and why not? I will be friendly with anyone who can help us. The British always talk too much when they've had a mug or two of rum, and the blacks know more about the town and the garrison than we do. They told me where the secret supplies of food for the soldiers are stored, and even where the weapons are hidden."

"We don't want to use guns," said Jambo.

"No, but we can get their help and work together. They want to get away from this miserable place as much as we do."

"It seems to me you have been doing a lot of plotting with your new friends," said Jambo.

"Not plotting—talking. They are a good-hearted lot, and like us, have no love of the British. Jambo, I think you should meet their leader."

Early the next evening, Jambo slipped away from the grave-digging detail and met Oliver on the edge of town.

"Keep your head down," he warned, as they crept across the swampy fields that separated the slave quarters from the guard posts that ringed Williamsburg's handsome brick mansions. "The British don't like us consorting with them."

If Jambo felt the Acadians' conditions were demeaning, he was shocked by the humiliating conditions endured by the slaves. Their homes were so crude—just tiny shelters of ragged palm thatch over earth floors—that they spent most of their time outside around open fires, warming their meager diet of rice and vegetables.

"Meet Bram," said Oliver. "He is like the head man here. This is Jambo."

The slave said, "Welcome sir. Sit here. Please, eat."

From a distance, the slaves had seemed such down trodden creatures that he was surprised to discover the grace of the man before him. How he, his wife, and five children survived in these dirt poor conditions, filled him with admiration, and as he quickly discovered, like the Acadians, they refused to be cowed.

"We have something in common, it seems," said Bram. "We too were kidnapped from our homes by the British and brought here against our will.

They even changed my name. They couldn't pronounce my African, name so they called me Abraham, but even *that* is too much for them, so Bram it is."

He paused and gazed at the rows of the sugar plantation that stretched away to the hills.

"They had two ways of packing us into the holds—either loose, which gave us room to move a little, but meant we were constantly being thrown against each other, or packed in tight. We were chained, ankle to wrist, to make sure we could not move. Even if we could, the hold was too low for us to stand up properly. It was hot, so hot that the sweat ran off our bodies and on to each other. We had buckets, you know, but imagine trying to use them tied up to another man. There were layers of filth on the ship's floor."

"I know what you describe," said Jambo. "Only too well."

"They would make us sing and dance on deck, even when we were chained together. We were the entertainment, especially when the ship was becalmed and they were bored. If they didn't like the performances, they would spice things up by lashing us. In fact, the more they degraded us the more they enjoyed the spectacle." Again the pause and the long study of the horizon. He slipped off his ragged shirt to reveal scars across his back.

"We men were lucky, but the women..." He paused and squeezed shut his eyes, rocking backward and forward. "The women were there for their use. First the officers would pass them around among each other. Then down the ranks to the seamen. My elder sister was assaulted day after day. It was sport for them. To say they behaved like beasts would be to diminish God's creatures." He opened his eyes and stared off as if into nothing.

"She went mad with the shame of it. During one of the dances, she got free and threw herself over board."

He said it so matter-of-factly that Jambo was not sure he had heard right. The slave's thick accent with its cadences and rhythms, unfamiliar words and swooping sentences were sometimes hard to understand but not as hard to comprehend as the horrors he related. "But then quite a few killed themselves, and the rest prayed for death. My brother went for days without speaking. He spent hours staring straight ahead, but he might as well have had his eyes shut because he did not see anything. He became quite unhinged. One night, he begged me to throttle him and put an end to it."

He paused again. For several long seconds. He passed his hand over his mouth as if willing himself to speak. As if he could not bear to recall the evil let alone put them into words. At length he pursed his lips, looked steadily, at first, Oliver and then Jambo and continued, "We tried to starve ourselves, but they wouldn't let us die. We were too valuable." He held out his wasted arms, which looked as if they could barely lift an ear of maize and then, he laughed bitterly.

"They had a special steel appliance which forced our mouths open, and they would pour water and gruel down our throats. It was only just enough to keep us alive, but when we got closer to land they gave us more food, even a corn mix, so that we would be fattened up and be worth buying. After all, who is going to waste money on a sick slave?"

It was the young carpenter's turn to be silent. He had understood that. He sat in numb disbelief, scratched fiercely at his mop of black hair and rubbed his eyes. For the first time he had realized that they, the exiles, were not alone in their suffering. Indeed, their pain was as nothing compared to the savagery inflicted on these people—these human beings that he had thought not worthy of his recognition.

"What makes them behave like that?" he murmured half to himself, not needing an answer.

"Money," said the slave.

"And power," said Oliver.

"Things that never concerned us Acadians," said the carpenter.

"But I do not understand why they treat you in the same way," said Bram. "You aren't even for sale."

Jambo smiled. "No, we are little use to them. The merchant who shipped us here made a fine profit, but really we were expelled because we owned land that they wanted. Their dream is to rule the world, and we were an

124

inconvenience that had to be removed."

"Our dream is to escape," said Oliver.

"Ours too. They call us savages, but the barbarity of these British is hard to comprehend."

Jambo strained to listen to the lilting tempo of his words which sometimes faded away into a murmur.

"Sometimes, when we are so hungry that we can hardly stand, we steal the food they throw out to feed their pigs. If we are caught, we get a whipping. If we are lucky. They think nothing of cutting off a hand. And, of course, without a hand, who can work? We are no use to our owners, so they are only too happy if we starve to death."

He shook his head. "Most of us were resigned to this hideous fate until we started talking to our friend, Oliver. We think that if we can reach French territory, and keep heading south, we might be able to catch a ship and reach the Indies. Maybe sail back to Africa. We might die in the attempt, but would that be such a bad thing?"

"We should plan something together," said Jambo.

"I think we should." He gestured at a lad of about 18. "This is my son His name is Jem. If you agree, he will be our go-between while we work out a stratagem that benefits us both."

The gangly lad stood and bowed. A smile of pure optimism lit his face.

When they were back in the ship's hold, Jambo and Oliver told the prisoners of their meeting.

Francois was immediately hostile, "We should have nothing to do with them. They are the lowest of the low and cannot be trusted."

Pierre said, "It sounds to me they have been cruelly treated by the British just as we have. Do we not have a common goal and a common enemy?"

"They have had a bad time of it, no mistake," said Oliver. "I find them to be trustworthy fellows."

Jambo said: "I found Bram, their leader, to be a brave as anyone I have met. The suffering those people endure, almost as if it is part of some natural order, is beyond belief. We would find it hard to bear what they have been put through and still maintain any kind of dignity."

Not only that," said Oliver. "They are essential to any escape plan we may work out."

"But, do they have any hope of getting away?" asked Pierre. "The blacks are hated by everyone — the French, the British — they will be caught and cut down within days."

"Maybe, but they want to try and I am not going to dissuade them," said LeBlanc."In truth, I would say the odds are stacked against us, too."

"But we have to make the attempt," said Oliver.

"I don't see how we can achieve anything while we are still on the ships," said Marguerite, ever practical.

"Absolutely," agreed Jambo. "We need to be on shore. We will have to persuade Dinwiddie to let some of us off. Maybe he will allow it for a few weeks."

"But why now?" asked Pierre. "He has steadfastly refused to let us stay on land."

"And he will be even less obliging after l-l-last month's little episode with G-g-gautrot," said Charles.

Marguerite said, "But think about it. Their fields are in a neglected state because so many of their men are off fighting. The maize has been left standing and will soon rot away. Their livestock is starving. Who is milking their cows? We could suggest that the fittest of us look after the crops and till the fields?"

At their next meeting with the Governor, Jambo was at his most emollient, and Marguerite even smiled at him.

LeBlanc said, "You know how sorry we are about Mr. Gautrot. We did not know he was embarking on the escapade. It was just that he was grief-stricken at the death of his wife, and he had some strange idea that his parents were on the ship that landed at Hampton." Jambo felt guilty at his disloyalty to the dead cousin.

"He had been married only one month," said Marguerite. "I am sure you can understand. We are not asking to be set free, not asking for anything other than the chance to camp out on land and recover our strength. Look at my little girl." Marguerite held Osite toward the Governor, who scarcely glanced at the child. "She has been feverish for weeks now. I fear she might not live the week." A tear ran fetchingly down her cheek.

"We do not want favors," said Jambo. "What we propose is that with so many of your men away on military duty, we do their work in the fields. Of course, we would not expect payment, but we are farmers and that is what we have done for generations. We can harvest the maize and tend to your cattle."

"You are a good Christian, sir," said Marguerite. "I am sure you do not want those crosses on the hillside to be your memorial."

The governor flushed, pursing his thin lips until they almost disappeared in his fleshy face.

It occurred to LeBlanc that the governor was as puzzled by his prisoners as he was annoyed by having them in his territory.

'He certainly doesn't what to make of you, my darling,' he said to Marguerite later. 'That talk of the crosses hit home.'

The Governor blew his nose.

"Very well. You are always telling me what fine farmers you are, so perhaps this is the opportunity to prove it. The fields do need clearing, and the cattle fattening up."

Washington glared at him but the Governor continued, "Lucky for you, I am not like my fellow governors who wish only ill of you.

"I will let you on shore. As you say, you can make yourselves useful. Not all of you mind, but in groups."

"Sir, we are more grateful than words can express." Marguerite, smiled and opened her intriguing eyes with a look that almost teased.

A furious Washington, stomped to his feet and interrupted, "My Lord," but Dinwiddie coughed and waved them, and the angry aide, away.

"Be off with you. Make this work and, who knows, maybe you can stay there until I can find some land to assign to you for a longer time."

In the course of the next few days, 60 prisoners came off the ships. They were chosen by lots or handpicked by Jambo, though to the plotters' surprise, most of the captives preferred to stay where they were.

"Too damn risky," said Marguerite's brother Joseph. "I'm not risking my family on such a hare-brained scheme."

They bivouacked along the shore, creating something of a holiday atmosphere with over-excited children playing on land for the first time in six months and families singing around open fires and tucking into fresh food while the men and women worked in the fields.

"I think we are entitled to help ourselves a little," said Marguerite, hiding handfuls of maize in her skirts at the end of their first day in the fields. "They will want us to stay well fed to do even more work."

For the first few days a platoon kept guard, but unexpectedly they were withdrawn leaving the surveillance to a couple of Rangers, who would wander past at dawn and dusk to make sure the prisoners were behaving themselves.

"It's the backwoodsmen," said Oliver. "They are flocking to the city from the frontier. Apparently they are a wild lot and cause trouble wherever they go."

"This give me an idea," said Jambo. "Is Jem here?"

The young slave used to creep into the encampment most evenings as dusk fell with suggestions from his father for the escape. Jambo took him to one side, ignoring the glare directed at him by Francois, and had a long, intense conversation with him.

The slave slipped away, returning much later, beaming with optimism. Jambo slapped him on the back, but did not share the information with his comrades except to say, "It's looking good."

However, the moment they saw the sloop they realized that Oliver's enthusiasm had run away with him. It was moored in a shallow cove surrounded by mangrove swamps. One on side was the mainland and the road that led to Hampton—the road that the soldiers had marched along when Gautrot was making his doomed flit—on the other a short headland, and beyond the straits that led to the Atlantic.

"It's not big enough," said Pierre.

"More like a fishing boat that's survived a month of storms on the Grand Banks," said Francois.

"We can't fit *sixty* of us on that little thing," said Marguerite.

"Is it meant to be leaning to one side?" wondered Marie.

It was listing unsteadily to starboard. As they stood and stared through narrowed eyes, their heads comically adopted the same angle as the sloping ship, it reminded Jambo of the times they had stood in class by the abbot's desk, heads to one side, peering over his shoulder as he went through their home work.

"We need to take a closer look," said Pierre. "Francois and I can wade out to it when the tide is low. We'll pretty soon get an idea what needs to be done."

"Keep an eye out for the alligators," said Marguerite.

Oliver, abashed by his comrades' disappointment at the sloop, concentrated on a pair of boots as if it was nothing to do with him.

When the two men came back, they took Jambo to one side.

"We can't go ahead with this," said Pierre.

"Madness," said Francois.

"It's badly waterlogged and the barnacles on the bottom will make it as slow as a pregnant sow," said Pierre.

"The ropes are frayed and rotting, and the water butts have been split. It would be better to haul it ashore and make a bonfire," said Francois. "It's like The Sarah and Molly after that first storm, but worse."

"Much worse, I fear," said Pierre. "No wonder the escapade of our cousins from Georgia ended in disaster if their boats were like this."

"At least the wheel and the rudder seem to work," said Francois.

"What about the sails?" asked Jambo.

"We couldn't unfurl them to check. Just have to hope," said Pierre.

The three men sat in silence.

"We can't give up now," said Jambo.

"Maybe we should," said Pierre.

"Never," said Francois. "How I'd laugh to get away from these bastards."

Jambo said, "If we can get out to sea and head south for just a few miles we can land, lose ourselves in the forests the south and make our way overland to French territory. It's our best bet."

"Our only bet," said Pierre.

"This is the plan," said Jambo to his comrades as they gathered around the encampment fire a few days later. "We make our escape in two days.

"What I have arranged with the slaves is that, just before dusk they start a disturbance in their camp. We have seen what happened with our guards the moment they heard of trouble on the frontier, so we hope some will be drawn in that direction to see what the noise is about.

"At the same time, we shall push off from here. As soon as the soldiers spot us, they will have to come after us, too. By dividing the soldiers, it gives us both a better chance of success—not much, but better than going it alone. It gives us a chance to get clear and the slaves to make for the cover of the hills."

Jambo took a deep breath to steady himself. He understood just what a risk it was they were about to run.

"The tide will just be starting to come in a little later than it is now, and it will be darker, which will help. We will have a very short time to get everything done, so we must move fast. Tomorrow we must pack away all the food, medicine, and spare clothing that we have collected and load them on board. But whatever happens, we *must* behave as if it is a normal day. We shall still have to work the fields and deliver the produce to the British stores as usual.

"At dusk the day after, those strong enough will wade or swim out while the rest—the children and women and the old folk —will be ferried boat load at a time to the ship. We know they never have more than two guards on duty, if any, and they spend most of the time in the guardhouse on the other side of the harbor wall. Sometimes they patrol as far as the sentry post on the road, and occasionally out on to the headland on the other side of the cove, but Oliver will be teaching them some new card games and that should keep them out of the way."

"Are you happy to be our decoy?" asked Pierre. "It could be dangerous."

"Of course," said Oliver. "I have come to know the guards pretty well. They trust me, because they think I am stupid."

"Good man. Now, have we had any luck finding poles we can use to push the ship into the narrows without using sails?"

"We, er, *borrowed* some," said Oliver. "They are building an extension for the governor's palace and there seemed to be plenty of fine ash struts lying around that I am sure they won't miss. They are about eight feet long, which should be long enough to reach the bottom, at least until we get mid stream."

"Francois and Pierre will row each group to the far side of the ship, away from the shore, where we will have already hung ropes over the edge. Jem here, in case you haven't all met him, is our messenger. He will be on shore, and just before the tide reaches its peak, I'll give him the signal and he'll race to the slaves' quarters. When he gets there, they will start the riot. It should take ten minutes, maybe fifteen, before we hear anything. Jem is a fast runner."

Jem grinned broadly, excited at the responsibility.

"As the number in the encampment gets smaller, the ones left behind will have to make as much noise as if we are still all here. That's a task for you Charles."

"My p-p-pleasure," he said. "It will noisier than a night in the t-t-tavern at home."

"In all, we will have about an hour to get everyone on the ship and be ready to sail. The moment we hear the slaves, we will let the ship slip from its moorings and hope the troops are confused enough to give us time to get away."

"It's risky," said Pierre.

"It is," said Jambo. "But we must try. It's only half a mile, maybe less, to the headland and the outpost. If we can get beyond that, we should be out of range of their gunfire, and then we will have a chance to reach open sea. It is only a chance, but at least it is a moment to take control of our destiny. For better or worse."

For better or worse. They toasted each other in rum that Oliver had been given by a tavern owner in return for *helping him out*, as he put it.

In the early evening, a procession of men carried the supplies above their heads through the dark water to the ship, while Pierre and Francois rowed the skiffs laden with the others across the short expanse of water.

"Thank God for this sea fret," whispered Jambo as he waited with the others for their turn to board the ship. All was quiet, just the occasional scared yelp of a child, or the squeak of the rowlocks, and then everyone was on board. The fires still burnt in the abandoned campsite and someone had left a cauldron warming, the smell of burnt food wafting to those crouched on the ship. There was just one boat left by the shore with two oarsmen waiting for Oliver. Jem hovered by them, waiting for the signal from Jambo.

A shot rang out. They were rooted to the spot. Had Oliver been caught? They held their breaths in trepidation. Then another. Both from the slaves' village.

"They have moved too early," said Jambo. "That's not the plan."

"They've betrayed us!" said Francois.

A racket of shouting broke out. More gunshots, yells, and screams. Flames leapt into the sky from the direction of the slave encampment.

Oliver appeared out of the dusk running like a hare. He tore down the beach, leapt into the boat, grabbing Jem as he went, and the crew rowed like demons, scrambling, panting on deck.

"It's the backwoodsmen," he gasped, glasses steamed with the exertion. "They have come into town from the border country and they're going crazy. They are all drunk, and the ones who aren't in the taverns are attacking the slave camp. It's just sport to them. A bloody game."

Jem was so close to Jambo that he could smell the animal sweat of his fear.

"*He* can't come," said Francois, and made to manhandle him over the side.

"We are not abandoning him now!" shouted Jambo and shoved Francois off the lad so hard that he tumbled on to the deck.

"Nothing for it," said Jambo. "We have to go."

"Not yet," said Francois, scrambling to his feet and looking for a second as if he was spoiling for a fight. "The tide is too high."

"Shut up, Francois. Grab a pole and do something useful. All of you men start pushing. Anchor up."

It made a squealing, rusty sound as it was raised. They held their breath. Surely the British would hear that, but no, the bedlam from the slave quarter drowned it out.

The ship slid silently from its moorings with Pierre standing at the wheel, and they let the current take them into the mid stream. If only they could get beyond the headland before they had to raise the sails, they might just be able to slip away unseen.

"The tide is still against us," said Francois, pushing his pole into the depths.

"The rudder's not working," hissed Pierre. "I can't control the thing.

It will only pull to starboard."

"I can't reach the bottom," said Francois, his pole slicing uselessly through the water.

"Nor me," chorused the men who had been trying to push the ship out of the shallows.

"Raise the sails," ordered Jambo, joining Pierre at the rudder, hoping his extra strength would help make the ship swing to port.

"It's the only way to fight the current. With luck, we can tack around the headland and out into the straits."

"The soldiers will see us the second we do that," said Pierre.

"We have no choice," said Jambo with a calmness he did not feel.

Jem clambered up the main mast and tugged at the furled sail while a cursing Francois, pole abandoned, braced himself on the deck, pulling at the ropes of the mainsail with all his furious strength. One furious yank and most of the sail came away from its fittings, flapping feebly in the stiffening breeze. *Catastrophe.* It was in tatters, mildewed and rotten.

Oliver shouted, "Here come the soldiers."

They raced around the harbor wall and he could see them reach for their muskets, crouch and take aim—the puffs of smoke billowing out an instant before he heard the crack of the shot.

"They can't hit us from there," said Jambo, "but if they reach the outpost before we do, we are lost."

The race was on. One man, he couldn't make out who it was, shinned along the bowsprit clutching a ragged square of canvas which Oliver held at the other end, flapping as ineffectually as the sail. It was a pathetic attempt to catch even a puff of wind.

In an even more desperate move Jem, clambered along the yardarm, where he tried to tie down remnants of the mainsail, while Francois continued in his unavailing struggle to keep what was left of the sail aloft, but still the ship kept yawing to the starboard and even Pierre's huge strength at the wheel was not enough to steer them away from the land.

"We are heading straight for the mangroves," wailed Oliver.

The current had taken over, driving them hard toward the shore. The men grabbed the poles and desperately tried to fend off the worst of the impact, but had to duck for cover as the bullets cracked and popped around them.

The white of the waves brushing against the land stood out in the dusk. Closer they came—in a rush now—almost as fast as the soldiers whose musket fire showered down on them.

A bullet cracked into the bulwark inches from Jambo's head, a splinter scraped his temple, another shot whipped into the cabin door, sending Pierre diving for cover. There was a scream from above. It was Jem. The young black was hanging off the yardarm arched backward. It looked for a second as if the sweet-natured lad was smiling—as always—but, no, this time it was a deathly grin from which his blood spewed on to the deck.

With a great grinding sound, the ship gave one final lurch and careened into muddy embrace of the mangroves.

It had been a tragedy of errors, all over within twenty minutes

They were kept on the shore overnight, wet and miserable, the dead Jem stretched out in front of them, eyes open to the dawn sky, his brains spilling on to the ground.

At the very least they expected Dinwiddie to march them off to the cells or demean them publicly with a whipping. Maybe he would have the ringleaders executed. Instead he surveyed the bedraggled Acadians, picked his nose, and gave a half smile.

"You seem desperate to leave," he sneered. "Some will never have the chance to try again." He kicked the dead slave. "Let his own kind bury him. You French, come with me, I have something to show you."

They were marched, still in their soaking clothes, along the track that led to the slave quarter. As they approached, they heard a discordant humming noise, which for a second Jambo thought was made by the swarms of cicadas that chirruped unceasingly in the undergrowth. As they came closer he realized it was the chilling ululation of mourning women.

They reached the compound and it was as if a door had been opened to reveal a chasm of evil. Every one of the shelters had been broken up and scattered in shreds of bamboo and thatch, their few possessions and their cooking pots had been thrown around, and their rice stamped into the ground.

But that was not the cause of their horror. Ten slaves, maybe more, were hanging from the trees, naked and mutilated. Some had lost a hand, some an arm, others had their ears cut off, one had had his nose sliced from its face, another had his head cracked open, brains spilling like seeds from a rotten pomegranate.

They had all been whipped, their scars congealing in the mid morning heat from the wheals on their backs, blood dripping slowly on to the ground. One had had his stomach ripped out, leaving his intestines to spill out and drape themselves like grotesque leggings. Already ants were swarming over the bloody corpses. The chickens came pecking, and the dogs sniffing, while vultures sat in the trees waiting their time. The carpenter found himself staring into the eyes of Bram, his mouth in the ghastly grimace that must have been his last scream of agony.

Except he was still alive. His eyes met the Acadian's and he tried to speak.

"This one's still breathing," said a soldier, and he rammed a bayonet into the slave's stomach. He gave a convulsive lurch, and his innards slithered to the ground in ghastly ribbons of grey intestines, blue veins, muscle, and gore.

His wife who was at his feet, rocking backward and forward in her desolation, did not stir as her husband's blood spattered on to her and the children who she had gathered to her.

"I am sorry," Jambo said helplessly, but he did not have the courage to tell her about Jem. Nor could he shake off the guilt he felt. In truth, he had always known the slaves had less chance of escape than the Acadians and he was ashamed that he had taken advantage of them.

Washington said, "This is what happens to anyone who defies us."

"You must have been mad," said Purreton, as he locked them up back on The Sarah and Molly. "What made you join forces with the slaves? They haven't got the brains to escape, and they don't know how to fight. They surrendered to the backwoodsmen within ten minutes. Now the ones left alive are trapped here forever. You too." He shook his head, his good eye so beady it looked as if he was winking. "And what on earth made you think Dinwiddie would leave a ship at anchor waiting for you to steal? Did you not stop to think the entire escapade might have been a trap? Still, now he knows for sure how loyal you are."

One morning in May as the blossom on the trees threatened to submerge Williamsburg in a forest of white and pink, Purreton summoned Jambo on deck. They had grown used to each other. The Englishman respected the Acadian's stoic determination to stay defiant, and Jambo recognized that the skipper was simply in government pay, doing what he was told as humanely as possible. They both realized they were caught up in something out of their control.

Purreton seemed embarrassed, chewing his tobacco with vigor before he spat it out. "You are on the move," he said.

"What do you mean?" asked Jambo. "Where are we going?"

"A long way, said the skipper. "You won't be coming back."

Book Two

FIFTEEN

Liverpool, England

Summer 1756.

Prisoners of War

"Come and look at this," said Pierre, his bulk blocking out the light as he poked his head down through the hatch.

They had clambered up the ladder on to the deck. *Land.* For the first time in more than 40 days. Land. But this dirty smudge on the port side was not like anything they had seen before. It lurked beneath a haze of smoke, which poured from tall chimneys. As they drew closer they could pick out a discordant clutter of wharves and warehouses crouching at the corners of streets whose houses stretched in long terraces as far as they could see. Boston had seemed dauntingly frenetic after the gentle open spaces of Acadia, but this ugly sprawl...once more Jambo was reminded of the abbot and the admonitory paintings of damnation he used to show them with its flames and sullen vapors that threatened to subsume the earthly paradise above.

He and Marguerite stood on deck in silent dismay. Most villagers were chattering and pointing, the relief at being released from their seaborne prison outweighed the apprehension they might have felt.

"So this is where we have finally been *removed* as that nice Colonel Winslow put it," said Oliver.

"Well, he said whatever part of the world. Remember that?" asked Pierre. "Though I can't see us being happy here."

"Or allowed to be peaceable," said Francois.

"Surely they won't keep us incarcerated on board like Dinwiddie did," said Marguerite.

"This time we will fight our way off," said Francois, but no one bothered to hush him. They realized he was as fearful as the rest of them.

Jambo drew Marguerite and Osite closer to him and held Jean-Baptiste's hand, while the sailors busied themselves, furling the sails, and readying ropes for docking.

"Is this the Liverpool you spoke of?" he asked the skipper.

"It is, my French friend. One of the finest ports in England. A tavern on every street, a woman on every corner, and so much money. You'll like it here." He laughed and hawked a mouthful of yellow spittle into the fetid water. "Now, out of the way, I've got to unload the cargo. You lot, in other words."

It was two months after Purreton's warning that they finally left Virginia. After the attempted escape, they had been locked away for all but one hour a day and their rations cut back to watery soup with a few grains of rice, so it was almost a relief when the skipper announced, "This is it. As I said, you are to be sent away. We have ships for you."

He pointed at new arrivals in the bay. "The council spent a lot of money on that lot and I am sure you will find all the comforts you have become used to." He gave his habitual half-laugh, half-tobacco cough. "This is the parting of the ways," he said. "My contract is up, and at last, I am being discharged, I am glad to say."

The governor's officials had already made a list of which family was to travel on which transport, and over the next two days they were ferried to different ships. Some families were split up, but their protests were ignored.

"You'll all end up in England," they said. "If you make it at all."

Jambo and Marguerite were bivouacked on the Carolina, while her brother Joseph and his family were taken to the Virginia Packet.

"I will see you soon," said Joseph to his sister without much conviction. "Don't you fear, you have a fine man to look after you."

She was tearful as they were rowed off, but that turned to laughter as Charles, Anne, and the children were ferried to a waiting sloop. The tavern owner stood up shakily in the rowing boat and shouted, "Keep s-s-singing. Don't let them break our spirit!" and broke into a chorus of *Mademoiselle, voulez-vous dansez, la bastringue, la bastringue?* conducting the others until a sailor told him to sit down and shut up.

Would Charles be waiting for them here? Perhaps they would be on the quayside with his other brothers and sisters.

He pushed the thought out of his mind. Better not to hope for anything. Disappointment always followed.

One thing was certain, they could not have survived the voyage much longer. At first, as the ship sailed away from Virginia, they had welcomed the illusion of freedom—anything had to be better than the calculating indifference of Dinwiddie and the unyielding Washington, anything to put behind them the shame of their ignominious escape attempt and the horror of the slaves' executions. Jambo was haunted by their slaughter, and had found it hard to shake off the guilt he felt at their fate.

"They would have taken the risk, whatever we said," argued Oliver. "They knew what would happen to them if they failed. It's not our fault."

"It was a throw of the dice, remember?" said Marguerite. "It failed. We have to put it behind us."

The refreshing breeze that sent them on their way turned into terrifying gales, sometimes for days on end, and the waves that began by lapping gently at the ship's bow in the shallow waters off the coast became towering mountains of sea that crashed on the deck with ferocity greater than anything they had suffered before.

They clung to each other, screaming as the gales whistled through the riggings and ripped the sails into tatters with their sheer ferocity, twisting the deck rails and sweeping away the lifeboats. The vessel plowed though great walls of water, danced like a dervish on the crest of the waves, and plunged like a diver toward the ocean depths only to be hurled back with every timber shuddering.

The Carolina was not equipped with the prison boxes that had contained them for seven months, but in those conditions they almost wished they were, for the prisoners were hurled around the hold, crashed against the rough bulwarks, and into each other with sudden violence. One boy fell with such force that he lay in a coma for two days, and old man Pierre Babin tumbled into the gangway and broke his pelvis. There was nothing they could do for either of them in such storms. They were left to lie there until it became possible to tend to him, but by then it was too late. The old, the young, they died where they fell.

"How quickly we have become accustomed to death," said Jambo. "Remember when Madeleine Daigre's baby was swept away during those first days at sea? We were horrified, weren't we? Tears, appeals to the Almighty, anger. We could not believe that we deserved such cruelty."

But that was in the first days of their expulsion, when they assumed that there would be an end to their torment. Now, in their mood of grim resignation, they were too sick and debilitated to feel even sorrow for those who died. When there was a death, they muttered a few prayers, did what they could to console the grieving relatives, and got back to the unrelenting business of survival.

Without realizing it, they had developed a shell of sturdy resistance that protected them against their purgatory. It held them in good stead. They stayed disciplined, learning to live together just as they had in Grand-Pré, helping each other through sicknesses, sharing their food and water, trying to respect another's foibles, and staying tolerant when sheer weariness or hunger made it easier to be selfish or aggressive.

Jambo insisted that they logged any kind of illness the moment a symptom appeared and to make sure that the sick were kept in a kind of quarantine near the stern of the ship, well away from the stinking privies, but there was always someone who was ill, whether from seasickness, or vomiting and diarrhea, or if not that from a griping constipation caused by the dirty water, and the lumps of salted meat they were occasionally treated to.

No one bothered to complain about the hacking coughs and sore throats that were as incurable as they were unavoidable in the stifling hold. They no longer noticed how filthy they were, or if they did, they were beyond caring. Sometimes, the sailors would open the hatch to let in fresh air, and lower down buckets of salt water for them to wash in, but it was never enough to clean the grime from their bodies, or prevent the infestations of lice that swarmed over them, driving them crazy with their itching.

"You need to love someone a lot to do this," said Marguerite as she combed through Jambo's lank hair with her fingers.

Then, scurvy struck.

"I'm surprised we didn't have it before," groaned Pierre. "What can you expect when we never have fresh food?"

The first victim was a lad of four, one of the Landry family from Canard. At first he had dysentery, which as they came to learn all too swiftly, was the signal that scurvy was not far behind. Soon his body was mottled with spots, virulent against his deathly white skin. His lips were blue, his chest heaved and his hands scrabbled in the air as if reaching for a hand to pull him from the shadow of his inevitable death.

His mother knew he was going to die—they all did—but she did her best to comfort him while his father sat staring at them both in helpless misery.

It fell to Jambo and Pierre to wrest the dead child from the mother's arms, murmur a prayer, and slip the body though a porthole.

"What hope do we have?" asked Marguerite as she held Osite close to her. "How can we survive this?"

When Jeanne Dugas gave birth during a heavy storm, she died with her child. Her husband Paul barely roused himself to nod in numbed agreement when Jambo said, "You must say farewell now. Let them go."

He could not bring himself to look as Jambo and Pierre took the bodies and dropped them into the sea. It was as if the mother resisted her final passing. Her arm fell from the shroud as the men held her at the porthole, and for a second she seemed to be holding on to a rope. Then, when they disentangled her and tried once more to push her out, her hand flapped back as if waving a macabre farewell. Dugas did nothing. Just stared. Stupefied by the horror of it.

Fifteen children died on the journey.

Marguerite shuddered, "Can you imagine those bodies falling to the bottom of the ocean? I can see monsters of the deep racing toward them with their jaws agape, ready to devour them."

"It's the children that get the worst of it," said the first mate on one of the days calm enough to allow the prisoners on deck.

"Many a mother has been thrown into the water with her child. In one crossing I was on 32 children died, God rest 'em. It's a bad business, but there is nothing to do but say a prayer and let the sea have them."

No one was spared the scurvy. Jambo woke up one morning, gripped with a fierce attack of diarrhea. As he clung to the rail that served as the privy, perilously perched above the waves, he felt the fever creeping up on him, and found himself fighting for breath. Within hours, his face and legs were covered with suppurating wounds, and his legs were swollen with internal bleeding. Spots on his thighs and legs made it agonizing to move, and when the disease reached his gums, his teeth were loosened and his eyes bled. Every muscle ached.

"We have to carry on," he mumbled between his bleeding gums. "We must, or we will all end up being thrown in the ocean."

Sleep was impossible. He lay awake, feverishly rewinding memories of Grand-Pré. Odd moments; one night he was haunted by the vision of the toys that had been trampled by the British into the mud at Boudrot Point. The bear he had carved for Jean-Baptise would have been swept out to sea, or maybe found by a soldier and given to his own son. Osite's little doll might still be lying there on the levee. Then he thought of their fields—how they would be full of weeds, how the orchards would be untended, fruit lying rotting on the ground and the game and the rabbits—how many would have been caught in traps and left to die in lingering agony with no one to collect them?

"We'll have to a lot of work to do when we get back," he thought, only to berate himself for such fanciful nonsense.

As the ship made its last manoeuvres to dock, the turbid water of the harbor washed against the ship's hull.

"Look grand mama," said Jean-Baptiste. "Dog."

So it was—a dead dog, bloated by water, its legs obscenely splayed out toward them. Mother, frail as a leaf, looked as if she would faint.

"And rats," added the lad's grandfather quietly, peering at the creatures scrabbling in the rubbish that floated alongside the quay.

"It is filthy," said Marguerite. "A cess pit. How can anywhere be so disgusting?"

They looked in dismay at the shipbuilding yards with their timbers piled high, the grimy warehouses, tall blackened buildings surrounded by the rubbish of the wharf—sacks that had split open to let sugar spill on the cobbled quayside, rotting vegetables, carcasses of putrid meat, fought over by tatterdemalion sea birds and crows, wild dogs, and creeping cats, while horses and heavily laden carts forced their way through the confusion of people.

As they clustered on the deck and stared down, it felt as if everyone on the dockside paused to glare back. The stevedores stopped working, shop owners appeared at their doors, street sellers stilled shouting their bargains, and raucous groups of men and gaudy women spilled out of the taverns to inspect the new arrivals.

Marguerite had spirit enough to hiss 'harlot' at the sight of their painted faces and outlandish clothes that did little to hide their bodies.

"Over there," said Pierre, pointing to a group that emerged from a warehouse.

More than 100 blacks were being prodded along by armed militia. They were covered in rags and manacled together by their ankles and wrists. The chains clanked and rang on the cobbles. Some held their heads high, but most slunk along, subdued and hopeless.

Unbidden, the images of young Jem, the blood dribbling from his gaping mouth, and his father Bram, ripped apart and left to rot for the delectation of vultures came to him.

"They must be slaves. Are they going to Virginia?" Jambo asked the skipper.

"Yes, the African trade. Big money. Off to America to do the work you wouldn't do. You had it easy compared to that lot."

"I fear you are right," said Jambo.

"Now I need to count you for my report."

One by one they made their way down the shaky gangplank.

"366," said the skipper, handing his bill of lading to a waiting customs officer. "Dated: June 30, 1756. French prisoners handed over to the safe protection of the Liverpool Harbor Authority." He signed it with a flourish. "Now off you go," he said. "Au revoy mes amis." Then, he surprised the Acadians. He paused, turned back, and took the young carpenter by the hand. "Good luck. God be with you. You'll need Him."

Jambo picked up Jean Baptiste, Marguerite clutched the baby, and with mother and father they tottered their way on to the quay as feeble as invalids. The bones in his hand had healed but the fingers had set almost at right angles to his arm, so he could not hold tight to the gangplank rope, and months cooped up without exercise meant his limp was worse. He swayed and almost fell over as he tried to get his balance on the solid, unmoving cobbles beneath his feet.

What next? What should they do? The refugees stood irresolute and confused—the men were bearded, gaunt, and dirty; the women were in their worn woolen clothes, scrubbed and cleaned so often that they were as thin as paper. The children clung to their parents, open-mouthed with anxiety at this world of squalor and hostility.

"Wait here 'til the officer arrives," said the skipper. "You'll be looked after."

"Who are this lot?" shouted one of the onlookers. "Warra they wan?"

It was in such a strange dialect that Jambo could scarcely understand what he was saying.

"They're French," replied the skipper. "Traitors. From America. Been sent to prison here to keep them out of trouble."

In an instance, from being mildly curious, the crowd turned into an angry mob, cursing the pitiable band as '*Papist scum, filth, Froggie swine.*' More of them tumbled out of the taverns, whipping themselves up into a frenzy as they threw stones and rotten vegetables at them. Some put their faces close and spat.

"Keep calm!" shouted Jambo, ducking as a brick almost took out his eye. "Do nothing to provoke them, or we will end up being thrown in the sea."

Just as it seemed the crowd would force them off the quay and into the filthy waters, soldiers on horseback came clattering down the wharf side and laid about the jeering throng with the flats of their swords. A carriage followed, out of which a stepped an official, a dapper fellow with a face so thin and a neck so long he reminded Jambo of the grey heron that used to pick around the shore at home. He looked distracted.

"My name is Commissioner James Langton from the Admiralty. Welcome to Liverpool, though I do not know what we have done to deserve this visit. You will be treated fairly, like prisoners of war should be. Who is your leader?"

Jambo stepped forward. "We are British citizens," he started, but his broken English and heavy accent sent the crowd into another round of catcalls.

"You don't sound very British to me," said Langton. "Maybe you can improve your command of the language during your stay here. No one told us you were coming until one week ago, so we have no special quarters for you. Even if we did, we would not be disposed to oblige you. No silk sheets here, my friends. There is a war on you know. Now gather your belongings and come with us."

"Be proud," said Jambo as they prepared to follow. "Remember who we are, and what we have gone through. We cannot show that we are defeated. Never."

Yet, what shame and anger the bewildered outcasts felt as in their rags, carrying the few pathetic bundles of clothes they had, they were forced to walk through the claustrophobic alleys of this squalid city.

Even that summer day there was a feeling of damp neglect about the streets, their cobbles running with waste and water as a steady drizzle fell from a leaden sky. They were shaky on their feet after months at sea, and by now their worn-out moccasins had fallen apart, and their wooden sabots kept turning their ankles on the rough surfaces. Many limped along with bare feet.

They seemed to tramp for ages, kept company by drunken louts and layabout lads who kept up an unending flow of hate-filled taunts, and a bombardment of stones and rubbish, until they left the last of the city behind them and reached the scrubby countryside where the crowd lost interest in their new diversion of Frenchie-baiting and slipped away.

On they went, prodded by soldiers along a muddy track through eerily empty fields for about five miles until they neared a small village. The soldiers halted the straggling line of deportees in front of a group of dilapidated buildings. The musty stench of neglect and abandonment hung over the dismal scene. Their roofs were stripped of tiles, gutters were left hanging, windows were shattered, and doors clung lopsidedly to their broken hinges.

"My God. Here?" Jambo stood in disbelief, his shoulders slumped. "It's a ruin."

Oliver dropped his knapsack and rubbed his glasses as if he could not believe his eyes. "We are to stay here?"

The children burst into tears. Marguerite remonstrated with the Commissioner, "Think what you are doing to these poor little ones by making us live here."

But all Jambo could say, in his incredulity, was to repeat: "This is a ruin. This cannot be."

"It is the best we can do," said Langton. "This is now officially designated a detention camp for prisoners of war. Better than you have any right to, I reckon. Now get in line so we can get your names, ages, and occupations—not that there will be much call for your skills here."

"You, you…" Francois could not find the words for his anger. Jambo saw his fists clenching and moved to restrain him. The plowman settled for his customary insults. "Bastards. Bloody cockchafing swine."

"This is shameful," said Jambo, recovering himself. "You may not accept our rights as citizens, but you must recognize that we should be granted the respect and dignity we deserve. We are not dogs, but we have been treated worse than them for eight months."

"We deserve better," said Marguerite.

"You deserve nothing," said Langton. "You are miscreants who have defied the king. Do you not realize that the war with your masters, France, was declared only last month on May 18?"

"Let me think," said Francois with heavy sarcasm, "May 18? Where were we then, I wonder?"

"Half way across the Atlantic," said Pierre. "There weren't many journals delivered to us."

"For us the war began almost one year ago," said LeBlanc.. "When we were expelled from Grand-Pré."

"I know nothing of Grand-Pré," said Langton, his thin face quivered with irritation. "And care less. Now, we will provide chairs and tables, and enough wood for you to light a fire so that you can warm up the food we have for you."

"And to sleep?"

He waved at the bales of straw in the courtyard, so matted and grubby that they must have been used as bedding for cattle.

"We cannot sleep on this!" protested Jambo.

"This is disgusting," said Marguerite. "Look at the rats droppings."

"There's cow shit all over the place," said Francois. "Bastards."

"There are no gates or doors," said Pierre with his trapper's eye for danger. "The people will attack us."

Langton ignored them. "We are obliged to give you bread, cheese, butter, peas, and beer. You will have an allowance, too. A generous one. Out of the kindness of His Majesty's heart, we will give you six pence a day, and three for each child. That is how we treat prisoners of war. With a fairness you do not warrant." His head rose on his long neck and he peered at them along his heron's beak as if sniffing out further dissent. "You are under a curfew. No one is allowed out of this area before six in the morning and after four in the afternoon. Anyone found drunk will be punished."

"Drunk!" exclaimed Francois. "I did not notice any hostelries selling spruce beer on the way here."

"Though most of the people seem to be roaring," said Marguerite.

Langton left without a word, carried out of the yard in his coach, leaving a dozen soldiers on guard.

"Are they to keep us in, or our new friends out?" asked Pierre.

They looked around with heart as heavy as they had been since they had been expelled in October. They were in a group of warehouses, which judging by the shards of china, disused work benches, and machinery, had been used to make pottery.

The walls were running with so much damp that moss and fern sprouted from the cracks in the bricks. In one corner, broken guttering spilled a steady stream of rainwater that had turned the ground into mud. The flagstones had been dug up and taken away, and most of the wooden beams were sagging and pulling down the ceiling with them. There was a well, but it was filled with rubbish. Only the huge, open fireplace with a rusty cauldron hanging from a spit seemed to be in some sort of working order.

Jambo jumped to his feet and stood on a pile of pottery.

"This is no time for wavering," he said. "Remember, our ancestors had less than this when they landed in Grand-Pré, and we can make a home of sorts here until we return to our own country. We have withstood months of adversity at the hands of the English, and we cannot be brought down now. Let us share out the space we have and make the beds—"

"Beds! My pigs had better," complained Francois.

"—as comfortable as we can. The firewood the generous commissioner has given us is soaked through, so let's see what timber we can find to warm up this feast of cabbages, even if they do look as if your pigs would turn their noses up at them, Francois. Let's hunt around for anything that will serve as benches and tables, because despite what Langton says, there is nothing like that here."

They found enough wood. The women lit a fire under the cauldron—having scrubbed it out under the water from the gutter—and cooked, while the men foraged for as much clean straw as they could for makeshift beds.

"Nothing like half-cooked cabbage stalks to cheer the soul," said Oliver. "What have you ladies got lined up for us tomorrow?"

Tomorrow. The day after. The days and months after that. What did the future hold for them? As soon as darkness fell, there was nothing to do but set their own guards against marauding locals, lie in the gloom and wait for dawn. There were no blankets, so they huddled together in their clothes, drained by the ugliness of the day, by the crowds, by the city itself and the fearful conviction that they were cut off from home and loved ones forever—a few lonely survivors with little to hope for. It was impossible to find solace in sleep.

"It's strange," said Marguerite. "I cannot get used to the fact that we are not on a ship. It doesn't feel right, not bracing myself against the twists and turns of the sea all the time."

"I fear we might have more than enough time to get accustomed to that," said Jambo.

The rain poured steadily down through the holes in the roof. Rats scuttled around as if they owned the place, and owls came swooping in after the vermin, startling the children with their clatter. They were all awake long before the soldiers came marching in, shouting at them to line up for the dawn roll call. They gathered round the feeble flames of the fire, grumbling, yawning, and stretching their limbs that ached from the hard floor of the warehouse. They finished off the last of the evening's gruel hunched close together, as if to ward off the rain that still drizzled down remorselessly.

"Today we start to rebuild these ruins," said Jambo. "We all have skills of some kind. First, we need to fix the roof."

"What is the point of that?" asked Francois, belligerent as ever.

"It might help to keep us dry," said Marguerite sweetly.

"It doesn't make sense to spite ourselves," said Jambo. "Is anyone else opposed to making this midden habitable?"

Francois grumbled something about doing the work that should be carried out by the '*lazy, work-shy, British swine,*' but the rest of them murmured their agreement.

"Don't you think we should see where we are, what the neighborhood is like?" asked Oliver.

"Why don't Oliver and I take a walk around and see what we can discover?" asked Pierre.

"Don't talk to anyone unless you have to," warned Jambo. "They don't seem to like us much."

They were back before the afternoon curfew. "We are in a ghetto in the middle of nowhere," said Pierre.

"It's a sort of no man's land," said Oliver. "The village is called Woolton, but it's a small, poxy place with a small church that doesn't look as if it has been troubled by the faithful, a couple of stores, and another disused pottery works. In fact, all around, it's as if the people just upped and left because many of the houses seem to have been abandoned and the fields left untilled."

"There are rats and flies breeding in the garbage, and pigs rooting around in the mud," said Pierre. "The only sign of habitation was on what we reckon is the main road back to Liverpool."

"We were almost knocked off our feet by a carriage," said Oliver. "And the nobs inside! Such finery. The men were so dressed up they looked as effeminate as girls at a dance."

"Not a problem we shall have here," pronounced Marguerite with gentle sarcasm.

Before Pierre could continue Oliver interrupted. "Tell them about our stroke of luck."

Instead, the burly trapper ducked down out of the sight of the guards and disappeared into the dusk beyond the walls of the ghetto.

He returned with a sack. In it was bread, cold meats, and three bottles of wine.

"There is a small tavern on the main road," said Pierre.

"And we found this nearby," said Oliver, all innocence.

"Shame to waste it," said Pierre.

For that brief moment, it seemed as if God was once again their side.

"I know what Charles would do if he were here," said Jambo.

"Let's sing!" said Pierre, and they began a chorus of *A la Claire Fontaine.*

Jambo put his arms around Marguerite and they laughed. It was the first time in months.

SIXTEEN

Woolton Detention Centre, Liverpool

Summer, 1756

The Speckled Monster

Jambo and the others sat astride a beam on the ridge of a warehouse, covering the holes with broken tiles and lengths of timber that they had culled from the empty buildings near the camp. Pierre had found some nails and Oliver a hammer—'*just lying around,*' he said artlessly.

"Does this rain ever let up?" said Pierre half-heartedly pulling his ragged cape of sacking over his head.

"And the fog. No wonder the English look so white and ill," said Jambo.

"And seem so angry," said Oliver, drying the condensation from his glasses. "They are going to be hard to do business with."

Since their arrival, the city had been covered by a low, grey cloud that hid the summer sky with a poisonous smog that stung their eyes and crept into their chests.

"I would give anything for fresh air," said Jambo. "My lungs feel as if they are full of muck."

"The rain is dirty, too. Have you noticed how grimy the clothes are when the women hang the washing out to dry?"

The buildings of their ramshackle refuge stood like rotten, blackened teeth, separated from the nearest habitation by the neglected common where neither green grass or crops flourished, and only a few stunted trees struggled for a foothold. To the east was a grey, greasy plain. To the west, the horizon was broken by the silhouettes of the city's buildings, and the masts of the barges moving along the River Mersey carrying coal and wool.

Oliver was playing with words—Mersey, merci, mercy. "There's no mercy here, that's for sure." He chuckled to himself for several minutes.

"The sea and the river are so dirty there's hardly a fish to be caught," said Pierre. "And what's happening in the fields? They are full of wheat and barley so stunted and bound with weeds it is as if no one has been near to tend them. There don't seem to be any laborers here, just beggars."

Wherever they looked from their vantage point on the roof there was machinery—pulsing, smoking, steaming, and stinking. In the distance they could see huge windmills, sails turning steadily as they pumped water or milled grain, and the factories of the chemical manufacturers spewing out toxic clouds. If the sun ever had a chance to peak through, it was blotted out by the smoke from the tallow-boiling works.

After a few weeks they decided to venture as unobtrusively as possible into the city centre during the hours allowed by their curfew. Oliver led the way, because he had already made the trek several times, slipping out of the camp when the guards weren't looking, but the moment they reached the main road, little more than a mess of potholes and puddles along which horse and carts careered recklessly, a gang of youths appeared, hurling whatever came to hand and whatever insults came into their mouths. The women bore the brunt of their obscenities, but they ignored them and strode out with their heads high.

As they passed the tavern where Pierre and Oliver had found the food and drink on the first day, the landlord came to the door joining the angry chorus and shaking his fist.

"Wonder what his problem is?" Oliver sniggered.

The narrow streets were almost as claustrophobic as the ship's hold. The air was filled with the cloying, throat-catching aroma of the sugar refineries. The smell from the salt processing plant mingled with the pungency of the herring-smokery and the whale oil refinery. All the time there was a gruesome olfactory undertow of the fetid odor from the streets of rotting meat, rubbish, dead dogs and shit. There was also the unrelenting bedlam—the braying of donkeys, the clatter of horses, and the carriages of the rich merchants dashing past and forcing anyone in the way into the gutter. There were grocers with baskets of vegetables balanced on their heads, women carrying milk pails across their shoulders, hawkers, and pickpockets weaving through the melee. The noise reached a crescendo on market days with stall owners haggling over deals, and street sellers shouting to be heard over the cacophony of cattle, sheep, barking dogs, and grunting pigs.

"It's worse by the docks," said Oliver. "It's one tavern and whore house after another, and streets overflow with spilt ale, vomit, and piss. They just go where they stand. Sorry Marguerite."

"Now I see where the incomers in Halifax learnt their manners," she said.

Despite the grossness of it all, there was wealth beyond their imagining. The Acadians marveled at the noble houses on Ranelagh Street and Duke Street. As Oliver had reported, "They are like castles. Some of them have ten rooms and as many servants," but they hadn't expected such solid grandeur, so many towers and domes, nor so many windows.

"But who would want to live in such strange buildings that are so tall and narrow, and all jammed together?" asked Pierre.

"Made of cold brick, too," said Jambo. "Chills the soul to imagine living in something like that."

A coach and four clattered past, splattering them with mud.

"I see what you mean about their gaudy appearance," said Marguerite. "That last one had a beauty spot on his cheek as big as a currant. Ridiculous."

"Mind you," said Oliver, his moneymaking instincts sharpened by such dizzying choices. "I have never seen so many shops and tradesmen. They've got everything—drapers, rope makers, grocers, tallow chandlers—and how many barbers and tailors does a place need? I think we shall be able to do business with them eventually."

"But how *wasteful* they are," said Marguerite, as she collected fruit and vegetables that had been thrown away and left to rot on the ground.

"There are so many down-and-outs like us, scraping around for leftovers," said Pierre's Marie, "There seem to be hundreds of homeless."

"There was a fight among about ten of them the other day over a sack of flour that had fallen off a cart," said Oliver.

"And that is between their own countrymen," said Jambo. "Don't they look after each other?"

"None of it makes sense, does it?" asked Pierre, hanging the last tile onto a rafter. "Don't they miss the quiet? The seasons? The rhythms of life? I know I would give anything to be out in the still of the night, hunting rabbits."

Despite official indifference and the downright hostility of the people, the Acadians had made great strides since they were marched to the ghetto one month before. The pump had been fixed, a permanent fireplace had been built, and the warehouses had been divided into makeshift cubicles using lengths of cloth for curtains, so that each family had some privacy. Some of the rubble had been cleared from the yard, partly to create a space for the children to play, but also to fill in the gaps of the walls where thieves crept through.

"The English are an odd lot," said Jambo, pausing to massage his damaged hand. "They don't behave as if they rule half the world. This pursuit of power does not seem to give them much pleasure."

"They seemed quite happy to drive us out of our country," said Pierre.

"I'm not so sure," said Jambo. "Yes, Lawrence was the devil, but Winslow seemed more apologetic than angry most of the time, almost depressed."

"And Dim-wittie just seemed irritated—as if his dinner had been interrupted," said Oliver.

"And now this Langton looks around him with the air of someone who would rather be elsewhere," agreed Pierre. "Certainly he doesn't want to waste his time on us."

"That's my point," said Jambo. "The English don't particularly care about us. They neither hate us nor fear us. We were just in the way. Acadia, the places Washington used to talk about—Ohio, Illinois—they were simply territories the English had to capture so that they could drive out the French and take control. They had virtually exterminated the Indians, so it was our turn."

"I think you are right," said Oliver. "I don't even think Lawrence disliked us as a people. After all, his officials were trading with your Uncle Rene right up to the end. No, we are like cogs in a water mill, but so small that no one noticed when the big wheels turned and ground us into little pieces."

"I don't suppose anyone knows we are here," said Pierre.

"France must, surely," said Francois. "I expect King Louis will come to our rescue."

"I doubt it," said Jambo. "He has a war on his hands. The truth is that we are trapped here and will be until the fighting is over, and that's if we are lucky."

"We've survived so much. It can't get any worse," said Oliver.

"I am surprised how resilient the children are," said Pierre, "Though I think the older ones suffer most, because they have some understanding of what is going on."

"And they can remember their old lives which makes things worse," said Jambo."

"Ever since I put those traps out in the wasteland toward the river, I've taken my Ignace with me when I go to check them. He really enjoys doing that, like any true Acadian," said Pierre. "But the little ones often sit in silence for hours, sucking their thumbs."

"And Jean-Baptiste has been wetting the bed since we arrived here," said Jambo, hammering vigorously at a beam. "By the way, I need to find something for Osite's birthday," he added. "To think, she is two this month, and has spent almost half her life in a prison of some sort. Oliver, anything you can magic up?"

"I'll have a little scout around." He laughed. "I have become quite friendly with a woman who has a stall near Duke Street who sells whistles and drums. Even a doll or two, though not as good as the ones you used to carve, Jambo."

"Right. That should stop the worst of the rain. Pierre, come and give me a hand with the gates, I want to block the hole in the wall where those lads broke in last night."

Marguerite came into the yard.

"Hello, my dearest. Look at our new roof." He held his arms wide as if acknowledging the cheers for winning top prize in the annual cattle market in Halifax. "All our own work."

One look at her face stopped him. She was as pale as a cloud.

Sudden panic gripped him. "The children," he asked, "Where are the children? Are they...?"

"You'd better come," she said"

Jeanne Aucoin lay on her straw bed. She was feverish, with sweat pouring from her forehead.

"It's as if my bones are on fire," she whimpered.

They tried to cool the fever with dirty rags dampened with water from the pump, and did their best to calm her as she writhed in agony and fear.

"I'll get a doctor."

Jambo ran the five miles to the quayside. "A doctor, where can I find a doctor?" he asked anyone he met in the street. All passed by, reluctant to acknowledge this wild-eyed young man with a foreign accent, until a sailor led him to a door with the brass label, *Sick and Hurt Commission.*

"They're meant to look after you," said the man who spoke in a brogue even stranger than the locals. "To be sure, these are the officials responsible for the welfare of deportees and prisoners. God be with you."

Jambo was just in time. The doctor was about to go out to dinner, and he waved the breathless stranger away impatiently until he took one look at the dread in the young man's eyes. That was enough to detain him.

"Come with me in the carriage. But be quick, I have an appointment. What does she look like?"

Jambo was vague. He had been in such a rush. All he could think of was *like death.*

The doctor stooped by the sick woman's bedside, but scarcely bothered to examine her. He knew instantly what was afflicting her.

In the time Jambo had been fetching the doctor, the wretched woman's skin had become like crepe rubber. Pus poured from the boils on her face, and they could almost see the blood leaking into her skin, wincing as she coughed up the bloody mucus as it flowed deep into her intestines.

The doctor took a pinch of snuff. "The speckled monster," he muttered to himself. To the people around the bed he said quietly, "She has smallpox. Boil water and keep her as clean as possible, but first move her as far away from everyone else as possible."

"May God have mercy," said Marguerite, almost as pale as the sick woman.

"What can be done?"demanded Jambo.

The terrified woman tried to sit up, but slumped back. There was no strength left in her.

"I am afraid it is too late now," he was talking softly, so the stricken patient would not hear. "The disease has taken hold. Now listen to me and there may be a slight chance of keeping the death toll down—for many will die, there is no doubt of that."

He took a few steps away. "This is what we call a virus. It can be passed on and caught at any time during the course of the illness, but it is *most* dangerous during the first week of the rash, when most of the skin lesions are intact. You see, here, on her arms and around her neck? These are the lesions. The chances of being infected decreases within seven to ten days when scabs form, but bear in mind that the infected person is contagious until the last one falls off."

The doctor, who was not much older than Jambo and clearly reluctant to get too close to his patient, was talking in a precise manner that contrasted with the panic that gripped the listeners.

"You have to realize that the disease is caught mainly through face-to-face contact with an infected person. The longer the contact, the more easily it spreads. Keep the children away from them, however distressing that might be, because that might give the little ones a chance of survival. That means anything up to about six feet, so keep your distance.

"It can also be diffused through contaminated objects such as bedding or clothing, so the moment anyone shows any symptoms, put them in isolation. Not just the patients, that includes anyone who has been close to a victim."

There was a brief silence, broken only by the anguished groans of the dying woman.

"Is there nothing we can do for her?" asked Marguerite.

"Pray. That is all, I am afraid." He paused as he made to leave. "Well, have heard of this new idea from China or somewhere in the far distant east. They are foreigners, so not to be trusted, but you might want to try, especially as the late King's Queen experimented with it. Variolation it's called. She tried it on four criminals, who were sentenced to die on the gallows, and it seemed to work judging by the agony they went through."

"Did they live?"

"In fact they did. She even had her own children inoculated, as we call it, and some of the wealthier class have followed her example."

"Well, come on, what is it?" asked Jambo, irritated by this lesson in medical history.

The doctor rummaged in his bag and brought out a flat stick. "Take a sample of a pustule from a victim like this," he said as he prodded it into the leg of the unfortunate woman. "It's not very scientific, but now that it is infected you can take it and stick it into your nose, or in a cut in the skin. It will make you ill—after all, it is smallpox—but not so much that you won't survive. It builds up what we call an immunization to the disease. That's the idea, anyway."

He took more snuff and sneezed noisily over the patient.

"That is all I can do for you. I shall notify Mr. Langton and the priest.

He won't be pleased to be made so busy, that's certain." He mounted his horse. "Remember: hot water and prayer."

They found themselves checking for symptoms of their own. Was that shiver a fever, or just a cold? Were those aching limbs down to tiredness? Was that only a headache, just a backache?

But there was no doubting the raised pink rash on the skin that turned first into pus-filled lesions, and then became crusty after eight or nine days. There was no mistaking the delirium, the vomiting, the diarrhea, and the bleeding.

They did try the doctor's variolation, sliding infected slivers of wood into their noses or mouths, but it had no effect. The carpenter even tried it on himself and spent most of the next day with a head ache, puking without control.

"Not me," said Marguerite. "I am too busy to spend a day being sick."

The next day, Marie Daroy was stricken down, then Jean-Baptise Comeau. Then Jacques Landry, Alexis Trahan, Joseph Vincent, Jeanne Daigre followed. It became a blur of death.

With so many to cope with, the sick were often left to die on the earth floors, and despite the advice of the doctor, whose visits were as short as he could manage, it was impossible to isolate the victims. They cleared a space in an outhouse on the edge of the ghetto where they laid the cleanest straw for beds, but there was little they could do to ease their agony. It was impossible to boil enough water to make it drinkable, or even safe enough to soothe their pain-wracked bodies. There was nothing to be done about the heat and the dankness of the warehouse.

"Medicine. We must have more." Again and again Jambo ventured to the offices of the Sick and Hurt Commission to demand help from Langton, but there was no comfort there.

Far from it. He was indignant that they had brought the disease with them.

"It could spread through the city. Just think what that would mean for a port like Liverpool, especially now the country is at war."

"Well, give us, I beg you, more food, some clothing. So much has been infected."

He waved him away.

"No clothes are to be provided," he said. "But we British are not uncaring, so I will award an extra allowance of 10 shillings for funerals."

It was a carelessly cruel rebuff, and one that LeBlanc would never forget, or forgive, as he and the ones left standing struggled to contain the remorseless march of the disease. Every day that summer there was a funeral, sometimes three or four.

He was carrying two pails of freshly boiled water across the yard when his father tugged at his sleeve.

"It's your mother."

"She was lying in her cot, a pitiful scrap, arms like sticks, her face pinched and grey. She was dying. "I'm sorry, son," she said.

He held his mother's hand, and felt the last flicker of life whisper from her body. She had never spoken of it but he understood that she had never recovered from losing her children. Her boys. From the moment they had been imprisoned on the transports, it was as if her entire life was undone. It seemed to her like God's judgment on her as a mother—that somehow she had failed, and that all the years spent caring for her family, her home, her village, had come to nothing. Her *sorry* was for him—sorry that there was not enough left in the world to make it worth staying alive. Sorry that even *he* could not lift her from her misery.

There were nine deaths that August day. Nine mothers, wives, husbands, fathers, or children. The survivors laid them out, covered them with sheets, and prayed.

They never had the materials or the time to make coffins, so the dead were wrapped up, laid on a disused door, and carried by four men in a melancholy procession across the blighted common between the warehouse and the church. The carpenter was kept busy. At every funeral he followed behind, clutching a small wooden cross, bound together by rope on which he had carved the name, date of birth and death.

The Scottish priest who had been *given* to them for their comfort, despite his objections to their *'foreign Papist inclinations,'* murmured a few half-hearted prayers, and the bodies were laid in their shallow graves.

The ones left behind were left with a searing sense of desolation. Every day, more empty beds, more spare places at the communal dining hall. There were heartrending piles of clothes, and little stacks of shoes. They cleared the bedding of the deceased, and set fire to it outside the compound, but often the hot summer's wind sent blackened flakes of the straw back in their faces. Children wandered around, the green snot of their misery hanging in tendrils. Some were orphaned, shoeless, grubby and unclaimed, but not neglected for long as an aunt or a friend's caring mother would gather them up, clean their faces, and give them their surrogate love.

"There is consolation," said Langton on his first and only visit to the ghetto during that time. "It means the allowances will go further and that will give you more food to share around."

The carpenter stared at him, his eyes blacker than ever with contempt, until the Commissioner, discomfited, cantered off, back to the safety of the city.

After his mother's funeral, his father took to wandering around the ghetto talking to himself—or maybe to his dead wife. He became vague and forgetful. Sometimes he would join the group around the cauldron to eat and demand a beer as if he was at home, only to stare at the food and drink he was offered and push it to one side.

He would ramble, "Where's Olivier? Where is the boy? I promised Jean-Baptiste we'd go fishing. Is Charles holding a *bal de danse?*"

Three weeks after mother was buried, Pierre came into the ghetto with the old man.

"I found him by the river," he said. "He thought he was home, walking by the Canard."

Father looked blankly at Jambo as if he had never seen him before. "I'm tired," he said, and his son took him by the arm and settled him in his palliasse.

By morning, he was dead. *It wasn't smallpox, it was surrender,* realized Jambo, as he and the men carried the body to the grave alongside his dead wife. Despite his apparent disregard for anything but a beer and crackling fire, none of those easy pleasures would have been possible without his wife. He seemed not to care much about any of the family, but in the dark days of exile he had come to understand that they were all that mattered to him. Who could he joke with, what could he gossip about, if they were not there? What was the point of making fun of his unmarried daughters if their mother, his wife, was not there to tick him off at his poor taste in humor? They all gave him meaning. Now there was not enough to make life worth the bother.

Jambo and Marguerite did not give up. The men kept the water boiling and foraged for clean straw for their bedding, while the women ignored the advice of the doctor by tending to the dying, cleaning and bathing the gruesome sores.

What else could they do? They had known each other all their lives. These were people they had gone to school with, played games with, and shared the work of the fields. They had danced at their weddings, and shared the delight as their children took their first steps. Some were simply good drinking companions. In times of pleasure or of pain, nothing could shake the kinship of an Acadian.

Like all the fit women, Marguerite and Pierre's Marie worked without break. They found a willing helper in Francois's niece, 20 year old Agnes Hebert. If one slept for a few hours, the others would take over, hoping against hope to save their cousins, but more often surrendering them to death with the heart-breaking rituals of folding their hands in one last resigned gesture, hiding their disfigured faces with a sheet, and murmuring the prayers.

They were all grey with exhaustion.

"You look awful," Jambo said tenderly as he kissed his wife's brow.

"As for you," she laughed, "I daren't let you near a mirror for fear of what *you* might see."

They held each other briefly.

"I was thinking of the orchards in the meadow on the lee of the hill," she said. "I had never seen such ripe apples as last autumn."

"I was wondering if that horse of mine was running free."

They smiled ruefully. Nostalgia was a comfort.

By October, more than 100 of the 366 Acadians who had landed in June had been buried. But then, one morning they awoke and there was no sound of tears. No screams of agony or fear. No panic-stricken relations rushing around crying out for cloths and hot water. No deaths. It was over.

"But beware," said the doctor in his precise, unemotional way. "There are still things that can go wrong. Often there are complications, like scars from the pustules, which can be really deep and pitted. Sometimes casualties are afflicted with arthritis and bone infections. Some catch pneumonia because they are so weakened. There could be severe bleeding, eye infections, and inflammation to the brain. It feels like your head is going to explode."

"Death might be a kindness after all," said Marguerite wryly, but the doctor had jumped on his horse and galloped out of the yard.

That night, for the first time in months, they draped the curtain around their shelter and made tired, careful, affectionate love. It was as much to prove they had not been brutalized by the months of death and loss as to reassert their feelings for each other. But then, nothing could weaken that.

SEVENTEEN

The ghetto, Liverpool

Winter 1756; Summer 1757.

The End

The first Christmas in the ghetto was a perfunctory affair. A few prayers uttered without conviction and mumbles of consolation for those who had lost someone they loved, which as Marguerite pointed out, was every one of them.

"But," she said, "We have to celebrate those of us who have been spared and be thankful that we are still here."

Here was a forlorn place. Everything had gone into fighting the plague. The result was that all their efforts to make their prison habitable had come to a halt. The pump had seized up, so there was little water to drink let alone wash with—instead, in the depth of that first winter, they collected snow and warmed it in their cauldrons. It rained, it snowed, and then the ice melted into puddles turning the floor of the ghetto into mud. Jambo had redirected some of the gutters so that the rain would pour into water butts, but they were so leaky that they made the mud deeper still. The latrines, which they had dug when they first arrived, iced over, and then with the warmth of spring turned them into a nauseating swamp of excrement where flies feasted.

They were still hungry—far from having more food to share, as Langton had so crassly claimed, their plight was made worse by the Commissioner sometimes forgetting to pay their allowances—and they were cold. However close they sat around the fires that filled the warehouses with more smoke than heat they did not have the clothes or the shoes to withstand the chill of a Liverpool winter. They used rags bound around their feet instead of their old sabots, which even Oliver had not been able to repair, and some even wrapped themselves in the clothes of the dead.

"More use to the living," said Francois bluntly and no one disagreed.

If they huddled together to keep warm, the lice that lurked in their beards, in their hair, in every corner of their clothes, crept like an invading army from body to body.

And rats—what a playground it was for them. The rodents scampered around the place, coming out at night to sniff the sleeping bodies. Marguerite woke screaming to find one nibbling her toes.

There was a kind of insanity about them. Some of the newly widowed lay on their mattresses, immobile with depression, some having conversations with their dead. The survivors were hollow cheeked and emaciated, skin hanging from bones that stuck through their skimpy, unwashed, clothes. They wandered around the ghetto in listless despair. As for the children, they clung to their mothers, waiting for a scrap of food to be spooned their way.

They would cook anything they found—the carcass of a stray sheep or a dead horse found lying in the ditches—and having eaten every inch of the flesh, they would crunch the bones into a paste and mix with stewed weeds, wild flowers, and nettles.

"Quite tasty," said Oliver, but he immediately doubled up and retched it back up.

Francois, almost hallucinating with hunger, started to eat mud. "There's grass in there," he croaked, his hair falling lankly over his face, his eyes mad and staring. "You can eat grass."

A group of them went scavenging a few times a week around the yards of the wealthy merchants, rummaging through the bins and risking a round of gunshot from the footmen.

One day, Francois came running into the compound with a chicken and a shoulder of mutton, which had been cooked for a feast, but barely touched and then thrown away. He was limping slightly.

"I was winged by shot," he said. "But never mind, it was worth it. "They're a bit green, but stick them in a stew and they will be delicious.

I found a half-full bottle of rum, too."

Meat. The prisoners were ecstatic and ignored Marguerite's warnings about eating rotten flesh—until the virulent bout of diarrhea that followed almost as soon as they had swallowed it.

"There were a few rats nosing around," Francois admitted as they perched on the unsteady pole that stretched over the latrine.

As they emerged from the darkness of the plague into spring, Pierre and Jambo tried to be more scientific in the search for food. They used their well-honed skills to make rough snares of sisal, stolen from the nearest factory, and distributed them around neighboring countryside in the forlorn hope of catching rabbits. They trapped mostly rats.

"Might as well skin them and put them in the pot," said Marguerite, ever the realist.

They dug allotments in the unused land close to the ghetto, and begged and stole seeds to plant. The first cabbage shoots were greeted with elaborate joy.

They kept alive their old sense of kinship and mutual respect by gathering around the graveyard most evenings and praying. Even the ones whose faith in a benevolent God had long been shattered understood that they owed it to each other to sit quietly together in communion and remember their lost cousins.

"It shows we have a bond," said Jambo. "If we can stay strong for each other, then we will be unshakeable."

They were encouraged by the latest communiqués from the war. So many of their guards had been sent abroad to fight that the ones left behind had relaxed their vigilance and had become tolerant of, if not altogether friendly with their shattered charges.

They no longer confiscated the few newspapers and pamphlets that the prisoners found lying around, even though it meant that the prisoners discovered that the British navy had surrendered the island of Minorca to the French in June—just before the Acadians had arrived—and that there were calls for the admiral to be tried for treason. British forces had been routed in America, where the French General Montcalm had swept the British aside and marched on Quebec.

"They took 1,700 prisoners," said Oliver, whose English had become fluent enough to read better than the others. "And they displayed the British flags in triumph in the churches of Montreal and Quebec City itself."

"Maybe it will lead to our return," said Pierre.

"Especially as the Empress of Austria has just declared war on the Prussians, who just happen to be Britain's most powerful ally." Oliver positively crowed, as if he had been promoted to be one of the Empress's own hussars—or better, head of her commissariat—even though he had never heard of her until that morning.

"A toast to the good Empress," said Francois."Whoever she is."

"The war will soon be over!" said Oliver "And we'll be free."

"Don't be so sure," said one of the guards as he broke off from his perfunctory patrol of the perimeter to pass the time of day. "The tide will turn against you Froggies now, because we at last have a leader who will change our fortunes. You wait, William Pitt is the man to see off anyone rash enough to stand in our way. He's a real firebrand."

When Langton rode in on one of his regular inspections, Francois grabbed his bridle and said, "We hear you are losing the war. Have you come to set us free?"

Not for the first time, Jambo wished his angry friend would keep his mouth shut. He had important business with the Commissioner, and before he could open his mouth it looked as if he was going to wheel his horse straight back out of the ghetto.

"Mr. Langton, a moment, please." He elbowed Francois to one side. "Why have you cut back on our allowance?"

"Because the English are being soundly thrashed and this is one way of getting your own back," jeered the plowman from a safe distance, though whether he was more wary of LeBlanc or the English official was uncertain.

"There can be no excuse for stopping our money," said Jambo. "After all, as you pointed out, there are fewer of us now."

"We should not be forced to beg," said Marguerite, her face set with anger. "You should be ashamed that you treat us like this."

Langton scratched his long neck, both irritated and embarrassed at feeling he had to explain himself.

"This war is bleeding the country dry," he said. "We don't have enough in the coffers. We give you 36 pounds a year, which is more than most of our own population earn if they can find a job, which is unlikely. Haven't you seen how angry the common people are? People are starving and rioting for food every day. Only last week, some broke into a mill and ransacked it for flour. No wonder they are resentful of you."

Jambo was about to say they were probably more resentful of their own politicians than a handful of half-starved deportees, but held his tongue. They had been shocked by the violence on the streets, much of it aimed against the government, which they blamed for its tax rises and food shortages. There were constant fights, many sparked by the press gangs bursting into the taverns to round up the drunks and 'volunteer' them for military action. On one bloody occasion, His Majesty's men even tried to seize the crew of a whaler and force them into service, but they were fought off with blubber knives and harpoons.

"They only pay soldiers eight pennies a day," said Oliver. "About the same as a loaf of bread. It's not much for certain death on behalf of a grateful country. Or do I mean indifferent."

"But," said Jambo to Langton, "we can help. There are fields left neglected all around us, and judging by the state of the homes there is scope for carpenters and good honest workmen. Our women can weave and sew—in our country they are famous for their skills—and if we can make a living, however small, it will save you *giving* us any money. We would rather not rely on charity, that is not our way."

Langton shook his head and replied as if he was reading from an official brief, "I fear not. The Sick and Hurt Commission in London has ruled that all you Neutrals are prohibited from working in case it upsets the laborers in the towns where you are being kept. I'm sorry, but there it is."

For Jambo, the Commissioner's statement was almost as telling as the moment in the church when Winslow had announced that they were to be *removed.*

And just like then, most of the Acadians were grumbling and talking amongst themselves rather than listening.

"In the *towns?* There are more of us?" asked Jambo. Thunderstruck, he took a step back from the Commissioner and with that characteristic gesture pushed the hair off his face, as if trying to perceive clearly what the man had said.

Oliver swiftly cottoned on to the momentous news. "Do you mean there are more of us in prison? Not in Liverpool, surely."

"Where? Where are they?"Jambo grabbed the horse's bridle for fear the Commissioner would gallop out of the ghetto, leaving the question unanswered.

Langton hesitated. "Not in Liverpool, no, but in other cities, maybe. I cannot tell you more. Not until the war is over and France is defeated."

"But you must tell us. It is our right," said Jambo.

"I cannot. You have no rights. And anyway, just think what confusion it would cause if you were to start wandering around the country trying to find your missing kin."

"But we have brothers, parents, and friends we thought were dead," implored Jambo. "At least tell us where they are so that we can write to them."

Langton shook his head. He said nothing else and spurred his horse out of the ghetto.

The carpenter just stood there, stunned, gazing after the messenger of such momentous news. He didn't know whether to feel cheered by the realization that they were not alone in this hostile country, or despair that he might never learn which of his old comrades was still alive, or—the unbearable truth—discover which were dead.

"We should send someone to find out," said Francois.

"Where do you suggest?" asked Pierre. "And who?" The most patient of men, sometimes he allowed his irritation with the *unthinkingness* of the plowman to show.

"Even if we knew, we would never get beyond the city boundaries," said Oliver.

"Precisely," said Pierre.

"We must ask questions of everyone," said Jambo. "The merchants in the port, the shop owners, the seamen. They are always voyaging to other ports in the country or talking to those who have. I'm sure they will have some information."

"There will be loose talk in the taverns, especially when a sailor drinks too much," said Oliver.

"Which they do all the time," said Francois.

"We could write to the Sick and Hurt Commission in London," suggested Oliver.

"Langton would seize our letters, read them, and burn them," said Pierre. "That would give him the excuse to stop our allowances again."

"If there are more of us alive we have to know," said Jambo.

"It won't make much difference to our lives here, will it?" said Marguerite, with her customary forthrightness. "There is more important work to do. I know you think that roof is fixed, but there was a leak over there by that guttering you just put up. And you call yourselves carpenters."

A few weeks' later on a warm July evening, Oliver came dashing into the ghetto. He was so excited he flung his gear on the floor—hammers, glue and nails flying everywhere.

"I have news," he said, eyes bulging behind his glasses. "Important news." He gave a flourish as if he was selling a pair of new boots to a discerning customer. "Meet my friend John. Mr.John Turney."

A stocky young man stepped into the courtyard. He looked around nervously and seemed shocked at the sight of the emaciated group that confronted him. They stared back. He was the first foreigner to have come into their ghetto, apart from their guards, Langton, and the doctor.

"You are welcome," said Jambo. "Have we met before?"

"John works on the ships that take timber along the coast, isn't that right?"explained Oliver.

"It is, to be sure," said the young sailor.

"I know," recalled Jambo. "You helped me find the doctor the night the plague broke out. I am grateful to you. No one else would stop to help."

He shook his hand.

"He's from Ireland," said Oliver as if that explained everything. "No great lover of the English."

The stranger nodded tentatively in agreement. "It was me. Happy to be of assistance."

Oliver said, "As you know, I have been fixing shoes down the docks for a few weeks now—ever since, you know, the plague ended and we were allowed out into the city again. I have got to know a skipper of a merchantman who works along the west coast. We play cards, and I let him beat me a few times. I always let the others win when I need something. Never fails. This lunchtime—he'd had a few glasses—I put it to him that we had heard from our fellow Acadians in London. Bluffing, see?" Oliver waggled his eyebrows knowingly.

"He looked at me and said, '*Not London, mon ami, I don't think so. No, they're in Bristol. It's a port, second only to Liverpool in importance. Very big in the African trade as well, though not as big as us.*'

"Before I could press him for more details, he downed another large port and fell asleep on the tavern settle. Well, John here was with us, and when he was sure the skipper was unconscious he told me that Bristol was only half the story. There are hundreds more in Falmouth and Southampton. Tell them."

"Take a seat Mr. Turney," said Marguerite. "I will make you tea."

The sailor perched uncomfortably on a bench while the Acadians gathered round. "Once a month we sail to Bristol, usually with timber, and then we often go on to Falmouth and sometimes right along the south coast to Southampton. They are all ports in England," he added in case they were in doubt. "As you would expect, the talk is mostly of the war, but recently I have heard about you French prisoners, how you came from the colonies. The locals are very hostile. What do you call yourselves? Neuters?"

"Neutrals," said Jambo. "We do not believe in fighting for France or England. We take no sides."

He could tell this was a puzzling concept for the Irishman who furrowed his brow and fidgeted with his cap as if waiting for the carpenter to justify such curious instincts.

"We have always been a peaceable people," added Jambo in explanation.

"There's many an Englishman I would happily smite," John said. "Unfortunately, Ireland is a hard place to make a living, and the English rule the country with a merciless hand, so I have to swallow my pride and work where I can."

"Well, my friend, what have you heard of our cousins?" asked Pierre.

"I cannot pretend it's of any cheer," he said. "None of the populace wanted them living in their backyards."

"That sounds familiar," said Pierre. He nodded, as if it was only to be expected..

"And they wanted them even less when the plague struck," went on Turney.

Jambo took a deep breath—more of a sigh—"So it hit them too."

"It was truly desperate by all accounts," went on Turney. "I heard that the authorities feared the death toll would reach 1,000. They believed it would kill nearly every one of you."

"If it was as bad as here, I'm not surprised," said Pierre.

"But how many died?" asked Jambo, not sure whether he really wanted to know the answer.

"Bristol was bad. I was told 300 landed there and over 100 perished."

"Dear Lord," murmured Marguerite, crossing herself.

Turney was struggling. "I'm a simple soul, to be sure, for me people are good or bad, I see things in black or white. I know the English are bad, that's clear, but I was horrified by what I discovered. It's hard for me to bring such dismaying news to you."

"Nonetheless, please continue," said Jambo. "Spare us nothing."

"I could not find out anything about the people in Falmouth," faltered the sailor. "The locals would not talk about what happened there as though they were hiding a dark secret."

"Our poor people," said Marguerite. "Is there no end?"

"I am sorry," said John. "There is no easy way to tell the story."

"Of course, not," said Jambo. "You are only the messenger. But can we find out more? It is clear that many have died, but there must also be hundreds who are still alive."

"Everyone I saw was in a wretched state," said the sailor. "The ones who survived the pox are forced to beg for food and clothing."

"That's something we also know about all too well," said Marguerite.

Jambo said, "Mr. Turney, we are grateful to you, even if the intelligence you bring is so disheartening. Please consider yourself welcome here any time you feel like being among friendly faces."

"Maybe you can be persuaded to carry messages from us next time you sail," said Oliver.

"Of course. I shall have to be careful, because our skippers are under strict orders not to let anyone fraternize with the enemy—I mean you people. But I am happy to help such an injustice. I sail next week, so let me have your letters and I shall do what I can."

"This gives us new hope," said Jambo, as they celebrated Osite's third birthday. They played her favorite game—he tossed a ball, which she was meant catch in a cup tied to the end of a stick, but giggling happily, the little girl missed every one. The grown-ups and Jean-Baptiste played ninepins with skittles that Jambo had whittled down, and a wooden ball that was so uneven it was impossible to know which direction it would bounce.

"We must find out the truth," said Jambo. "If we can be sure that our cousins are safe—and which ones still live—then we have something to hold on to."

"As well as each other," said Marguerite, cuddling Osite who had fallen and cut her knee.

Two days later, when he and Marguerite were tending to graves whose crosses had been knocked over by vandals she said, "I feel faint. It's nothing but I think I'll lie down for a while. You finish here. Wake me in twenty minutes."

He left her for half an hour before he went to their corner of the warehouse. She didn't stir when he pulled back the tarpaulin they had hung around their little space for privacy. He held her by her shoulder and turned her over to see how she was. He knew instantly.

The blood had drained from her face. Her eyes, those odd eyes he loved so much, were like stones in her grey face, opened but struggling to focus. Her breathing came in great gasps. Death was sucking the air from her lungs.

Surely the plague had left them. What terrible mockery was this? How had he not realized how frail she had become? They had become so preoccupied with the day to day challenge of staying alive that he had not noticed how sharply the bones stood out down her back and her shoulder blades. Her cheekbones stretched her face above her sunken cheeks. She was unrecognizable from the healthy, adventurous, young woman who only two years before had been working in the fields with a baby in a sling around her shoulders.

She had never shown weakness. From the moment the soldiers arrived and ripped their lives apart, she had stood up to Dinwiddie, helped others through the terrors of the Atlantic crossing, tirelessly ministered to the dying.

She had always been so strong. For him, the children, and for her friends. Now she had nothing left to give. Once again the futile ritual of damp cloths. Once again the unavailing words of comfort.

Jambo kept the children away from the bedside, but they knew what was happening. No one needed to explain, because they had already watched as their aunts and uncles, so many of their little friends, had been taken from them.

How she fought the inevitable. For a while, he thought she would not succumb to the monster that gripped her. He sat by her cot for hours, day after day, as she resisted death. One moment it seemed she had slipped away from him, the next she was back, gasping for air and life.

But after six weeks of the fight her breathing became little more than a rattle, her white, white, face a horrible translucence disfigured by the spots that burst in bloody, pus-filled, eruptions. Her fair hair, which once cascaded around her face and shoulders, had become matted and black with sweat.

One evening, she suddenly sat up and looked beyond him. "The roof. It's leaking."

"No my love, we have fixed it." He gazed—no, more of a glare—he glared at her as if his fury at her sickness, at God's neglect, could somehow translate into that wracked body and bring her back to him.

"I can see the light through it. The stars." She reached out a hand. "The children. Where are the children?" And then, "I love you. Remember…"

She fell back, a flow of blood and mucus ran from her mouth, down her cheek, and on to her neck. She was dead.

He methodically wiped her face and shut her eyes, and then held her emaciated body. He was stricken to his soul, but no tears came. She would not have approved of him weeping.

'Do not forget what you have been saying every day since we were expelled,' she would have reminded him. *'We must be strong if we are to be unconquerable.''*

The women brought him to his feet, and he took the children into the courtyard while they cleaned the corpse.

The men helped him carry her body to the graveyard where he hammered in one more cross to add to the scores already there. He carved her name as tidily as he could:

Marguerite LeBlanc
August 1731—July 1757

As he threw the first clod of earth onto the coffin, the cold dismissiveness of Commissioner Langton echoed in his ears, '*No clothes…but ten shillings allowed for funerals*'.

EIGHTEEN

Liverpool

Summer and Winter, 1757.

Distant Voices

For weeks he scarcely stirred from the corner of the warehouse that had become their home. He drew the curtain around to create a dark void, and lay on the straw bedding, gazing at the holes in the roof that Marguerite had chided him for not mending properly. Yes, there were a few pinpricks of light, like the glimmer of stars.

He forced himself in the mornings to get the children dressed, and make sure they were fed from the communal cauldron of porridge in the courtyard. Then he sat them down for the daily classes, where Agnes Hebert taught some of the young ones French, the scriptures, and what little English she had picked up.

"We're learning together," she said. "In fact, Osite knows almost as much English as I do."

Agnes, too, had been distraught at the death Marguerite, whom she had come close to during the darkest days of the plague, so it seemed the most natural thing in the world that she took over looking after the children. The morning after Marguerite's funeral she was there, dressing them, combing their hair, making sure they ate properly. She was affectionate and calm, doing the best she could to bring consolation to their shattered young lives.

They responded to her with trust, especially as they were so bewildered—not just with their own grief, but with the sadness of their father who had been rendered as helpless as they were. Osite snuggled up to him, her nose runny, snuffling *mama, mama* in a soft undertone, while Jean-Baptiste would either sit on the edge of the bed and rock backward and forward, or creep into the crook of his father's arm for solace. It was almost as if they were comforting him.

They hardly spoke.

The children had seen so much death that they felt it was the natural order, but this was a mystery that their father could not begin to explain to them. He could offer them no comfort from the teachings of the Bible, no prayers, no easy phrases. God had refused to spare someone who had done so much good, who had been a caring mother, and a loving wife. Why take *her* of all people? *How many lives did this confounding deity want?*

Remember, she had said with her dying breath. Remember what? Her? He would never be able to forget her, or any moment of their lives together, though sometimes he thought it would be better if he could wipe clean all memories of Marguerite, Charles, his parents, Grand-Pré—his entire past. He was so crushed, that for the first time in the year and a half since the expulsion, he gave up. He barely talked to anyone apart from the children, and he stopped working. When he was asked to help repair a door or fix a door back on its hinges, he waved them away and said, "Ask Pierre."

Every day, the three of them would walk across the scabrous wasteland outside the ghetto to the graveyard where he would sit and share his thoughts with his dead wife.

The graves were so thinly covered with earth that dogs and foxes had come scavenging for the bodies that lay below. One night he caught a fox gnawing at the arm of a corpse it had dug up. He had howled at it with the rage of a mad man and hurled clods of earth in its direction until long after the creature had slipped away.

Jean-Baptiste would solemnly help as his father covered the graves, tidied the verges, and straightened the crude wooden crosses which were already slipping at angles, many defaced and torn out of the ground by the local ruffians. Osite pulled up dandelions and clumps of rose bay willow herb to make little posies.

The others tried to rally him. Pierre and Marie would bring him bowls of stew and chatted aimlessly until he told them to leave him alone and spare their sympathy. Francois would gruffly try to cheer him up by talking about the old, lost, days in Grand-Pré—the harvests and the hunting—and Oliver would recount the latest gossip from the docks, but the widower was not listening.

Most mornings Agnes would come across the yard while the children were having breakfast with a mug of tea and bread for him. Every evening she would bring him supper before telling the children stories and singing Acadian favorites before tucking them into their cots.

He wished they would all leave him alone.

A few months later, Commissioner Langton rode into the yard. It was unusual to see him, because the British seemed to have lost interest in their charges. They had reduced the guard to a few half-hearted soldiers who just poked their noses around the gate every now and then, made sure all was quiet, and moved on. So convinced were they that the prisoners posed no threat that they had even stopped harassing them if they strayed out of the ghetto during curfew.

Langton did not dismount.

"LeBlanc. A letter."

He said it as if it was the most natural occurrence. He did not stop. He did not explain. A letter. The widower reluctantly got to his feet and came blinking from the warehouse gloom into the courtyard. He gazed blankly at the envelope, which had obviously passed through so many hands that it was in tatters. After a long pause, he tore it open with trembling hands.

Brother,

Brother? It was from Charles. He was alive. The date and address was scrubbed out.

We heard that there were some of our people in Liverpool, so I thought I would write just in case you or one of our family and friends are there. I don't know if this will get to you, I am relying on the good will of an inspector from what they call the Sick and Hurt Commission. Seems to be a decent man—at least he does not treat us like dirt. We are in a port called ███████ *which is a grim place, but with some fine houses—though only for the rich, of course. The English have put us* ████████ *barracks. This place has a small harbor with very few ships, though I'm told there's a wine trade with Portugal. You never know your luck.*

For the first time in weeks Jambo smiled to himself. His brother was as incorrigible as ever.

The soldiers tell us that ██████████ *has the healthiest air in England, but in that case I fear for the rest of the country, because many of us are indeed sick and hurt.*

You'd laugh—the aristocracy come here to bathe in the seawater because it is meant to be good for them. They believe it cures bites from mad dogs. Can you imagine? Just splashing around, not fishing or anything useful. The locals are all very excited because the Prince of Wales, son of the King apparently, comes here. I thought they were talking about whales, like the ones off the Grand Banks.

"Anything important has been censured," he muttered to himself.

██

████████████████████████ *but we LeBlancs are still here, brother, and I am still singing.*

He tried to decipher the dateline. There was a J. June, July. January? The letter could have been sent as long ago as one year. Maybe Langton had impounded it, the swine. July would make sense. They would certainly have landed in this port at about the same time as the Carolina had reached Liverpool. Wherever they were—Turney had mentioned Bristol, Southampton and Falmouth—they were alive twelve months ago.

Anne and the children send their true affection and give mother and father my respects.

I will write again soon and please, if you receive this, write to us as soon as you can.

Your brother, Charles.

True affection. The widower thought his own inner darkness had obliterated all his feelings, yet now he had to summon all his will not to break down. He put down the letter and realized that a small audience had grown round him as he read.

"Cousins, I am sorry for not sharing this with you. It seems that the Admiralty has relented and allowed letters to be sent. It is from brother Charles. Almost one year old since it was written, I believe, so a great deal will have passed since then. But at least, in this, all seems well with him and the family. Let me read it to you."

"It is comforting to know that Charles and his family are well," said Agnes after she had blessed the children good night.

"It is. Yet I worry about him—all of them. We don't know if they were stricken by the plague as we were. Is that what he means by *'many were sick and hurt?'* The worry is that his letter is out of date. There will surely have been deaths, though God forbid their suffering was not as horrible as it was here."

He stopped. It was the most he had spoken for two months—just a few *'thank yous'* and grunts of appreciation had fallen grudgingly from his lips.

"I suppose there is not much more we can do than try to be positive and wait to hear more. Meanwhile all we can do is make the best of what we have here," said Agnes.

"I have nothing here," he said.

She replied with surprising asperity, "You have your children, and you have your comrades—Pierre and Marie, Oliver, Francois—stalwart friends with whom you have shared much hardship. You of all people should know that we have to stay united against all adversity. Isn't that what Marguerite would say?"

Her fierceness made him start. "I know. I am sorry. I am thinking only about myself."

It was two months after Marguerite's death. For the first time, he had the strength to write in his cramped hand to Charles, even though he was not sure where to send it:

My dear brother,

I write you these words to tell you that my very dear wife has left this world to pass to the other. I will tell you that she had been sick eight weeks, but she received all the aid that a dying person can receive at death. As for me, I am in good health as well as my two children. I beseech you to pray for her and to commend her to all our good relatives and friends.

I remain, in grief, your servant and brother.

He gave the letter to Turney to see if he could find where Charles was imprisoned and deliver it, but heard nothing in reply. *It won't have been delivered,* he thought pessimistically. He had little faith in the go-between who every time he asked for news reacted with, what he felt, was a shifty evasiveness.

"I do my best," he said. "But I have to be careful. We are forbidden from fraternizing with foreigners, and I rely on a third party, like someone in a tavern to pass on the letters. Have to bribe them with ale."

"We shall have to recompense you," said the carpenter, frustrated that their only link to the wider world was proving so ineffectual.

John had taken to calling by when he wasn't at sea, and the carpenter found it irritating the way he lurked around the ghetto, talking to Agnes and Marie, and being particularly attentive to Madeleine Hebert, whose husband had died in the plague. One day he fancied he saw them holding hands, but dismissed the thought. She had been widowed less than a year and it would not be seemly for her to remarry, and quite out of the question with a foreigner.

He mentioned it to Agnes, who surprised him by blushing and saying, "Heavens no. Nothing like that."

But he had lost interest in the matter even as he asked the question.

Despite his lack of confidence in the messenger, he wrote to Charles again. *We are always hungry,* he scribbled. *What a happy day it is when there is enough cabbage and potato peelings to make one hot meal. We are always dirty. Always tired out and short of energy, but unable to sleep at night when this ghetto of ours echoes to the cries of the children, 'Mama, I cannot sleep. Mama, I am hungry.' It is so sad to hear."* Above all, he tried to explain how they were gripped by emotions that swung from hysteria to sluggish despondency.

Even Francois has been brought down, he wrote. *He goes around saying 'I am going crazy with all this' and climbs up on to the roof of the warehouse shouting curses at the outside world. There is no one to hear, and though some of the younger ones laugh, we know that really he is living out the madness that we all fear we are falling into.*

Instinctively, they focused their hate on a common foe to help them stick together. The British, naturally, were the subject of both their despair and their disdain. Quite a shanty town had grown up along the road to the city, and every time they walked past, the layabouts who lived in its collection of lean-tos, as depressingly squalid as the slaves in Virginia, would amuse themselves with a barrage of filthy curses.

"They say the same things every time," said Pierre's Marie contemptuously. "You'd think they could change their insults every now and then."

Worse was the way passers-by in the city streets, often quite genteel types, took pleasure in spitting on the ground when they came near. Sometimes the soldiers would remember they were the masters, and quite arbitrarily sling a couple of them in the city jail.

But it was Liverpool itself that sapped their souls the most. It seemed to them to be a baleful, physical being, like some brutish creature lurking outside their gates, and it was the city they hated more than any person.

They only ventured into the centre when they had to, and then only when the market had closed, to scavenge for food and to beg—but they never got used to the catacomb of dense streets with their ugly rows of terraced houses. Their heads ached with the constant whir and clatter of machinery, and they walked everywhere with a cloth clamped to their faces to block out the noxious smells.

They were repelled by the ferocious, hard-faced energy of the place.

"Every brick of this town is cemented with the blood of an African," said Francois as they watched another shipment of slaves being marched off to auction.

They were alienated by the self-obsessed, busy-ness of the city, which overflowed with tanners and wheelwrights, drapers and blacksmiths, and yet whose streets were lined with laborers who could not find work, and beggars who fought any Acadian who trespassed on his patch.

Only Oliver prospered, polishing shoes, playing card games in the docks, and fleecing gullible drunks.

They looked to each other for support and gave it willingly. It did not take much for any one of them to be overwhelmed by their plight—something trivial like a lost shoe, a broken pot, or a leaking gutter would feel like a catastrophe—but instead of letting their cousins fester in neurotic impotence, the ghetto dwellers rallied around, made a new shoe, fixed the pot, and repaired the guttering. It was the way they would have behaved in Acadia, and it helped them cope with their degradation with dignity and strength. Amazingly, if proof was needed of their resilience in those grim confines, even the widowed found love.

There were two marriages in the first summer after the epidemic. Pierre Trahan married Marguerite Duhan, and Etienne Darway wed Francoise Trahan. And, miraculously it seemed, they gathered for a baptism—that of Jean Peter.

It had been only a month before that Marguerite had died, but even the carpenter could see that the birth was a portent of hope and renewal. The infant's parents beamed with joy, and even the churlish priest seemed to welcome their happiness and conducted the services with some enthusiasm.

Yes, there was new life, but reminders that death was their closest companion were never far away.

Turney called in after one of his voyages. Instead of joining the prisoners around the fire, he approached Jambo. He looked ashen.

"Mr. LeBlanc, Jambo," he muttered awkwardly. "This is for your, er, wife." The carpenter looked at him uncomprehendingly. The sailor was holding a letter. It was marked for Marguerite LeBlanc, Jambo and Family.

He opened it. It was from Marguerite's brother, Joseph, who he had last seen waving goodbye from the deck of a ship—the Virginia Packet, he seemed to remember—when the exiles were split up in Williamsburg.

Bristol, July, 1757.

The censure had overlooked the dateline. This was a recent account, written—he noticed with a catch in the heart—the very month his wife had died.

Dear Sister,

I trust you are well, and Jambo and the two little ones are flourishing. We recently heard of there being cousins in Liverpool, and there are rumors of more in ▊▊▊▊ *and along the coast.*

We arrived here almost one year ago now. What a year it has been. The journey ▊▊ *an undertaking.*

There were many women and children on board, but thank God, Marie and the children were among the survivors. We still have heard nothing of father. Indeed, so many of our cousins from Grand-Pré are missing. I pray that they are well.

When we reached the port, we had to stay on the ship for three days ▊▊▊▊▊▊▊▊▊▊▊▊▊▊▊▊▊▊▊▊▊▊▊▊▊▊▊▊▊▊▊▊▊▊▊ *I dread to think what we looked like. There was an inspector who said* ▊▊▊▊▊▊▊▊▊▊ ▊▊▊▊▊▊▊▊▊▊▊▊▊▊ *he felt nothing but sympathy for us—and I believe him—but even when we were allowed off the ship* ████████

██

████████████████████████████████ *It rained most of the time. All we had was a daily ration of soup and bread—mind you, that was better than the muck we had during the crossing.*

Eventually the mayor was persuaded to let us live in what they said were large warehouses just out of town. Nice and airy, he said, built around a spacious courtyard ██

████████ *Very choice, I tell you. We were given the same food and provisions as a prisoner of war, and a small allowance for clothes, though where we are meant to spend this fortune we have not discovered. They ordered us to be in indoors by eight o'clock every evening and "not to be found drunken." For some reason, that made me think of Charles.*

A lot of us were sick. ████████████████████████████████

██

████████ *. All we needed was broth and water with good nursing and wholesome air.*

How wrong they were ████████████ *ox.*

Ox? Must have been smallpox. Yes, judging by this:

Little Anastasie Boudrot, only nine, was the first to go. Then old Marie Scanatt—remember how she would make us sweet dumplings when we were children? Then, dear sister ████████████████████████████████

████████████████████████████████████ *But, sister, thank the Lord we have been spared and I pray you and our cousins wherever you are still alive.*

Write to us if you can. Bring some cheer to us.

Your loving brother, Joseph.

PS. With undying love from Marie and the children to you all.

There was a separate sheet of paper.

I know you will be wondering how I found out that there were cousins in Liverpool. Do you remember that young lieutenant in Grand-Pré, the one with the wooden leg? He is here, and now that he does not feel he has to behave like the enemy, he turns out to be an uncommonly helpful character. The authorities do not like us to write letters, so he helped me write most of this and negotiated with the censor, and then arranged to get this delivered by Mr. Turney, who seems a trustworthy fellow. Watson remembers you. He always thought Jambo was making fun of him by limping around. We laughed at that. J.

He was trembling when he finished reading. To be reading a letter to his Marguerite, who had been in her grave for such a short time, from someone whom he had assumed was dead, was like some ghastly hallucination. It was as if he was being mocked by a cruel world, and a God who took pleasure inflicting pain, and then making it unbearable with a savage twist.

He took to his bed, his arms wrapped around his body, legs curled up to his chest, as if to hold himself together.

Agnes tried to comfort him but he sent her away.

Two days later. Another letter. He left it on the table where Agnes had left it. He had no need of more letters.

She said, "It's from Southampton."

It was from Charles, and this time there was no date—not even one to censure. It almost fell to pieces in his hand.

Dear Brother,

How go things with you? I pray you and Marguerite and the children are well, though I fear for you. Indeed I fear for all of us. Write to me brother, I beg you.

"Pray God they are still alive," said Agnes.

"I imagine this was written last summer," said Jambo. "Look how many of us have died since then. How many of them will be alive today?"

When the next letter arrived from Southampton, he did not have to open it to know that it would bring unwelcome news. He left it where it lay for a day, as if gathering his courage, and then abruptly, he broke the seal.

Brother,

My beloved Anne has died. She was taken from us swiftly. The pox has now claimed scores of us. There were...███████, we landed in ███████ country and now there are...███████████—Curse the censor—*The ones who still live are sick and starving.*

My Anne made me happier than any man had a right to be, as you know best. She gave me a meaning to life that I did not have before, but I will not be defeated by this. I have told the children that we are Acadians and we cannot allow ourselves to be beaten down. Write with to me brother, I have yet to hear from you.

I am so sad. For the first time I am weary of life.

Your brother, Charles.

He took the letter and sat by Marguerite's grave until dusk filtered through the lowering Liverpool sky and turned to dark. He had no fight left. He wanted to end it, to surrender and be reunited with his dead wife. In his hand he held the knife he had taken from their table the day they had been expelled. He fingered its blade.

A figure slipped out of the ghetto and flitted through the shadows to his side. It was Agnes. "I think you need to come back to us," she said. "Your children need their father. The men need you to work, and to show them the way."

He looked at her blankly as if he did not understand what she was saying.

"Come," she said.

He got to his feet and placed the letter carefully in his jerkin. "You're right. I have let you down."

"And you need a shave," she said. She took him by his damaged hand and led him back into the prison camp.

The next morning she said to them, "Let's go for a walk by the river where the air is cleaner. We'll spare the children their lessons today." She picked up Osite and plonked the girl in the handcart they used to collect firewood. "Come on Jean-Baptiste, let's see what adventures we can have. Maybe we will see the swans in their nest by the weir."

NINETEEN

Liverpool

January 28, 1758.

On the Towpath

Agnes was sitting quietly by the big communal fire darning one of Osite's smocks. Jambo found himself watching her as she kept her head close to the needle, radiating a calm self-assurance that contrasted with the disconcerting mix of depression and scarcely contained hysteria that gripped many in the ghetto.

In profile, he could see the outline of her firm jaw and a little nose that turned up at the tip. She was softly curvaceous. He had never really looked before. Whereas Marguerite had let her fair hair run riot from her bonnet, Agnes had her tight brown curls tucked away tidily. Every now and then, she gave him a quick look with her perceptive grey eyes, and continued with her work without speaking. She was 22. Had she been in Grand-Pré, she would have been married by now to some nice lad and had at least two children.

There is a luminous purity about her, he thought, and as he did, he felt a curious pang. Of what? Surely not jealousy. He had noticed her having intense conversations with Turney, which irrationally annoyed him. How could there be anything for him, a grieving widower, to be jealous about?

No, he must be confusing that flutter in his stomach with the palpitation of loss he had felt every day since Marguerite had gone. He poked at the fire. Yes, that was it. As he had been doing so often to comfort himself, he let his mind wander to the day they had married.

August 2, 1750. He had been trembling with nerves and excitement as the abbot blessed them, but the moment their vows were exchanged his agitation disappeared and he kissed his bride, first on her brow, then her beguiling, eyes, and finally on her lips with an enthusiasm that made everyone smile.

In the months before the wedding, as tradition demanded, the villagers had helped them build their home, laying the shallow foundations, delivering cart loads of stones, and helping saw timber for beams. All they expected was a flagon of ale as their reward. Come the day, they crowded in with food and drink for the party and gifts of hens, cattle, and sheep. His parents presented them with a cart, and Uncle Rene promised a horse. He had struck a bargain with an English merchant, he said, pleased at his negotiating skills.

The party started, and it seemed as if the everyone from Grand-Pré was there, drinking and singing, beating kettles and blowing horns.

"Come on," said Charles. "Time for the b-b-broomstick. You know you have to do it. Bad, b-b-bad luck if you don't."

While he and Marguerite's brother, Joseph, held the broom, the new couple jumped over it to the cheers of the crowd, she with her skirts held high, he with an elaborate nonchalance, both trying to hide their embarrassment. Then breathless with the joy of it all, the bride stood while the guests pinned money on her veil and dress.

It was dawn before Marguerite and Jambo had time to themselves, slipping away to their bedroom, and much later before they were seen again. The party went on without them, their guests polishing off barrels of spruce beer, wine, and cider in a way that would have left the Bishop of Quebec fuming with disapproval, until the couple emerged to cheers and affectionate ribaldry that made him blush more than Marguerite.

Those first few months were so intense, so thrilling for such an inexperienced fellow whose only experience with a woman had been when his Uncle Claude took him drinking one night in Halifax and pushed him into a room where a German prostitute lay waiting for him. It was over so quickly he did not admit to Claude, or any of his cousins, how disappointing it had been.

But with Marguerite…he was shocked at how uninhibited she was. Even when they were working together in the fields, or when he was out fixing traps, she would bring a picnic and lead him into the forest, where to his embarrassment and excitement, she would often swiftly seduce him.

He stifled the memory and went back to repairing a chair Francois had found on a rubbish trip near one of the merchant's homes on Hanover Street.

"They seem so happy," Agnes said.

For a second he thought Agnes was talking about him and Marguerite, but her eyes were following Etienne Darway and Francoise Trahan, the newly-weds, who were laughing and holding hands as they walked across the courtyard. Already she was carrying a child.

"Early days," he said.

"You cynic." She laughed.

"I don't mean it," he said. "Of course, I don't. Though I do wonder what kind of a world the child will be brought up in. No, those two give us hope. Marguerite's last word was *remember,* but for months I could not understand what she meant but now I do. When things were bad, we would urge each other to stay resolute, whatever sadistic trick the British or the fates had for us. Etienne and Francoise are proof that the human spirit can overcome anything."

"The human spirit," she said. "And love. " She looked at him steadily with her grey eyes.

He could not hold her gaze and looked away, studying the flames. "I'm very grateful to you," he said.

"For what?" She looked away then, the faintest of blushes feathering her neck.

"You have been so kind to the, um, children." He was flustered, though he could not tell why and pushed his hair, which had grown much too long, off his face. "They seem more settled now."

"They need affection," she said, needle poised as once more, she held his gaze, eyes widening. "Like everyone."

"I neglected them, I know," said the carpenter.

"You were sad. More than sad," she replied and smiled softly, "It is allowed. You loved her."

She put down her sewing. "I am going scavenging for driftwood along the canal. Will you come? The children are in Bible class for another hour, and the fire is looking in need of cheering up."

She took his arm, and wrapped her shawl against the bitter wind that came in from the Atlantic and whistled up the River Mersey.

"Almost like Minas Bay in winter," he said.

"Can you imagine living out our days in this? I know we never had much by way of money or possessions in Grand-Pré, but we had a rich life. This is so, so…" She struggled to express herself but the best she could muster was, "Empty."

They walked along the muddy towpath, he in his tattered jerkin and she in a shawl and skirt that had been darned and dyed so many times there was hardly a stitch of the original garments left. Instead, they relied on the old coats, trousers, and dresses they found when scavenging the bins of wealthy merchants, and either adjusted them or used the material to make new clothes. An embarrassed Jean-Baptiste had to wear an ill-fitting pair of shiny pantaloons, discarded by the son of some grandee with a jacket made of sacking.

To stay as warm as possible, they stuffed straw inside their jerkins.

"Maybe we could hire ourselves out to stand in the fields and frighten the birds," Agnes said.

"What they must think of us," he said, scratching his beard—already flecked in grey—with his damaged hand.

They walked past two men who sat begging by the lane and she said, "I don't know what to make of them. There are so many poor people."

"You gorra penny to spare?" asked one.

"We need to eat," said the other, getting to his feet. They were thin, questing, like hungry foxes about to pounce on a chicken, and dirty beyond care. The older had a straggling moustache that almost hid his mouth, but not enough to disguise a hideous scar that made him look as if his lips reached across the right side of his face in a ghastly smile to his ear. The younger had a withered leg that made him off-balanced and forced him to stand side-on to the Acadians. He glared at them through a curtain of greasy hair.

"I fear we are no better off than you," said Agnes, holding tightly to Jambo's arm.

They looked at her with a mix of astonishment and hostility at what they obviously thought was a lie.

"This is a rich city, why can't you get work here?" asked Jambo.

"I s'pose you think we beg because we like it," said scar face.

"No one begs by choice," said Agnes quietly. "No one should be dragged down so low."

"Where do you live?" asked Jambo.

"Here," said the older, his hands trembled as he pointed to the hedgerow. "We sleep where we bleedin' drop."

"Some of the lucky buggers 'ave walls and a roof," said his companion." I say 'lucky' but they end up under canvas in the shanty shit heap over there, or in cellars where the water runs down the walls and the floors are covered in piss."

"We all die just as quickly," said the younger. "My name is Boot, by the way."

They looked puzzled.

"Because of his leg," said his companion with the scar. "Has to 'ave his boot built up with wads of leather so 'e don't fall over."

He laughed, revealing black teeth that stood out from his smiling scar like dead flies on rashers of bacon.

"You can call me William."

"But why are things so hard for you?" persisted Agnes.

"We have been kicked off our land," said William. "From when time began, people like us have lived on commons. You know, we grazed our livestock, kept a few hens, grew some veg. We lived well enough. The land gave us firewood, fruit, nuts for pig fodder. But then the bastard landowners demanded that we prove that we had *rights* to be there. We had to show 'em legal documents."

"They know we can't read or write," said Boot. "They know there is nothing wrote down in law."

"Just the rights of hundreds of years," said the older man.

"Then the fuckers—sorry ma'am—made us pay the costs of hedging and fencing and then the small farms—even the ones with all the bleedin' documents in the world—couldn't stand up against the wealthy bastard landlords, and they had to sell up." Boot lent against a tree to steady himself.

"The *Enclosure Act* they call it," said the older man, enunciating carefully so that his listeners would understand. "En-fucking-closure Act. It is the curse of us poor sods of laborers."

"What could we do? We had to search for work in the city," said Boot, "and even if I weren't a cripple, I know nothing of lathes and machinery."

"And anyway," said William, smiling in that grotesque, miserable, way, "there are no bleedin' jobs."

"So please give us money," said Boot. "We know you have government 'and outs."

He shuffled sideways toward the couple. "Or food. I beg you."

"We have nothing with us," said Jambo. "I am sorry."

He made a play of opening his pockets to show how empty they were, but a farthing fell out.

William groveled in the dirt and grabbed it. "More. Give us more."

They were threatening now. They would not be able to stop themselves crossing the thin line from desperation into savagery. They reminded him of the wolves that had prowled around him when he had been trapped in the blizzard. The same staring eyes, mad with hunger.

Boot picked up a brick, while the older man hurled himself at Jambo.

He sidestepped, stuck out a foot, and hit him on the side of head, sending him sprawling. "Run!"

The two beggars chased after them, but faded away into the dusk as they came close to the ghetto.

The first flakes of snow were falling as they paused to recapture their breaths.

"Come on, let's get back inside," he said, gasping for air. "We will have to set a watch out for those two tonight. They are men without hope, and all the more deadly for that."

They turned to go into the ghetto, but Agnes, who had been standing, hands on knees trying to regain her breath, slipped on the icy bank. He caught her, and as she fell toward him, without quite understanding what he was doing, he kissed her.

They stood looking at each other for several seconds. This time he did not look away. For a second his broken hand rested on her arm. She took it and kissed his fingertips. Then her body was hard against him, her mouth sought his again.

He was breathless with joy. It was as if his heart had paused for breath, and in that second been stormed by this sweet girl, but even as he felt himself being swept away he was seized with guilt. He remembered his pledge to Marguerite when they were reunited in Virginia. *My compass and my lover,* he had called her. *How could you doubt my constancy?* He had promised, *I would never be with another.*

All he could think to say was, "We'd best be inside."

They walked back into the ghetto, keeping a safe distance between them, and trying to look as casual as they had when they left.

He was surprised no one noticed that something, *everything,* had changed between them. As they sat through the meal with the others at the communal table, he felt he had a sign emblazoned on his forehead: *Agnes and I are in love,* or was it: *Marguerite, forgive me?* He put the children to bed as usual, while she went to her quarters in the area set aside for the women.

He waited until all was still and the children breathing steadily before he crept through the warehouse and slipped through the curtains to her bedside. She was waiting for him, eyes wide with anticipation and apprehension.

"Never such love," he moaned as he gathered her to him, burying the echo of the same words he had made to Marguerite. He came hard into her as if he had to exorcise the memory of his dead wife, as much as prove the fervor of his passion. He did not even hear her cry out in painful surprise.

The second time he was gentler, and her cry was of pleasure.

They were married on January 28.

"Why wait?" said Agnes, showing the straight-forwardness that took him time to get used to. "We know what we are doing."

They took their vows in the courtyard of the ghetto with uncle Francois—on his best behavior, not a curse all evening—as the best man. There were none of the riotous scenes of his first marriage, but they sang and danced to the old songs. Oliver, bless him, had *come by* a barrel of wine and Pierre's Marie made a cake.

Later, they held each other and she said, "We might never get back home, we might be forced to live here for the rest of our lives, but we have each other. We are prisoners, but you and I are free."

He felt as happy as he had been when he and Marguerite had been together, though Agnes could hardly be different. Calm where the other was fiery. Demure where the other was demanding. They created a life centered on their new-found love.

They were a partnership. She encouraged him to concentrate on skilled work, like repairing furniture and even carving toys and figurines with his good left hand, and with the little money he made he bought cotton, which she made into sheets and sold in the market.

If Agnes lacked the exuberance of Marguerite, she had the dead woman's determination to stand her ground when she felt it important, as he was to find out when they had their first argument. He had found her and Marie talking intensely with her cousin, Madeleine, whose husband had been taken by the plague. As he came near, the widow almost ran from the yard in tears.

"Why did she leave so suddenly?" he asked.

Marie said, "No reason."

Agnes said, "She has fallen in love."

"Well, that's fine," he said. "She should remarry."

"Should, maybe," said Marie. "But the man in question is not one of us. Not an Acadian."

"Then who?"

"It's John. John Turney." Agnes looked warily at him.

"But I thought...no, this cannot be. He is a good man, I am sure—good enough, anyway—but we are Acadians and must stay so. We cannot marry outside."

Agnes rounded on him. "For one thing, do not forget he dislikes the English almost as much as we do. Look at the way he has risked his livelihood for us, delivering letters to our cousins. For another, we cannot stand in judgment on people's feelings."

"She deserves our blessing," said Marie.

"This is outrageous!" said Jambo. "We must hold a council meeting."

"Don't be ridiculous," said Agnes.

He looked at her with amazement. He would have expected it of Marguerite, but not of sensible little Agnes.

"A council meeting. How pompous can you be? We may be prisoners, but we should not be fettered by some ancient custom that was applied in another time and another place." She went on, "*We* have found happiness, you and I. Do not begrudge them."

He stormed off, only to be crashed into by Francois as he plunged through the gates of the ghetto.

The burly plowman was bleeding from a wound on his head, and leaning so heavily on Pierre and Oliver for support, that the cobbler almost disappeared beneath his bulk.

"What have you been up to?" asked Jambo.

"We were walking back from the docks when some sailors started taunting us," said Oliver.

"I thought they had got bored treating us like aliens," said Pierre. "But no, they'd heard reports from Acadia, which they thought were amusing, and couldn't wait to mock us with."

Francois said, "The bastards told us that the British have seized Cape Breton and Prince Edward Island, as they call Ile St. Jean. Now they control the St. Lawrence all the way to Quebec. They rounded up and expelled 6,000 of our people. All of them. They are in transports on their way to France."

"This is the storm season, and nobody in their right mind crosses the Atlantic at this time of year," said Oliver. "It is far, far more dangerous than when we crossed."

"You can imagine what a great joke the swine thought that was," said Francois.

"They were taking bets on how many would survive," said Oliver.

It was several weeks before they learnt the heart-breaking truth. As well as the few letters that arrived from their cousins around the country—all of which were still censured if there was anything controversial in them—they had assiduously collected newspapers and notices, anything that might bring enlightenment about their fellow castaways. Just as diligently, they eavesdropped on any sailors or merchants as they regaled each other with idle talk from the colonies. Oliver often came back from a day at the docks with gossip. Some of it true.

But it was Pierre, scavenging for leftover food at the end of market day, who found a copy of the Pennsylvania Gazette lining the shelves of a stall. Crumpled and stained, it had obviously crossed the Atlantic some months before.

Oliver propped the paper up in front of him while he supped his turnip and cabbage soup, and read out loud.

Extract of a Letter from Captain William Nicholls of the Duke William Transport, Penzance, Cornwall, December 16th, 1758.

Under the greatest Affliction, I acquaint you. I have been obliged to leave the Duke William, with 300 French inhabitants on board, from Prince Edward Island, North America, to sink about 35 Leagues from the Land's End, Wednesday the 13th inst. about 4 o'clock in the afternoon and believe she could not keep above water till eight at night.

"May they rest in peace," murmured Pierre's Marie.

"Amen," they said, crossing themselves.

"His prose is too clumsy," said Jambo. "Cut to the chase, Oliver."

"This Captain Nicholls told the authorities in Prince Edward Island that it was impossible for his vessel to sail and expect to arrive safely in Old France at that season of the year, but he says, he was under orders, so three transport ships, the Duke William, The Violet, and the Ruby, set off with their prisoners locked away below decks."

They flinched as they recalled their own traumatic experience.

"They sailed from the island on November Fifth and struggled through the gales, which were, he says here, as bad as any of the sailors could remember. On the 29th the ship sprung a leak, and within minutes five feet of water filled the hold." Oliver took off his spectacles and blinked.

"It was do or die. Both the crew and the prisoners set to, bailing out the water in the hold, and for eight exhausting days kept the ship afloat. When the storm eased up, they were able to fix the leak. They thought they were safe. But no, ten days later, only 30 leagues from the English coast, the leak broke out again and this time it was impossible to staunch.

"My God, listen to this. They actually saw two ships steering toward them, so they hoisted a distress signal and fired their guns to attract their attention, but the ships ignored them. They even cut down the main mast to show what difficulty they were in. The captain says, *'One ship got so close we could see the men on deck but it sailed away.'*

"Cockchafing cowards," said Francois thumping the table and earning a reproving look from Agnes.

"How could they have been so heartless?" She said.

"It's unforgivable," said Pierre.

"It's murder," said Jambo.

"It says how the French—that's our people, I think he means—were then resigned to death. The captain writes that they had behaved with the greatest fortitude. '*They came and embraced me, saying that they realised that I, with all my people, had done all in our power to save the ship and their lives, but as I could be of no further service to them, begged I would save my own life and my men*'. He took the priest with him in the lifeboat and says, '*All we could hear were their cries. Some even waved to us to begone. It almost broke our hearts*' Oliver paused to let his horror-struck audience imagine the scene.

'*The Duke William disappeared beneath the waves. As for us, it pleased God to conduct us safe to this place.*'

"Typical of a priest to save his skin," said Francois. "Perhaps he will find the time to pray for the victims he deserted."

LeBlanc took the paper. "The other two ships went down," he said. "The Violet took 500 with her and another 300 perished when The Ruby was swept all the way south to the Azores and smashed against the rocks of an island."

"I am sorry I said that about Madeleine and Turney," he said when the children had been put to bed. "The drowning of those poor souls is a reminder that we have to seize what little joy we can. All of us. You're right. We cannot stick with old rules if they make people unhappy."

"The more who can find joy in this place, the more certain I am that we can survive," she said. "It is a way of laughing in the faces of the British."

TWENTY

Liverpool

Winter, 1762.

In the Spinney

Oliver was drinking coffee and reading a journal that John Turney had brought with him from Bristol. He loved to sit, eyes glinting behind his glasses, regaling the men gathered around the big dining table with anecdotes. One of their favorites had been the exploits of a French privateer from Brest who had the daring to base himself on the Isle of Man and lurk off the coast where for two or three years he had been harassing the English merchant ships.

"*Vive la France*," Francois would toast the pirate's latest success with a beer.

"What do the English put in this stuff?" He reached for another mug. "It's as weak as piss."

"Uncle Francois," admonished Agnes. "Children."

"This is good," said Oliver, his grubby polish-stained fingers prodding at a page. "Listen. The editor writes, *During their abode here*—this is Bristol, mind—*the Acadians have behaved in a decent manner and by their industry and civil deportment they have gained the esteem of all ranks of people.* Esteem!"

"I don't see much *esteem* coming our way here," said Francois."

"To be fair, their feelings toward us have changed a great deal—even as long ago as '59 when they took Quebec," said Jambo.

"*Be fair*," expostulated Francois, slamming down his mug. "Fair? We've been here almost six years. When have these bastards ever done the decent thing by us?"

Jambo ignored him. "That victory sealed British power in America. After that it didn't matter whether we supported the French—as they liked to insist we did—because France was done for. In America anyway."

"They are winning the war in Europe, too," said Oliver. "They have been blockading French ports for months now and are laying siege to Cadiz in Spain. "

"That's the least of it," said Jambo. "They have captured territory around the world. I don't know where they are, but they've taken a place way out east called Manila from the Spanish, and another called Pondi-something."

"Pondicherry. It's in India. That's another blow for the French," said Oliver.

"And haven't they seized Martinique and Havana in Cuba?" asked Pierre.

"Bastards routed the French when they tried to get a foothold back in Newfoundland," said Francois. "Will the swine never be satisfied?"

"Maybe when they have conquered enough territory it will mean we can go home," said Jambo. "They will need our skills in Acadia to work the fields. I don't suppose there is a levee which won't need repairing."

Whatever he hoped, the reality was that after all the years of banishment, they were as far away from realizing that dream as ever. Instead, what they had achieved was to re-assert their traditional Acadian values of family and community in the ghetto. The walls of warehouses had been rebuilt, the roofs were sound, and the fires gave out a great blaze and kept the cauldrons bubbling all day. They had built stores and pantries, and made a play area for the children. Chickens and geese were fattened for the pot.

Jambo and Pierre had found a stretch of river which was not too polluted where they fished and occasionally caught a few perch or a muddy pike, and the trapper would sometimes arrive triumphant at dawn with a brace of rabbits. He might have caught more, but the starving indigents from the shanty town used to skulk in the undergrowth and raid the traps. Langton had long relaxed the rules about working, so the men went out every day to look for odd jobs on the docks or the factories. Others stayed in the ghetto where Jambo had set up a cooperative to share the work, repairing furniture for the rich, fixing their chaises, and making toys for their children.

"They accept us more because we do better work than the locals," said Pierre.

"And we charge less," said Jambo.

The women were making such a success of mending clothes and sewing simple garments that they bought a small loom from a woolen manufacturer in the city. It was short work for the men to make it right, and soon the women were weaving coats and jerkins and outfits smart enough for the wives of gentlemen to wear. So successful were they, that they could afford to hire a stall in the market and every now and then a maid from one of the merchant's mansions summoned them to display their wares to the lady of the house.

They had repaired a broken down cart that had been abandoned, and bought a nag from a farmer who omitted to mention it had broken a leg the year before, which meant it could only pull half a load.

"Still, we are in better shape than this lot," said Pierre as they rolled past the lean-tos of canvas, rags, and branches, which were home to an ever-growing feral underclass who sat around getting drunk on potato spirit, devoid of purpose or hope.

Jambo thought he saw the two men who had threatened them on the riverbank, but the cart gave a lurch in a pothole and when he recovered his balance they had slunk out of sight. What did it matter? They were nothing to him.

One evening he was near the docks heading for home after repairing a merchant's roof when he paused to watch a cock fight. One rooster had just dispatched a rival with a swift, final blow of the blade attached to its leg. Blood from the torn neck dribbled across the dusty ring while the crowd howled their approval. Money was changing hands as they laid their bets on the next contestants, which were straining and squawking to be released from their owners' grasp.

"God, these British," he thought as he hastened on, disgusted by the sight, only to hear his name called out.

"Mr. White. Er, Monsieur LeBlanc."

Monsieur. He did not think he had heard correctly, but turned to see an Englishman of about his own age looking at him quizzically.

My God. Brooke Watson, the limping lieutenant from Grand-Pré, who he had last seen exhorting the villagers on to the boats at Boudrot Point. He was about to ignore him and turned away, but Watson stepped forward.

"My dear, er, chap." He extended a hand, which Jambo, in his surprise, shook. "Fancy meeting you here."

Jambo could not think what to say. His immediate instinct was to rage at him. He felt tempted to smack him in the face, but even as he felt the urge he understood that violence was pointless. Indeed, to his surprise, he found that he felt more embarrassed than antagonistic. So much had happened to them in the seven years since that day, that he had long ago realized that the harm men do to each other is rarely of their own free will or born out of their own conviction. Mostly they were taken by the flow of events and the obligation to carry out orders. Watson was just a cog in an unrelenting war machine, just as the carpenter was an unremarkable player on the side of the vanquished.

Watson was unabashed. "Come and have an ale. We have much to talk about."

They settled in a corner of the tavern called the Hole in the Wall. Even at that time of the afternoon, the low-beamed drinking house was a hubbub of sailors and dockers as well as prostitutes on the prowl for early custom.

Watson ordered the drinks and continued. "I am on my way from Edinburgh, where my, er, new wife resides, to London, and I stopped here to attend to some business. I plan to trade with, er, Nova Scotia when the war is over. I have been on a tour visiting some of our ports to see which is the most suitable as a headquarters." He paused. "But you, you and your family, how are you coping here? We had no idea, er, then, that you would be sent to England. None at all. The plan was to deliver you to the colonies where you could become part of society there. Find employment, you know, settle down, and become good British citizens."

"There was no chance of that," said Jambo.

"We felt for you. Colonel Winslow, remember him?"

"Indeed, I do," said the Acadian, pursing his lips as if to prevent an outburst of the bitterness that swept over him. "I am not likely to forget."

"He said it was a bad business—the worst he had been in. I saw his journal once, and he wrote how it was *very disagreeable to my natural make and temper.* But, you know how it is, we get caught up in things."

"Ah, yes." Jambo. He could not believe he was having the conversation. It was altogether bizarre. "What can I say."

"We had no option. I hope you understand now. How could we have a country—French speaking to boot—which would not agree to take up arms on our behalf? If you were not for us, I'm afraid the governor felt you were against us."

"That much is evident," said Jambo heavily.

"But fate always deals a hand, doesn't it? Did you know that Lawrence is dead? Caught a chill in 1760. Only 51 years old."

"That is some kind of justice, at least," said LeBlanc. He supped the beer.

"He was a man without pity," confessed Watson. "He would not entertain disagreement."

"What of you?" asked Jambo. "Where did you go after the expulsion?"

"Me? In '58 I was the commissary under General Wolfe at the siege of Louisbourg. That was, er, unfortunate. Not defeating the French, obviously, but the drowning of those poor fellows who were, er, moved on in the ships.

"The captain really did not want to make the journey, he knew it was dangerous, but Wolfe insisted. Odd cove I must confess."

Jambo said, "You might not remember him, but you met my wife's brother—my late wife—in Bristol. At least I think it was there, it is hard to be certain because our letters are censored. Name of Joseph Trahan."

"I met many of your unfortunate fellows in my travels," said the former soldier. "I must confess they were treated badly. I don't think I remember him, but I did help one or two write letters and made sure they were delivered. Maybe in a way I wanted to make some amends."

"Well, he wrote and said you were very helpful. Thank you. These travels of yours, did they take you to other ports?"

"They did, yes. I went to Southampton. What a hole that is. Nothing happens apart from a few dances in the spa, though our royal family seems to like taking the waters there. Heaven knows why."

"I wonder if you met my brother Charles?"

"I don't think so."

"You would not forget. He likes to play the lute and sing."

Watson reflected and took another mouthful of ale. "Does he have, er, a stammer?"

"That's him," said Jambo eagerly, though hardly daring to ask more. "When were you there?"

"Er, last year," said his old adversary, brow furrowed as if he was trying to remember events that had occurred in some distant country, in another life. "No, the year before. '60. Yes, that's it. Two years ago."

"So, it was, you know, after the plague," asked Jambo, again, terrified to hear the answer.

"Definitely. Let me think. Ah yes. Charles. Always joking."

"That's him," said Jambo eagerly.

"They were all making do as best they, er, could," went on Watson. "Many had died, as I discovered, but he was the one who kept up everyone's spirits. I admired his resilience."

"He always preferred to laugh than feel sorry for himself," said

Jambo. "He needed to," said the Englishman. "It was terrible there. Terrible."

"They did here, too. Try to stay cheerful, I mean. More than one hundred were taken by the pox alone."

There was a silence.

"Let me ask you." The beer had made Jambo mellow. "The leg?"

Watson laughed. "It was bitten off by a shark in Havana harbour. You know Cuba?"

"I have heard of it."

"Beautiful island. British now, of course. I was in the crew of an uncle's merchant ship. I was only 14. But it was the life for me. Well, it was until my, er, swim." He gave that barking laugh that Jambo remembered from Grand-Pré.

"Took a chunk below the calf of my right leg, then came back for more and took off my foot. My shipmates pulled me out. Blood everywhere. Couldn't save the leg. Caught the shark though and cooked it. Tasted horrible." He smiled. "You limp too. I noticed that in Grand-Pré. I thought you were being, er, satirical."

Jambo explained the night of the trap.

Another silence, as if they both felt they had been too expansive with each other.

"When do you think the war will end?" Jambo asked.

"Soon, very soon, I think. France has been pretty well thrashed right across the world and is suing for peace."

"I heard that your William Pitt has been removed as first minister."

"Indeed he has."

"But isn't he the man responsible for your victories? The war was not going well until he came to power."

"It's true. Some say he is a great fellow."

"But others, perhaps, are envious of him?"

"That could be the case." Watson was being careful. "I think he is a man who does not suffer fools."

"You mean there might be fools ruling the country."

"All countries," said Watson, and they laughed. "Ours is not to reason. Just do what we are told."

"Even if you are first minister."

"Even more so, I would say," said the lieutenant. "The new king, that's George the Third, said Pitt had the blackest of hearts and preferred others to advise him. So that's him finished. It's all so random, is it not? We are all at the mercy of someone else's ambition or their envy."

"What will become of us, do you think?"

"I cannot tell—even if I knew. It could be that because you no longer appear to be a threat that you are in a stronger position than you realize. The government might be charitable because, let's be honest, you do not matter to them. What little I know of Langton is that he is a fair-minded fellow, but don't forget, he is a way down the chain of command so it will not be his decision.

But let me tell you this." He drew the Acadian to one side and lowered his voice. "There is a French emissary coming to London soon. A man called Nivernois, Duke of somewhere or other. Very important. Close to King Louis, I hear. You should get a message to him, or better, *see* him. Now I must go. Good luck my friend."

With that, he stomped off along the quayside and Jambo set off back to the detention centre.

He had hoped to hitch a ride on the cart, which usually left town in the early evening, but he was so late he had to walk. As he approached the beggars' encampment he saw a crowd of his fellow prisoners, who seemed to be squaring up to a bunch of ruffians. Curiosity turned to panic when he realized that they were gathered around the cart, and that they were not fighting, but trying to help a woman who was lying on the ground surrounded by scattered vegetables.

Agnes saw him and came running up. "It's Marie."

His sister lay on the ground. He could not comprehend what had happened. Why did she not get up? He turned her face to him and he saw a neat blue bruise on the side of her temple from which blood ran.

"It was those men," said Agnes. "They started shouting horrible things at us—well, we are used to that and took no notice—but they had slings with stones, which they shot at us. One must have hit Marie because she just gave a little cry and toppled off the cart."

Some of the shanty town dwellers hovered, eager to help, one brought water, another dirty rags to serve as bandages, but a group of sallow-skinned men, sunken-eyed with filthy hair that hung over their shoulders, sat on the bank just above the road, swigging alcohol and jeering at the distressed Acadians.

"Serve you right, taking our jobs."

"Greedy French bastards."

"One down. And that's just the start."

He recognized two of them as the pair that had attacked Agnes and him. There was no mistaking the scar or the man with the crippled leg. They looked even meaner than before. Hungrier than wild dogs.

He made a move toward them, but they scrambled to their feet. He saw they had cudgels pitted with nails in their hands.

"You again, the fucking Froggie," said the one called Boot. "Is that your missus?"

"You 'ad her as well as the young tart you took walking?" Said William, the scar face, pointing with his cudgel at Marie.

"Nice looking piece, isn't she," said Boot.

"Bit old for you," said William.

"Still like to have 'er," leered Boot, drinking from his bottle.

"Alive or dead, it's all the same," said William, his rotten teeth leering though the grotesque smile of his scar.

"Me, I like a bit of action." Boot had put his hand down inside his frayed breeches and jerked it up and down obscenely. "Could do with some now. Lovely bit of Froggie meat."

Jambo leapt up the bank toward them—to his surprise joined by two local men—but the wretched specimens disappeared into the crowd and off into the stinking alleys of the slum.

"We're sorry mate," said one of his unlikely allies.

"They're scum," said the other. "Worse than scum. We're not all like that."

"They think because they're poor, they can cheat and steal. Some of us have pride, you know."

"We'll sort 'em out," said the first.

"I'm grateful," said Jambo. "Maybe you can help us track them down. They can't attack women like that and get away with it."

Agnes was pulling at his elbow. "Not now," she said urgently.

"How is she?" he asked, eager to pursue the two men. "Have we called the doctor?"

Agnes looked at him and shook her head slightly. He looked again at the mark on her temple.

"Sister. My God, I hadn't realized." He cradled her head in his arms. Apart from Charles—and he did not know for sure if his brother was still alive—she had been his only surviving relative. Parents, uncles, brothers, and sisters were all dead or scattered to oblivion. "Does Pierre know?"

"Oliver has gone to look for him."

The trapper came running followed by Joseph-Ignace. The young man sobbed uncontrollably as his father stooped and held his dead wife's body in his hands, as if nurturing a fledgling that had fallen from a tree.

He said nothing, but squeezed his eyes tight as if holding back the tears, or maybe conjuring up their life together, before picking her up and leading the small crowd back to the ghetto. Still not speaking, he gave her to the women to be prepared for burial, picked up his shovel, and went to the graveyard where he steadily and quietly dug her grave.

So arbitrary, thought Jambo as he sawed and hammered together a rough coffin. *Without reason. What had she done—or Pierre for that matter—*

to be abandoned by God like this? They buried her the next day. Pierre stood by the grave with their seven children. While they were red-eyed with weeping, he remained expressionless. Nothing showed on his face except a slight tic that caught at the corner of his right eye. Jambo put a hand on his broad shoulders, but could think of nothing to say. He left the melancholy group to make their last farewells, the clods of earth thrown into the grave thudding on the coffin.

Pierre spoke little in the following weeks. In the daytime he would draw his family around him like a cloak against the mystery of a wicked world, and in the evenings he would head off with his traps, returning at dawn.

Jambo suggested they inform the Commissioner about the killing, but the trapper merely shrugged.

"He won't be interested. It is just one traitor, as he would call her, killed by the rejected dregs of his city. It doesn't amount to much, does it? As far as he is concerned, none of us qualify as members of the human race. This is for me to deal with."

Jambo assumed he meant coping with his heartache, particularly as he continued, "How can I grieve more than anyone else? You have been through this. You were strong. I had twenty years with Marie and I am blessed with our children. We never faltered, she and I. She was taken before her time, of course, but then, our time is never when we want it."

"I admire your fortitude, Pierre," he said.

The trapper said nothing.

One morning he returned with a brace of rabbits.

"The snares are always being raided by the vermin from the slums, but I caught a couple of the beggars last night, gave them a whack, and frightened them off."

Agnes brewed coffee and they sat quietly for a while.

Pierre asked casually, "Would you recognize the killers?"

"Of course. Only too well," he said.

"Old friends of ours," said Agnes.

"Let's take a walk," said Jambo, and they ventured up to the main road to the rancid shacks of the settlement.

There were a group of men lounging in their usual position on the bank.

One spat noisily on the ground.

"Don't make it obvious by staring," said Jambo. "But see the two by the water pump?"

"With the flagons of ale?"

"That's them."

For a second it looked as if the trapper was going to confront them, but he hesitated. As he did so, the two Englishmen who had tried to help LeBlanc on the day of the attack came up. "You the husband?" asked one.

"Yes," said Pierre. Nothing else. He slumped, his powerful, muscular frame seemed to shrink and he averted his eyes from the two strangers. But then he pulled himself upright and looked steadily back. "Yes. I am."

"Bleedin' shame, mate, that's what it is. Those two are the lowest. Always causing trouble. If you ever need any help just ask."

"I will," said the trapper."Thank you."

A few days later, he said, "You should come with us tonight. Francois and I are setting some more traps."

"Take your knife," said Francois, who was carrying a shovel and lengths of rope.

"Why?" asked the carpenter.

"To skin a rabbit," said Pierre grimly.

"Or two," said Francois.

The moon was high in a clear sky, and the way was well lit. As they walked quietly along a path that led to the spinney where Pierre laid his traps, two men shimmered out of the dark and—as if it had been planned—fell into step with them.

He was about to ask, '*What's going on?*' but one of the arrivals said,

"You keeping well, mate?" so he replied with incongruous politeness, "Yes. Thank you."

But what *was* going on?

The five of them walked in silence until they reached a clearing.

"Now," said Pierre without preamble. "Nearly every night those two killers have raided my traps. I have let them get away with it, because I wanted to make sure they kept coming back."

He pulled two live rabbits out of his sack and tiptoed into the clearing where he lay them, twitching, each in a trap.

"I have lined the clearing with traps strong enough to hold a bear," he said. "I should catch one of the swine if we are lucky. Maybe both. Then we can decide what to do with them."

"No doubt about what that will be," said Francois, his eyes glinting dangerously.

"Put these masks on."

The five pulled woolen hoods with holes for their eyes over their heads.

Jambo did it without thinking, as if it was the most natural thing in the world. They were to teach the men who murdered Marie a lesson they would never forget. There was no discussion. No opportunity for him to argue in his rational way that the matter should be handed over to the authorities.

For so long the leader of their troubled community, now he was doing what Pierre wanted. The fact that the trapper had been quietly planning his revenge, building up his resolve since the attack, gave him the power.

The five men crouched on the edge of the clearing so that they had a clear view of the path that led from the beggars' quarters. They did not have to wait long. They could hear them trampling carelessly through the undergrowth, whispering loudly, and laughing drunkenly. There were four of them.

"They've left the rabbits for us," said one.

"How very kind," said another

"They're so bleedin' stupid," slurred the third.

"Hang on I need a piss," said one on the other side of the bushes from Jambo. He was so close he could hear him unbuckle his trousers and hear his sigh of relief as he let a stream splash near the carpenter's boots.

As he did so, one of his accomplices stepped into the clearing. With a crack like a whip the snare caught him by a leg and sent him sailing into the air and left him hanging head down from a tree. The one behind, too drunk to react, stepped straight into another trap and was dragged to the ground, scrabbling like one of the rabbits he had come to steal.

The third intruder was Boot, the young man with the withered leg. With surprising alacrity, he turned to run, but was met by Francois who stepped from his hiding place to hit him smack on the head with his shovel. He went down without a sound.

The man relieving himself stumbled as he tried to escape, pulling at his trousers as he went, but Jambo grabbed him round the neck and pulled his knife. He nicked the miscreant and blood spurted over his hands. He shoved him into the clearing with the others.

Uncannily composed, Pierre inspected the faces of the men.

"This one, I think," he said grabbing the struggling wretch on the ground by the hair and holding the face toward Jambo.

It was William, his raw, red scar smiling back up at him.

"Yes," said one of the Englishmen before LeBlanc could answer.

"And this?" He dragged Boot into the light.

The Englishman nodded.

Francois, with his knife in one hand and his shovel in the other, was quivering with venom, "Let's beat them to a pulp."

"Wait." Pierre came close to the one Jambo was holding. His blue eyes pierced through the mask at the captive who was shaking so much the carpenter had to use all his strength to keep him upright.

"Pathetic." He looked at his naked bottom half. "You talk big for such a small man." He ripped his trousers into shreds. "Get out."

Gibbering with fear and relief, he fled half naked from the clearing, the white of his behind absurdly dappled by the moonlight. One of their English accomplices kicked him as he went. Pierre turned to the one hanging head down from the tree. He cut the rope and sent him sprawling.

"You are lucky to be alive," he said, lifting his head six inches off the ground and pushing his hooded face close to the terrified creature. "We know who you are. We know where you live. If I see you again—that's all, I just have to see you—consider yourself dead."

"I promise," he spluttered. He had soiled himself in terror, excrement running down his legs. "All I wanted was a bite to eat."

"And tell that to your friend. He might think of changing his mind when he gets his trousers back on. Now go."

The moon was at its highest, shining down on the clearing, illuminating the grotesque scene. The younger captive was groaning as he came round from Francois's blow, the other lay still, realizing that the more he tried to wriggle out of his bonds the tighter the ropes that held him would become.

Pierre was talking very quietly and methodically. "You killed my wife. This man's sister," he said. "You insulted her, said vile things about her even as she lay dying in front of you."

The younger man was now fully conscious and whimpering like a wounded dog with fear as it dawned on him what was to happen. "It was a mistake," he gasped. "We didn't mean it. Honest. I'm sorry. Anyway, *he* threw the stone."

"Liar, it was *him!*"

"You're pathetic specimens," said Pierre, quietly matter-of-fact.

"Cowardly bastard!" yelled Francois, hitting him in the ribs with his shovel.

The older man with his ghastly scar seemed to smile as he squealed in terror, "'He did it. Not me. I tried to stop it."

The other tried to get to his feet as if to attack him, but he was knocked down and as he fell, the ropes tightened around his legs and his arms. If he tried to kick them off, the violent movement tautened the rope around his arms, and when his arms jerked, the noose around his neck tightened. Jambo had seen Pierre catch a bear like that. Francois dragged the two doomed men so that they were side by side. Then a madness took over.

For the rest of his life, whenever the images of the next few moments came involuntarily into his mind, Jambo pushed them aside. He would not let himself see them. Eventually, it was as if he could not be sure what really happened. Just as he had schooled himself to be strong and sensible, now he deliberately obscured the memory. That way no blame could be laid. No one was guilty—or they were all guilty. It made it easier to bear.

It was all so quiet. So methodical. The light from the moon flickered. Shadows came and went as the wind made the trees sway. They became hazy, indistinct figures, like ghostly warriors in a war dance as they gathered around the whimpering victims.

Francois was cursing them under his breath as he wrung his huge hands around one man's neck. The two Englishmen were kicking them. Pierre was pacing around the clearing muttering—*or maybe praying,* he thought later. Jambo heard the words '*Marie* and *understand.*' He could feel the frenzy growing. They were getting out of control as each one's need for violence and revenge spurred on the other. He still had his knife in his hand. He *wanted* to use it.

The men on the ground were crying out for help, for forgiveness, for their lives. Their faces were bloodied. Their shirts had been torn off to reveal a mess of scars and bruises.

In the chaos an English voice said, "Let's shut them up."

"Hold this one's mouth open." It was Pierre, calm, matter of fact.

A hand gouged out earth with a knife and carefully mud was funneled into his quarry's mouth and into his nostrils.

"Now him."

He did the same to the older man, ramming it in tight, deep into his throat. "There will be no more insults from you," said one of the attackers. Was it Pierre? Francois? Jambo himself? It was moving so fast. So dementedly. So calmly.

"You and your filthy gobs."

Pierre hunkered down and took off his mask.

"You might as well see who has put an end to your pointless existence," he said and they stood around them, five figures, macabre and terrifying in the glimmering half-light. Gazing down at their victims. Silent.

The Acadians waited and watched as the two men struggled to free themselves. Tied up as they were, all they could do was jerk spasmodically and work their heads desperately in an attempt to let air into their windpipes. Unrecognized sounds came from their throats as they grunted, gurgled, and whimpered.

"Their Adam's apples worked convulsively as they tried to clear the obstruction. Their eyes bulged and popped. Blood seeped from the sockets. It seemed to take forever. If they managed to spit out a morsel of the earth, or swallowed, more earth would be steadily rammed back down their throats and inserted it into their nostrils with the care of a surgeon.

"Hold that one." One of the victims had wriggled a hand free from its bindings, but he had no chance. A knife flashed in the moonlight. It went through the palm of his hand, nailing it to the ground.

The howl of pain—like a demon expelled from hell—was caught short by hands being clamped over the mouth with its grinning scar. He writhed, kicked, and spluttered for what seemed an eternity but was only a few minutes. He gave a ghastly groan. His legs twitched. He was dead, smiling as he went to his damnation. Then the other was seized with shuddering hiccups that made his body quiver. Silence.

The sweat was pouring from Jambo. He was shaking with the horror of it, but Pierre and Francois were unmoved.

The two Englishmen were crouched, talking and laughing quietly to themselves as if they passing the time of day. One got up and kicked William's body. "He attacked my daughter. Filthy swine." He kicked him again. "That's why I'm here, mate."

They dug a shallow grave into which they threw the bodies as if they were carrion.

"Serve 'em right, mate. Worse than shit."

They headed back to their home in the slum. Partners for just that one night.

"See you around." Said one.

"Good night's work, mate," said the other.

The Acadians returned to the ghetto as dawn rose and slipped in unnoticed. *How relaxed we seem,* Jambo thought.

Agnes sensed something. "You've cut your hand," she said.

"It was the rabbit. The knife slipped when I was skinning it."

She knew he was lying, but she could have had no inkling what her sensible, steady, husband had done.

Two days later, Langton called by with a platoon of soldiers. "There's been trouble in the slums," he said. "Two of them have been murdered and one gang is blaming the other. I am going to have to enforce the curfew for a few days—as much for your own sakes as anything else."

"What about us?" demanded Francois. "Are you not going to investigate our loss? This man's wife was murdered by one of those scum."

"I know, and I am sorry. We are trying to find the killer but these people are beyond the law." He pointed with his whip toward the shanty town. "We thought we had a couple of suspects, but there's no one to trust to tell the truth."

"What of these dead people?" asked Jambo. "Two of them, you say?"

"It's odd, I don't know what to make of it," said the Commissioner scratching his long neck ruminatively. "It looked like they had been caught up in traps in the spinney near the river. One had been hit on the head with a stone, and there were wheals on their arms as if they had been tied up, but it was hard to tell what happened because foxes have got at them."

Pierre sat impassively and Francois, for once, stayed quiet.

Jambo said, "The men from the slum were always raiding our traps which is why we now set them as far away as possible. We haven't put them in the spinney for ages."

"They know about the curfew," said Oliver. "So they reckon they can take their pick whenever they like after dark."

"We have nothing to do with them," said Jambo. "They are like savages, outside the laws of civilization. You say they stick together, but I imagine they are always fighting and betraying each other."

"Very probably," said Langton. "It was odd though, it was almost as if they had been laid in graves."

"That will be the foxes," said Jambo. "They drag their prey to a safe place so it is well hidden. Always digging."

"And their mouths had earth in them."

"I've eaten mud," said Francois without missing a beat. "We all have. Hunger drives you crazy. You hope there might be a root or a blade of grass buried away. Or even a bug."

They never talked about it again. It was as if their deadly hunting expedition had never happened. Pierre continued to keep to himself by day, and disappeared at dusk to tend his traps, though now he came back with rabbits more often than before.

Before. Jambo tried to make sense of what the five of them had done. The old village priest had taught them to meet an eye for an eye, and that was what they had done. But was that right? Marie was avenged. Her killers were dead. No one knew who had done it, and judging by Langton's reaction, no one cared. Their victims were disgusting creatures dredged from humanity's cess pool, but they were probably more pathetic than evil, driven into violence and murder by the miserable circumstances of their life.

Was he now any better?

Like them, he had endured years of disappointment and neglect. Now, like them, he had been party to a killing. He had become as brutalized as them. He had put aside the rational behavior that he had worked so determinedly to cultivate. Think first, then talk, then, perhaps, act. That had been his way. Now he had behaved like an unthinking savage.

Yet, what disturbed most was that he could not feel any guilt.

Every night he stayed awake, agonizing, until as dawn approached one morning, Agnes said, "It's distressing the way people treat each other."

"What do you mean?"

"Those two men who were killed. You would have thought the piteous families in the shanty town would stay loyal to each other. Like we have."

"Yes. Adversity has kept us strong." He wasn't sure where the conversation was leading, especially as she stayed lying on her back staring at the roof. In the grey dawn light he could see her face was inscrutable.

"I feel no sympathy for them," she said. "At first, when those two attacked us on the canal side I felt more sorry for them than frightened. The world was against them."

"Like us," he ventured.

"Yes, like us. But now I feel that they could have made something of their lives. *Like us.* Instead they gave up, turned to drink, and violence."

"And murder."

She kept her gaze focused on the roof. "Whoever killed them, they deserved it. They had surrendered their right to life." She paused and reached for his hand in the bed. "In a way, the killings were a recognition that goodness and evil exist," she said. "They were bad people, they were punished."

"What about us?" he said. "We are not bad, yet we have been punished time and time again. We have not been able to take revenge on the British, on Lawrence, on Dinwiddie, on any of the sadistic swine who have brought us to this place."

"Not on them, no. But when bad people die, are killed, it does something to redress the balance. It tells us that ultimately God is on our side. Deaths like this should keep us strong."

"So you think —"

"I think God knows what is right and wrong. And you know what is even more important? The only thing that matters? It's that we are still alive." She turned to face him, wrapped her arms around him and kissed him.

He woke the next morning as clear-headed as he had been before the night of the killings. "We must have a meeting," he said. "I have much to disclose."

As they gathered, Pierre joined them. He seemed as solid and unflappable as ever, except the tic that hovered over his eye.

Jambo explained his meeting with Brooke Watson and the disclosure that there was a French delegation heading for London.

Pierre said, "Why have you taken so long to tell us? Isn't this important?"

"It is," said Jambo with a ghost of a smile that only Pierre and Francois would notice. "It is also clear to me that we must get to see this Nivernois. I don't suppose he even knows we are here, and even if he does I doubt he cares very much."

"How can we contact him?" asked Pierre.

"We shall have to write," said Jambo.

"Langton will open every letter," said Pierre.

"You're right. Most of the missives we get from our cousins are still censured."

"We shall have to go to London, find the French embassy, and deliver the letter in person," said Jambo.

"We would not get one hundred yards," said Oliver. "The nearest post chaise to London goes through a place called Warrington, and that's about 20 miles away. We'd never get past the guards at the city gates, and our English is not good enough to fool anyone who might challenge us on the journey."

Agnes said, "Why not ask John Turney?"

"What a good idea," said Jambo. "He would be ideal."

The council bridled at that. Not all had been won round to the idea of an Acadian marrying an outsider, and Madeleine had been warned that if she married she would not be allowed to live with him in the ghetto. The young couple were defiant, and despite the pleas of Agnes and the women of the ghetto, she and Turney were banished. Worse, because he was not Acadian, the British had then deprived the couple of the new wife's refugee allowance.

"Would he go?" wondered Oliver. "After all, we have treated him and Madeleine unkindly."

Jambo said, "Let's ask him."

"And Madeleine," added Agnes. "You owe her that."

The sailor strode in to the warehouse with his wife and the couple stood warily before the assembly.

"John, welcome to our gathering," said Jambo. "This is a little embarrassing, because of what occurred before."

He saw the sullen expression on the sailor's face.

"Well, more than embarrassing. We were at fault. First we would like to apologize. Most sincerely. Now, we would quite understand if you refuse, but we have a favor to ask of you."

He explained about Nivernois and how grateful they would be if he acted as their emissary and take a letter to London.

The Irishman paused before he replied. He held his wife's hand tightly.

"We have had a hard time of it since we wed. We were not welcome here and, to be sure, the English are not exactly friendly. When I am at sea Madeleine has been left alone for many weeks, which has been frightening for her. I can see no reason why I should help unless—to be frank—unless there is some benefit to us."

"We have been harsh, cousin John," Jambo used the affectionate Acadian soubriquet. "I repeat, I cannot say how sorry I am. We all are. I think we have now all learnt the importance of friends and allies staying together. More important than sticking to old customs."

The sailor shuffled, momentarily tongue-tied but Madeleine said, "Yes, *cousin*—she used the word with heavy sarcasm—you have been harsh. More than harsh. It was shocking that such prejudice existed among us when we ourselves, all of us in this detention camp, have been treated in just the same, callous way. If it had not been for the help and loyalty of the sisters here, I don't know if we would still be alive."

Agnes put her arm around her. "Of course," she said. "You are welcome to come and live here—if you can forgive us."

Jambo shot a quizzical look at her. Francois grunted disapprovingly. So the women had rallied around without telling their men—another custom that had been ignored. It was one thing to give women the vote in council matters, but quite another for them to go against the will of their men.

Jambo let it pass. Their world was changing. "We should have done this months ago," he said. "I know we are in the wrong."

"I will do it," said Turney. "For the sake of Madeleine, who is expecting again. She has been sorely hurt by her treatment, and I expect that by doing this we shall be admitted back into your community and allowed to live here."

"We would pay you to go, of course," said Pierre.

"I would expect five guineas for my expenses," said the sailor.

"Agreed."

"I think ten is more appropriate," said the carpenter.

He was back within three weeks.

"It was an odd affair," he said. "That Nivernois! He thinks he's very grand, which is surprising when you remember his side has just lost the war. I had been travelling four days by chaise in the bitter chill, but when I handed in the letter he kept me waiting all day in the servants' quarters, offering me neither soup or a place by the fire. In fact, at first, I don't think he understood why I was there. They had been dining, and well, judging by the legs of chicken and cuts of mutton that still lay on the table, not to mention the empty carafes of wine. In truth, he's an arrogant sod, no better than the British bastards who run this country. He's got those glasses on a holder, which he peers through as if you were a speck of dog shit at the end of his foot.

He slighted me in front of his comrades, showing off, I thought. '*So, you are an Irishman*', he said. '*An Irishman who is pleading for a small group of French-speaking people imprisoned in some God forsaken place who say they are British subjects. What is that to me?*' They all laughed. '*Acadians?*' said one of his audience. '*Never heard of them.*'

"I told him that you were innocent victims of the British who were loyal to France and had been subjected to unimaginable hardship since being expelled from your homeland. He seemed not to be listening, but he finally agreed to read the letter, studied it for a few moments and immediately left the room to consult with his officers, leaving me in this huge room by myself with just one aide to talk to.

"He hadn't heard of you either but he did say something about there '*always being a place for citizens to serve the King in his distant dominions.*' I'm afraid I was so peckish I could not concentrate on anything but helping myself to as much food left on the tables as I could.

"I reckon Nivernois had been playing some sort of game with me, because when he and his men came back there was quite a change of heart," said the Irishman. "He was almost polite. Offered me food, which made me smile since I had already been stuffing myself, and said, as much to the company as to me, '*I feel for these Acadians. They need our help. And to be treated the way they have, locked away in this by the unspeakable British— that must be closer to perdition than hell itself.*' There was much laughter at that.

"But he stilled them. '*No,*' he said, '*This is serious, these people need us. I will see what can be done.*' He turned to me and said, '*I shall send my best man. De la Rochette, step forward.*''"

"A singular character pushed his way to the front of the group that surrounded the duke. He was a real spark, dressed up to the nines in velveteen and silk and my God you should have seen how he crawled to High'n'Mighty Nivernois.

"The Duke ordered him, '*Get to this benighted outpost as soon as possible. And you sir*—he turned to me—*tell your Acadian allies that France and its most noble king is coming to their rescue.*'"

TWENTY-ONE

Liverpool

December 31, 1762.

Two Evils

It was New Year's Eve, and the ghetto was as cheerful as the refugees could make it. They had clubbed together to buy mutton, potatoes, turnips, and even extra casks of porter.

Jean-Baptise and Osite came dashing into the compound.

"There's a Frenchman," shouted Jean-Baptiste, bursting with importance at being first with the news.

"With a big hat," explained Osite stretching her little hands as wide around her head as she could.

"He's coming to see us." The boy emphasized the *us* with disarming gravity.

Ever since the British had stopped patrolling the detention centre, the Acadians had their own vigilantes to protect them from outsiders. The moment they knew the stranger was approaching they gathered suspiciously by the main gate.

"Messieurs. Bonjour."

It was an extravagant figure who stood before them. Turney had warned them that the French emissary had seemed to him to be an ostentatious and slippery character—'*a man less trustworthy I have yet to meet*'—he had declared, and with one glance at the greasy individual with an absurd wig and a moustache that curled up at the ends in a permanent simper, the prisoners thoroughly agreed. Their visitor was fashionably dressed in a dark blue coat and waistcoat with deep cuffs edged with fine embroidery, and his hair was tied back under the wide-brimmed tricorn hat. He paused, carefully checking where he should plant his dainty shoes as if to ensure their buckles of false stones would catch the light of the lanterns and send little flashes of color around the dingy warehouse.

"This is Monsieur de la Rochette," said Turney. "We met in London."

The Frenchman did not waste a glance on the Irishman. "I am indeed Alexandre de la Rochette, a plenipotentiary of no less a personage than Louis Jules Barbon, Mancini Mazarini, Duke de Nivernois, Grandee of Spain, Peer of France. A friend and confidant of King Louis himself."

"Welcome," said Jambo, disguising his instant antipathy to the posturing plenipotentiary. "Please come in. Agnes, tea for the gentleman."

"Do you not have something stronger? The journey from London was the very devil, and these English hostels are so uncivilized."

"You can try the dances at the Assembly Rooms with the city's finest," joked Oliver. "We are always made most welcome and find the wine of the highest quality."

De la Rochette gave his moustache a contemptuous twirl at the sarcasm.

"We are prisoners here," said Jambo. "I fear you find us in a place not as civilized even as the humblest hostel. We are destitute, and we eat and drink what we can, but I am sure we can find you a flagon of porter."

"Porter? That disgusting English brew. Still, I suppose it is better than nothing."

He fussed about with his handkerchief, brushing down the bench the Acadians had pulled out for him to sit on. "Now, tell me your story."

When Jambo had finished, even this louche character was stilled for a while.

"I had no idea," he said. "All that way. All those deaths. How you must hate your oppressors." He gathered himself. "My friends, you can be assured that King Louis himself knows of your imprisonment here, and that he has promised his loyal subjects land and money. You will never starve again, that I pledge. From now you will have the full protection of France. That is my solemn oath."

Some of the exiles clapped and cheered, and cries of *Long live the King* echoed around the prison, but others like Jambo kept their mouths shut and their thoughts to themselves.

De la Rochette stayed for two days, eagerly trying to persuade the Acadians that their future lay in Old France. He painted a picture of steady work, green meadows, good hunting and fishing, and happy families in solidly built homes.

"Just the way I imagine your Acadia to be. It will be a new start."

"We want to go home," interrupted Francois with typical bluntness. "That is all we want from you."

"Of course, of course," he said soothingly. "But first we must get you out of this." He waved his handkerchief at their dismal quarters.

"You will find the Old Country very pleasing, believe me."

Jambo was unimpressed by the glib persuasiveness of the man who had no real understanding of the calamities the Acadians had endured, or how fierce the pull of their homeland was.

"I plan to visit your cousins, as you call them, in Bristol, Southampton, and Falmouth if I have the time, and I will return. I beg you, though," he said as he made to leave, "do not tell anyone what we have discussed. I am sure British spies know that I have been here, but discretion is all."

The moment he had gone they held another meeting.

"He is a secret agent," said Francois.

"Why should we trust him?" asked Pierre.

"Why indeed," said Jambo. "On one hand he says he had no idea how much we have suffered, while on the other he says the King of France has our best interests at heart, as if he has been fretting about us for all this time."

"But," said Oliver. "If he can get us to France, won't that be better than languishing here?"

"Maybe," said Pierre. "But it is *Acadia* where we want to go, is it not?"

"Agreed," said Jambo. "Nowhere else. He did not understand the depth of our feeling. Or chose not to. I think a meeting with Mr. Langton is called for. Let's hear what he has to say."

The Commissioner said, "I know, of course, that you have had a visit from a Mr. Rocket. I have no doubt he made you many promises, but this long war is at last coming to an end, and Great Britain has swept all before her. We are the world power now. France's fleet has been destroyed and we rule from India to the West Indies, and, of course, we have our greatest prize, North America. All ours. I seem to remember you telling me when you arrived that you were British citizens, so now you must see your interests clearly lie with us."

"But what would we do?" asked Jambo. "You have locked us away, stopped our allowances, and banned us from work. What is there for us here?"

"All that is changing. You can see how the city is growing. Soon it will be second only to London for wealth. Here is just one example; we will need men to build a new canal to link Liverpool with the middle of England. I shall make sure you get the best posts and the best pay."

"There will be jobs in France," said Oliver. "And allowances."

"Don't be fooled," said Langton. "Do not believe for one minute that the French will not abandon you once you are in their country. This man Rocket—" Langton seemed to enjoy mispronouncing it, "—did he show you his credentials? I thought not. What proof do you have that he really speaks for the government?"

"Why would he lie to us?" demanded Pierre.

"What is the point of him coming all this way to spin a yarn?" asked Oliver.

"I'll tell you exactly why. If France is lucky when peace is declared, and the treaties are signed, she will be given a few poxy islands in the West Indies in return for the great territories we have wrested from them. They will need bodies—and I mean *bodies*—to build fortifications and harbors. That's where you will come in. Fancy another trip across the Atlantic do you? Your so-called countrymen will try to send you to their colonies of Guyana and Haiti, two places so wretched that even renegades with a price on their heads hand themselves over to be executed rather than step foot on their primitive shores—the heat, the disease, the squalor.

"You might have felt you had cause to rail at the conditions here, but I tell you, this is a paradise in comparison. Go to France, by all means, but you will be fodder for their ambitions."

"That is not quite how Monsieur De la Rochette puts it," said Jambo. "He tells a different story."

"Naturally. But not all of your people are as impressed as you seem to have been. I am sent all the intelligence about what happens, so I know the true state of affairs. I have heard already that the prisoners in Bristol told Mr. Rocket to leave them alone. They told him that all they wanted to do was return to Nova Scotia. Mind you, I think they might have overplayed their hand somewhat. They have demanded that their possessions be returned to them, and that they be compensated for their loss. In return they have agreed to sign the oath of fidelity and not to bear arms against anyone."

"That's nothing new," said Jambo. "We have always agreed to that."

"It didn't stop us being expelled," said Pierre.

"So what is your alternative to De la Rochette?" asked Oliver.

"Stay here and become proper British citizens, or follow the lead of your Bristol comrades and take a new oath, agree never to take up arms, and King George will send you back to Acadia. He will hand over your homes, your farms, and supply you with livestock."

"How can we believe you?" asked Francois. "I have never known an Englishman to tell the truth yet."

"I will leave it with you," said Langton, refusing to be ruffled.

Who to follow? The argument went on for days.

"We should listen to Langton," said one. "At least he is holding out the chance of returning home."

"But I don't understand why they would want to do that," said another. "They kick us out and then welcome us back. It doesn't make sense."

"Surely the British would have moved their own people in by now."

"And what about all those incomers like the Germans who had started to settle around Halifax?"

"They could never replace us. They will still need our skills. Do Germans know how to fix a levee?"

"If they haven't allowed other settlers in by now the place will be a wasteland," said Jambo, the memory of the blazing houses still as sharp in his mind as it was on the day they were expelled.

"At least, we will be welcomed if we choose to go to France," said Oliver. "There must be relatives of our forefathers still living there."

"That would certainly help us make a fresh start," said Jambo. "But only if he is telling the truth about the farms and the homes."

"That's a big *if*," said Pierre. And off they went again rehearsing the pros and cons.

"If we agree to go to France, surely we will be in a stronger position to beg King Louis to help us."

"He might negotiate with the British to let us home—if not to Grand-Pré, then maybe to Quebec or New Brunswick."

"But we know France has been humiliated in America. You should hear them crowing in the taverns. The only territories the French have left are the St. Pierre and Miquelon Islands."

"And they are just lumps of rock in the Atlantic. We'd starve."

"Perfect place if you are a seal."

"Not much to choose from, is it?"

"Still," said Jambo. "We have to decide. One or the other."

"How strange that as freedom beckons we feel so trapped," said Agnes.

"I don't trust De la Rochette," said Francois. "Creeps around like a puffed-up snail."

"Very good, Francois," laughed Oliver. "Puffed-up snail. Wish I'd thought of that."

"I certainly would have no truck with him," said Pierre. "But then, who could have faith in Langton?"

"Especially as it is not his decision," said Jambo, remembering what Watson had told him. "Our fate will be decided in London."

Nonetheless, Langton became a frequent visitor to the ghetto. He hoped their allowances were now up to date. He enquired solicitously about their conditions. Then the priest, who had served as their chaplain with scant interest for seven years, took to preaching sermons that encouraged his charges to take the oath and vote to return to Acadia.

For the first time since he had been obliged to minister to the dying during the plague, he did his rounds of the ghetto, chatting to the older couples, offering them comfort, and persuading them to follow God's will and throw in their lot with the British.

"I've heard that more than fifty of the old timers have agreed to go home," said Oliver.

"It's the right thing to do," said one of the Comeau brothers. "I'm 60 now, I don't want to be sent off to start all over again in a foreign country, because that's what France is to me—*foreign.*"

"Home, that's all I want," said Jean Saunier. "When my wife died I lost everything. I agree with the priest, the best we can do is sign the oath and return home."

"I don't even mind saying that we will take up arms for them," said Charles Boutarit.

"Good God, man," scoffed Francois, "You're so old and feeble you can hardly walk. I don't suppose the British will be rushing to conscript you."

As even some of the most skeptical began to hope that the return to Acadia was a possibility, it was, once again, Oliver, the gossip, the talker, the friend to so many, who discovered the truth.

"We have been deceived, cousins. This priest has been promised he will be appointed parochial dean of all the Catholic villages in Acadia if gets us to take the oath, but we shall not be going with him. That is not what Langton plans at all."

"So it is a trick," said Francois. "See what I mean about an honest Englishmen?"

"But why go to all that bother and deception?" asked Pierre.

"Seems a lot of effort to get us to build a canal," said Oliver.

"Are we so important to them? It is not as if we are standing in the way of them conquering the world," said Jambo

"Like we were in Grand-Pré," said Pierre ironically. "With our mighty force of braves."

"It's as though we are unfinished business," said Jambo. "They want us to be totally subservient to them, to give up our religion, to sign the oath. This is about power."

"They would rather have us here under their control, than give us our freedom, or even let us go to France," said Agnes.

"It's like one of your card games, Oliver, there is only one winner."

The cobbler smiled uncertainly, not sure if that was a compliment, "Maybe Monsieur De la Rochette has the better pack after all."

Langton called by soon after Oliver's revelation. He trotted into the ghetto all smiles, confident that his arguments had won the day, but after the briefest of exchanges he raised himself in the saddle, his beak of a nose flashing angrily at the prisoners.

"You fools. You do not understand what you are letting yourselves in for. This is insubordination. I shall cut your allowances. I shall throw you in prison. You will pay for this."

"As if we have not paid for the years we have been here," said Jambo.

"As if this is not a prison," said Pierre.

Francois started forward, but Agnes clung to her uncle's arm, as she did so often, to stop him hurling himself at the Commissioner and said scornfully, "You should be ashamed at such deception. We have had enough malice at your hands without this."

"Think about it," said Langton, recovering his poise. "You have been misled by mischievous gossip. My offer stands."

De la Rochette reappeared later in February on the very day the treaty that ended the war was signed. The city was in celebration—the church bells rang, bunting hung from every street corner, and the pubs were overflowing with celebrating sailors and soldiers. The prostitutes were busier than they had been for months.

"What a vile place this Liverpool is," sniffed De la Rochette, "The streets are running with gin and piss, the gutters are overflowing with drunks and harlots. My friends, I have again come to *rescue* you from this city of savages, and to free you from the cruel dominion of these people.

"I have visited all your countrymen, and wherever I have been I have seen hardship and neglect. And death. So many deaths." He flapped his lace-ruffled wrists melodramatically. "What a time I have had. I have to tell you truths, even though I know you will grieve to hear them. I must make you face the evil of these Englishmen. I have the figures in black and white that tell a tale of such calamity that I find impossible to comprehend."

More flapping, more lace.

"I think we can handle the truth," said Jambo. "The letters we received were often censored, and the worst of the detail obliterated, but we do know that many have died."

"Perhaps more than you imagine," said the emissary. "The British are proud of the way they have rid themselves of you. They boast that 14,000 of you were expelled from Acadia between '55 and '58 and that as many as 8,000 have since perished."

He waited to let the figures sink in, but the Acadians were too overwhelmed to react. They would all have lost someone they knew.

"I hesitate to tell you that of the 340 of your fellows who were sent to Southampton, only 219 are still alive. And in Falmouth I can scarcely believe what happened. The locals were so ashamed that they would not talk about it, but there is a churchyard where 60 of your, I mean *our,* cousins lie together in one grave. Unconsecrated. Uncared for. I was told that the ones spared the plague were forced to dig the pit themselves, and then the military threw in the dead as if they were dumping trapped rats into a ditch."

Jambo noted the way he had embraced his audience with that *our* and felt even more hostile to the glib emissary.

"Just one sad patch of earth with a field of crosses. There are only 159 of you still alive in that miserable port. Everywhere I went I found that the government has discontinued our people's dole money, and the streets are full of widows and orphans, mothers and babies, begging for alms.

"The way they treated the prisoners in Bristol will redound to their eternal shame. Let me tell you that 289—maybe more, the figures are confused—arrived on a ship called the Virginia Packet, and when I was there last month only 160 were still with us.

What a time they had of it. Apparently, when the Packet hove to the Admiralty, doctor came to check them for disease and said he had never seen such a pitiable mass cowering below deck. They were obviously sick, but he was under orders and said it was just a *passing malady,* and that all they needed was a diet of broth and gruel, nursing, and the wholesome sea air of the West Country. The ones who survived the voyage on the ship, which was too small to cross the Atlantic with so many on board, were clinging on to life."

He shook his pompous wig with what was intended to be a show of sympathy.

"But far from being taken ashore immediately for food and medical treatment, they were kept on the ship for three days because the mayor wouldn't let them land. '*Too expensive,*' he said. "Then they were kept on the quayside for another few days while the city decided what to do with them before they were marched to a concentration camp, which had been used during the last war between England and France and still had rusty manacles hanging from the walls."

*That must have been the **airy** warehouse around a courtyard that Joseph had referred to,* decided Jambo, *though the mention of manacles and the behavior of the mayor had been deleted.*

"Did you know there were Spanish prisoners in Bristol as well as our cousins too?: said De la Rochette. Again that glib, jarring *'our cousins.'* How dare he?

"There were 700 of them all thrown together in the one jail where they lay wallowing side by side, infecting each other with their mutual stench and effluvia."

He repeated *'mutual stench, effluvia,'* with relish, as if it was an incantation to the devils of neglect, as if he were bringing his own brand of melodrama to their plight.

He's enjoying it, fumed Jambo inwardly.

"Hardly surprising, the pox struck within days," continued the emissary. "Horrible. Well, you know all about that. To be fair, some of the local officials wanted to help. Apparently they begged their Lordships at the Admiralty in London to give them shoes and stockings to distribute and for a small allowance to help them pay for clothes but they never got an answer.

"One doctor was charged with neglect. A priest told me that they decided there was no point trying to save lives when the plague struck, because so many were too weak to save, and they were all traitors anyway. And then there was the corruption. One of the so-called officials was caught falsifying the accounts and making a very handsome profit. He was removed, but the prisoners did not eat any better."

"And Southampton?" asked Jambo. "What of them?"

"Just as bad. They were imprisoned in a store that had been used as a powder magazine, and were thrown into the streets when a tsunami swept in from Portugal destroying everything in its way. Incredible—a once in a lifetime tragedy. They had to live outside for weeks. In winter, too. They were eventually allowed to work. Not using the skills that I have come to know you Acadians have, but to build a turnpike using picks, shovels, and bare hands to clear the way and level the road. Hard labor for such talented people. Many died where they stood."

The figures whirled through Jambo's mind. There were about 1,200 who had sailed from Virginia. According to De la Rochette, more than 400 had perished and many more would be ill and hungry. Which of their friends and relatives had survived? Who had died?

"The way you have been treated is a shame and a scandal," said the Frenchman. "The British are a disgrace to a civilized world. Luckily your people all know what is best for them now. They have placed themselves under the protection of the king. Wherever I went they cried, '*We are French and the king of France must decide our fate*'"

"You must understand," said Jambo. He still refused to be overwhelmed by the easy plausibility of the man, especially after Langton's contradictory claim about the reaction he had received in the other prison camps. "Our ambition is to return to our homes in Acadia. That is all that matters to us. Can France help achieve our goal? Commissioner Langton says he can arrange it. We don't know if we can trust him, but let me be frank, we cannot be sure of you."

"Remember," said Pierre, "Though we speak French, none of us have been to France. We are not French."

"My friends," said the envoy, spreading his plump be-ringed hands as if to surrender all responsibility. "You must decide. Delegate two representatives—perhaps you, Mr. LeBlanc and one other—and we shall go to London where you can meet the Duke de Nivernois himself. Ask him what you like. Get the answers you want, and that you deserve, and then you must accept the offer. Or reject it."

It took the French emissary, LeBlanc and Pierre five days to reach London, bumping and swaying along rutted, muddy highways, changing coaches and staying in public houses where, if challenged, they pretended to be representatives of Prussia, Britain's ally against Spain and France.

As the coach raced through the hurly burly of London, they gazed open-mouthed at the crowds, the beggars and dandies, the gentlemen on horseback, the ladies picking their way along muddy streets. Some of the streets were filthier than Liverpool, with gin houses and pawnbrokers and shops with broken windows that had been boarded up. Then they trotted through oases of elegance and wealth with magnificent houses that lined wide streets. At the end of one, a huge, white mansion filled their horizon.

"It's where the Queen lives," said De la Rochette. "Buckingham Palace. Not a patch on King Louis's court at Versailles."

The meeting did not take long. The Duke was a sharp-faced individual who was immaculately and expensively dressed. As Turney had said, he did peer at them through pince-nez as if they were tradesmen who had been mistakenly let in from the streets, but he was polite to the shabby visitors and made sure they were fed and rested before summoning them to his gracious study, lined with gilt edged mirrors and velvet seats, to insist that the welfare of King Louis' loyal servants was his sole purpose.

"Whatever is best for you," he said. "I will ensure shall be done."

Jambo watched his eyes as he talked. They were still, calculating. This was not a man who would feel any sentimental attachment to these servants unless it was to his advantage.

"Will France claim us as her subjects?" asked Jambo. "We want rights as citizens. It is not allowances we want—it is not in our nature to accept hand outs—what we need is work and decent pay."

"Will we get a home to live in?" asked Pierre. "With land. As we had in our country."

"As Monsieur De la Rochette has promised," added Jambo.

"My dear fellow citizens," said the Duke, shooting an irritated glance at his aide. "You say you do not want allowances, but nonetheless we will offer help to get you on your feet. There are parts of northern France near the ports where there is land going begging. Land that needs *your* skills. Monsieur De la Rochette has been telling me what fine farmers you were in your homeland. *Men of the earth.* It is just what Old France needs now. We will give you free food and tobacco for three months—just to get you settled—and we will give you livestock and farm implements. More, you will be exempted from taxes for fifty years. Fifty!"

He obviously expected them to be impressed by this display of largesse and apparent good will, but Jambo declared, "This is all very well as a temporary measure, but all we want is to return home—to Acadia."

As if there had been a signal from the Duke, De la Rochette stepped forward. The self-styled plenipotentiary said, "We understand your desire to return home. But, I have to tell you the hard truth. It will not happen. You have been lied to, but that is no surprise, the English and the truth are strangers. Here—" He held out a clutch of papers. "—I have some documents relating to the peace process.

"In Canada, which as you know was surrendered to the British with the unfortunate fall of Quebec, our commander, the Marquis de Vaudreuil, presented his British counterpart, the Baron Amherst, with 55 articles that had to be signed to finalize the peace treaty.

"Let me read: Article 39 asks that the French in Canada must not be deported to England or the English colonies. What does Amherst have to say about that? He writes in the margin, *Agreed, except as regards the Acadians.*

"Now here: Article 54 demands the guarantee of a safe return to officers, militiamen, and Acadian prisoners in New England to their respective countries. Again, the Lord Amherst writes, *Accepted; but with reservation to the Acadians.*"

"They hate us," said Jambo. "But I do not understand why, now that the war is over."

"My dear man," said De la Rochette airily. "This is not about Acadians. This is about power. The British are building an empire. They want North America for themselves, and quite simply they cannot have another nation, however small, within their borders. France would do the same."

Nivernois interrupted. "I do not think you understand how important you are to King Louis. Only this January, a few weeks ago, he refused to sign the armistice unless Amherst allowed you to return to Canada, or failing that, to France.

"But this is Amherst's reply," he continued with what LeBlanc felt was a note of satisfied vindication, '*No to Canada.*' But he yielded to the plea for you to return to France. So our offer is the only alternative for you. I am sure you will agree that we have done the best we can."

De la Rochette added, "Whatever your man Langton has been telling you in Liverpool is simply untrue. What he wants is for you to foreswear your religion, turn your back on your country, and work for him like slaves."

"There is no choice," said Jambo as he and Pierre made the journey back from London. "We have to accept the French offer."

On June 7, 1763, the exiles packed their possessions and prepared to leave the ghetto for the last time, and make the walk through the drab streets they had come along seven years before.

He paused for a few minutes in the graveyard with its scores of crosses and makeshift headstones. He put a little posy of wild flowers on his mother's grave, and straightened the cross on father's. Weeds had started to grow across the burial plots and puddles had formed where they had started to sink below the level of the ground. Soon they would disappear, over run by nature, and no doubt, by buildings. As he had so often, he sat by Marguerite's grave. It broke his heart to think he would be leaving her in this lonely yard and tears started to his eyes. But no. '*Remember,*' she had said. '*Be strong*'. He touched the earth where her heart would have been and limped out.

Agnes was waiting for him. She understood.

They were assembled on the quayside where Langton held a roll call. As the last refugee clambered up the gangplank on to the sloop L'Esturgeon, he shouted, "224 of them—that's the lot. "I wish you well," he said. "Though I know you have made the wrong choice."

He paused. "Maybe there will be more rabbits for you to snare." He looked hard at Pierre and then Jambo. "Ones that the foxes won't eat."

They held his gaze.

"Take them away." He spurred his horse off the quayside, his heron neck stretching out as if in search of fresh prey.

"Just think," said Jambo. "There were 366 of us when we arrived. We have left more than 100 crosses behind."

Agnes said, "Have you not noticed how many children there are? Look at them running around the deck playing. There were forty births in that ghetto. Forty new lives, forty new Acadians."

"You are right, it is a kind of miracle," he said.

"I have another miracle for you," she said. "I am pregnant."

Book Three

TWENTY-TWO

Morlaix, Brittany, France

June, 1763

New Hope Betrayed

His feet had barely touched the cobbles of the quay when a voice shouted, "Jambo! B-b-rother!"

It was Charles. The two men fell into each other's arms in an embrace so tight it was as if they were trying to exorcize the pain of their years apart.

"Alive. You are alive!"

"And k-k-kicking.".

"Who would have thought we would see each other again. I felt sure we would die in our British prisons."

"Well, h-h-here we are."

They embraced again. Then, embarrassed by such an extravagant show of emotion, they slapped each other on the back and then held each other by the arms.

"Welcome to France and f-f-freedom."

"Free," said Jambo. "Free of the British. Free to go where we want and do what we please."

What lightness of heart he and Agnes had had felt the moment L'Esturgeon had sailed away and out of the sight of Liverpool. The pall of smoke and misery that had hung over their lives faded into a dirty smudge on the horizon and disappeared forever. For the first time in almost eight years they felt optimistic. They were going to a country that wanted them, with people who would be friendly, help them find work, build homes, and settle. Who could tell, as the animosity of war faded, they might find a way back from France to their homeland.

"Whatever this Morlaix place is like it will never replace Acadia, but at least we can live peaceably without fear of soldiers or bitter citizens," Jambo said, holding Agnes around the waist. He could feel the baby growing already. Couldn't he?

"We'll never go hungry again," said Agnes. "The children will be properly fed, they will have new clothes, and be able to play without walls to hem then in." She became increasingly animated. "Imagine, for the first time in almost eight years they will live in a home of their own, be able to go to a proper school, learn to read and write, and be happy."

Her eagerness was almost as childlike as her two young charges, who were dashing about the deck with unfettered joy, their pale cheeks burnished with the June sun.

The French coast came close and the ship sailed past a huge fortress built out in the sea.

"To stop the British invading," said Oliver. "According to the first mate they tried two hundred years ago."

"And will no doubt try again," said Pierre.

Then, with most sails furled and buoyed by a racing tide, the ship glided swiftly along a deep valley with woods rising on either side.

"My goodness, it's busy," said Agnes as they bumped gently against a wharf.

It was as if the whole town had come to greet them. A huge French tricolor hung from the town hall. In front were scores of exiles, a crowd of faces that he had not seen since the day they were expelled, shouting greetings, calling out names, and waving. Where had they been? Had they suffered as they had?

Who would be missing?

The two brothers, arm in arm, were interrupted by one refugee after another. First Pierre Terriot, then old Germain Dupuy who tore him out of his brother's grasp to ask, "How is your father? And Rene?" He took one glance at the carpenter's face and muttered, "I'm sorry," and squeezed him consolingly on the shoulder. Here was Francois Aucoin, his cousin Joseph, and Olivier Boudrot. "Hey Jambo," Oliver shouted. "Heard from those brothers of yours? Claude still owes me for a pig I sold him in '55!"

Questions were swiftly followed by a look—not so much of embarrassment at the inevitable answer, but of understanding. After all, they had all endured the same calamities and knew there would be mothers, fathers, and children lost at sea, wiped out by the pox, or taken by exhaustion and hunger. Explanations were not necessary.

Charles drew him to him one side, away from the crowds. "Well," he said, making no attempt to hide the tears that streamed down his face now that they were out of the public gaze and he no longer felt he had to put on a show. "You look b-b-better than you should. I like the grey b-b-beard. But your hand?"

"An over zealous British sailor. I will tell you all. But you brother, you look like no worse than if you were recovering from a long night in the tavern."

He was thinner, true, and his face was deeply pitted with pockmarks, his cheeks rimmed with stubble, but even now Jambo could not help noticing the softness of his muscles. Clearly prison had failed to toughen him up, and—how strange, how familiar—he still had the smell of drink and tobacco about him. And his eyes; they still had that old gleam of mischief.

"I had a bout with the pox—makes me look a little distinguished, don't you think? But I was lucky, and I found the best way to get through was to l-l-laugh it off. What will be will be, as father used to say. Yes, I suppose I have to say I was b-b-blessed." His eyes clouded again as if he had not altogether convinced even his optimistic self.

"So you have not heard about mother and father?" Said the younger brother.

"Don't s-s-say…"

"Mother died in the plague—she had become so weak and unhappy—she missed you and our brothers so much it was as if she lost enough reason to live. I honestly believe if the pox had not killed her she would have faded away from the way she neglected herself. She didn't eat. She didn't care. And father, well, it was as if he too gave up once she had gone," said Jambo. "He drifted around the ghetto aimlessly, forgetting where he was and what he was doing."

"Dear mother," said Charles. "I cannot bear to think of her going like that, she was such a f-f-fighter. But our brothers, what of them?"

"I have heard nothing. They were not in England, I'm sure."

"Maybe they t-t-too have perished." He hesitated. "You heard about m-m-my Anne? Did you get my letter?

Jambo said, "I did, but only one year later. We mourned for you, and I did write back many times, but I fear the British postal service was not reliable. How have you managed without her? The children?"

"The l-l-little ones are well. They are here, somewhere. But, my g-g-goodness, who is this?"

He made great play of pretending not to recognize Jean-Baptiste who had run up to him and thrown himself into the arms of his favorite uncle.

"My, how you have g-g-grown. Jean-B! You must be, let me think, ten years old"

"Eleven. Eleven and three months," said the boy.

"Almost a man," said his uncle, and he gave him a mock salute.

He looked expectantly beyond Jambo, ignoring Agnes who stood patiently to one side.

"Where is M-m-marguerite?"

"She is dead. I lost her six years ago. Almost to the day."

"Brother, I had no idea, though so many of us have gone I might have g-g-guessed. How sad. I am sorry." Recovering himself, "But how f-ffortunate we are. You and I. Still alive, still with hope. Some, at l-l-least."

"You are right," said Jambo. "I thought there would be no more joy for me. In truth, I too gave up. But, even in the depths there can be a rebirth. Here is my wife—Agnes."

Charles looked blankly at her.

"You must remember her. Agnes Hebert. We have been married now for five years."

"My goodness. Jean's daughter, and the niece of Francois Hebert, if I am not mistaken. Let me look at you. I'm s-s-sorry, I didn't recognize you. How l-l-lucky you were not to inherit your uncle's looks."

"Or his temper." She laughed.

"I too have an an-n-nouncement," said Charles. "Jambo, Agnes, Jean-Baptiste, and you too little Osite—though not so little now are you,? Quite the sweet heart—I thought there would never be anyone to r-r-replace my Anne, but this is M-m-madeleine. She is the daughter of Pierre and Marie-Joseph Gautrot—they had the farm with all the d-d-ducks down by the river, remember? Her husband was taken by the plague. We m-m-married in '60."

A thin, rather severe woman, her greying hair pulled tight back over a forehead lined with worries, stepped forward and gave a polite bow.

"Madeleine, of course. The Gautrots, how well I remember you all." Jambo was flustered. "How happy I am for you. For both of you."

It was a difficult moment, both embarrassing and poignant. An image of his wedding to Marguerite flashed into Jambo's mind. He could see Charles cheering them on as they carried out that silly tradition of jumping the broomstick. '*Come on, higher, higher.*' he had exhorted. '*The higher you jump the longer you'll be married and the more children you'll have.*'

What was Charles thinking of his younger brother now? He could tell from the furrow that briefly creased his brother's brow that he had been taken aback. Without saying a word, he was asking; had his younger brother made the right choice? And Jambo, too, was finding it hard to imagine Charles without his beloved Anne. Could he love Madeleine as much? Maybe he did not have to. Maybe the important thing was not love—not the impetuous, daily reawakening of that shivering passion that he and Marguerite had enjoyed—but something that was both prosaic, yet more daunting; duty.

They had to care for each other, to share the challenges and unite against their enemies. But more, underlying everything, they had to meet the atavistic, undeniable need to have the children that would become the next generation of Acadians, the ones who would eventually replace the scores who had died before their time.

As for the women standing on the quay that warm summer's day, they both understood how different their lives would have been if they had not been touched by tragedy.

Agnes said, "I remember the ducks. When I was little, me and my friends took their eggs and threw them in the air to see how high they could go without breaking when they hit the ground."

She laughed nervously.

"We thought you had told your father, because he came rampaging to all our parents' houses to complain. My papa was so angry he locked me away with no food for 24 hours".

"What a tell-tale I was." The older woman smiled, her face softened, her worry lines receded. She looked almost pretty, thought Jambo.

"I have been so lucky," said Madeleine. "I don't suppose you knew my first husband, but we had three children in quick succession so I have them to remember him by.

"And then Charles came to my rescue. He made me laugh again. "She smiled, recalling the jokes and the songs and tall tales that had won her over.

"As for you, cousin Agnes I seem to recall you were a pretty little thing who seemed always to be surrounded by the village's eligible men."

They both laughed at that and the two brothers stopped their own reminiscences to watch with pleasure, and relief, as Madeleine took the younger woman's hand in a gesture that was as much of understanding as friendship.

"Agnes is expecting," said Jambo.

"Congratulations my dear," said Madeleine. "I, too, have another on the way."

"That will be our third?" asked Charles. "All under four. What with the others, that's quite a h-h-handful." Charles smirked as his younger brother hit him on the back with a complimentary thump.

"Well, you have been busy," he said.

"I am doing my best to keep the flame b-b-burning," he said. "As one Acadian dies, another is born." He put his arm around his younger brother's shoulders and grabbed one of their hold-alls. "Now, we had better get you to our quarters as soon as p-p-possible. We are in barracks until they find us better homes. At least, that's what we are told. The ones who came here from Louisbourg after the expulsion of '58 are constantly grumbling at their plight, but then they didn't have six years in English c-c-concentration camps to compare it with."

"After Liverpool, this is paradise," said Jambo, puffing a little as they climbed one of the steep hills that rose from the port and protected it from the storms of the Atlantic. "Fresh air! My lungs don't know what to make of this. Blue sky. Clean sea. Even the way the tide races in reminds me of the Bay of Fundy."

The barracks were tidy and dry, and the French commissioner promptly doled out their allowance of six sous a day, and dished up the free food and tobacco they had been promised.

"We will soon find employment for you," he said. "And we want you to sign the children up for lessons."

The brothers sat outside their new home, looking down on the bustle in the harbor, smoking the strong local tobacco, and recounting their experiences since they were separated in the bay off Williamsburg six years before. Their children played with each other as if they had known each other all their lives.

Charles strummed a lute.

"Where on earth did you get that?" wondered Jambo. "Surely you didn't carry it all the way. No, I know you didn't."

"It was left hidden in the Bristol prison," said his brother. "It had been used for Spanish prisoners of war. One of them must have smuggled it in. Remember the last time we played?"

Of course he did. That night in the tavern during that noisy party Charles held just before they were expelled. How could he forget.

But he was rattling on. "There must be a thousand or so of us here. Most of the Southampton and Bristol p-p-prisoners were sent to St. Malo, which is not far, just along the coast. We only arrived last month, about the same time as the Falmouth contingent. There's Simon Granger, remember him?"

How could he forget? Marguerite had led him to believe she had rather liked the young Granger before they had started courting—though later she admitted she was playing a game to quicken his pursuit of her. Granger greeted the new arrival with an embarrassed shake of the hand.

"I am sorry to hear about Marguerite," he mumbled.

"Thank you." Neither man could think of anything else to say.

Charles jumped in. "Meet M-m-michel. He has a story to tell."

They were joined by Michel Comeau, a survivor of the 1758 expulsion, the news of which with the sinking of the prison ships had so shocked them in Liverpool. He explained how he and his family had fled Grand-Pré the night before the fateful meeting in the church.

"When that notice went up—we were all gathered round, remember? —and your Uncle Rene was telling us how badly things could go, so I decided it was time to get out even though Charles wanted us to drink our worries away in that tavern of his. The British had a few soldiers keeping guard, but they weren't expecting anyone to make a flit and spent most of the time in their encampment.

"We hid in a barn on the edge of the village—you know, the one near the saw mill that belonged to the Melancon brothers—waited until one patrol came past, and ran as fast as we could into the forest and away. Our plan was to get to Prince Edward Island where my wife had family, but there were so many soldiers around that we ended up in Cape Breton. Still, we thought we would be safe there.

"The fortress at Louisbourg was new and well equipped. *Impregnable,* the French reckoned. Surely there could be no threat from the British. But in the summer of '58, they sailed into the bay with a huge fleet. We counted about 150 transport ships and 40 men-of-war. Later we found out that there were 14,000 soldiers on board."

"We did hear accounts of it," said Jambo, but the newcomer was in full spate.

"What a battle. The French hit 'em hard from the battlements with cannon shot. Should have seen the landing boats capsizing and breaking into pieces. The water was full of dead British soldiers, but their warships blasted back, and then it was the French whose bodies were filling the bay." He shivered. "The waves were pink with blood. They left a bloody line on the shore where high tide reached. The British waited until one of those thick sea fogs came down, crept around the headland and tore the town apart. There was nothing for it. The French surrendered. Even then we thought that if we laid low we would be allowed stay on, but we underestimated the British."

Another man, who Jambo dimly recalled used to have a smallholding just off the road to Halifax, broke in. "Nothing stands in their way, does it? They needed Louisbourg to protect their fleet when it sailed on Quebec, though we did not know that then."

"*We're neutral,*" we told them," continued Comeau, slightly put out at being interrupted. "French, British, we support neither."

"Did no good," said the second speaker. "They rounded everyone up, as many as 6,000 of us. '*Here you are,*' they said, as if doing us a favor, '*Ships to take you to your homeland where you belong. France will welcome you with open arms.*'

"Well, winter was coming on and we did not think for a moment they would make us set sail," said Michel. "God, what a crossing. The biggest ship was the King William, but it had no chance in seas like that. We saw it go down. Just like that. Toppled over by a wave as high as the cliffs of Blomidon and sucked down in a flash. But we were lucky."

"Our ship was blown miles off course," said the other, as if determined to show he had suffered just as much survivor. "To some islands called the Azores. We lost 100 of our cousins."

"You have had a time of it," said Jambo, wondering if the pair would ask him about his own misfortunes. Perhaps the years of adversity had made them all more preoccupied with their own predicament.

Granger said, "Did you hear about the priest, an Acadian priest, on the Prince William who jumped into a lifeboat to escape with the sailors?"

"Yes, the captain's account was in a journal," said Jambo.

"But do you know what happened when he turned up in Falmouth to take communion? We turned our backs on him. Ostracized the coward completely. He became crazed with guilt and took to standing in the square preaching for hours on end about the need to forgive our enemies, but no one paid any heed to him. Then he disappeared. His body was found hanging from a barn way out in the country one year later."

"Fear makes cowards of us all," said Pierre.

"And heroes," said Jambo. "It has only been our determination that has brought so many to this happy home."

Charles said, "Now that the war is over, we should be hearing more about those who did survive. Bad enough that the British censored our l-l-letters, but who knows how many they t-t-tore up?"

"All I have heard from the colonies is of Uncle Rene who was in New York," continued Jambo, who described the bizarre meeting with the Melancon brothers and Lajeunesse in Virginia. "But that was seven years ago."

"We heard that too," said Charles. "He then persuaded the authorities to send him to Philadelphia where he and his wife, M-m-arguerite, were reunited with three more children, but it ended badly—he died there."

"He would have been 73," said Jambo. "I thought he would have lived much longer."

"The extraordinary thing was that some of the Acadians in the city actually sent a p-p-petition directly to King George about the way he had been treated," said Charles. "They said it was a c-c-common calamity—that's what they called it—and regretted he had d-d-died without any more notice being taken of him for his many years' labor and d-d-deep sufferings for His Majesty's service."

"The British never did understand that we were not their enemies," said Jambo. "Least of all Rene. He did so much work for them. They could not grasp that, by staying neutral and using our skills, we would have made Acadia even more prosperous. For them as well as us."

"We shall not see his l-l-like again."

"I'm not so sure. He had 150 grandchildren. One of them will raise the old man's standard in the years to come."

Morlaix was a busy port with quaint, narrow streets of timbered houses and overhanging eaves.

"Cozy," said Agnes.

"Cramped," Jambo grumbled. "Not enough room to breathe."

Until the refugees had flooded in, its citizens had been content and busy, manufacturing sailcloth, cotton, paper, and leather. There was even a small tobacco factory.

"But," said Simon Granger, interrupting Jambo when he was enthusing about starting out as a carpenter again and earning good money. "The town has declined with the war. Now there is hardly enough work for the locals, and they are already beginning to resent us incomers. They say we are a threat to what little labor there is."

"That sounds familiar," said LeBlanc.

"You won't find a thing here," survivors of the Louisbourg expulsion would tell him with depressing certainty. "We've been here for five years now, do we look like people who are flourishing? Have you seen any of us actually with a job? And those barracks—a temporary home? Don't make me laugh."

"But we were promised work, homes, money," said Jambo.

And, as if in a chorus, they would reply, "And you believed them? All you will do is join us begging in the streets, shivering around open fires, and trying to feed a family with one bowl of soup a day."

"They're right, there is less opportunity here than Liverpool," said Oliver after three weeks tramping the quayside with his repair kit. "So far, my total is precisely two jobs, and one was a pair of sandals so broken it would have been cheaper to buy him a new pair."

Simon Granger said, "It might seem strange, but by the end many of us did not want to leave Falmouth. It had been a nightmare at the beginning, locked away in an old barn that had been used as a prison camp in some other war. The damp, the dirt—well, I am sure it was the same for you."

"It was," said Pierre. "You begin to think starvation is normal."

Granger went on. "We hated the British because of the way they treated our dead. Did you hear about that?"

"We did, cousin," said Oliver. "The shame of it."

"I will never be able to rid myself of the sight of bodies piled on each other. People we knew, many we loved, dumped in ugly, tangled heaps. But then a strange thing happened—we became haunted by that grave. It kept such a hold on us that when it came to leaving, we felt as if it would be disrespectful to abandon the dead there with no one to care for them or remember them."

He shook his head. "And the British changed too. Maybe they felt some pity for us, because after a few years they let us lodge in the houses of shop owners and farmers. Some of us were given apprenticeships as carpenters and stonemasons, some worked in the port, others in the fields. The women were making a decent living by selling sheets and mending clothes.

"In a way, Falmouth was similar to Grand-Pré. They farmed and fished just like us, and we found we had much in common, more than we had with that De la Rochette character who we did not trust one little bit."

"Couldn't agree more," said Jambo. "But he told us how enthusiastic you were to leave for France."

"Far from it," said Granger.

"That cheat," said Francois.

"Rather than join him and come here, two of my brothers escaped to the countryside because they liked it so much there," said Granger. "One of them had even fallen for a local girl."

"I don't blame them," said Pierre. "I am well pleased to be away from England, but this is not the land of milk and honey we were promised. I don't see much demand for a trapper in these cobbled streets."

Francois said, "I have walked ten miles into the countryside on every lane every day this last month to see if anyone needed a plowman. Nothing."

"They have to find something for us," said Jambo. "That was what Nivernois pledged."

Granger said, "I think we will find that the *something* is not here in Morlaix. The Duke and his cronies have already come up with plans that will take us further afield. I have visited an island two day's sail away that they have in mind for us to settle, and there is talk of transporting us to far-flung territories. I fear we shall be on the move again."

Oliver called by to say, "There is a meeting in the town hall tonight. It's about jobs and new homes."

"Well, thank God for that," said Jambo. "Progress at last."

"But guess what?" said the cobbler, bobbing from one neatly-shod foot to another with his usual delight at being first with the news. "It is being held by the Abbot Jean-Louis Le Loutre, no less."

"Le Loutre," Jambo was amazed. "I thought he must have been long dead."

"He's trouble," said Francois.

"The man might be a priest, but, frankly, he's a lunatic," said Jambo.

"He came to St. Charles once to give a sermon. I've never seen anyone be so excitable. He's a fanatic. Always stirring up trouble."

"Wasn't he the one who persuaded our cousins to join the Indians and fight the British at Beausejour in '55?" asked Pierre.

"I heard he actually paid for the scalps of any B-b-british soldiers that his Indian allies took prisoner," said Charles.

"Remember how he escaped when the siege collapsed, dressed as a woman? Almost got away with it, but they caught him and stuck him in prison on the island of Jersey," said Oliver. "Just over there," he added, waving vaguely out to sea.

"Should we listen to a ranter like that?" asked Francois.

"The Duke de Nivernois will be there too," said Oliver.

"Our noble friend. Be interesting to hear what he has to say this time," said Jambo.

They gathered in the town hall. On a stage sat Le Loutre, as jumpy and tense as de Nivernois was calm, nerveless and effortlessly superior, occasionally eyeing the ragged crew before him through his pince-nez. The priest insisted on prayers. He gave thanks for their salvation, he drew down curses on their enemies, and he besought God's blessings on all their projects.

"I was born here, in this very town, 54 years ago. All my life I have fought for truth and justice, and today I pledge to do everything I can to bring peace and prosperity to you outcasts." His eyes blazed in his broad forehead, his mouth worked and revealed alarming yellow teeth. His arms were flailing so wildly that at one point Jambo thought he would fall off the dais.

Agnes whispered, "Is this the man to lead us to a promised land?"

"Well, the British did call him The French Moses." Oliver chuckled.

"I'm sure he is sincere," said Pierre

"That's what worries me," said Oliver.

Nivernois looked on, amused and cynical, until Le Loutre had finished and addressed the crowd with a kind of weary forbearance, as if greeting home runaway children. "My dear Acadians, fellow citizens of

France," he said. "Welcome to your *true* homeland. As I undertook when some of us met in London, we have plans to find you homes and steady work with the rewards you deserve. As you have probably seen already in your short sojourn here—"

"Get on with it," muttered Francois, just loud enough to earn a stare of reproof from the abbot.

"—this beautiful city of Morlaix is not big enough to assimilate you all. But with such a mighty empire as ours, there are many opportunities to be had abroad."

"Are you sending us home to Acadia?" shouted someone from the back of the hall to cheers and a chorus of '*Hear, hear.*'

"Because that is all we want."

"That, of course, is not possible," continued the Duke smoothly. "But we have fine new territories in Guyana and Haiti in the West Indies. They are crying out for skilled workers. New ports have to be built, fortifications erected, and most important, the possibilities for farmers such as yourselves are limitless. There are cocoa plantations that need to be planted, coffee, and sugar to be grown. These are projects that will take years to develop, and will guarantee a living for you and the generations to come."

"Cocoa," said Francois dismissively. "We plow fields, we grow wheat."

"What we understand is sheep and cattle," said Jambo.

"We are trappers and fishermen," said Pierre. "What do we know about coffee?"

"We can build levees to prevent the sea flooding our lands, but we are a peaceable race, we know nothing of building forts," said Jambo.

"And the c-c-climate?" asked Charles. "I imagine it to be unbearably hot."

"Warm and delightful," said the Duke. "You will never need to wear an outer garment."

"We had a taste of that in Virginia," said Jambo. "We were sick most of the time. We Acadians like the pure air of the north. If we were to settle in your southern territories, we would lose more than half of our people through some kind of pox, I am sure of that."

"Well, my friends," said Nivernois. "Think about it. The Indies are full of riches for young men with ambition, and we are looking for volunteers. But hurry now, because many adventurers from other countries are eager to join these great enterprises. You can become masters of a new world with wealth beyond your dreams. It is your decision."

Instead of the enthusiastic reception he clearly expected, the Acadians stayed silent.

"Empty phrases," said Pierre.

Then LeBlanc got to his feet.

"You may remember we met in London earlier this year," he said.

The grandee looked at him though his pince-nez. He showed no sign of recognizing the carpenter.

"We agreed to come here—reluctantly it must be said—in the hope of rebuilding our lost country, of creating a new Acadia in what we thought, indeed what we were told, was a friendly country. We do not ask for much. Give us some land, tools, seeds, perhaps a few cows and we will do the rest. We are men of the land, we know what we are doing. Your investment will be repaid within months."

He paused and stared steadily at the men on the dais. "Do not fob us off with vague promises of 'limitless opportunities' in alien lands."

There were cheers at that but Nivernois, clearly irritated at such obduracy, got his feet, snapping shut his pince nez and swept out of the hall to his waiting chaise.

In that first summer they waited in vain to be moved into the new homes they had been promised. They searched without luck for work, and every day became hungrier, while the clothes they had been given when they first arrived soon fell apart at the seams, keeping the women busy with their needles. There was nothing for it. Agnes and the children joined the other women begging on the quayside and outside the factories while, Jambo limped from house to house asking for odd jobs.

"Oliver was right. There was more work in Liverpool," said the carpenter as he and Agnes waited for another meeting in the town hall where they had been summoned to hear of a scheme that *'all would want to join.'*

This time a businessman called Antoine de Bougainville had a scheme to settle some islands called the Falklands far south in the Atlantic.

None of the listeners had heard of Bourgainville let alone the Falklands, but the way the Parisian described them they were a very heaven.

"The climate is cool, which will be to your liking," he said. "The countryside is green and beautiful, and the farmland rich. Furthermore, the seas are filled with enough fish to fill every Frenchman's stomach for a year. Do not delay. I have two ships arriving in the port within the month. Who will be on them?"

To Jambo's surprise, about 20 hands went up.

"They must be mad," said Francois.

"Surely we have all had enough of life on board without embarking on another nightmare voyage across the world," said Jambo.

"He is just in this for the money," said Oliver. "All he is looking for is cheap labor and a quick profit."

"How do we know there are farms and fish?" demanded Pierre. "None of us have heard of the place. What guarantee is there?"

Granger said, "These schemes are two a penny. Any greedy bastard who wants to make a fortune finds a willing patron like that Nivernois character who greases a few palms, and persuades the government to give them a license. They dazzle us with a vision of Utopia, but once they get us there, pay the absolute minimum—if that—and pocket the profit. They make a mint."

"What is the alternative?" asked Pierre when they met outside the barracks for an evening drink and smoke.

"Nothing," said Francois, who by now claimed to have walked every byway in Brittany in search of work and had become increasingly morose and introverted.

"I tried to set a trap in what I thought was common land, but was chased off," said Pierre.

"All I have managed has been one day working on new decking for one of the Falkland transports," said Jambo.

"Sometimes it seems there are more of us begging than there are people living here," said Agnes.

"No wonder they haven't welcomed us," said Jambo. "Remember how we resented those Germans and Scots when they arrived in Halifax. The locals here must think we are like leeches."

Within months of their landing, the pretence that they would be moved from the barracks and resettled was abandoned. For some of the older exiles, the realization that they had been persuaded to exchange one miserable existence for another proved unbearable, and they simply gave up and slipped away to an early death. Newborn babies were greeted by their parents with joy and with despair—another mouth to feed, another little soul that would most likely starve and be buried long before its time.

Even an official in Nivernois' bureau admitted to Le Loutre that the Canadians, as he called them, *'languish in the most frightful misery.'*

"He understands," said Le Loutre. "I understand. You are burdened with debts and without means to subsist. He asks me to pass on the sadness he feels to see you perish from hunger without being able to provide any relief for you here."

"That's all right then. At least he feels *'sorry'* for us," said Oliver sarcastically.

"It's not sympathy we need, but action," said Francois. "The bastards have let us down.

"We have been b-b-betrayed," said Charles.

"There is no point of staying here if there is no help for us," said Pierre. More and more of them were volunteering for the schemes that

Le Loutre suggested, even though they believed they would end in disappointment.

"I have heard that another 90 signed up to go to this Falklands place," said Jambo. "And more than 1,000 have agreed to sail to Guyana."

"They're d-d-doomed," said Charles.

"They are desperate," said Jambo. "But then, aren't we all?"

"The truth is, the future is so bright for us Acadians," exhorted Le Loutre at one of his regular meetings. "So many opportunities. With God's blessing, the King has located 20 different places across the empire for you to start anew. They must be seized before they are granted to others. I urge you to consider the island of Corsica in the Mediterranean. It is rich and warm. An *enviable* place.

"Then there are the moors around the seaside provinces of Guyenne and Gascony to the south that need clearing. With government aid you could establish yourselves there—they may be wastelands now, but with your skills you could build your own homes and harness the land for farming. Maybe you could even build ports and establish trade with the West Indies. You could become prosperous."

The crowd stared at him—contempt mixed with indifference.

"I have heard Corsica is as granitey as a grave," said Pierre.

"As for Gascony, it is a marsh, a soggy mess with as many mosquitoes to bite you in one day as they would in a year in Grand-Pré," said Granger who seemed well informed about Le Loutre's *opportunities.*

Nivernois visited again, and this time he was accompanied by an even grander personage, the Duke de Choiseul, who had been France's foreign minister until falling from grace at the end of their disastrous war.

"My fellow Frenchmen, my *dear* Acadians," declared Nivernois.

Francois looked as if he would leap on the stage and throttle the silkily elegant grandee. "Fellow Frenchmen. Pah."

"I would like to introduce one of our country's greatest men—the Duke de Choiseul."

"Isn't he the one who is what we might call over-friendly with the King's mistress?" whispered Oliver. "Madame de Pompadour."

"The royal strumpet," said Francois, making an obscene gesture with his hand.

"Sssh, uncle," chided Agnes. "Behave."

"It's true though," said Charles. "It's common knowledge that King has one m-m-mistress after another. He spends all his nights and most of the days in b-b-bed with some whore or another."

"And his spare time fighting wars that he always loses," added Pierre.

Choiseul nodded graciously and rose to his feet with an air of majestic self-importance. "My friends, cousins, I have come all this way from Paris, where I have completed peace negotiations that have been more beneficial to France than could have been hoped for. Now we look to the future, a future in which you can and *must* play a part. I exhort you to join our great and patriotic cause in rebuilding our empire in the West Indies. I cannot stress what tremendous possibilities there are. These are havens to be happy—a brave new world for you who have endured so much. The King wills it, and so do I. Volunteer now and you will not regret it."

This time there was a smattering of applause, and while some stepped forward to take the papers of enrolment, most scornfully left the hall.

"They are exploiting our weakness," said Pierre. "We must stay united against their persuasion."

"We cannot join these bastards," said Francois.

"Little chance of that," said Jambo.

"I have another proposition to make to you," announced Nivernois a few months later. "Sardines. I happen to own a small island off the Brittany coast called Bouin. It is, from what the good abbot has told me, a smaller version of Prince Edward Island. The climate is similar, and within a few years, fishing could become the biggest industry in the area. The King himself has approved the scheme."

"I can imagine the King settling down to a banquet of sardines," observed Oliver, "Nicely arranged on his silver platters."

"And fed to him by *one* of his l-l-lady friends," said Charles.

"Not so much a Lady of the Bed Chamber but Mistress of the Sardines." Oliver twinkled with amusement at his own wit.

It was more than sardines that Choiseul, Nivernois, and their cronies sat down to at the feasts organized by the mayor when they came calling with their latest schemes. Jambo recalled the mouth-watering anticipation he had as a child when mother would make him wait before she treated him to cinnamon rolls as he peered through misting windows at the procession of soups and stews, mounds of vegetables, boiled fish, and meats arranged around a grand centerpiece of peacock pie and suckling pig.

"Look at that," said Oliver as the servants brought in replicas of castles and pastoral scenes of windmills on green icing fields surrounded by sugared fruits, sweetmeats, jams, jellies, and creams.

"Greedy boot-licking bastards." Francois was beside himself, kicking at the wheels of a carriage until a whack across the shoulders from a guard sent him on his way.

"We must be a great disappointment to them," said Pierre. "If we don't join their schemes and help them make them more money, they won't be able to afford to live in such luxurious ease for much longer."

"You know what it says in the Bible about the rich man and the eye of the needle," said Le Loutre to the irritation of his hungry flock. "I believe we shall prosper eventually. I have another scheme," he went on. "This, I believe, will be the place where we can, *at last,* build a new Acadia."

"Another one," spat Francois. "Spare us."

"The Duke has won special permission to let you settle on Belle-Ile-sur-Mer, just a little way off the coast to the south of here."

Before he could continue, he was interrupted by Simon Granger, "Let me tell you about this Belle-Isle. This plan was suggested last year when we first arrived, and as heads of our families Honore Le Blanc, Joseph Trahan and

I were taken to look over it. Frankly, your reverend, I assumed the idea had gone away.

"This is the scheme I have mentioned to some of you before. At first it seemed ideal—meadows that were waiting the cut of the plow, fishing, plump cattle. We met the governor of the island who was most welcoming. He could not wait for us to settle."

"That's a bad sign," said Francois.

"But then we learnt that the island is more exposed to foreign attacks than *any* other place in France. It has been conquered by many countries, including the British who took it only two years ago. Just because it is in French hands again does not make it safe. The British could recapture it and we would be back in one of their detention centers.

"We were there in the summer, but even then the wind threatened to flatten the place—gales the like of which we never had in Grand-Pré—and when we stuck a spade in the ground we realized that the soil was flinty and barren, so different from the rich lands of our homeland. It is just not suited to the way we farm."

"And," said Trahan, "we were there only for a few days, but the locals made it very clear that we were not welcome. Some of them had just returned to the island after fleeing from the British and saw us as another bunch of troublesome foreigners coming to interfere with their livelihoods."

"Wherever we go, we are the enemy," said Agnes.

"Furthermore," said Granger, "The food is disgusting. We would have to eat fish and drink cider instead of the milk and bread we are used to."

"I quite l-l-like the cider," said Charles later, and Jambo had to admit that any regular food would be better than the gnawing ache of hunger they had become used to.

"It's another plot to get rid of us," said Francois. "What was it that your uncle Rene called it?"

"The destruction of a people," said Jambo.

"Exactly," said the plowman. "Clear us away—anywhere as long as we are out of sight."

"And out of m-m-mind," said Charles.

"The truth is," said Jambo, "with Agnes about to give birth, we cannot go anywhere. I don't see that we have any choice but to stay in Morlaix. There may be work preparing the ships that arrived last week to transport the volunteers to Guyana."

For a few weeks his skills were called on to help refit the holds so that they could carry as many of the emigrants as possible.

Almost as bad as our prison transports, he thought. *Still, I am being paid.* He jingled the few sous in his pocket as he strode up the hill to the barracks. The ships were ready to sail the following morning, and the port was overflowing with desperate volunteers waiting to embark. *They look worn out already,* he thought, and was amazed to discover that many of them had walked for weeks across the continent from as far away as Germany to join the expedition.

Three young men blocked his way.

"Fucking Canadian parasite," said one.

"Foreign bastard boat-licker," said another.

"Good evening," said Jambo, so taken aback at the language he could not muster an adequate reply. They loomed toward him.

"Your money. Give it here."

"Even if I had any, I would not let you have even a sight of it," he said levelly, wishing his hand was strong enough to let him fight with two fists.

"You owe us," said one, pulling out a hammer from his jerkin.

"I can't see why. I don't know you."

"You're taking our jobs," said the first.

The third man pointed an iron bar at him. "We are starving, yet you foreign scroungers get an allowance."

"It is not fair. We deserve our share," said the man with the hammer.

They had the same feral despair as the two men they had killed in Liverpool, but these were armed with iron bars and he was alone. They came close, one of them pushing his face right up to Jambo. He stank of drink and dirt, greasy hair pulled back in a pony tail, his eyes red with hate. Could he kick him in the groin and hit the other before the iron bars came crashing down? In the second before he could decide what to do, a figure erupted out of the dusk, roaring and cussing.

It was Francois. He shoved the leader away from Jambo and punched him smartly in the face. His hammer fell to the ground. The carpenter picked it up and struck his accomplice across the knees. That was enough. They fled, one limping so badly that Francois caught up with him and kicked him down the hill.

"My God, Francois. You saved me. Thank you, my dear fellow. But what you doing here?"

The plowman looked shame-faced, almost shifty. Irascible, he certainly was, but he was an honest fellow and could never dissemble. He tried to hide a sack he had with him by pushing it behind a wall with his foot.

"You are leaving us. Guyana."

"I couldn't tell you, cousin," he said. "There is no hope here for me. How many acres of meadow are there to plow? None. I have begged for work at every farm in the district and beyond. Nothing. I have no family. There is no reason to stay."

"But there is *every* reason," said Jambo. "You cannot leave now, not after all we have been through. We owe it to each other to stay together. Look what we have shared."

"Death and misery," said Francois.

"Yes, but we have survived. You and I, Pierre, Oliver, all of us are part of a story that is still being written. These are your friends, Francois, comrades who you have battled alongside for years. And then there is your niece, my Agnes, who is about to make you a great uncle. That's another chapter you cannot miss."

"I know. I shall never have friends like you and Pierre. And having Charles back with us is a tonic. As for little Agnes, I am overjoyed for both of you, but I have to go. There are 12 ships waiting to take us, and I hear the number ready to sail has risen to as many as 1,700. I have no great hopes of the venture, my friend, but think it is the best chance. Can it be worse than this? Than Liverpool? Virginia?"

Jambo's throat constricted with the sorrow at losing his old companion. "I hope not my friend. God be with you. Good luck."

They embraced and the plowman slipped out of sight toward the port and whatever destiny the morning tide would bring him.

They named the baby Pierre-Etienne. When he arrived they were happy with this confirmation of their love, but that brief moment was soon overwhelmed by the reality of having another mouth to feed without the means to fill it.

Le Loutre christened the child in the barracks chapel, and as he held him Jambo said, "We were told, '*You will never starve again, you have the full protection of France*,' but all we have been offered is the chance of an early grave in a tropical hell hole, or catching sardines for King Louis. What future does this infant have?"

Le Loutre, for once at a loss, promised to pray for the family.

"Prayers are not what we need," said LeBlanc, and showed the priest to the door of their cell.

To be fair to the abbot, he was indefatigable. He made regular visits to the barracks where he would comfort the sick and hold small prayer meetings, he harassed the authorities for food, and invariably he would tell them about projects that he *knew* would transform their lives.

Jambo could not abide the man, but he listened when he met him in the docks when he was looking for work, and once again the priest returned to the idea of them settling on Belle-Ile, this time promising that they would be guaranteed ten acres of land each.

"The grant has been increased too," he said. "King Louis is offering 56,000 livres and an additional five years exemption from tax. Don't forget there will be a horse and a cow provided to help you make a start."

"I will let you know," said Jambo.

"Maybe it is a risk we should take," said Pierre.

"I will talk it over with Agnes. The baby might be strong enough to make such a journey, but he is a frail little thing."

That very evening, as he came through the barrack gates, he found the children waiting for him. Jean-Baptiste solemn as stone was holding his sister firmly by the hand. She was whimpering, nose running.

"It's the baby," said the boy.

Agnes was sitting bolt upright with Pierre-Etienne in her arms, looking straight at the door. She started as his silhouette blocked out the light of the doorway and shivered, but she clutched the child tight as if she feared he would be taken from her.

The infant was eight months old, but he never had a chance.

"No child can grow up in these conditions," said Jambo as they laid the body in the graveyard. "Never enough to eat."

"Or a proper home," said Agnes. "Just rags for clothes."

They sat by the grave that evening while the children, in their sweet and childish ways, tried to comfort them. Osite collected flowers—just as she had for Marguerite—and arranged them on the new earth. *How young to be so familiar with the rituals of death,* he thought.

Agnes did not weep. She sat quietly, playing with a small spray of daisies the girl had picked and then, violently, said, "What a *pit* of a place this is! Is this really the best we can hope for?"

He told her about Le Loutre's latest plan.

"It does sound more sensible than most of his suggestions," he said. "I think Pierre has decided to go."

"When do we leave?" she said with that sudden decisiveness of hers.

One morning in October 1765, they joined 77 families on the quay to board a ship that was to take them to Belle-Ile. Le Loutre stood by the gangplank and blessed every one of them as they boarded.

"It's n-n-not for me," said Charles. "I have never plowed a field in my life, and islands make me nervous. They are hard to escape from. So f-f-farewell for now, brother. We shall m-m-meet soon, and I know where you are this time."

"Nor me," said Oliver, bobbing around and nervously wiping his polish-stained hands on his apron as if he feared the disapproval of his old comrades. "There will be even less shoes to repair there."

TWENTY-THREE

Belle-Ile-Sur-Mer, the Brittany Coast

November 16, 1765.

Benighted Isle

"It looks very pretty," said Agnes as they sailed past a small port with brightly painted houses.

"Yes," said Jambo. "And we shall soon find out if it is the paradise that le Loutre insists it is. A new Acadia? Don't forget what Granger said. Somehow I don't think we will ever be as blessed as we were back home."

Agnes was holding the rail with one hand, and the new baby in the other. What a surprise that had been! Hardly had they buried little Pierre and decided to throw in their lot with Le Loutre than she had given birth to a girl they christened Blanche.

"We have to be positive," she said. "This will be a better place to bring up a baby, and I am sure the children will be happier here. It is their first real taste of freedom. Just think how much of her life Osite has spent locked away in some dark cell. I cannot believe she and Jean-Baptiste are so...so normal. Look what fun they are having being taught how to tie knots by the sailors."

The last time he saw his children laugh so much was when they sailed into Morlaix more than two years before, and what a mockery of hope that had turned out to be. God forbid they were going to be let down again. He was moved by their artless joy as they dared each other to get as close to the prow of the ship as possible before the waves splashed over them. He wished he shared their happiness. Instead, he was beset with anxiety.

"What if Langton was right?" he said. "Fodder, he said we'd be, and everything the French have done so far makes me think he might be right."

"Yes," said Pierre. "Go and build a harbor there, clear the swamps here."

"All those meetings that he organized—"Jambo nodded toward Le Loutre who was standing, legs firmly planted, eyes straight ahead, as if he was leading them to a promised land, "—none of us trusted anything that he or Nivernois said, did we?" asked Jambo. "Yet here we are, with only their assurance that this is the place we can build a new Acadia."

"Yes, here we are," said Pierre. He steadied his wife as the ship lurched in the waves. "But we have to make the most of it. What choice do we have?"

His wife! Jambo was still recovering from the surprise of the evening a few months after they arrived in France, when Pierre had stopped by after another fruitless day spent knocking on doors for odd jobs. For a man who had been driven away by gamekeepers from every woodland he had tried to lay traps in, and as a widowed father with hungry mouths to feed, he seemed unwontedly cheerful.

"I have something to tell you." He had said it the same matter-of-fact gravity as he had when he had asked his friend to come with him the night of the killings.

"You've met Francoise?"

Jambo hesitated. *Francoise? The Daigre woman?* Ah yes, she had been on the voyage to Boston in the early days of the expulsion. Her sister's little boy had fallen overboard, and, he recalled, how moved he had been by the way she had spent many hours consoling the woman. He hadn't seen her since Virginia, but apparently she had been widowed in Falmouth and shipped with the other exiles to Morlaix. A rather dumpy woman in her thirties, she looked worn down with her loss, and the hurt that reflected in her eyes made her look permanently on the verge of tears.

"Nice woman," he said carefully. "Sad."

"Less so now, I hope," said his friend. "We are to marry."

"My dear Pierre. Congratulations. I am pleased for you."

"Are you sure?" He could tell Pierre was desperate for his old friend's approval, after all it was his sister as well as his wife who had been killed in Liverpool.

"Of course. One thing we have surely all learnt is to find happiness where we can, and as often as possible. If Marie and Marguerite could speak to us now, that's exactly what they would say. Come my friend, my dearest comrade, let's have a mug of cider to celebrate."

And now Pierre was not just standing with his arm around his second wife, but gazing proudly at their first-born. Jambo could see that the look in her eyes was of newly-kindled hope.

"I do wonder why they sent us to Morlaix, knowing there was nowhere to live and no work," said Jambo.

"They must have known that the locals would be as hostile as they were in England," said Agnes.

"Maybe that is the point," said Jambo. "They told us anything we wanted to hear, so that then they could say, '*We are sorry, circumstances have changed, this place cannot support you after all, but we have a demi-paradise waiting for you on the other side of the world, so sign here; how can you resist?*'

"They relied on us being so down trodden that we wouldn't summon the will to say *no* to them," said Pierre.

"It works, doesn't it?" Jambo sighed. "Who would have thought Francois would go off like that?"

Already, the carpenter was missing his old comrades. Of the five that had survived the years since they were taken from Grand-Pré, only Pierre had joined the expedition to Belle-Ile.

Oliver had decided to try his luck in Nantes. "It's a port, and there are always people needing shoes repaired in a busy city like that," he said confidently. "It's the kind of place where strangers with ambition and money pass through. I can help them achieve one by relieving them of the other."

And Charles, well, who could tell what his big brother would get up to, but Jambo knew he would laugh his way through all the difficulties that came his way. He would survive.

He fretted about Francois. Would he be banging heads together in the swamps of Guyana as the work force set about building the defenses for the new French colony? *Rather,* reckoned Jambo, *he would struggle to cope.* He had long understood that behind the plowman's fierce exterior, all that cursing and fist thumping, he was, at heart, plagued by doubt and insecurity and as fearful as the rest of them. He would resent any form of authority, especially if the angry Acadian felt it was unfair or cruel, and his notorious short fuse would be exacerbated by the heat of the tropics.

"I fear for Francois," said Agnes, as if divining his thoughts. "If only he had waited. He would have been kept busy plowing the fields here."

The ship tacked through increasingly choppy water toward the island's port, a nondescript town in the lee of a mighty fortification that loomed grey and massive above it.

"It was meant to be impregnable," observed Pierre. "But Le Loutre was telling me that the British took the place easily in '61."

"They're good at sieges, aren't they?" said Jambo ruefully. "Beausejour, Louisbourg, Quebec. They just seem to walk in."

The ship gave a lurch, threatening to spill the passengers across the deck. They laughed nervously and grabbed the children for safety, but it happened again leaving the ship leaning at an alarming 45 degree angle. Water lapped over the deck on the port side.

"Out of the way." The sailors were shouting and dashing about in panic. "The current has got us. We are running aground."

"My God, we are heading for those rocks!" shrieked Agnes.

The crew dragged down the sails amid a pandemonium of orders and screams and hurled the anchor into the sea. An image of the farcical—the nightmare—attempt to flee Williamsburg flashed into Jambo's mind. "Dear God, don't say we have come this far just to drown," he prayed.

Everyone was shouting , sailors and passengers alike, all in a frenzy of fear.

"Hang on."

"Let go."

"This way."

"That side."

"Don't jump. Help is coming," yelled the skipper. "Stay calm."

"Jump," exhorted the first mate.

"Quick, in the boat," said Jambo as the first of a flotilla of coracles bobbed alongside.

The ship had listed so far into the water, that it was easy enough to lift the children into one of the rescue crafts.

"Agnes, get in this one!" He held her hand until the oarsman made sure she was safe before handing over the baby and the sack that contained all they owned in the world. The ship shifted alarmingly beneath his feet, the waves reached as high as his knees.

"Nothing for it," he said to himself. "Time for a dip." He plunged into the chill sea and scrambled over the rocks and on to the beach where he caught a last glimpse of the ship before it slid beneath the waves.

They were all alive, shivering with wet and cold on the shore around Le Loutre, who was wringing the water from his robes.

"The Lord is smiling on this enterprise," he said, baring his yellow teeth to show his pleasure at another small miracle. "He has once more spared us from the waters."

"Did you say the British called him French Moses?" asked Agnes, teeth chattering, trying to calm the screaming baby. "I wish he wouldn't practice on us."

"Welcome to Belle-Ile," said the priest as if such a narrow escape was a daily occurrence. "The Beautiful Island. It is well named, I can promise you. Soon I will introduce you to the governor, Baron De Warren, who understands your plight. He is a Scottish gentleman—from the north of England—and he fought against the British in the war. He has set aside the land for you and built homes for what is to be a splendid future. Meanwhile, he has arranged that you to stay in some rooms—just for the night. Follow me."

He led them up a steep hill to a group of grain warehouses alongside some disused barracks, still littered with spent cartridges left by the British.

Jambo and Pierre smiled wryly.

"What magnificence," said Jambo.

"I haven't seen such luxury since our stay in the Palace of Liverpool," said Pierre.

Before they could change out of their wet clothes Le Loutre was back amongst them. "Here he comes. The Baron. Wait in the courtyard."

There came the clattering of a chaise up the cobbled street, and out sprang a man with little legs and a body like a farmhouse loaf, his small round head perched on top. It was bizarre—he appeared to be wearing a skirt woven in many colors, which as he leapt to the ground caught on the door handle of the chaise exposing a sight which made the women gasp, though Agnes said she was sure some giggled.

His entourage, who had followed on foot, assembled obediently behind him, a few wearing the same plaid-colored outfits, which Le Loutre later explained were called kilts.

"Worn in Scotland," he said. "They have many odd customs. Speak strangely too."

"They look a thuggish crew," said Jambo, but Le Loutre had dashed off to welcome the new arrival.

The Baron, unperturbed by his surprising arrival, pulled himself up to his full height, which amounted to all of five foot four inches, to display a motley array of medals and sashes.

"My friends, welcome to Beautiful Island," he declared in a strange, high-pitched accent. "I understand your plight and the shameful way the British have treated you, because I too have fallen foul of that ruthless race. I know you come here with eagerness and longing to create a new Acadia, and I salute you. I can see you are robust, courageous, and in good health. You will prosper here, my friends."

"The King has fulfilled his promise," said Le Loutre.

The Baron, irritated by the interruption, glared at the priest. "His Majesty always keeps his word. As well as paying for a house to accommodate each family, he has given you a horse and a cow each, and in every parish there will be a bull and a stallion.

"Remember, there are no taxes to pay and sufficient food rations to last three months. Most important of all, for you men at least, I have arranged an allowance of 110 pounds of tobacco per month."

There was ragged, if skeptical, cheer from his audience.

"Now, you will understand I'm sure, that though some families fled the island when the British invaded, there are still many living here. There was talk that you incomers should be kept together in an enclave at the end of the island, out of their way, but I feel that we must all live in harmony.

"In short, you—and them—should become as one. A single people. To that end, I have decided that you will be distributed among the parishes and not be settled in one place. I am sure you will all co-exist in a good, Christian spirit."

"To put it another way," muttered Pierre. "They want us off the island as soon as possible."

At dawn next morning they set off with Osite perched on top of their new wagon, while Jean-Baptiste chased around with a stray mutt of a dog they had brought from Morlaix.

"He's a bit like us, the way he goes sniffing around for bits of food and left-overs," said Jambo.

"It's time he had a name," Jean-Baptise said. "Let's call him Sniffer."

"They don't seem too keen to see us," said Agnes as the few islanders that the new arrivals passed either ignored them or swiftly disappeared into their cottages, slamming their doors as they went.

They walked along a small valley, and up a gentle slope for a mile or two until they reached an open plateau. It was covered in gorse and marked out with wild hedgerows, but instead of being reassuringly cultivated there was an air of neglect. The roofs of some farmhouses had fallen in, fences had come down, and the fields, which were overgrown with weeds and thistles, had not been plowed for many months.

"I guess this is because so many of the people fled the British," said Pierre.

A chill wind whipped across the open spaces where trees had been blown horizontal to the ground like penitents on their way to prayers, and the sea mist that scudded across the empty landscape wound around them like ragged shrouds.

Two huge figures materialized like ghostly apparitions out of the clouds.

"What are those?" asked a fearful Jean-Baptiste, scrambling back to be near his father.

Two granite stones over ten feet high stood as if guarding the way.

Le Loutre said, "They are heathen altars. Some say they date from pre-historic times when they were put up to glorify pagan gods. The locals call them Jean and Jeanne. If I had my way, I would pull them down and use the stone as foundations for new houses."

After three hours of walking along country paths, he raised a hand in a signal to them to stop. "Now, halt here and admire." He waved toward a gaggle of cottages, "This is your village. It is called Kerlédan. See, there are your homes." He pointed with pride at the low-lying dwellings that had been painted in cheerful reds, blues and greens. "Right, Le Blancs. Five of you, I believe. This one has been set aside for you."

Jambo was impressed, despite his skepticism of the priest's plans. The cottage was as solid and as snug as if it had been brought all the way from Grand-Pré. There were the cow, and the horse and the bull, and the fields awaiting the first plunge of the plow. In the distance, the haze of the sea.

Their hearts soared, and for a moment Jambo had a miraculous sensation of flying, as if he was on an imperceptible curve of the universe with the straight lines of the paths arrowing across the plateau, over the meadows, high above the woods, and away into the sky.

"We shall be happy here," said Agnes, and she kissed every one of her family as if in blessing.

"We will," said Jambo. "Le Loutre was right for once. It does remind me of Acadia."

He seized Osite and twirled her around, much to her embarrassment.

"I am too old for that, father," she reprimanded him gravely. "I am eleven now."

The very next morning, just after dawn, Jambo was in the fields, pacing up and down, measuring them and checking the soil. He started to chop down branches for firewood, and put aside the stouter timbers to for fences.

"Can't have cattle wandering everywhere," he said to Pierre, who had been given the next smallholding.

"The soil is stony, isn't it? Said Pierre, prodding it with his new fork. "But I think if we can get down deep enough, it will be enough for a decent crop of wheat."

"We have to make it work," said Jambo, whose spirits were higher than he could remember. "After all, this island is where our children will grow up, independent and free. It is *their* Acadia."

"Yes, at last somewhere we can call home," said Pierre. "I'm going to build a chicken house over there and add to the stables—they are too small."

But before they could get started, winter was upon them. The homestead was open to the blast of the wind, the ferocity of the rain, the sleet, and snow that whistled in from the Atlantic. Such was the chill that it was impossible to force a plow into the ground. Indeed, there was little they could do except wait for winter to pass.

They had their allowance, but it was a rare Acadian who would accept a benefit without trying to earn his way, so they would slog through the blizzards to the port to find work. They tried to fish the frozen sea, braced against the gales on the nearest jetty. Pierre and Jambo set out every dusk to set traps, but Pierre grumbled when he came back empty handed, as he did most mornings, "There are only about five rabbits on the entire island."

Once again, they called on the spirit of self-reliance which had seen them through so many ordeals. They worked together to clear the land of the wild brambles and gorse, reinforced the fences, and made the barn watertight for the storage of their first harvest. They were ready to transform their land into fields of plenty.

"Come and look at my chicken run," said Pierre.

"A noble edifice," said Jambo. "I didn't know you had chickens. Where did you get them from?"

"I haven't yet," said Pierre. "But Le Loutre said he could get some from the mainland."

The moment spring arrived, softening the iron earth, they worked like demons from dawn to dusk, plowing and planting seeds.

"Isn't that a fine sight," said Jambo as they surveyed their fields with the fuzz of the nascent buds making straight rows of green stretching out before them.

"The first harvest since Grand-Pré," said Agnes joyfully.

"I think that calls for a flagon of cider," said Pierre.

When it didn't rain they were unconcerned. They had stored water in the butts all winter long and had plenty to help ripen the crop. But the days turned into weeks, then months.

"Surely today," they would say, gazing out to sea for signs of rain clouds. "Surely today."

But no. There would be storms with dramatic flashes of lightning flashing in zigzags across the livid cloud-filled skies, but barely a drop of rain.

And so it went on all that first summer. The promise of the green shoots disappeared, replaced first with brown tufts, and then with empty furrows that mocked their endeavors. The cows, with ribs that almost pierced their hollow shanks, stopped producing milk, and many dropped from starvation, even Pierre's hens, which Le Loutre had indeed delivered, clucked and fussed, but could not find enough scraps in the hard earth of his yard to keep them laying.

The bright paint on the houses that had so cheered them when they first arrived peeled and faded, leaving them looking as desolate and neglected as those they had seen when they landed.

And the villagers—red-faced and blistered from the heat with cracked lips and light headed from thirst—would sit despairingly in the shade of the trees, smoking their pipes and waiting.

"At least this pernicious wind does some good," said Pierre. "It has blasted the trees so hard and forced them so low they make for perfect shade."

However, they did not give up. As winter approached, once again they plowed, prepared, planted and prayed. In case they were afflicted by another season of drought, they dug wells and laid irrigation gullies, anything that might save water. By the time of the first spring rains they were rewarded, once again, by furrows of green.

But just like the year before, no sooner had the shoots appeared than the rain stopped and the sun came out, shimmering remorselessly on the fields. And like the year before, the entire crop wilted and died in the onslaught.

One morning in that summer of '67 as Jambo and Pierre were attempting to coax life into the few cabbages and potatoes they had managed to grow on their smallholdings, they were brought to their feet by the sight of a group of islanders coming down the lane.

"Good day," said Jambo cheerfully.

"We would like a meeting with you and your fellow citizens," said the head of the delegation. This was clearly not a friendly visit. The incomers had been subjected to a few of these meetings by the islanders who came to see if *'Everything was in order and if there was anything they could do to help,'* but, insisted Agnes, they were spying missions to discover how the Acadians lived and what they, the locals, could do to make their lives difficult.

"Of course," said the carpenter. "I shall round up who I can find and we could meet in the barn. It should be big enough to hold us all. Agnes, bring some cider for our friends."

The visitors sat along one side of the barn on the long benches the Acadians had made while the newcomers took up the other wall. *Like a village dance,* thought Jambo wryly.

Agnes and Francoise brought in jugs of cider and handed mugs to their guests.

Their guests looked around disapprovingly at the half-empty building which had seen so little use. There were a few sacks of seed, lengths of fraying rope, rusting tools, feed for the chickens, which clucked in and out of the door which had never shut properly, and, in the middle, the cart which the villagers shared to make visits to town.

"Mr. LeBlanc, gentlemen," started their spokesman, a man with fleshy, unnaturally red lips that leaked spittle, and a squint that made him look as if he was looking past the carpenter into some gloomy future.

"And ladies," said Agnes and Francoise in unison.

His eyes swiveled in surprise, focusing on the source of this interruption, and he mopped a fleck of saliva from his mouth.

"Ladies! Good God!" He recovered himself. "As some of you might know, my name is Jacques Foucquet. I represent the Baron's interests in this parish. To come to the point. You have to understand that most of us—the ones who have lived on the island all our lives—were not altogether happy about you coming here."

"Not happy at all," said one of his companions.

"It is not personal," said another. "But we go back for generations. This is our island, but in recent years we have been attacked by the Dutch, and conquered by the British who drove away many of our families, leaving the island neglected and desolate."

"Now we have you Canadians," sniffed Foucquet.

"Acadians," corrected Jambo. "We understand your concerns but we were told that we were welcome. The Baron said we were, what was it, *robust and courageous'*

"That's as maybe," said Foucquet. "But you do not seem to be making any attempt to fit in with us and behave like true Bellois. Your language is impossible to understand, and your customs are, well, not French."

"That is because we are not French," said Pierre. "True, our ancestors came from Poitou, which I believe is not far from here on the mainland, but that was more than 150 years ago. We are Acadians, we owe allegiance to none."

"Though we are very happy to be on your island," Jambo, eager to keep the peace. "We feel privileged."

"But you have your own council," said Foucquet.

"It is very informal, and we meet to discuss unimportant matters like where to mark the boundaries of our smallholdings," said Pierre.

"I've heard that the women are allowed to have a say on this council of yours," said one with an air of mystification.

"And a vote," said Agnes. There was a palpable stir at such a bold interruption.

"Here, women keep their mouths shut," said Foucquet.

"And their legs open," muttered another to the sniggers of his companions.

It was such a gratuitous remark that the villagers thought they must have misheard. Surely these people would not display their boorishness so openly. Even Foucquet seemed discomfited and blew his nose noisily.

"The Lord De Warren much admires your women," he said, trying to placate Agnes and Francoise who held him with an icy glare. "In a respectful way, of course." His delegation fell to tittering again. "But a vote? That is going too far."

"I am sorry," said LeBlanc. "We have always allowed women to help make decisions before council takes action. Even when the British were our masters they did not object, and now we are amongst friends we see no reason to stop."

"What about our jobs?" asked another.

"I don't understand," said Jambo.

"You are a threat to them," he shot back.

"How can that be?" asked Pierre. "We are trying to do the best we can, and do any tasks we are asked to do in the town as well."

"I have seen you doing carpentry work," said Foucquet.

"Well, I am a carpenter," said Jambo.

"But you can't be a carpenter as well as a farmer." He brought his eyebrows together in a frown but his perplexing gaze went off in different directions. "Me, I am a pharmacist. That's what I do, that's all I do."

"I also know how to trap and fish," said Jambo.

"We all do," said Pierre, to tuts of disapproval from their audience.

"That is not the French way," said the pharmacist."Here we have one trade and we stick to it."

"That's why we cannot not allow you to use the boats," said one of his henchmen. "As Mr Foucquet says, you either farm, or you fish."

"You are either a shepherd or a trapper," said another with an air of finality. "Not both."

Foucquet chipped in, glaring at the far wall of the barn, "I have been informed that you do not carry your identity papers with you at all times."

"We do not approve of them," said Pierre. "It is an infringement of our rights. Even the British did not insist on that."

"You are not allowed to hunt or fish without one," said Foucquet.

"That is what we have done for generations. It would be discrimination to stop us," said Pierre.

"So you are not prepared to embrace our customs? Even though you are living on hand-outs at the expense of the King," said Foucquet.

"We want nothing more than to be your friends and co-exist

peacefully," said Jambo. "As for the allowance, we prefer to earn our keep, though that has not been possible so far."

Pierre said, "If you had experienced what we have in the last twelve years, you might be a little more tolerant."

"Now," said Agnes. "If you have finished your cider, we have work to do."

As she noisily collected up the mugs, all of which had been drained— *They didn't mind us pouring cider for them, did they?'* she huffed—their visitors rose angrily, doubly affronted by being talked by a woman in such disrespectful tones, and stamped out of the barn.

Foucquet paused. "I am sorry you refuse to embrace our customs, my Canadian friends. You will find you have made an error of judgment."

"Pompous ass," said Francoise, loud enough for him to hear.

The delegation made sure the islanders knew of the immigrants' *'bloody-minded'* refusal to fit in with their way of life and worse, and spread rumors about the *'wanton bitches who showed men no respect. No better than trollops. And maybe worst of all, 'They have a vote! They actually have a say in the running of their affairs.'*

Instantly, they were ostracized by the locals.

Doors were shut in their faces when they enquired about jobs, notices appeared on warehouse doors and farm gates reading: *'No Canadians'* and some of the stall holders by the port stopped serving them.

It was as if the confrontation gave De Warren's men a license to bully the incomers. They arrested them for no reason, beat them to confess to some trumped up charge and confiscated their provisions. Worse, they felt free to taunt the women with the crudest of sexual abuse. They would circle them in predatory bands, clutching at them and jeering.

"I hear you Canadians can do two jobs at once. How about doubling up with us," said a pair of them as they lurched out of the tavern and raised their kilts in tumescent salute.

"The shocking thing is that some of the women laughed," said an angry Agnes later. "It's not just undignified of them, it might encourage the foul-mouthed pigs to think they can get away with it, or even to imagine that their vile behavior is welcome."

TWENTY-FOUR

Belle-Ile-Sur Mer

June, 1769.

Defiled. Defiant

"We must have more water for drinking and washing," said Agnes. "I know what little we have has to be used growing vegetables and watering the cattle, but this place is getting to be as unhealthy as the ghetto. What about the babies? They need more than a mother's love to survive. We need water to keep them clean and food to keep them alive."

She had given birth to two more children in quick succession since their arrival on the island. Joseph, born in 1768, gave Jambo the boy he had wanted he and Agnes to have together but it was Marie-Francoise, born the year before, who had stolen her heart. They could tell at a glance that something was badly amiss with her. She had a curve to her spine, a bulging forehead, and her little legs were bowed.

"Rickets," said Francoise bluntly. "It's caused by lack of proper food. You've not been eating enough."

"Well, that's true," said Agnes, who found her directness disconcerting, especially as Pierre's first wife Marie had been so sweet natured. "But then, none of us have, have we," she said, angrily throwing open the door to the empty pantry.

Agnes adored the misshapen scrap. She held her, stroked her crooked spine, massaged the skinny, bandy legs, and breast fed her until there was no milk left in her own under-nourished body.

She would strap the infant to her chest and talk gently to her as she went about her chores, sharing all her thoughts with the uncomprehending infant; how she eked what she could from their meager supplies to produce at least one meal a day, how she worried about Jean-Baptiste who was showing his growing independence by skipping his lessons with the abbot, preferring to work with his father in the fields or hanging around with the other lads.

"There's papa," she would say looking through the window at Jambo, who still went about his work with the same calm determination that he had always shown, limping around the ravaged fields, his damaged hand by his side, balancing the bucket of feed against his hip. "But," she told the girl, "He's not the same, he is losing his appetite for the tussle. But he won't give up, you can be sure of that."

"And as for Osite. She's just 15 and she is *so* serious—as strong a character as her mother," she confided as she watched the girl dutifully setting off for her studies with Le Loutre. "She can look after herself, that one."

"You have to know how to read and write in this country," Osite said. "It is the only way to keep up with them—as you will discover, dear brother, when they overcharge you in the market because you can't understand their figures."

Early one morning Jambo and son were in the field behind the cottage, calling in the cattle while Agnes watched from the window.

"They are looking serious," she said to Marie-Francoise. "I wonder what the matter is today."

In the field, Jean-Baptiste was saying, "The cows are looking thinner than ever."

"It's no surprise," said his father. "We ran out of feed months ago, and the islanders are not going to help."

"It's not that," said Jean-Baptiste, "There's something wrong with this one. And look there."

Three cows were lying down with saliva drooling from their mouths.

"Check their hooves," said Jambo urgently.

"They're blistered," said his son.

"Dear Lord," said Jambo despairingly. "Foot and mouth disease. Why this? Why now?"

"What can we do?" asked his son.

"Not much," said his father. "They might recover, but they will spread it to the other cows and to the sheep and goats. It takes months to recover, and even if they do, their milk will eventually dry up.

"The best thing to do is kill them, and bury the carcasses in the hope that the disease passes."

It was too late. Within weeks, most of the cattle on the island were stricken, dying where they fell. The Acadians dragged their hulks away and burned them on huge, stinking pyres that spread ash across the countryside, covering the dark green conifers with their grey dust, and filtering into the houses—just the way it had been when the burnt flesh had floated from the ruins of Grand-Pré and seeped into the ships. Jambo shuddered.

The dog's growling made him start. For a second he thought it was dear old Poutu, whose barking had been almost the last, forlorn, sound he had heard above the cries on Boudrot Point all those years ago, but it was Foucquet and his cohorts.

"You are destroying our livelihood," Foucquet said, his squint glaring dangerously over Jambo's shoulder. "We've never had this disease before. As a pharmacist and a scientist, I know about these things. Your farming methods are to blame. You do not understand how to look after cattle.

"The fact is," he went on, "You don't have to bother to work properly or responsibly, because you have such a generous hand-outs from De Warren. This has gone on long enough. It is time you stood on your own two feet just as we have to."

Within weeks, the Baron announced an end to their allowances.

"You have had every chance to succeed," he said. "You have been here almost six years. We cannot support you forever."

He and Jean-Baptiste leant on a gate and watched the crows dancing on the body of a dead horse, picking away its eyes and foraging in the soft folds of its mouth. Its bones stuck out of its skin as it lay on the cracked earth of what should have been a meadow of rich grass.

"We are wasting our time," said the younger man. "We can't go on. Look at it."

In the years since their optimistic arrival, the island had become a devastated heath where even the thorns and gorse wilted. The streams were rocky tracks through brown fields that should have been rich with maize, wheat, cabbages, and potatoes, but instead were graveyards to withered crops, stunted plants, and starving livestock. The few scrawny cattle left alive limped around, their bells tolling in melancholy dissonance.

Jean-Baptiste threw his hoe on the ground. "We have to get off this cursed place," he said.

Jambo had started to say, *No, we must keep going just as we always have*, but he bit his tongue. He knew that the authority was ebbing from the likes of Pierre and himself, and that the young man and the new generation of exiles were beginning to assert themselves. They did not share the increasingly idealized memories their elders had of their homeland. They could not understand why they should tolerate further indignities at the hands of their French hosts merely to hang on to the dream that they might help the Acadians return to a country they had never known.

His son's anger worried away at him so much that he resolved to talk things over with Agnes on an evening when he knew that son and daughter had taken the horse and cart and gone to town. The young man said he had heard that one of the ships that called by regularly with supplies for the islanders needed caulking, and was prepared to defy the hostility of the locals to apply for the task. What he did not admit to his parents was that the port had become a meeting place for the young immigrant lads to loaf around and pick fights with the islanders.

Osite had one of her regular reading lessons with Le Loutre. With her cloud of red hair, the young woman had her mother's outgoing personality, fierce blue eyes – both the same color unlike Marguerite – and a poise that turned the heads of island's young men but she was too serious to let their admiration deflect her from her course. She could already read and write better than anyone had ever managed in the LeBlanc family, and was reaping a reward for her talent. Increasingly the refugees were receiving letters from their relatives in the American colonies, and Osite was called on to read their messages, and for a few sous write a reply.

To his surprise, as he came in to the yard, he saw the horse and cart were back, though, to his annoyance, not tethered safely to the gate.

"How many times do I have to tell you to tie up the horse" he yelled. "It will trot off and be stolen by an islander."

He burst into the tiny living room, but was instantly struck silent. Osite was doubled up on the palliasse. She was hysterical. Uncontrollable sobs tore though her, making her body shake in violent spasms. Her hair had come loose from her bonnet and flew in all directions, her lip was puffed and bleeding, and she had a swollen cheek the color of a rainstorm. Agnes had wrapped a blanket around her and was trying to make her drink a cup of wine.

"What?" He stood there helplessly as Agnes tried to calm her. The blanket slipped to show that the young woman's chemise had been ripped from shoulder to waist, revealing an arm covered in scratches and bruises. He was embarrassed and horrified to catch a glimpse of her breast, which had been scarred with what looked like teeth marks.

"Osite. Agnes. What has happened?"

Jean-Baptiste, who was sporting an eye that that was an array of black and purple, mopped blood from his nose and lip, and said, "De Warren's men set on the girls."

Osite, her eyes dilated with anguish, her face working as she drew breath in great, wheezing, gasps, blurted, "We had finished studying with the abbot and were waiting for Jean-Baptiste to bring us home. We were set on by three men as they came out of the tavern. They started saying disgusting things about us. Called us prostitutes, said they would pay us well, and how grateful we would be because we were so poor and hungry. Then they started to manhandle us. I cannot bear to recall what happened."

"Don't say anything more, my dear," said Agnes, pulling the blanket around her. "I think it best that you go and lie down."

But the girl continued her faltering account, "Anne Granger hit one who tried to put his hand up her skirts, and then one got hold of me. He was pawing me. He was all over me. *God,* he stank of beer. Look."

"My darling, the marks around your neck," said her distraught father. "Your arms, those bruises. You poor ..."

"He was strangling me." She gulped for breath between her sobs. "He said this was the best of both worlds—pleasure for him, profit for me. I hit him, but he dragged me to the ground by my hair and starting hitting and biting me. And..."

"Come, Osite," said Agnes.

The girl wiped her eyes, but instead of obeying her stepmother, her gaze hardened and she suddenly became as angry as she had been anguished. "I kicked him. Hard. Hit him, scratched and bit. He won't forget me." She gave a harsh laugh that became a gulp of anguish.

"My sweet girl," said Jambo. He felt hopelessly inadequate.

"Don't worry about me," she said. "Or any of us. After everything we have been through, we cannot be intimidated by cowards like that. We are *better* than them."

"Well said, sister," said Jean-Baptiste through swollen lips. "And well kicked too. The coward could hardly stand after that."

She fell to weeping again, her hands shook as she wiped away the tears, and then she slumped into the arms of Agnes, her defiance extinguished by the shock and the pain of her injuries.

"Do you know the attackers?" asked Jambo. "I shall get the men together and teach them a lesson."

"I do," said Jean-Baptiste. "One of them was that Foucqet character who has caused so much mischief for us. He's the ringleader. He and his mates are always hanging around the port. The trouble is De Warren's men think it is their right to have any woman they fancy. They are like a private army, and they treat the island as their fiefdom."

"We cannot allow it," said Jambo. "I shall go to the castle and see De Warren. He will sort his men out."

Jean-Baptiste said, "It's a waste of time, believe me father. I spend more time in town than you do, and everyone knows that the Baron himself is one of the worst offenders. The man is a barbarian. They are all in it together. He boasted to his cronies that he prefers Acadian women to the locals because they are '*big and rustic.*'

"The shame of it," said Agnes, who was busying herself with basins of hot water and towels which took into the darkened back room. "I knew they are crude and treat women vilely, but I never thought they would match their cowardly insults with such an awful deed."

"Not as shameful as you might imagine," said Jean-Baptiste. "How do you think the Robichaud family lives so well when they have never lifted a finger to do any work? Have you ever seen the husband out in the fields? I think not."

"What are you saying?" asked Jambo, almost as appalled by such a shocking assertion as he was by his son's insouciance that such squalid possibilities existed.

"You must understand father, we all have to survive the best way we can. And what the Robichaud wife and her daughter do is just another way of paying the bills."

"It is *disgusting,*" spat Agnes. "To think that any woman should feel compelled to do that."

Jean-Baptiste said, "Poverty and hunger make savages of us all."

"It does not have to," his father said. "I shall protest to the Baron."

"He will laugh at you," said his son. "Then he will put you in prison."

"I will, at least, talk to Le Loutre. He must have some influence over this Scottish heathen."

"That man is nothing more than a damned nuisance," said the-young man. "He has no power. He does what he is told. Damn him. Damn de Warren. Damn the lot of them."

Agnes flinched at his language and started to remonstrate, but instead stayed her tongue and joined the family in miserable silence.

"It is intolerable enough that nature is against us, but when the men sent to protect us are worse than those who feed on carrion then we have to find our own solutions," Jean-Baptiste went on, his voice rising. "We cannot beat them, but we can leave them behind. We must get off this benighted island."

Jambo realized that he was looking at the image of himself at that age—17 years old, confident, determined, and unafraid.

"You are right," said his father. "They give us no choice."

TWENTY-FIVE

Belle-Ile-Sur-Mer

July, 1769.

For Pity's Sake

As Jean-Baptiste forecast, Le Loutre did not want to hear what his father had to say. His stuttering rage was met with embarrassed sympathy, much wringing of hands, and invocations to God's understanding in the face of such evil. He could not bring himself to condemn the attackers though.

"He's a fool and a menace, but I almost feel sorry for him," Jambo had told his son as they walked over the fields to confront the priest. "Look at him. He is as haggard and worn out as I am. His hopes have been as blighted as ours. He's in his sixties and he has spent his life in forlorn quests—bringing the gospel to hostile Indians in Nova Scotia, most of whom thought he was mad, trying to rally them and us Acadians to fight the British invaders, then spending years on the run and longer in prison. And for what? Everything he has done in the name of his faith had been for the good of others, or so he thinks, but so little has been achieved."

"Now all his plans have come to nothing," said Jean-Baptiste, "To make it worse for him, he is expected to condemn the vile behavior of the very men who he thought shared his dream of a fine new world here."

The priest had been expecting them and ushered them into his dwelling. Just one room, with a cot, a chair and a table with a brass bound Bible, it was what they expected of a man of such self-denying sincerity but far from behaving like the protector of his flock, he was agitated and evasive.

"I will see De Warren," he promised. "It is a pity."

"A pity." Jambo seethed at the feeble response. The attack on his daughter had revitalized his spirit, and his eyes were black with contempt under his beetling eyebrows. Whatever sympathy he might have felt for the priest had gone. "For De Warren or my daughter? Or for you? Just a pity?"

Jean-Baptise chimed in. "It is a scandal, a crime against my sister."

"Can you imagine her agony? The humiliation? A *pity* you call it." Jambo seemed to tower over the priest. For second Jean-Baptiste thought his father was going to pick him up and shake him.

"Forgive me...I mean. Your daughter. Tragic." The priest was incoherent in his agitation. "God will find the answer. He will never desert us."

"What do you mean *never desert us?* He has never been with us." LeBlanc looked around wildly. He reached for the priest's heavy Bible, and looked as if he was going to hurl it at him, but instead, with all his fury, slammed it down on the floor.

"Not once in the past 13 years has he shown us any mercy," said the carpenter, his voice rising again. "That's a *pity,* all right."

Jean-Baptiste had never seen his father lose control.

"I agree, I do," said the priest, scrabbling on the floor to rescue the Bible. "Please do not misunderstand me. Of course, this is a shameful misdemeanor. But, meanwhile it is best to keep the young people away from the port. There is always trouble there."

"So it's their fault is it?" barked father.

The priest started to speak, realized that whatever he said would make things worse, gave a half bow and walked out of his own house.

A few days later he rode up to the LeBlanc cottage. "I have spoken to De Warren," he said. "Or at least to one of his men. He promises that nothing like this will happen again. He has apologized and says the guilty men will be punished." He hesitated, awkward. "How is the unfortunate girl? Osite was one of my most promising pupils. So bright. Now, tragically ruined."

Father and son did not speak, but simply stared at him with disdain. Fearless when it came to spreading the word of God, he was at loss for the right words now. He swung himself back on his nag. "I shall pray for you all," he said. "Maybe there is a solution. I have details of a scheme that will take us away from this island. That might be for the best in view of ..." His words trailed away. "I would like to tell you about it."

Jambo was about to speak but Jean-Baptiste interrupted. "I think not."

Nonetheless, some weeks later they reluctantly joined their fellows in the church to hear of a settlement that was planned for them on the mainland. The priest had recaptured some of his old conviction.

"This region is being specially set aside for immigrants like us," he enthused. "At last, somewhere we can call home which will be free of drought and hunger. An end to discrimination."

"He's always talking, talking. Just talking," said Jean-Baptiste to Osite as the family sat together at the back of the building.

Since the attack the two had become closer. In fact, Jambo remarked to Agnes, the effect on the young man had been profound.

"He's grown up overnight," he said.

From the day after the attack on Osite, he stopped hanging around the lads in the port, getting drunk on potato wine, and, indeed, chasing the girls, but instead, he followed the example of his younger sister by agreeing to have lessons in reading and writing – and actually attending them.

As for Osite, she had stayed in her room for several weeks—too devastated to face the family and her father—but eventually she had joined them, her face still bearing traces of the gruesome medley of bruises. She was still so shaky she could hardly stand, but she was content to sit and study, breaking off to help in the house and encourage Marie to walk on her wobbly, bowed legs.

"I pity the priest," Osite had said when they were deciding whether to go to his meeting. "He is so blinded by the certainty of his own beliefs that he has lost all sense of reality. He still believes all this nonsense about '*new lives*' and '*great opportunities.*'

As the priest tried to enthuse his indifferent audience—there was mention of a '*benefactor, a Marquis, no less*'—the older man shut his eyes, squeezed together as if he was hanging on to the old belief that somehow they would be saved from this perdition and taken back to Acadia.

"This is just more of Le Loutre's nonsense," he whispered to Agnes, who was holding his hand, massaging the damaged fingers that now ached from arthritis. "I cannot bear to listen."

He was worried that since the night of the attack, the boy and his stepmother had become estranged.

"She blames me in some way for the attack," he had complained to his father. "Even before it happened, she was always nagging me, '*You are spending too much time down by the port; you are mixing with the wrong types*', And saying things like, '*It makes me nervous to think that you might let Osite out of your sight when you get together with the other lads. Your father needs you in the fields. He's got too much to do without your help.*'"

"She doesn't blame you son," He had put his arm around his shoulder. "Not one bit. It has been hard on her too. We would not have got through this ordeal without the calm way she handled everything."

He did understand, though, how badly it had affected her. Already slight of build, she had become as thin as a rail. Her face became lined with worry and her mouth turned down. Her grey eyes, once so steady, were as dulled as a dawn mist.

Now everything went into the care of Osite, the girl she loved as much as if she had been her own and, just as Jean-Baptiste had felt excluded by his mother, Jambo felt as if he, too, hardly mattered to daughter or wife. A morning or two after the attack, when he was in the yard feeding the hens he overheard Agnes saying, "Whatever happens, your father must never know the truth. The shame would kill him. He keeps asking, '*Are you all right, are you all right?*' but I have told him that the shock has brought on some malady unique to women and you will have to rest".

"Did he accept that," asked his daughter.

"Well, in truth, he was too embarrassed to ask more questions," said Agnes." It has been almost as painful looking after him as you, my dear."

She must think I'm stupid, he thought, making sure he made enough noise to alert them to his return. *I know what the truth is and there is no shame to it. I know my girl. Just like her mother, she will not be defeated.*

And Osite herself asserted, "Nothing that has happened should beat us. We shall rise above these people and their vile ways. As for me, I will go to town whenever I want, even if my attackers are there. No, particularly if they are there. I shall shame them. Above all, I shall continue my studies. That will be my victory and my escape." She struggled to her feet.

Her father put his arms gently around her and kissed the top of her head. "Just like your mother," he said so quietly that only she heard.

Le Loutre was in full flow. "The Marquis de Pérusse has raised enough money to build scores of homes some miles from Nantes. There are hundreds of hectares that will be divided equally into three acres for each household. It will be called the Acadian Line, so that there can be no doubt who it belongs to.

So like her mother. He let the priest's words pass over his head. *I have not been the same since she died. Not that defiant optimist I used to be. I have become like a man walking head down into a gale without any idea where I am going. Who'd think I was only in my forties? My hair is starting to turn grey. I can tell when I walk the fields with Jean-Baptiste when he sees the limp getting worse and that damned hand flapping at my side, that he feels sorry for me. He even helped me over a stile last week. I was the strong man of the ghetto. Now...*

The priest was still talking. *Would he never stop?*

He enthused, "The houses will be as well built as we were used to in Grand-Pré—good solid mud on a flint base with a thatch. There will be two bedrooms, a fireplace, a pantry and a small barn to keep all your farm tools.

The Marquis will supply you with four oxen, two cows, two plows, and a cart. What's more, there will be a communal pasture."

As we were used to ... Increasingly the older man had taken to sitting on the bench outside their cottage with his comrades, smoke his pipe, and reminisce. They warmed themselves with weary nostalgia.

He could see the cottages scattered on the hill side from Grand Pré down to the sea and the levees—how proud they had been of their levees—the smoke swirling from chimneys, the sounds of children playing.

He would conjure up the whir of the saw mills and the creaking of the water wheels. There were the men coming back from the forest with the game they had trapped, and the fishermen beaching their coracles, laden with fish. The meadows were rich with their swaying crops of wheat and barley, and the orchards were heavy with fruit.

"Have we not heard all this rubbish before?" asked Pierre abruptly, starting him from his reverie.

"Why mock us with false hope?" asked Jean-Baptiste.

A voice from the front of the church shouted, "Cousins, do not go near this place. It is another scheme to exploit us!"

The speaker was one of the young Trahans from the nearby village of Bangor. "I have a cousin on the mainland who has been there, and I tell you that none of the houses have been built, the ground needs clearing, the soil is marshy. It will be impossible to grow a thing."

Le Loutre was abashed by this and started to marshal his reply when Jean-Baptiste got to his feet and cried, "Do not believe what this priest has to say. There is no point. I do not know a thing about this place, but I do know he has learnt nothing from the mistakes he has made, and does not seem to understand that these barons and rich bastard entrepreneurs have only their own interests at heart. *Theirs,* not ours."

It was a brutal intervention and one that brought cheers from the crowd. The meeting broke up. There were no takers for Le Loutre's latest plan.

"He is not a bad man," said Jean-Baptiste that evening, "Maybe I was harsh, but he is driven by a crazy idealism which has made him trust men who are without scruples. He is a fool, no match for De Warren, this Marquis, all their despicable ilk."

His father said, "The French Moses—that's what they used to call Le Loutre. Remember when the ship bringing us here foundered in the bay? Sometimes I think we would be happier if the waters had closed over our heads and we had all gone down with it."

As the family paused in pained reflection, Osite said, "We cannot feel sorry for ourselves now, not after everything we have been through. Father, you know that best of all. As Jean-Baptiste said, we cannot rely on priests or dukes or businessmen to help us."

"Or wait for them to exploit us," said her brother. "The shocking truth is that we exiles are as lost as we have ever been. In the ghetto we knew the enemy—well, I should say, father, *you* knew the enemy and stood up to them—but now we are subjected to hate and discrimination by the very people who are meant to be our saviors."

"Father, you were the hero then," said Osite, fingering the bruise that still blushed the side of her face. "Now we alone—this family—have to be just as brave. Decide what is best for us and make it happen."

It was as if the ghost of Jambo's first wife was in the room.

"Hurrah little sister, well spoken," said Jean-Baptiste. "I say *no* to Le Loutre. We need to find a place that we want to live in, not an *invented* community like this Acadian Line. A place where we can become part of a real, living society. Yes, it is up to us. We have to take our fate into our own hands."

"Where shall we go?" asked Agnes.

"I am told Quimper is a pleasant town with plenty of work," said Jean-Baptiste.

"I have heard the same," said Osite.

"Let's go there," said Jean-Baptiste.

"Yes," said his father.

TWENTY-SIX

Quimper, Brittany

The summer of 1772.

Tales from Far and Near

"Yes," said Jambo. "Quimper is indeed a pleasant place. Prosperous. And the cathedral—I have never seen such a fine building."

"We will be able to pray for our salvation," said his son drily.

"The market has more food than I have seen since mother took me to Halifax for the Michaelmas Fair," said Agnes.

"There will be work here," said Jean-Baptiste as they strolled along the riverbank where barges that made the daylong trip to the Atlantic were moored. The alleys were lined with flourishing little shops, some selling pork and butter, for which they learnt the town was famous, and one street that was packed with cobblers and leather workers.

Jambo half expected to find Oliver there, enthusiastically fixing shoes and taking a sou or two off passers-by in a card game with rules that only he understood.

In their optimism, they chose to ignore the running sewerage in the side streets and the primitive cottages with ragged thatch roofs from which hangdog peasants skulked like conspirators, gathering on street corners smoking and grumbling about their lot, the government, and '*these cursed incomers*'.

"Look at the pottery for sale here," said Osite, peering through a shop window. "I didn't know that there were craftsmen capable of making things in so many colors."

"And so delicate," said Agnes.

"We'll have to earn a lot of money before we can afford anything like that," said Jean-Baptiste.

It had taken longer the family longer than they anticipated to extricate themselves from the island they had come to hate. There were arguments over rents; De Warren demanded payment for the livestock he had provided when they first arrived; Foucquet insisted they owed him a tithe for their use of the lane that led to the port and even Le Loutre tried to insist that all exiles were 'obliged' to settle in the new settlement, the Acadian Line.

What's more, in the midst of all the wrangling, Agnes gave birth to a boy, Simon. It was almost as if it was an act of defiance to all the hostility that surrounded them but, insisted the new mother, despite her eagerness to put it behind her, "We cannot travel with a baby. We'll have to wait"

Jean-Baptiste grumbled, "At this rate we'll never get off this damned island."

Even Jambo was fretful. "Osite wasn't much older when she was dragged half way round the world," he said to his wife. But she would not shift until the child was more than six months old.

"He'll be strong enough now," she said.

Eventually, two long years after the family gathering when they had decided to leave, De Warren washed his hands of them.

"Fuck off and good riddance to you, you leeching Canadians," he said as they boarded the ship that was to take them the few miles to the mainland.

From there, they travelled by barge to Quimper and rented a cottage on the outskirts of the town, just off the old road that led to Brest in the north and Nantes to the south.

There were eight of them packed into their new home.

Osite and the two girls – Blanche, seven, and Marie-Francoise, five, shared one room, while baby Simon cuddled up to his parents—though more often than not Marie-Francoise would drag her awkward little frame into bed with them as well, complaining of aching teeth and bones. Sometimes her frail bowed legs would give from under her and she would break a bone, but she was heroic in her determination to keep up with her brothers and sisters when they played, and eager to listen as Osite read her stories from the Bible. Soon she could remember passages from the New Testament, and would stand precariously on the kitchen bench to recite poems that her clever big sister had made up for her.

Jean-Baptiste and Joseph, four, slept where they could until Jambo built a small outhouse from discarded timbers he had found in the town's boatyard.

To the carpenter's surprise, Pierre had thrown in his lot with Le Loutre's scheme and set off for the Acadian Line.

"Francoise is pregnant again," he had said. "We need the security. It cannot go wrong this time, can it?" He did not look convinced.

The LeBlancs, on the other hand, were full of hope. Jean-Baptiste, who had turned 20, had become increasingly forceful. "Yes, mama, if you want pottery like that, we men had best get to work. Father, I am told they are building a new turnpike to Nantes and are recruiting laborers."

"I shall get a position in the school," said Osite with surprising confidence. "Not many people can read and write as well as I can."

"And I will, no doubt, spend my time looking after the lot of you," said Agnes.

So it was father and son who went looking for work on the turnpike, where they found that their chances depended on the whim of the foreman who chose his favorites from the gaggle of men who congregated outside his office at dawn every day.

He was a sallow, shifty, character, with thin shoulders that rose above his neck as if he was permanently shrugging. He had a pursed little mouth, through which he stuck his tongue like a greedy lizard chasing flies.

"What do you want?" he demanded the first morning they joined the queue of waiting men.

"Work," said Jambo firmly.

"Of course you do, but why bother me? You're foreigners." He held up a ledger like a shield as if to repel them.

"We look after our own kind first," said one of the locals waiting to be chosen.

"And last," said another.

"We live here," said Jambo. "We have been in this country for nine years. We have a right."

"A right! Hear that—he has a *right* to a job," said the first laborer, who looked as ill-kempt and gaunt as the two Acadians. "Listen, monsieur, none of us are entitled to anything here, we're just the poor, bloody workers. Except there ain't no work."

"I can't take on cripples," said the foreman, who had been observing the carpenter as he limped toward him.

"It makes no difference to the way I swing a hammer," he said, keeping his right hand tucked into his waistcoat. "I can break stones as well as any man."

"We can do anything you want us to do. We will labor hard from dawn to dusk," said Jean-Baptiste.

"Even if we did take you on, it's lower pay for foreigners," said the foreman, sensing a useful money making opportunity.

"As long as it's fair that's all right with us," said the carpenter before his son could bargain with him.

The foreman did not hesitate. "Very well. Start today."

The locals were indignant.

"You can't do that," they chorused angrily at the foreman. "You've given our jobs to outsiders."

"Now we'll all be paid less in the future," said one.

"Foreign bastard cheats," from another.

"Margins are tight." The foreman's tongue flickered. "I have to do the best I can for the investors."

"We know what that means," sneered one of the spurned workers. "You charge your bosses the old rate and keep the balance for yourself."

The foreman shut his ledger. The two Acadians said nothing and joined the working crew. Nonetheless, when winter arrived they were the ones who were the first to be laid off and forced back on the streets, scouring the town and nearby countryside for labor. Anything would do—thatching barn roofs, fixing fences, loading the barges.

Jean-Baptiste talked himself into a job as caretaker in one of the pottery factories, and Osite took on a cleaning job at the school. If Agnes could not find the time to make garments to sell in the market, what with all cleaning and cooking, she would take the little ones to the main street and beg.

They were used to it. They felt no shame. In fact, the children, led by a theatrically plaintive Marie-Francoise, would sometimes put on a show of crying and holding their stomachs so pitifully that a few extra sous were thrown in their direction.

"They will grow up to think dishonesty is the way to prosper," Jambo complained to Agnes. "The people will not believe us when we really need help."

"The only shame is that we have been reduced to such a plight," she said. "We have to get food and money by whatever means we can. As long as the children realize it is little more than a game, I do not think they will grow up to be felons."

Sometimes he would hear of a job out of town and set off on foot, or squeeze in among the produce on the back of a cart and head for La Rochelle or St. Malo, but as often as possible for Morlaix where he would stay with Charles.

His brother, Madeleine, and their children—'*five of the b-b-blighters now,*' he laughed—were living in what was little more than a lean-to shed in a refugee settlement that had spread out from the old barracks on the hill overlooking the port.

His feckless older brother was as cheerful as ever, "It's a fine position up here," he said. "We d-d-don't have quite enough food, but we can at least admire the view. Now, bring me up to date with everything?"

Before Jambo could open his mouth he continued. "I heard rumor that our brothers Olivier and Pierre were in Philadelphia, or somewhere in P-p-pennsylvania. And Claude was spotted in Massachusetts, but I have no idea if that is true."

Jambo said, "I was told hear that soon after our sister Madeleine and husband Paul were sent to Massachusetts in '55 he died, and their children were indentured to an English landlord. I think she is having a hard time. But as for the others...we can only pray they are still alive."

"Well, yes, pray, but we have to f-f-face up to reality," said Charles. "We may never see them again, and although I miss them as k-k-keenly as you, here we are and here we will s-s-stay." He took a sup of cider. "We have to m-m-make the best of things." And then, shrugging off the fate of his family with typical insouciance, he said, "There is plenty to entertain us here. No end of g-g-gossip. Have you heard about Jean-Baptiste Hebert?"

"Go on, tell me."

"I don't know if he is a relation to Francois—God save him—but he became a pirate."

Jambo laughed at yet another of his brother's tall tales. "A pirate!"

"Of course, he is not called that, because actually he is hired by the k-k-king, no less, but his job is to seize ships—English, Dutch, doesn't matter—and bring back whatever booty is on board. There are quite a few involved in that g-g-game here. Believe or not there's a Joseph LeBlanc. He must be one of our family, I suppose. In fact, I thought it was *you*, Jambo, when I first heard. Maybe you'd finally stopped being so d-d-damned sensible and gone m-m-mad. They get a cut of what they capture and m-m-make a decent living, which is more than the rest of us do.

"See that big house there? Belongs to Patrice Trahan who used to help p-p-poor Pierre Landry in his mill, but now he sails the seas in pursuit of treasure. Cuts quite a f-f-figure, I must say. Mind you, it's not all easy pickings. There was one—can't remember his name, a Granger, I think—who was b-b-beheaded for trying to smuggle out some adventurers who, the King said, were guilty of sedition. Protestants, probably."

"But how are you getting by?" asked Jambo.

"I help in the docks, but it is too much like h-h-hard work for me. Madeleine does some mending and washing, and she takes the children b-b-begging. What else can we do? We cannot afford to live on the government allowance." He took a draught of cider.

"But it does pay for the occasional drink," said Jambo.

"It does." He paused and laughed, unabashed by his brother's irony. "A man needs a few p-p-pleasures." Then he was off again, "Do you remember Anne P-p-rince?" he asked. "The one who married Sylvain LeBlanc? Very sad. After he died in the plague she was left with four daughters to bring up. Well, she was living on the heights over there on the other b-b-bank with one of them—Anastasie it was—when late one night they had a knock on the door.

"It was a P-p-protestant p-p-priest fleeing from the authorities. The government is very hostile to Huguenots as they call the Protestants in France, you know. Banned 'em. Anyway, they felt sorry for the runaway, but no sooner had they taken him in than a couple of town officials also came c-c-calling. They arrested them all and sent them off to Brest where they locked 'em up. Of course, they found them g-g-guilty and g-g-guillotined them."

"That's dreadful," said the carpenter. "Such cruelty. Our lives have been quiet in comparison. By the way, did you hear that Le Loutre died? "

"Has he indeed?" For once Charles was behind with the news.

"Yes," said his brother. "Only a few weeks ago, in fact. For a man so certain that he had God on his side to cause such mischief was a tragedy. For him and us."

"I say good riddance," said Charles. "These priests are a m-m-menace. Remember the Bishop of Quebec? How he wanted to have the tavern closed? Mind you, the s-s-scandals some of us have been mixed up in would benefit from an absolution," he said with relish. "Disgraceful. One or two of the women have been caught going with the sailors. They've been d-ddisowned by the Acadian council here, but they are still p-p-lying their t-t-trade. Well, it's easy money and they are desperate. I think some of our holier-than-thou councillors stop by occasionally to savor their wares."

He pushed the jug to Jambo. "H-h-have another mug of cider, brother. It's a bad b-b-business, of course, but after all we have been through we have learnt to make the most of our chances where we c-c-can, and how we can. I shall not judge."

"You are right," said Jambo. "Every single day of the last—what is it now, 17 years?—has been a trial, so if one or two of us has sinned then I think it best to let God be the judge."

Perversely, Jambo was cheered by his brother's garrulous accounts of bad behavior and venality, if only because they reminded him that even as they eked out their existence from day to day they could aspire to the ordinary. To be greedy and concupiscent, even downright stupid, was somehow a triumph.

He managed to get a few weeks work in Morlaix—first in the tobacco factory, which was badly paid but did give him sufficient to save a little and fill his pipe for a month, and then he helped with the repairs to a ship that had arrived from South America, much buffeted by the gales.

One evening after work, he got talking to a fellow on the quayside.

"You're Joseph LeBlanc, aren't you?" asked the man. "Jambo."

"I am."

"I'm Anselme Boudrot. Used to be friendly with your youngest brother, Jean-Baptiste."

The image of two young lads larking about in the yard at home sprang into Jambo's mind, but this Anselme was dull-eyed and weary. *I must look the same,* he thought.

"Remember when we arrived in France we were told about a chance to rebuild our lives in the Falkland Islands?"said Boudrot.

"The first of many '*glorious opportunities,* '" said Jambo. "Ah yes."

"You spoke out against it," said Boudrot.

Jambo shrugged. "I think we realized pretty soon that the French were as duplicitous as the British."

"You were right, cousin. Too damned right." For a second the other man showed a spark of the spirit he must have had as a youngster. "Were we warned about the three month voyage in some of the worst seas ever known? Far, far more terrifying than the Atlantic crossing, cousin, I can assure you. Were we told that there were no houses for us to live in once we got there? Just stone huts with their roof tiles blown off by winds fiercer than the gales that would whip up the waves in the Bay of Fundy."

"So not a land of plenty?" interjected Jambo.

"Only rock," continued Boudrot. "Rock with a few swamps in summer and hardly any trees—just a few shrubs kept flat to the ground by the infernal wind. Of course, there were no fences, so when we landed with the few cattle and sheep that survived the journey they promptly scattered across the island. We were forced to hunt seals for food and clothing. Then, one morning, we woke up to find, guess what?"

He did not wait for his audience to answer. "In the bay, a British man o' war, and on the harbor wall, a platoon of red coats. Even there, thousands of miles from the nearest land, there was no escape from the bastards. They claimed it was their territory, and needless to say there were more of them and better armed than the pathetic French who cowered behind the timber walls that passed for a garrison. It took them about ten minutes to round 'em up, stick 'em below decks, and take 'em away."

"The British—"Jambo started to say something about their relentless quest to dominate the world, but the refugee was in full spate.

"Then Spain decided it was *their* territory. More soldiers, more fighting. Well, the islands were wretched enough without it being a battleground as well, so we managed to get a ride on a Spanish ship and work our way home. Been to some places, I can tell you—Argentina, Uruguay, Brazil—none of them suitable homes for a civilized people. We only got back last month."

"Well, you will have discovered that it is not much better here," said

Jambo. "A lot of our cousins went south to Poitou, where they were promised land and homes in a settlement, but from what little I have heard that particular project has been a failure. Another one."

When work on the ship was completed and he was laid off, he bade farewell to Charles and trudged back to Quimper, where he was met at the cottage gate by Agnes. For once, she had a smile on her face. "It's Pierre and family."

"My friend, dear Pierre," said the delighted carpenter. "It must be over a year. Welcome. And Francoise. How have you fared? I confess I never did understand why you went off to Poitou like that. Still, here you are."

"You were right," said Pierre. The trapper seemed reassuringly unchanged, though the carpenter noticed as he lifted a mug of coffee to his lips that his hand shook, and the tic that had started on the day of Marie's death was more pronounced.

"Of course we were," said Jean-Baptiste with a stinging certainty that took the trapper aback. He was unfamiliar with this grown-up, straight-speaking, young man. "We know without you opening your mouth that the Acadian Line has been a disaster. Let me guess, it was another one of the government's *perfect societies,* which turned out to be a shambles of lies and incompetence."

"Exactly," said the trapper. "When we arrived we discovered that the Marquis, who Le Loutre so eagerly backed, had nothing like enough money to build the homes for us, so that left about 3,000 people on land that was little more than a swamp. The Marquis had not worked out the titles for who owned what—remember the abbot said we would get three acres each?—so we refused to clear the fields. What was the point? We might have worked away and found the land belonged to somebody else."

He looked more resigned than angry.

"We sat and we waited, but nothing happened for six months. We were hungry and likely to get more so with winter coming on. We weren't prepared to hang around, so we got out. I've heard since that some of the younger ones went crazy."

"Yes, there was a riot," interjected Francoise, who seemed delighted at the thought. "Serve Mister Marquis right."

Pierre smiled at her forthrightness and squeezed her hand affectionately. "They threw stones and timbers down the wells to block them up, smashed the windows and tore down the thatch in the few houses that had been built. That must be the end of the Acadian Line. Everyone has headed to Nantes. Hundreds of them. God knows what they will do for work."

He sipped his coffee.

"But you will never believe what the Marquis said. He blamed *us*. He accused us of being an intolerable, slothful breed who wanted to sponge off the state rather than work. Apparently it was all right for us to be getting an allowance when we first arrived, but not now."

"It's not as if our conditions have improved in all the years that we have been here," said Jambo. "We are still struggling to find work, and the local people continue to resent us. If they had been hungry for all that time they might think differently."

TWENTY-SEVEN

The 'Parasites Inn', Quimper

Spring, 1773.

Of Life and Loss

Some evenings Jambo would stroll around the cathedral precinct and stop at the tavern where the exiles used to congregate. The French called it the Parasites Inn because they resented the way their own government subsidized the foreigners while they were just as short of bread, just as unfairly treated by the landlords, and just as badly paid. Occasionally their resentment would boil over and they would lob a burning flare into the snug or break the windows.

The older men would reminisce and grumble while their sons would tell each other where they might find work, which factory owner was taking people on, who was laying workers off, or where a farmer might want extra help.

It was here that that reports trickled in sporadically of cousins scattered far and wide in America, France, and the West Indian colonies which helped reconnect the exiles to their scattered community.

They knew from De la Rochette when he had visited them in Liverpool at the end of the war that thousands of their countrymen had died at the hands of the British—either directly or as a result of their enforced wanderings—and as Jambo said, "We must all have lost someone close, but what makes it unbearable is that we don't know who is still alive and who long gone. The doubt is as disturbing as the certainty."

Nonetheless, over the years, thanks to a mix of gossip, rumor and actual fact they had put together an inventory of life and loss. Sometimes a traveler from St. Malo would call by, and in conversation would let slip that so-and-so who they remembered from their school days had become married, or a wanderer from Nantes, passing though in the hope of finding a bed for the night, would announce that the Heberts, the ones whose parents used to live on a farm on the River Gaspereau, had produced twins, or that one of the Boudrots had been killed in a fight outside a tavern.

But the most news came in letters delivered to the inn as the place where at least one regular would recognize a name.

A missive would arrive from a brother, thought to be dead, but no, he was scratching a living in an American colony. Another told of the sickness of a mother in Massachusetts, and the birth of a boy in Pennsylvania.

"Heavens, I'm an uncle," would go the cry. "A toast to another Acadian."

Many were sent by relatives who had heard that there was a cousin in France without quite knowing where. Often, if there was no one to match the name on the envelope, the tavern regulars would prise the letter open and share the contents because, as Pierre declared, "We are bound to know them, aren't we? Even if the letter is not for any one of us."

That was how they heard about Gabriel Lajeunesse, the blacksmith and his lost love Evangeline Bellefontaine. They broke the seal on a letter addressed to The Family Bellefontaine, Nantes, France, which judging by its ragged state had already been delivered to many households in search of one of their relatives.

It had been written by a Bellefontaine, who was working for a landowner in Pennsylvania, scraping along with his wife and six children. There was a lot of chatter about their daily woes, but there was a postscript, *Sad tidings of our niece Evangeline, I fear. She searched unceasingly for her Gabriel, the man she was to marry before the British tore them apart, but finally she had resigned herself to never seeing him again and became a nun, tending to the sick in Philadelphia. There, by some miracle, she found him, but he was so sick that he lived only long enough for them to be reunited on his deathbed. I heard recently that she followed him soon after to the grave, utterly heart-broken.*

Jambo recalled her standing distraught on the shore at Boudrot Point and then Lajeunesse in the maize field in Virginia, swearing, "I will find her. I won't give up."

What consolation was it to be reunited in death?

He heard from Jean Melancon. After their meeting by the graves in Williamsburg, he and his brother Phillipe had headed south and set up homes on the banks of the River Mississippi in Louisiana.

They even have levees here to keep the river at bay, Jean wrote, *You could almost imagine we were back home, except the weather is like the hottest August we had in Grand-Pré all year round, and we are pestered by bugs, mosquitoes, and alligators, fearsome creatures with teeth like something out of our old saw mill.*

The great thing is that Louisiana is now ruled by Spain. Not sure why, something to do with the treaty at the end of the war which got rid of the French.

"The same one that banned us from returning home and got us sent here," said Jambo as he read the letter out.

The authorities have been welcoming and seem happy to leave us to our own devices, unlike those bastard British.

"Or the bastard French," said Pierre with unusual asperity.

Maybe life is good over there in France, but you should think about joining us. There are so many now that it is almost like a new Acadia. The Spanish make us smile. They speak so oddly they can't pronounce Acadian properly, so they call us Caydjuns.

They were hearing a lot about this Louisiana.

"It seems that some of our cousins who were transported to New York after the expulsion were the first to move on and settle there," said Pierre.

"Way back in '64, I heard," said a regular.

"As long ago as that?" wondered another. "Still, anywhere must be better if it is not under British rule."

"My brother has not seen his children for ten years—lost to some landlord in Pennsylvania," said another, sharing the contents of his latest letter. "In the end he gave up trying to find them and trekked south to Louisiana and is happily living there. Well, as happy as a man can be who has lost his family."

"Why would the Spanish be so keen on us settling there?" wondered Pierre.

"I can guess," said Jambo. "Knowing how ruthless these great powers are, my guess is that they want us to populate the frontiers. They know what fine farmers we are, and how well we would cultivate the land for them, but more importantly, we would serve as a sort of human shield against the British. One thing is for sure, they won't have let our cousins in from the goodness of their hearts."

"There's a motive for everything and it is never to do with the goodness of their hearts," said Jean-Baptiste. "I bet if Le Loutre was still alive he would be holding meetings to tell us about the brilliant deal he has struck with some new Spanish friends."

"He'd have his lining on the quayside for the barges to take us to coast," laughed Jambo. And then serious, "No, Charles says we are probably better off here and I fear he is right."

The carpenter had long resigned himself to dying in France, and some evenings the shades of the past and his dulled resignation about the future would draw him to the cathedral graveyard.

It was a ritual he used to follow in Grand-Pré when he would simply sit near the graves of his forebears and feel, not sad, but conscious of the sense of continuity the old stones gave him—that season would follow season, that the villagers' existence would remain unchanging and uncomplicated as the living replaced the dead.

Those still moments spoke to him of the way each generation had striven to guarantee the future of their beloved homeland. *If only I could feel that comfort now,* he reflected as he looked at the alien names on the gravestones.

A voice said, "Jambo? Yes, it is. Joseph LeBlanc. The one we called Jambo."

A frail old woman, leaning on a stick, white haired and staring hard at him, came out of the gloom.

"My God." It was one of his aunts, Marguerite-Marie LeBlanc. The last time he had seen her they had been struggling to stay upright in the mud of Boudrot Point. She had been picked up by a soldier and hurled on to a skiff. Then she was wild haired, hitting out and screaming defiance—now she was stooped, drained of feeling, eyes as listless as muddy puddles.

He was about to say, *I thought you must be dead,* but instead said, "My dear aunt. This is a miracle."

She touched his face as if checking that he was flesh and not a vision. "Jambo, how are you?" she asked.

"Still alive, as you see," he said wearily. With a flash of the old defiance he added, "Still undefeated. Did they think they could so easily destroy us?"

They sat on a bench in the graveyard and she told him her story. She had been loaded on to a ship bound for South Carolina.

"Remember that Winslow character had said he hoped we would be a '*peaceable and happy people?*' She fluttered her hands across her forehead as if trying to block out the memory. "That was not the way the Governor saw it. He hated us. '*Traitors,*' he called us. '*Papists, riff-raff*.'"

"Ah yes, the usual insults. They have such a limited vocabulary when it comes to hate," said Jambo.

"He wanted us off his territory and out of his way, so he gave us a fleet of small boats—some of them not much bigger than coracles—and a few bags of flour and said, '*Off you go. Wherever you like. We won't stop you*'. Our plan was to sail back to Acadia but most of the boats sank within days.

Some of us made it to a harbor in Virginia."

"Virginia? But that's where we were." Jambo was shaken by the coincidence. "We were kept in the transports for months off Williamsburg. Was the port called Hampton?"

"We never got to know it well enough to call it a name." She screwed her mouth in concentration. "Maybe Hampton. Yes, it could be. We did hear that there were some unfortunates nearby being held as prisoners, but we weren't sure if they were slaves or Acadians. My Pierre—do you remember him?—was all for sneaking off to find out, but I put a stop to that."

So close. And yet what if the two groups had been reunited? What if poor, half-crazed Pierre Gautrot had escaped the patrol, what could they have achieved beyond the reassurance that there were more of them still alive? Nothing. The British would have been on to them in minutes, rounded them up, and used that as an excuse to shoot them.

"The British did not want us there either so they sent troops to scare us back out to sea," said his aunt. "There was nothing for it. On we sailed. The boats were waterlogged and impossible to steer through the inlets and the mangrove swamps, so we took to foot, travelling along the border with Old France, sleeping by day, walking at night. So weary, our bones ached.

"To make things worse, the Indians and the French were just as likely to attack us as the British. Everywhere we went we'd come across bodies left lying in the mud after some bloody skirmish. Have you ever seen a scalped man? Brains scattered, picked over by a black storm of crows? Hideous."

She shuddered at the memory, her hands waving away the image.

"The British took some of us prisoners, and others handed themselves in. It was too much for them to bear. We were so hungry we ate what we could—roots, rats, anything. If we were lucky, the men would catch a rabbit, or even a deer, but even then we did not dare light a fire long enough to cook them, so we ate the flesh raw. Scores of us died. I lost my beloved Pierre, my mother, and two sisters—they were too weak to survive such an adventure— but some of us did make it. We got to the shores of the Bay of Fundy, and there on the other side, we could see Grand-Pré with the smoke curling from the houses. We were so happy. Home at last.

"But our joy did not last for long. There were soldiers everywhere making sure that the borders were closed to us. Our little village is now a British settlement. Acadia is not our country anymore. It never will be."

She looked at Jambo and started to sob, dabbling at her eyes with the sleeve of her shabby jerkin.

"We kept going to Prince Edward Island," she went on. "It was then still in French hands. What an ordeal it was to get that far, hiding from the British, crossing rivers up to our necks, hacking through forests, and paddling over the straits in tiny coracles. We felt safe for a year or so because we knew so many people there, many outcasts like us, but there was to be no peace. The British invaded Louisbourg—you must have heard about that—and we were shipped to France. God, that was a crossing."

"From what I have heard you were lucky to survive," said Jambo.

"Lucky? I'm not so sure." Again, the nervy flip of the hand, the dab at her eyes. She explained how she had made one more attempt to return home. In the peace treaty that ended the war, France was allowed to keep only one possession in North America, the barren St. Pierre and Miquelon islands off the coast of Newfoundland.

"They aren't much, I admit," she reflected. "But they are closer to home than here, so I volunteered to go."

She had joined the convoy that had been arranged between the powers and set sail in 1763 only to be confronted, once again, by the British.

"Despite everything being agreed, they sent us straight back," she said. "I cannot understand why they stay so hostile toward us." She hid her face behind her hand for a second, paused and then looked up at him as if she was trying to remember something. "My sister. Jeanne. Your mother. What of her? Is she still with you?"

"No. Mother died in a Liverpool prison. She did not have the strength to endure any more sorrow. Just like father, who died soon after. She missed her boys. She never saw them again after they were imprisoned on the ships. She had me and the two little ones, but we were not enough."

"And that lovely wife? Marguerite?"

"She was taken from me."

She gave a jerk of her shoulders, almost a shrug, as if that was what she had been expecting to hear.

"You poor boy," she murmured.

When he recounted the story to Agnes later that evening, it seemed as if his aunt's travails summed up the futility of the twenty years to which they had been so casually condemned.

"It also shows how cussedly determined we've been too, doesn't it," said his wife.

TWENTY-EIGHT

Quimper, Brittany

February, 1774.

Havens to be Happy

Jambo's leg had become increasingly painful, making heavy work arduous, so he had begun to concentrate on his carving to raise extra money.

"I made you a doll once," he told Osite, "but it was lost in the sea the day we were being expelled. A soldier trampled on it."

"You've made me lots of dolls," she said and kissed him.

"But that was the first," he replied.

Nonetheless, he was particularly pleased with a little tableau of Indians in full regalia that he had sold to a stall holder, so decided to find Jean-Baptiste and celebrate with a mug of cider. As he strolled into the tavern his son was playing cards and talking loudly about a deal he and the owner of the pottery factory, had completed with a wealthy Parisian.

"These city types think we're stupid country clodpolls, but we took him for twice what we'd charge normally."

He had grown up quite different from his father. He was sharp witted, a little cold, but clever. Since the galvanizing effect the attack on his sister had had on him, he had learnt to read and write, swiftly realizing that there were easier and better paid ways of making a living than to follow his father and his friends toiling away in the fields for a few sous.

He had thrived in the pottery factory, combining hard work with a range of cutting put-downs and a refusal to tolerate fools, with a subtle understanding that if he was to overcome prejudice he would have to pay lip service to the superiority of his employers. He had been put in charge of the night shift, and picked out by the owner as worthy of yet further promotion. He had even caught the eye of the owner's niece. In fact, he had high hopes of marriage—a detail he had not shared with his parents.

He broke off from his game to embrace his father and elaborate on the cleverness of the deal he had masterminded, but as he raised his first mug of ale to his lips, Jambo's eye was briefly caught by the bedraggled tramp of a figure hunched in one dark corner.

He looked in a bad way—no doubt one of the many itinerant Acadians who stumbled though the town in search of old friends—and he brought his head down close to the flagon on the table as if he could not trust his trembling hands to lift it to his mouth.

"That man is staring at you," said Jean-Baptiste a few minutes later.

Jambo looked at him again. There was something strangely familiar about him. Above his matted beard the skin was drawn thin, and his eyes were blank, almost without color, as if he was going blind. But the scar, white and ragged against his reddened features...

"Francois?"

"Jambo." It was the plowman. Once tall, strong, and fearless, now he faltered toward them with the timidity of a starved beggar.

"Jambo LeBlanc. My friend."

"Francois, is it you?" He hardly recognized him.

"Comrade," said the apparition and held on to one arm while shaking the other. His hands, once so powerful from days thwacking his oxen into pulling the plow, were emaciated, their bones stood out, entwined by livid veins.

"And this is Jean-Baptiste," he said, pulling his own damaged hand out of the plowman's trembling grasp.

"It cannot be," said Francois. "A man. You were just a lad." He staggered and clung to the back of a chair.

"You are coming home with us," said Jambo. "You need food and rest."

He ate like a starved wolf, and slept for ten hours. When he awoke, Agnes said, "Here is coffee and porridge, uncle. Tell us your story."

"When I left you that night, Jambo, I damn near turned around and came back," he said, his hands quivering so much that he spilt the coffee down his filthy jerkin. "If only I had. The quayside was heaving with people. We had been told there would be maybe 1,700 of us, but the place was full of émigrés who had come, not just from France, but as far away as Alsace and Bavaria.

"They had walked all the way, tempted by the bounty that the French had promised them. How soon that would prove to be a lie. Worse than a lie, the enterprise was a betrayal." He was shaking as he spoke.

"I was surprised that there were families on board. I assumed it would just be men—miserable sods like me with nothing to lose—so that meant the ships were as crowded as they were when we came this way. So much for Le Loutre's promise of a comfortable passage across the Atlantic. What of the *good* abbot by the way? Is he still alive?"

"No, he died in '72," said Jambo.

"Shame. I would like to have told him what I thought of him. Bloody, damn fool. He told everyone Guyana was going to be like Grand Pré in the spring—warm and temperate, good soil. Perfect. Remember? How could it go wrong, especially as it was the *king himself* who promised each of us three years of food and free land?"

"The kind of promise that make all the time," said Jean-Baptiste. "And then break."

Francois glanced at him, taken aback by the young man's assertiveness. "By the end of 1765 there were 13,000 or more unsuspecting foreigners who made land at a place called Kourou, just up a river from the capital, Cayenne. The plan was to build a settlement with a fort and a harbor, but that was impossible. There was no equipment, no bricks, or mortar. We had to chop down the trees for timber—difficult without enough axes to go round.

"But that was the least of it. Right from the beginning, it was just a matter of staying alive. Hell would have been an improvement. It was the rainy season. Not just a good honest downpour like we used to have in Grand-Pré, this was a steady sheet of water that came down day after day. Night after night. There was no shelter. No food. Well, a bowl of warm water with a grain or two of rice. The promise of houses, built and ready for us, was a lie. What we had were lean-tos made of palm leaves and bamboo. And we were the lucky ones."

"Fancy that," said Jean-Baptiste. "The same old story."

"We sat in the mud and filth of the jungle—really, the place was just a quagmire that ran into the sea—and waited for the rains to pass. Within days everyone had diarrhea. You can imagine what that did to our luxurious accommodation. The stench was unbelievable, and—forgive me, Agnes—it was impossible to tell where the shit ended and the mud began. We were ankle deep in it." He closed his eyes for a moment.

"Have you seen anyone with cholera? It is something all should be spared. You could always tell if a man was coming down with it because his skin would change to a sort of bluish-grey, then the contents of his bowels would pour out, followed by the uncontrollable retching from deep in the guts. We were already stricken by thirst and dehydration, which made every limb in our bodies ache." He took a gulp of his coffee and savored its almost-forgotten taste for some seconds.

"Smallpox was terrible," said Francois, becoming almost incoherent as the horrors he had experienced came flooding back. "But this cholera was worse than the early days of Liverpool, Jambo. Much worse. There was something outlandish about it, monstrous, the way it ate away at your insides until it erupted in a bloody flux that could not be controlled. No wonder we quickly we became like brutes ourselves, fighting over the bread rations, eating roots, shitting where we stood. Dignity? We lost that soon enough."

Agnes flinched.

"I apologize for my language," said Francois. "But you have to understand what we went through. When did I leave? Summer of '63, wasn't it. Within months there were 800 in the hospital. Hospital! Just a clearing in the jungle covered with bamboo. It stank more than a shit house in August. Sorry. I was told that 9,000 died in the first few months, but I wouldn't be surprised if the figure was greater than that. What little rations they found were given to the poor sods in the hospital, though to be honest, it was wasted on them—they were going to die anyway."

"It is shameful that the French have behaved as cruelly as the British," said Agnes.

"Worse, in some ways," said Jambo. "Francois is right. It is the greater betrayal."

The plowman picked up the saga that evening in the tavern. With a plate of sausages and a flagon of beer in front him he recaptured some of his old zest and anger, especially as he had more of an audience.

"What was even more wicked was the behavior of the governor and his men. Their hobby was to pick out someone weak for their amusement, especially the slaves. God, we were treated badly, but the savagery *they* endured. The soldiers liked to whip the men, and then put salt on their wounds and watch them scream for mercy, or they would send them running through the jungle and take pot shots at them. When they hit a target they would leave him where he fell, and we would wait to nightfall to crawl out and try to save the poor sod. We were usually too late, the wild animals got there first.

"Needless to say, the governor turned a blind eye to what their men got up to. They were just as wicked themselves. There were always parties in his mansion—laughter, music, banquets of quail, fish, whole roasted sheep. And women. They would send out to the encampments for young girls to be brought in to serve at the tables, and then they would rape them and threw them out when they had finished with them. Bastards. None of the women were safe. The soldiers did not go short either. They would come marauding through the camps and pick out their victims. Once, we were kept at gunpoint while four of them assaulted a woman in full view of us. They seemed to enjoy it more with an audience."

The men in the tavern were quiet. Even the tavern owner stopped cleaning the glasses and listened.

"When there are no rules, there are no limits to the bestiality some men are capable of," said Pierre levelly.

The rictus smile of the dying beggar flashed into Jambo's mind. He took care not to catch the eye of the trapper.

"One of their favorite games was to stretch a woman out on the ground, strip her, and tie her down. Then they would cover her in molasses, right, you know, up between her legs, and watch as the ants attacked. Big red bastards the size of my finger they were. The women would writhe and cry out, but the guards just sat around and laughed."

He gulped and, with uncharacteristic quietness, hissed, "May God and syphilis rot their pricks."

He pushed the last of his sausage into his mouth and stabbed his fork with such ferocity into the table that he bent its handle. "In between his festivities they tried to persuade some of us to go to Haiti, the other place the *blessed* Choiseul talked about—one of his *'havens where you can be happy'*— remember that? The French were building a naval base there, a massive harbor with a breakwater that was planned to be the biggest in the Indies."

He paused while his mug was refilled, but before he could continue a voice came from the shadow of the snug.

"Ah, the havens to be happy. So many fell for that didn't we?" A stranger leant into the light of the fire. He was a stringy old man, his skin, scarred with pock marks, stretched tight across his cadaverous face. His hair, wispy and white. His eyes sunken, glittering crazily.

"I know what you are talking about. I was in New York when the war ended. The French circulated a letter from some sort of official telling us that King Louis had our plight at heart, wanted to help us flee the clutches of the British, and come to the safety and care of France."

"Sounds familiar," said Pierre.

"This character, De la Rochette was his name—"

"Rochette. Him again," said one of the regulars, an old Liverpool hand. "That trickster."

"So he tried the same game in America as he did with us," said another.

"Ah, so you know of the gentleman," said the intruder.

"Unfortunately, yes," said Jambo.

It was getting dark now in the low-beamed tavern and the shadows seemed to press in on them. The men huddled closer to the flickering light of the candle that the stranger had in front of him, reflecting the crazed white of his eyes.

"I don't how it was for you," he went on, "but we weren't in any position to argue. What was the choice? To die in penury under British rule, or take a gamble with the French? I had lost my wife, and my children were stolen from me to be apprentices. They were nine and ten years old, but they were made to work twelve hours a day and locked away in stables at night. They were fed once in the evening. Or not at all.

"What could I do? I had no money to buy them out, and no way of rescuing them. Anyway, where would we flee to? I went to visit them one day and was told they had been sold to a factory owner in Pennsylvania. I haven't heard of them since. So when France sent ships to take us to Haiti, I signed up. It was the same story for us as it was for you, my friend. All they wanted were bodies—bodies to work like slaves for a few months, and then die so that there was no extra expense.

"In truth, most of us craved the release of death within weeks of landing. Just as you found, there were no homes as they had promised, no fertile acres, but there was malaria and yellow fever. Hundreds died where they lay." His hands shook as he tried to relight his pipe but they were too unsteady and the pipe stayed cold.

"What made it worse—if that were possible—was the corruption. The French hired an American by name of Hanson to set up the shipments of us homeless. That's all we were—cargo. He was a cheating, double-crossing criminal. He had the nerve to take his fee from the French, and then charge each Acadian for the privilege of being transported to that haven, not of happiness, but of hell.

"Many escaped the encampment and disappeared into the hills. Who knows what became of them? Maybe, like true Acadians, they started smallholdings, built homes, and bred a few cattle. More likely they died. There were a few who stowed away on ships that were going to that Spanish colony, Louisiana. We heard nothing of them. Dead too, I imagine. Havens to be happy! The devil would flinch at such places."

This time, he managed to get his pipe glowing, and he slipped like a specter back into the dark fastness of the inglenook.

For a few moments the men sat saying nothing, their drinks untouched before them. The stranger's intervention had disquieted them even more than Francois's lurid account. No one knew who he was. Later, some said he had just wandered in by chance, others swore he lived like a hermit in a disused barn off the road to Nantes. It didn't matter. They all had stories like that, and they would be telling them, and hearing them, until they died.

He spoke for himself. He spoke for all of them.

But not quite all. Jean-Baptiste tugged Francois's fork out of the table and held it up as if it was a talisman.

"It's over now, old man," he said. He looked toward the darkened corner where the stranger sat. "We don't need any more of these stories. We have all lived through them. We know what has happened to us. Now, it is time to start anew. To look ahead. Francois, my boss's brother runs the quarry on the Nantes highway, he needs a good worker. I'll tell him you will be paying him a visit."

He replaced the fork on the table, its prongs toward Francois like a challenge.

TWENTY-NINE

The Lanes of Brittany

May 23, 1774 to September 1776.

A Marriage, a Journey, and a Death

"Mother, father," said Osite one morning. "I have someone I would like you to meet. He said he would call by later."

"He?" asked Jambo.

Agnes smiled.

A young man appeared at the door, and it dawned on Jambo that he had often seen him skulking at the end of the lane, taking what seemed an unusually intense interest in the hedgerow.

"Mister LeBlanc, I am very pleased to meet you. I have seen you in town, of course, and um, around. My name is Jean Houart."

"I am happy to meet you too," said the carpenter, and though he guessed what the answer would be, he asked, "What can I do for you?"

He was gravely correct, "I would like your permission to marry your daughter, Osite."

"What do you do?" he asked the suitor.

"I am a sailor," he said. "I have lived in the town all my life. At the moment I work on the barges that take the pottery from the factories to the sea. It is a decent living. I earn enough to look after your daughter and make her happy."

She smiled beguilingly as she held the sailor's hand, and Jambo could not but feel a mixture of gladness and loss.

"Jean remembers us the day we arrived in Quimper," she said.

"I had just started out as an apprentice on the barges," he said, gaining confidence. "You landed on the quay in front of me and walked past. I noticed Marguerite."

"We shall have to give you a true Acadian wedding," he said as his daughter kissed him happily.

"You mean as extravagant as ours?" asked Agnes, and they laughed the memory of their austere day in the ghetto.

He watched as Osite walked with Houart to the top of the lane and not the first time she reminded him of Marguerite. Her face was flushed, full of hope, and the possibility of her next adventure. Her hair was so thick that she found it difficult to keep its blaze of red coiled beneath her bonnet, and just like Marguerite, that promise of wildness sparked in her eyes.

Osite had inherited her strength. She had handled her ordeal at the hands of De Warren's men with an anger that replaced her hurt, and disdain that turned to pity. '*Not forgiveness*', she would emphasize, '*but compassion for their pathetic, emotionally stunted lives.*' She had used the trauma to achieve a moral superiority, and to become even more focused in her ambition to leave behind the confined world of the exile and become a teacher.

She was helping out with the very young at the school, but there had been opposition from the school governors who disapproved of employing a girl who had not only started her career as a cleaner, but was a foreigner. They were no match for her – as her father could have told them. She had developed a way of disarming people, making even the most ill-disposed to feel that in her hands everything would work out for the better. Just like her mother.

"She can convince anybody of anything," Jambo would say proudly "She knows how to make people feel calm. She has a generous way that fills a room in a gentle way, but which leaves no one in doubt who is in charge. No wonder the children adore her."

"She has been well taught herself, that's why," said Agnes.

He looked puzzled.

"Remember what you have said to us time after time, '*Always appear strong. Never be defeated'.* She listened to you."

"And now she is going her own way," he said mournfully.

After the wedding he felt more desolate than he had for years. Not since Marguerite had died in his arms 17 years before had he felt so troubled.

The day had gone with a flourish. How had Agnes conjured up the trousseau? She had transformed Osite's best, but undeniably threadbare, dress into an extravagantly embroidered gown, bedecked with lace, ornamental tags, bows, and tassels. He marveled at the way she had managed to spend many secret hours sewing such a creation. There was barely enough time in the day looking after the family, yet somehow she had achieved the impossible.

How beautiful Osite looked standing in the church by her groom. He chided himself for feeling so bereft at the thought of her leaving home.

The young bargee had followed the local custom by calling at his bride-to-be's house early on May 23 and escorting her to the church along the lane under canopies of blossom-laden trees. Jambo had recruited a couple of the regulars from the tavern to lead the way, playing their lutes while the bride, the guests, and the groom followed.

"Why have we stopped?" he asked when the small procession came to a halt. The dog barked with pointless enthusiasm.

"It is a wedding day tradition in this part of the world," said Agnes. "The village children block the couple's path with white ribbons, which the bride must cut. It is a way of showing that they will overcome all their obstacles together."

"If only it was so easy," he murmured.

"Sssh. She has suffered enough already," said Agnes. "She will be happy now."After the ceremony, the wedding party went home to celebrate the great day. Agnes had prepared a huge fricot, the old-fashioned Acadian stew of chicken, potatoes, carrots, onions and dumplings, which puzzled the groom's family, and they ate cream-filled pastry puffs until they felt queasy.

The couple toasted each other from a two-handled cup of wine before heading to the bedroom. No sooner had they hidden themselves away for their first night together, than the crowd from the neighborhood came clamoring, clanging pots and pans, ringing bells, and sounding horns.

It reminded him of his own wedding in Grand-Pré with its noise, the good will, all the hope and optimism in the world.

"We did her well, did we not?" said Agnes as they cleared the leftovers from the revelry.

"We did." He sighed. "Though, in truth, I had wished for something more of the old country."

"So my fricot was not enough for you," said Agnes and she pretended to hit at him with the ladle. "The truth is, husband, it is not just our new French in-laws that think it is a quaint old-fashioned dish, but so do our children. They know we used to eat it all the time, but they have no memory of the old ways. Only what we tell them."

"And then they don't listen," he said.

"Osite and Jean-Baptiste think we are stuck in the past," she continued. "You and I will never really settle in France or adopt their customs. We will always be outsiders, but they feel that *this* is their country now, and they don't understand why we don't feel the same way.

"Jean-Baptiste is making a good living apprenticed to the pottery, and I think he has a girl he is sweet on, though he is so secretive and never says what he gets up to. As for Osite, well, she is now a citizen of France, though she has seemed like a local, born and bred, for some years."

"She even talks like one," he said. "She doesn't even have an Acadian accent. When I can't understand her, she jokes that I am going deaf."

"That's her way of telling you what, deep down, you already know…that we have been in Quimper for more than two years, and we are destined to stay her until—"

"—we die. Yes, I suppose we are," he said gloomily. "The trouble is, I still yearn for Grand-Pré."

"I know," she said, and kissed him forthrightly, unusual for her. "But we know we won't be going back. This is our home." Then, with an uncharacteristic girlishness, she said, "You should yearn for me, nothing else."

"Not even your fricot?" He smiled a little, and she laughed.

"Well maybe that as well."

He had long since stopped taking it as a personal affront when he was laid off or rejected by some miserable foreman. When it came to foreigners, any Frenchman in authority would have been brought up in a climate of fear and prejudice that would make him treat the likes of Jambo with distrust, even hatred. It was the way. There was nothing to do about it.

He spent the summer days of '74 limping from farm to farm, building site to building site, looking for work, shrugging off the slammed doors, beating off the dogs that were set on him, and ignoring the insults and the threats.

There would be an odd day's laboring here or there, but Jambo was only one of the many desperate to earn a few sous. It was not just the immigrants who were treading the same path, but the local men. They were as badly treated in the France of the 1770s as they had been in the last century when his ancestor Daniel had sailed to Acadia to escape the same demeaning poverty and begin anew.

Unexpectedly, the carpenter found a kind of release walking the country roads, whether his wanderings found him work or not. Osite and her husband Jean had not been able to find a home they could afford, so they were staying with them, making nine of them crammed into the already overcrowded little cottage.

"I am going to have to look further afield," he said to Agnes. "The rents have been put up again—that's five times in two years—and the only way we can pay is by raising a loan at huge interest rates. And who arranges the loan?"

"The landlord," she said.

It had become a familiar exchange between them, uttered in a mix of frustration and resigned acceptance that they would never catch up with the arrears on the payments for the cottage. That, in fact, they would never earn enough to rise above the relentless routine of their poverty.

"I hear there is a lot of rebuilding in Rennes," he said. "There should be need for a carpenter. It's where our forefathers came from, or at least from the country in that direction, so I might meet someone who remembers our families."

"We'll come with you," said Agnes instantly. "I hate it when you go away, and the children miss their father. Not only that, we'll save on the rent."

"But how would we survive? I often sleep by the road or in a barn. It's not for a family."

"This is no life for a family either. We spend every day begging or scavenging from the market, and come back to this shack of a place where we don't have even enough room to sit. With Osite and Jean taking up our bedroom, well, a barn sounds rather inviting."

There was no argument. They set off, the carpenter pushing a hand cart in which the four children who by then were aged between three and nine, were loaded in a wriggling, fractious heap.

After a few days they reached Lorient, where to Jambo's surprise, he immediately found work in the naval shipyards.

"You're lucky," said the foreman. "The King has decreed that this should be the most important dockyard in the country. Trade is opening up with the American colonies now that they are falling out with their British masters, and the far east is booming, so we have to build ships big and strong enough to sail the oceans."

"Our luck is changing," said Jambo at the end of the first month when he came home from work, spreading his pay on the table. "Look at that— almost 700 sous. For once we can have a proper meal a day and afford these luxurious lodgings."

They laughed. They had been able to rent two dingy rooms above a grocer with a smoking fireplace, and one tiny skylight that let in a sliver of light for about 20 minutes a day. It cost half his wages. Winter crept up on them at the end of November with freezing wreaths of mist that lay over the town, hiding the church steeple, and covering the streets with ice. Occasionally, a flicker of weak sun in the middle of the day would mock them that the worst was over, only to slip away into the chill of night.

It snowed for almost two weeks in December, making work impossible, and the men were laid off for weeks on end.

"I've never been so cold," said Agnes as the family got as close to the fire as they could without actually setting fire to themselves.

"Worse than '54 when Fundy froze over. Remember that?"

When the yard was reopened, Jambo was put with a working group of ten. Some were friendly—at least, they were sociable enough for people who had been brought up instinctively to resent immigrant labor—and they had rubbed along, until one morning they were joined by three others. They swaggered into the yard behind a burly figure with a fierce red birthmark down the left of his face. It ran down his neck and merged grotesquely with a lurid tattoo of the devil emerging from flames as crimson as his disfigurement. He had a hammer in his hand and headed straight for Jambo.

"Ah, the *Canadian.* Heard about you. Why is he here?" he asked the foreman, who shrunk back as the bullying newcomer poked him in the chest with the hammer. He jabbed it toward Jambo. "Why should he earn so much when my brother—a true Breton—cannot find a day's work?"

"As a skilled man, I am entitled to at least 30 sous a day," said the carpenter levelly. "I do my job, and I do it well. I don't want any trouble."

"Don't worry about him," said one of the friendlier laborers, whose name was Alain. "He is well known in the town, though more for complaining and stirring up trouble than for actually doing any work. Typical of him to turn up once the bad weather is behind us."

"We think he belongs to some secret workers' cooperative," said one of his mates. "Fighting the rich, you know the sort of thing."

He didn't, in fact, but it was true that while most of them considered themselves lucky to have enough to eat every day, the aristocracy luxuriated in vast estates that could only be glimpsed at the end of tree-lined drives, or hurriedly sidestepped when they swept past in their carriages with a retinue of footmen trotting in front to clear the way.

"The gap between them and us is widening all the time," said the bully, who was called Duparque. The radical, as he called himself, was holding forth during their brief lunch break, his red splash of skin aflame with anger. He reminded him of Francois—though without the plowman's inherent decency. "Most of our pay goes in tax to support these swells. Something has to be done."

"It's true," said one of his cronies. "They do nothing while we slave our guts out."

"Have you heard about our new king, Louis the bloody Sixteenth?" He dipped his bread into a mug of astringent wine and pointed it at the group to emphasize his argument. "Shaping up to be as greedy and lazy as his father. He has been driven half way across France in a ceremonial coach for his coronation in Paris, and wherever he has gone, his rich ass-licking friends have showered him with presents."

He shoveled the bread into his mouth. "There was a piece in the news journal which said '*he received the most dazzling, the most sincere and already the most deserved proof of love from his peoples.*'"

"Not by anyone round here, I'll be bound," said Duparque.

"Is there anything about him not being able to swive that Queen of his?" asked one.

"That Austrian bitch, Marie Antoinette?" asked Duparque. "He can't get it up. That's what everyone's saying."

"Doesn't take after papa, then," said another. "He spent his entire reign fucking prostitutes."

"What do you think, LeBlanc? asked the bully. "You a keen supporter of the king?"

"It's not for me to say. In my country…" He stopped.

"*Your* country," said Duparque, all menace. "So this is not good enough for you?"

"All I was going to say was that we had governors who were either French or the British, but for many years we were able to forge our own lives without interference, and at least we lived as equals. We were lucky because the land was so rich."

"Well, why don't you fuck off back there then?" asked Duparque.

He sighed. *How many times?*

"Leave him alone," said Alain. "He's not doing you any harm and there's nothing we can do here to change a thing."

"We can fight," exclaimed the trouble-maker, clenching his fists as if ready to take on any aristocrat foolish enough to come near him. "Fight for our rights."

"What, march to Paris and storm the palace at Versailles?" Alain laughed.

That infuriated Duparque. "We can start right here," he said, coming up to Jambo, his hammer swinging. "We can get rid of these foreign scabs."

His face was so close to the carpenter's that he could see the bread crumbs that clung to his obscene birthmark, smell the garlic and wine on his breath. Jambo caught his gaze and held it.

Duparque raised the hammer as if to strike, but was pulled off by Alain. The two men rolled around the yard fighting. His two cronies joined in, and soon the yard was a turmoil of cursing, punching, and gouging men. Only Jambo stood back and watched.

"What the hell is going on?" asked the foreman.

"He has been abusing the new King," said Duparque, breathlessly scrambling to his feet. "I was trying to defend his honor."

"Is this true?"

"No it's not," said Alain. "It's Duparque up to his tricks. Yapping on about our rights and picking fights. As usual."

"I can't be having this," said the foreman. "We have a contract to meet. LeBlanc, you'll have to go."

"But." His ally started to intervene on his behalf, but Jambo took him by the arm and said, "There is no point. I am used to this."

"I am sorry," said the foreman. "Just having you here causes trouble, whether it is your fault or not."

When he stamped up the steep stairs to their rooms earlier than usual, hurling his tools into the corner, Agnes gave him a look of perfect understanding, embraced him, and without bothering to ask, silently started to pack.

Luckily it was warm, that summer of 1775, as they walked the by-ways of Brittany. They stayed a few days in Rennes, but could find nowhere to lodge so moved on to Angers, and on, and on, drifting through the countryside picking up the occasional job, sleeping in barns—"It could be worse," said Agnes. "At least it's dry and warm."—and making a dash for it when an angry farmer caught them.

The roads were full of itinerants listlessly wandering from one disappointment to another. Sometimes the LeBlanc family would meet other Acadians, but they had little to say to each other apart from sharing their grievances and frustrations.

"I can't bear to listen to anyone else telling me how miserable they are," said Agnes.

They kept to themselves, a tight-knit group, sheltering under the carapace of self reliance that they had adopted in the Liverpool ghetto. On they went, the children either larking about in the meadows and taking it in turns to push the cart, or whimpering with weariness, strings of snot trailing from their noses, dirty and forlorn.

They would walk past a cottage where a fire burnt and stand outside sniffing the wood smoke and imagining the families feasting inside. In truth, the families were as impoverished and hungry as the LeBlancs, but that did not stop them knocking on the door and shamelessly ask for food.

The cart often skidded off the muddy tracks into a ditch. On one occasion Marie-Francoise, who had tumbled in after it, came screaming back. "Body! A dead body!"

There it lay, a young man who had slipped and banged his head, or been attacked by a wanderer even more desperate than he. Perhaps he had simply given up, enfeebled by hunger. His face had been torn in half by a wild animal, and what was left of his body was blackened with frostbite.

Without hesitating Agnes stripped him of his outer garments and searched his pockets. One sou.

"I will wash them," she said as Jambo looked aghast at her. How could she have done that? How did he let it happen? But then he remembered how Francois had briskly taken the jacket of a dead man in the ghetto. *'More use to the living,'* he had said defiantly and the carpenter had acquiesced, so he kept his silence and covered the body as best he could with handfuls of mud and leaves and murmured a brief prayer.

She said, "It does not matter to him. If we can't sell his clothes, we can use them to keep us warm next winter."

She was right. It did not matter. Nothing much did. The only important thing was to live for the day and for each other. What else was there? If they were losing their sense of right and wrong, well, what the hell.

On they went. After each day's hike, he would lie awake staring at the stars imagining God, or the lost ghosts of their past, looking down at the pathetic little caravan of souls picking their way through a world that did not care about them or even notice them.

Yes, the clothes would help keep them warm

"I'm pregnant," she said.

He was disconcerted.

"We had better head home," he said.

"I know it's not the best of news," she said. "I am sorry."

"Don't be silly, my sweet one," he said, doing his best to sound enthusiastic. "Another LeBlanc."

"I know," she said, a little gloomily, he thought. "But let's not give up and go back to Quimper. It's early days and I feel well. Let's keep on to this Nantes place where you say that the shipyards are busy."

A few days later, they stopped in the small town of Chatellerault on the River Vienne where he knocked on the door of a church to plead for food only to be sent on his way by the house maid.

He found Agnes lying by the road side, clutching her stomach. A priest was by her side splashing water from the culvert in her face.

"She fainted," said the priest.

"Thank you father. Is she all right?"

"Of course. But her condition should not be a mystery to you, surely," he said. "Judging by this lot." He gestured to the children.

"I know, but we have had to keep moving to look for work and somewhere to stay."

"You had better come to the house," said the priest.

He helped Jambo carry his wife to the rectory and sat her down before dashing off, returning with sweets for the children.

"You must eat," said the priest, a middle-aged man with surprising long wisps of white hair, watery blue eyes and a mouth that twitched with suppressed tension. He nervously asked the housemaid who had turned the LeBlancs away to tend to the pregnant woman, and jumped, when, duty done, she bad-temperedly banged bread and cheese on the table for the family.

"Tell me, do, where you have come from and where you are going?" asked the priest.

Jambo explained their predicament.

"LeBlanc? That sounds a familiar name," said the priest. His mouth twitched as he tried to remember.

"We are Acadians. Our ancestors came from this part of the world."

"Ah yes," said the priest. "I believe many of you tried to settle in this area a year or so back. The Acadian Line, I think it was called. There was an abbot—a rather, what shall I say, *excitable* fellow."

"Father Le Loutre, perhaps?"

"The very one."

The two shared a moment of amused complicity.

"The immigrants who came here had a bad time of it," said the priest. "I feel for you, especially as some of my forbears also went to Acadia. I am a Robichaud. My name is Father Jean. I have been at this church for five years."

"We knew all the Robichaud families at home," Jambo said. "Though many disappeared when the British removed us."

"Well, I cannot allow you to be removed from here with your wife in this condition, um, happy though it is. I can find room for you in an outhouse—rather humble, I'm afraid."

The baby was born on a sweltering day in August and he was christened in the priest's church. Charles was a sickly, grizzling little scrap, reluctant to feed, invariably racked by a chest ailment or stomach pains, and always demanding his mother's attention.

Father Jean had Jambo doing odd jobs around the church, and helping his needy parishioners cutting firewood or collecting water from the well. It was unpaid, but the family was fed and sheltered.

"I don't see you at mass very often," said the priest one morning when the carpenter was repairing a wooden cross in the graveyard.

"I am so busy," Jambo said evasively.

"But even God rested for one day a week," replied the priest. "What will your children think if you are not by their side in church? Little Charles, um, needs your prayers."

How could he explain, to this man of anyone, that he had long lost his faith? God had let him down. His friends, brothers, sisters, and parents had all been taken from him. Marguerite had died in his arms. He had in turn put himself out of God's reach. Stealing had long since ceased to trouble his conscience. He had killed.

"I find it hard," he said.

"Hard?"

350

"To believe. I don't understand any more. When I was a boy in our village church, everything was clear. We listened to the Bible, we were brought up to love one another and treat each other as equals. The last time I went to your church was when the bishop came a few Sundays back. He preached a sermon about the feeding of the five thousand to a congregation that was starving, apart from the local gentry who were sitting comfortably in their elegant pews."

"We are all equal in the eyes of the Lord, aren't we," said the priest, but with no conviction.

"Indeed," said the carpenter. "You have done much to prove that. You are a good man, one of the few, and I am grateful. But the fact is, most people lead the most miserable of existences, while the rich, the ones in those gilt-edged pews of yours have lives of well-fed comfort."

The priest was silent for a while. "There is truth in what you say. But it would help me if you were to come more often. Just once a week."

"Help you?"

"Those people in the rich pews are influential in the area." His mouth was working. "They decide what happens in this community, and in this church. My living is in the gift of the landlord. The truth is, um, they don't understand why I am letting you—a foreigner—stay here."

"Because you are a good Christian, perhaps?"

"Perhaps, but I am not a brave one." His watery eyes glistened as if he was about to burst into tears.

"I shall do whatever is best for you," said the carpenter, but next morning he knocked on the door of the rectory.

"Father, I have been thinking over what we talked about yesterday and my wife agrees with me. We must move on, we have prevailed on your kindness too long."

The priest could scarcely contain his relief, but, mouth twitching, said, "I am sorry to hear it. I know of many of your people in Nantes. I shall give you a name of a family that has decent lodgings. And here—" he pushed 100 sous into his pocket, "—this will help for the journey."

The rooms were in the slum district of Chantenay, down river from Nantes itself, but despite the docks working flat out, there were so many refugees left homeless by the ill-fated Acadian Line experiment that there were no vacancies.

But then a stroke of luck, or so it seemed.

"Guess what," he said one evening. "I met Oliver. Oliver Terriot. Hardly recognized him. He tells me he has done well, and I have to say he looks remarkably prosperous. He had a waistcoat and a hat."

"Well, he was always clever," said Agnes. "In a shifty way."

"He runs a cobbler's shop apparently, and seemed very pleased with himself, selling shoes as well as repairing them. Anyway, he said he would find me work as a sort of partner as soon as he comes back from a business trip."

"A business trip? How very grand." She sniffed. "There was a time when a 'business trip' meant him going to Halifax to mend shoes at the annual fair."

"I know, made me smile. Still, I think we should celebrate." They spent a few sous on a carafe of wine and a cod cutlet.

They waited to hear from him in vain. Eventually, Jambo walked to the city centre and found the shop, only to be told that its owner, Monsieur Le Propriétaire Terriot, would not be back for a month. Maybe more. He was very busy. Important matters to deal with.

Jambo was dismayed. It felt as if the cobbler had thrown off the years of shared comradeship, and because of his success had felt ashamed of his old friend.

"He was always good at fixing deals," said Agnes contemptuously. "But mainly for himself."

He did not have the opportunity to brood about the slight for long. The baby, Charles, died just before his first birthday in the August of 1776.

Agnes grieved for him in a way she never had for Pierre Etienne, who had died almost exactly ten years before.

Jambo shared her sorrow but was puzzled by its profundity. Maybe in some atavistic way she was compensating for her lack of emotion at the time of the first death. Then she had wept, briskly gathered herself together, and gone back to the humdrum matter of staying alive.

What had helped her then to be so resilient? he wondered. *Had the days and nights tending to the dying in the ghetto inured her to misfortune? Had she been numbed by the bitter letdown of Morlaix?*

"I was younger, too," she said "Stronger. And there was no choice. There was no time to stop and mourn."

But Charles—she could not let him go. Once a week she would pick flowers from the hedgerow and sit for an hour or two by his grave, returning home silent and depressed. She felt a failure. Two babies were dead, and one was a cripple.

"What's wrong with me?" she would ask her husband, not expecting an answer. In truth, he had none to give. He held her and tried to sooth the pain but his wife had become impenetrable to him.

"This time, I really do think we should go back to Quimper," said Jambo. "Jean-Baptiste has written to say there is work in the docks, and that Osite and Jean have found a small cottage just outside of town.

"No, no. I can't go." Her eyes widened with terror and she took her head in her hands and shook dementedly, as if to she wanted him and his common sense to go away.

"But why?"

"My Charles. I cannot leave him here."

"We must be rational," said Jambo. "Think about it. We have lost so many of our friends and family since our travels began that we could be forgiven if we crept away and died in a ditch—like the man we found. But we haven't. That's what has made us strong. That's why we will survive."

She said, "I know you are being sensible, but I cannot bear the thought of him left here. You of all people must understand that."

"I do," he said. He could see the yard in Liverpool where he had left Marguerite. By now, the cemetery would no doubt have been covered by the ever-expanding shanty town of beggars and vandalized by miscreants. "But we *must* go. If we are going to overcome this sadness, then it is best to be near the ones we love. We can visit the grave once or twice a year, and I shall ask Oliver to look after it."

"Oliver. Huh. A *sort of* partner. We can rely on him can we, judging by the way he has treated his oldest friend?"

"Who knows," he plowed on. "Osite herself will be having her own children soon. The circle of life will keep turning."

THIRTY

Return to Quimper

1776 to 1783.

The World Moves On, and Stays Still

He prevailed. She grieved. "I should have used the garlic," she scolded herself. "I ignored the old ways. My mother's ways."

The garlic. To Jambo's dismay it had been the cause of a bitter spat with Osite. All Acadian mothers-to-be had grown up believing in the power of garlic cloves held in a saucer above the stomach to prevent miscarriages, and to guarantee good health during pregnancy.

"You know it is just a superstition," said Osite calmly as if there could be no argument. She had called into the old family home as soon as the family returned from Nantes to cheer her stepmother but, instead, found herself unexpectedly embroiled in a fierce argument. "No French woman would consider such nonsense, nor should we. Not anymore. Not in 1776."

"It was good enough for all the women in my family. I believe in it," returned Agnes. "And anyway, *I* am not French."

"There is no evidence that it works though, is there?" asked Osite. "It did not work for Pierre, did it? Look at poor little Marie." It was meant only as a common sense statement, but it cut deep and it was uncharacteristic from someone who usually showed such generosity of spirit. Agnes was distraught, but Osite was cut to the quick with mortification.

Jean-Baptiste, who had kept his thoughts to himself, tutted irritably, stuck a new hat on his head, and strode out of the house, leaving a disheartened Jambo to cope with this unprecedented falling out. They all, in their separate ways, realized that this was more than simply an argument about some arcane method of childbirth, but a remark that expressed the growing divide between the generations, and the frustration the young Acadians had with their elders.

Nonetheless, he felt he had to say something to Osite. "I shall talk to her. That is a mean thing to say."

But Agnes tried to dissuade him. "No don't. She was more upset than I was. Who knows, she is probably right. She was trying to be rational—as her father taught her to be. Remember? Maybe it is absurd to hang on to our traditions."

"It is nothing of the kind," he said. "They have helped make us the people we are. We should be proud of them, and Osite should, at least, respect that pride."

The next afternoon, he bumped into his oldest daughter talking to Jean-Baptiste. She was teasing him.

"You're looking very smart, I must say," said Osite. "Not just the hat, but I do believe that is a new waistcoat?"

"The boss and I were having a meeting with a buyer from Poitiers. Have to put on a show." He shrugged with careful nonchalance.

"Quite the establishment figure, aren't you?"

"I don't know about that," he said with the air of a young man very aware of where he saw his place in Quimper society. "Just moving with the times—unlike our dear mother and father."

Jambo pretended not to hear and before he could speak Osite put down the school books she had been carrying and hugged him "Papa, I was wrong, so wrong, to say what I did. I am sorry. I have just come from mother and we have made our peace."

"Thank goodness," said her father. He tried to laugh it off. "It is so annoying for you the way we old folk constantly hark on about the old days."

How the two young people radiated optimism. They could see a future and it was here, here in France, and not, he could hardly bring himself to frame the thought, and not Acadia.

Not only have I become sucked dry of optimism, I won't listen to reason, he reflected. *At least, that's what they think.*

He rallied himself. "Shall we go to the tavern, son."

Not now, father," replied Jean-Baptiste. "It will be the usual crowd. They all gather and talk about the old times, and I just nod along. Most of them are unaware that there is a world out there, and the few that are don't feel it has anything to do with them.

"They still see themselves as exiles, a band of rejects who have no place in France and who are just passing through.

"Come sister, I'll walk you home to that husband of yours and I'll carry your books like a proper brother.'"

Osite kissed her father. "You go, papa. Pierre will be there and, of course, Francois."

But instead of going to the tavern and its *band of rejects* he limped off home relieved that peace had been restored.

"I don't blame her, really. It is so hard to make sense of anything when you have endured what she has," sighed Agnes. She was talking about herself as well, Jambo understood that all too well. He knew that Agnes felt diminished, ground down by their poverty, the drudgery of tending for the children, the weary routine of taking in the washing, repairing clothes, and when all else failed, joining the beggars in her usual place on the corner of the market square. She was exhausted by the sheer endeavor of scraping together enough to provide one meal a day for her hungry family.

Underlying it all was her grief at the death of Charles. It had grown more, not less, palpable, so encompassing that it was beyond Jambo's powers to reason with her. She became more introverted, more lost in her woes. She reminded him of his mother; how she had given up.

She neglected her appearance, leaving her clothes unwashed for weeks, and letting her hair hang un-brushed from her bonnet. The lines around her pursed lips gave her a look of permanent disapproval, and she lost so much weight that the curves her husband once found so delicious faded into an unalluring gauntness. As for Jambo, he did not have the energy to cope with her misery. He too was worn out. Admittedly he was in his late forties, but he felt twice that age. His heart sank when he was hired to break stones in the quarry or shift the clay for the pottery, because his arms and legs shook and all the time his hand ached. All he could do when he got home was sleep or hide away in his outhouse.

He knew it was unworthy of him, but he was irritated by what he thought was Agnes's extravagant mourning. *It was not the Acadian way to surrender to misery,* but, even as he thought it, he was troubled by the realization that he felt nothing for the loss of Charles. Worse, there was little he did care about. Without noticing, he had slipped into some sort of emotional twilight, devoid of feeling.

If anything, he felt ashamed that the love that had flared so intensely in the ghetto had long faded, like an autumn leaf fading and falling into a stagnant puddle.

They hardly spoke. They never touched. He spent his time putting his energies into carving an Acadia in wood. It soothed him to recreate his familiar world of trappers, fishermen, sweet maidens, lute playing lads, and Red Indians in hand-to-hand combat with British soldiers, who leapt from his old carving knife as if they had a life of their own. Demand for these quaint North American characters grew so much, that instead of selling to a middle man, he set up his own stall in the market and often made more in a day than a week breaking stones.

He had stowed away his gear and gone to the tavern to meet Pierre. It was packed with the usual crowd, with Jean-Baptiste, despite his contempt for that '*band of rejects*,' leaning against a barrel, holding aloft a newspaper.

"Has anyone heard the latest?" he asked, but the few who heard him above the hubbub kept talking. His old aunt Marguerite-Marie LeBlanc, who had become quite crazed thanks to the trauma of her travels, was telling and retelling her story. She had come to the part when she had reached the shore of the Bay of Fundy, looked across at Grand Pre and realized it was forbidden, enemy, territory. "All lost, all lost," she was moaning.

Francois was drinking his cider, and cursing the unfairness of the world after he had been laid off yet again. Others were discussing the rebellion by the American colonies against their masters in Britain.

"The Americans have declared Independence," said Jean-Baptiste, "but the British are bound to thrash them. They have already driven the rebels back up the St. Lawrence and sent 'em flying. The colonials have had to give up any thoughts of conquering Canada."

"Shame, they might have let us home if they had won, especially as the French have been sending their navy to help fight the British," said Jambo.

"They beat the hell out of the rebels in New York, too," read Jean-Baptiste. "Their general Washington was forced to retreat."

"What, is that *our* George?" wondered Pierre.

"Must be," said Jambo.

"He was a piece of work and no mistake, wasn't he?" Said Pierre.

"Very tricky character indeed," said the carpenter. "Not sure who I want to win there. British, the colonials, French—none of them friends to us."

"All bastards," growled Francois.

"Another night with the debating society," Jambo said drolly as Pierre pushed a beer toward him.

"The world is changing fast," Pierre observed. "But not for us, I fear. We old timers are stuck."

"Yes, it's the young ones go their own way," Jambo said. "Much more than we did. Or would have dared."

"And parents don't follow their children," said Pierre. They sat in silence, sipping their beers. Old friends. So much history shared.

"Your Jean-Baptiste is doing well for himself, isn't he? And Joseph-Ignace has regular shifts on the barges. They seem content."

"The real revelation is our Marie-Francoise. *My,* that girl is bright. Nothing stops her. I wouldn't be surprised if she takes to teaching too in a few years. And as for Osite, she is moving up at the school, and of course there will be children coming along soon." Jambo managed a small, tight, smile.

"A generation who will be far removed from Grand Pré." Pierre said.

Jambo's smile tightened into a frown. "A generation who already call France home."

Yes, the world was changing, but for them the years had rolled on in the same untidy, aimless, round of making-do, without ambition to change, with no chance of release, seemingly forgotten by their French masters. Wages fell, costs rose, and the landlords kept a merciless grip on their tenants.

It was in '82, no late summer of '83, and a chatty carter had given them a lift back to town after a day harvesting a vineyard.

"Life," he declaimed cheerfully, "is shit."

"That's the only way to put it," he said with relish. "S.H.I.T. Here we are in 1783, and things can only get worse. Yes, we're in for it, all right. We've had the worst drought for years, and the freezing winters have hit the wheat crops. Have you seen the price of bread?"

They had, but their helpful companion did not wait to hear their views on the economy. "People can't afford it any more. Bread. That's our staple food but we can't afford it."

"We're all as hungry," said Jambo. "Did you hear about the attack on the bakery mill last week? It turned into a riot and the army was sent in. At least two were wounded."

"Can't blame 'em," said the carter. "We live in violent times. Look at all these wars we've had. You wouldn't know, being foreigners, but we seem to have been fighting forever. And how do we pay for wars? By taxes. And who pays the taxes? We do—the hard-up, bloody, working class. *Working,* that's a laugh.

"Here's a fact for you—did you know that it's 98 percent of the people who raise the money to help our nobles and the royals live in such splendor. Five meals a day, fine wine, and silk sheets to recline on when all that guzzling makes 'em weary. And the clergy, we pay for them too. We starve while they scoff away at lavish soireés and banquets." He paused to take a swig of wine from a leather flask and handed it to his passengers.

"You'd have thought we'd have made something out of the American War. We fought on the side of the colonials to help them win their independence, but what did we get out of it? Nothing.

"My naval chums in Nantes tell me the British are as thick as thieves with their old enemies, keeping all the trading agreements, while we have had to go hang. We haven't even kept any territory worth having either. Some place in Africa—Senegal, is it?—and an island or two in the West Indies. Good for the slave trade, I suppose"

"Makes no odds to us," said Pierre.

The carter took another swig, but this time did not offer the flask around. "You're the Canadians aren't you?

"No," said Pierre. "Acadians."

"Have you heard about the petition some of you Canadians have got up in Nantes?"

"No. Petition?"

"Seems like you want to go home. Don't blame you. What did I say? It's shit here." He laughed so uproariously that he spilt wine down his front.

They were dropped on the edge of the town, and though he had promised Agnes he would come straight home, he and Pierre called in at the tavern to tell Francois that there was more work in the vineyard.

"Hello father, Pierre." Jean-Baptiste cut a dashing figure with yet another new waistcoat and tight fitting breeches, and had become so confident that he rather intimidated the two older men. Jambo thought he detected a whiff of scent about him. "Have you heard about this petition?" asked his son.

"As a matter-of-fact we have," said Jambo.

Jean-Baptiste looked positively affronted at his father knowing something he thought he had to himself, but he went on. "It says in this paper: '*The Acadians in Nantes have delivered a petition to King Louis asking to be sent home.*' Listen, they say, '*28 years after the loss of our property, we find ourselves in poverty and misery. The landlords daily refuse to house us and without his Majesty's pay we cannot live. We are grieved that we are a burden,'* and so on and so on."

"Waste of breath," said Francois. "There is nothing this king will do for us. If his father could never be bothered why should he? No, we have to accept that we will die here."

Jean-Baptiste said, "You're right, Francois. We cannot expect help from the king, or from anyone for that matter.

"I'd go further, there is no point complaining like these petitioners. Waste of breath. It's up to us to make the best of what we can, because, yes, this is where we will end our days."

Later, well fuelled with strong dark ale, the quartet were walking home along the street of cobblers and leather workers when they came across a group around a figure who was using an upturned barrel as a card table.

"Take one," he said to the passersby. "You have to bid for tricks using a trump card. If you win enough tricks, you get a bonus, and you can claim your winnings. It's called quadrille. Very popular with the ladies in society. A bit complicated, but the winner can take home quite a pot. Place a bid—a sou is enough—and who knows, you could be rich."

The speaker was hunched over his cards, dealing with a blur of dirty fingernails, his little eyes flashing behind tightly fitting spectacles.

"My God," said Jambo. "Oliver Terriot."

The cobbler scrambled the cards under his cloak. "Who the? It's you Pierre, Francois, er, Jambo. You made me jump. I thought you were the gendarmes."

Francois and Pierre were delighted to see their comrade and dragged the cobbler back to the tavern to celebrate their reunion. Jambo did not share their enthusiasm. He ignored Terriot's outstretched hand and stepped away from his embrace. He had not forgotten how the cobbler had let him down.

Oliver could not help but notice and said, "Jambo, dear friend. I have never forgiven myself for not seeking you out in Nantes. I was called away on urgent matters. You know how it is."

"Well, no," he said, and became silent.

Oliver was briefly unnerved, but was soon rattling on as blithely as ever. He was well dressed. A smart suit and a collar. Shoes as shiny as a mirror. Only those grubby finger nails betrayed his years as a humble repairer of boots.

"Cousins, I confess that I thought that I would find you here. I did not come all this way to play cards, you know. I am on my way to St. Malo and Morlaix. I have a scheme that will free us from this servitude and spare us from the demands of our French landlords, and above all, take us to a new homeland."

"No, no." Jambo interrupted angrily. "Not a new homeland. We have played that game."

"You are talking to the wrong people," snapped Jean-Baptiste.

"Has no one told you about Belle-Ile?" said LeBlanc impatiently.

"Or the crooked Acadian Line?" added Pierre.

"We have had more than our fill of *schemes,*" said Francois. "Let's play cards and drink."

"No, this one will work," said Oliver. He was unmoved by the skepticism. He was still the same, still full of wheezes, blinking away with enthusiasm as he always had, though now the glasses were as thick as the bottoms of wine bottles. "Did you hear about the petition?"

"The one to King Louis?" asked Jambo. "Yes. Not interested."

"No, wait, listen. I was in my shop—"

"You have a shop?" asked Pierre.

"It is one of the best cobblers in Nantes, you know. It's bigger now than it was when I met Jambo, er, I mean, before." He seemed both embarrassed and pleased at his good fortune. "Anyway, this man walks in. Smart. Obviously got some cash."

Pierre said, "What, like our Marquis? Look what happened there."

"His name is Coudrenière—'*Call me Henry,*' he says—says he wants to buy shoes for his wife. We get talking and it turns out he is married to one of our cousins—Jeannette something or other. Can't remember. I quickly realize he is not there by chance. He's heard of me—as I say, I have done quite well out of the leather trade—and he asks me to go into a venture with him. Well, I listen of course. He's a local man, but he is just back from seven years in Louisiana where, he tells me, he made a fortune trading sugar and timber."

Oliver paused for effect. You must have heard that Spain owns the country, well, he reckons he can do a deal with them to settle us there."

"Stop there, Oliver," said LeBlanc. "We have heard all this kind of thing before. It is the same story—all he will do is win himself a hefty grant from the Spanish government, and we'll be sent off to some God-forsaken hole. Francois, tell him about Guyana."

"I have heard the stories about Guyana," said Oliver a mite testily. "Louisiana is nothing like that. I have yet to hear an argument against it. Everyone tells of the well-irrigated farmland, and the gentle climate. It's not a place for *savages* like Guyana, the people there are civilized, and the governor, who is an enlightened fellow, is on our side. He's genuine—not like our French masters.

"You must have heard how hundreds of our cousins moved there at the end of the war. There is a reason for that. Only last week I received a letter from my sister telling me how the governor had promised he would supply her family with money and tools, and guess what, he did just that.

"The crops are leaping out of the ground. Our people are allowed to live in peace, unhindered by authority, along the banks of the River Mississippi, which is as wide as the English Channel.

"There are levees, irrigation, rich soil, all the things we Acadians understand. Furthermore its capital, New Orleans, is one of the most elegant cities I know of."

"You've never been further than Nantes." Francois scoffed.

"Isn't this pure fantasy?" asked Pierre, but the cobbler was unfazed.

"The Spanish want the settlements to succeed. Think about it. It's in *their* interest for you to be happy and successful."

"And your Mr. Coudrenière," said Pierre. "Don't try to suggest that he will be interested in anything other than earning his commission."

"He does not deny he will make money out of the undertaking," said Oliver. "Of course, he hopes to. But he will have to raise the capital, and it is a mighty tricky project to get off the ground. I have faith in the man, that's why I am taking this petition to be signed by as many cousins as I can find."

"What does it say?" asked Jean-Baptiste.

Oliver took a much-fingered parchment from his hold all and declared, '*We implore his Catholic Majesty to grant the Acadians permission to go to Louisiana in order to rejoin our relatives and to establish ourselves among them.*' I have already had it signed in Nantes, Rennes, Caen, and Cherbourg."

"How many signatures so far?" demanded Jean-Baptiste.

"Well," the cobbler shifted uncomfortably. "Quite a few."

"Let's have a look," said Francois. He grabbed the document. "One, two, three, four, five!"

They laughed at the cobbler's discomfiture.

Jean-Baptiste took a closer look, "And one of them is yours."

"Count me out," said Pierre.

"I am sorry, Oliver," said Jambo. "You and I have been through a lot over the years—sometimes together—but you have to accept that while you might be tempted to go to Louisiana, we are not going anywhere. We stay here."

"Tell you what," said Oliver, tucking the parchment away but refusing to be discouraged. "Why don't you come to Nantes and meet Mr. Coudrenière?"

When they journeyed to the port a few weeks later, they discovered that Oliver, for once, had not been exaggerating his own success. Since Jambo's unavailing attempts to contact him when they were living in Chantenay, the shop had moved to one of the smartest streets and was twice the size. Shoes lined its walls from top to toe, and as they paused to read the sign which read **Terriot: Cobbler to the Gentry,** they were impressed to see several smart ladies emerging with boxes of new shoes. Inside the emporium was a buzz of activity with two apprentices bent over their lathes repairing footwear. There was no sign of Oliver.

"He's in the back," said one of his helpers.

Oliver was sitting with his head in hands. He could hardly bring himself to look at his visitors.

"So, Oliver, said Jean-Baptiste. "Where is your Monsieur Coudrenière?" He pretended to seek him out behind a stack of boot soles.

With his head in his hands he muttered, "It's a scandal, a conspiracy. He has been thrown into prison."

"That says all we need to know," said Jambo. "You haven't changed."

"Either that, or your friend is a trickster after all, just the same as the others," said Francois.

"Not so," protested Oliver, his glasses misting with frustration. "It is not my fault. Not his either. He has been accused of being a secret agent of Spain, but it is a trumped up charge by the local landlords who fear we will leave without paying our rents."

Jean-Baptiste, with an air of triumph, said, "Sorry Oliver, but I have found out. I have made a few enquiries about your Mr. Coudrenière. I have friends among the merchant class in Quimper society, and I have to tell you that he is indeed well known. He was so successful in Louisiana that he became bankrupt. That's why he's here. He is trying to get his money back, and using you to help him."

"I think we'll be going home," said Jambo.

"Do stop by for a chat and a game of cards," said Francois.

THIRTY-ONE

A family gathering, Quimper

Winter 1785.

Oliver's Last Throw

The cobbler did turn up on the LeBlanc family doorstep a few weeks after the Christmas of '84 but it was not cards he clutched but sheaves of papers.

He was completely unabashed by the farce of their last meeting, and still blithely indifferent to the hurt he had caused the couple when they were desperate for help.

"You managed to find us this time," said Jambo with a heavy sarcasm that Oliver either ignored or did not notice.

"Great news," he said. "It is now definite. We are going to Louisiana. Mr. Coudrenière has been released, and the Spanish consul in Nantes has commissioned seven ships to take our people across the Atlantic to our new homes. At no cost. It's all arranged. There's one called the Bon Papa, tied up to the quayside getting ready to sail you away."

"Oliver, there is no point," said Jambo. "How many times do we have to tell you, your man Coudreniére, the Spanish—they are not to be trusted."

Agnes bitterly added, "To be truthful, we have no great cause to rely on *you* either, do we?"

Oliver was undeterred. "The stumbling block turned out to be the debts that of our cousins owe their landlords. That is the main reason the French government have not agreed so far to let us go and that's why they caused that, er, embarrassment with Mr. Coudrenière. So hear this; Spain has agreed to pay all your debts. There is nothing to stop us now. Hundreds want to leave. There will be room for 1,500 on the ships, and I have more than 1,000 volunteers already.

"Your brother, Charles, has agreed Jambo, and so have the Boudrots, the Aucoins, and the Broussards. You must put your names down, my dear friends, or you will miss this opportunity. Just remember what we have been through. Would I mislead you?"

"You might," said Agnes.

"All right, all right," said Jambo. "We will think about it, but I know what the answer will be."

Later that evening as they squeezed into the living room of the cottage, there was a tumultuous banging at the door. It was Charles. With him, Madeleine and the children.

"Here I am. I wouldn't have m-m-missed this. Oliver told me all about this last m-m-month when he was in Morlaix."

"Oh did he?" asked Jambo as he embraced his brother. "Not so fast. I don't think we are going anywhere."

"Well, he c-c-convinced me." He was more stooped than the younger man had noticed before and his hair was only a wisp or two stretched across his head. *Heavens,* thought Jambo. *He must be 58 now. Looks 70!*

The older brother was as irrepressible as ever, though.

"I always thought I'd die here—well, you know that Jambo, we talked about it often enough—but I do think L-l-louisiana is the answer, especially as Madeleine has heard from her sister. She says it is a new Acadia, but with s-s-sun instead of s-s-snow."

"He hasn't convinced us," said Francois, gloomily. "You know how Oliver gets carried away. Remember the sloop in Virginia?"

There were so many in the living room they could hardly move. Charles made it almost impossible for them to settle down by whirring around the room greeting and kissing everyone there. "It's been so long. Jean-B, what a man. Look at you!" he hugged the LeBlancs' eldest, Blanche.

"Twenty years old already! Impossible. Little Marie-Francoise—— well not so little——you must be, er ...."

"I'm 18 uncle." And she put her thin arms around him.

"Isn't it amazing," said their garrulous old uncle. "Joseph you must be 17 and little S-s-simon, well, not so little, you are, let me think—14!"

"Well done, uncle," they chorused.

"You only understand how time m-m-marches when you see how others change," he said. "Me, I still f-f-eel as if I'm still 20,"

"Yes, yes, Charles," said Jambo. "Sit down and be quiet. We have much to discuss."

He and Agnes perched at one end of the table, while the children scattered themselves on the ground. Pierre, Francoise, and their four doubled up on chairs with Charles's brood, all as quiet as if attending a Bible reading. Francois sat scowling in the inglenook, a beer in hand.

Jean-Baptiste leant against a wall by the door, looking as if he was about to leave, while Osite and her husband sat slightly to one side. Separate.

Oliver came bustling in, and Pierre whispered to Jambo, "Isn't that a new jacket he's wearing?"

Jambo nodded. "Looks expensive."

"Well," he said, as sprightly as ever. "Have you decided?"

Pierre spoke first, "I think we can agree that we are all very wary about these schemes."

"You can say that again," said Jean-Baptiste.

"Every time we have been made an offer like this, we have been betrayed," said Francois.

"So why would we want to risk this venture of yours, Oliver?" asked Pierre.

"This isn't like one of your card games," growled Francois. "We aren't playing loo now, you know."

For once the cobbler stopped his whirling and blinking and became serious, hands on the table in front of him, spectacles straight, "You have to ask yourselves if you are content with the situation here. Surely, none of us can say that France is a place fit for us. Never has been, never will be. Even for someone like myself who has made a success of the situation—" he positively preened "—the discrimination that we have faced from day one still exists. We are poor and getting poorer. We are not alone in this, the rest of the so-called working classes—their very own countrymen—are bleeding."

"That's true, the rich are stuffing their faces with venison and swigging bottles of cognac," growled Francois. "What did that bitch Marie Antoinette say? *Let the poor eat brioche.* Fat whore."

"Uncle," rebuked Agnes. "Language."

"That's my point," said Oliver. "We are second class citizens."

"Third," said Francois.

"You're right, Francois. Third class. There is too much stacked against us for us ever to prosper," said the cobbler. "You have been in Quimper for more than ten years..."

"Thirteen," corrected Pierre.

"Thirteen years and it still feels like a prison, doesn't it? The bars are invisible, but we are still in some sort of ghetto. We are still treated like foreigners. Aliens."

"Certainly, many of the locals resent us just as much as they did when we first landed in Morlaix," said Pierre. "There was a rally outside the town hall last night demanding *'the Canadian spongers'* be sent home. Where do they think home is for us?"

"Even now, we are insulted by the bosses and hired and f-f-fired at their whim," said Charles.

"I met that slippery bastard of a foreman the other day," said Francois. "He still calls us *poxy parasites.* Thinks it a huge joke."

"It's not just the peasants who resent us, their hate is spreading to the children," said Francoise. "Our two youngest boys were sent back from school the other day because a group of local lads set on them."

"It is prejudice, pure and simple," said Oliver, sensing the tide was going his way. "Then there are the taxes. The salt tax. Salt! Basic to everything we eat."

"And that's n-n-not all," said Charles. "Look at the way we have to pay a tenth of our income, or what we p-p-produce, to the church."

There was a brief pause while they all considered just how much the shamelessly lazy Charles might have contributed to the episcopalian exchequer.

"Then there's the land tax to the state," said Oliver.

"And, on top of that, a t-t-tax on the number of people in the family. And in the good times—"

"Good times! Remind us of those good times," said Francois.

"—then we have to pay more t-t-tax."

Pierre said, "When the harvest fails, as it did last year, it means the people starve. So many of us are dying before our time."

"Just like Jambo's aunt Marguerite-Marie," said Agnes. "After all her struggles, she died a pauper."

"God rest her," said Oliver offhandedly. He hadn't finished his litany of complaints. "Rents go up every quarter, and we are forced to take out huge loans to pay them off just to maintain a roof over our heads."

"Which means we will never p-p-pay them off," said Charles.

"Precisely," said Oliver, as if that clinched the argument."That's why this Spanish offer is so good."

"Yes, I agree it is a struggle here," said Agnes. "But I am not sure about this plan. Jambo, what do you think?"

The carpenter stayed silent, lost in his own private argument.

"I mean, we know how much we have suffered at the unfairness of it all," Agnes went on, pouring wine and looking nervously at her husband for a sign of his feelings.

"Yes, we are always hungry, but why should we think Louisiana will be any better? Despite everything, we have put down deeper roots here than anywhere else we have lived, not that that is saying much. But here's Jean-

Baptiste—he is a success at the pottery, and Osite is one of the best teachers in the county. She did that herself. She defied the snobbery and hostility and rose above it. It is as great a deed as our own ancestors building Acadia."

Jean-Baptiste interrupted. "Well said, mama. We have proved there are opportunities for anyone prepared to work. Look at Blanche with her cleaning job at the big house. Even Marie-Francoise is taking classes at the school."

"What do you mean *even?*" Agnes laughed as she hugged her misshapen daughter to her. "She's the cleverest of us all. The fact is, we are happy here. Well, maybe not *happy,* but when I compare it with Belle-Ile and Morlaix, not to mention pushing a cartload of belongings around Brittany, there is, at least, some glimmer of hope. There may not be the kind of work that we think is right for an Acadian, but we have had to adapt, and we do. I am selling more of my clothes and Jambo is doing roaring trade with his figurines."

She paused. "And there's little Charles. He is so far from us. I cannot bear the thought of his corner of the cemetery left lonely and cold with no one to say a prayer and lay flowers. I have only managed to visit grave once a year since he died. The last time it was covered in weeds, and his cross had fallen over, but at least I could tidy it up, pick flowers and say a prayer."

Osite reached across and held her hand as she blew her nose and dabbed at her eyes. The room was hushed.

Pierre brought them back to reality. "There are big question to answer," he said. "Can we rely on this Coudrenière character? How do we know that the Spanish will treat us any different to the French? How will they profit from this?" He did not wait for the answer. "They did not win one of the biggest empires the world has known out of generosity of spirit. They are just as bloody and ruthless as the British and the French."

"How much are you getting out of it, eh Oliver?" asked Francois, cutting, inimitably, to the chase.

The cobbler flushed slightly. "Some expenses, nothing much. I'm doing it because I want to help. What you must understand is that this is not just some rich aristocrat like Nivernois who cares only that he gets his dividends. Henry believes in this project, and he believes in you. There has been so much praise for the way Spain governs the country.

"They have already welcomed thousands of our cousins. They have helped them settle, given them grants to start farms and build homes. Only last month I heard from my cousin Simon who has settled on a bayou, I think he called it, a sort of creek, where he has a smallholding. He sold his first harvest of maize this year. He's making money."

"Are you sure you are not confusing him with your sister who has been so well looked after?" asked Jean-Baptiste sarcastically.

"No one is saying that the Spanish have never, er, made any mistakes, though they are hostile to Britain, which is in their favor. The difference is that they want us to settle in areas that have little or no population, and create new Acadian communities.

"Jambo," he reached over and gripped the carpenter by his arm. "Remember when we were children? Remember all those stories about our forefathers when they first landed? They arrived with nothing—empty pockets, no tools, owning only the clothes they stood up in—and built a new country. Louisiana can become our new Acadia."

The carpenter stirred. His mind had drifted from the cramped room and lighted on random memories, like the night Pierre had rescued him from the wolves, drinking in the tavern with Charles just before they had been summoned to the church to hear their fate, and—guiltily, because Agnes was holding his hand—he was thinking of his dead wife.

"My aunt Marguerite-Marie." It was the first time he had spoken since they had all gathered. "You know that she was lying dead in her room for three days before anyone noticed. That wouldn't have happened in Grand-Pré. We knew when people were ill, we looked after them, and we stayed by them until they recovered, or until they died. My God, we even did that when the plague struck so many of us down in Liverpool. We are losing track of what it means to be Acadian. Making figurines, repairing clothes—that's what we have been reduced to.

"We don't notice the contempt when our women beg in the streets, we no longer protest when we are laid off—even when we are the best workers for the job—we accept that our children will be bullied at school. Prejudice, discrimination, downright cruelty. We live with it. It's not that we have lowered our expectations—we no longer have any.

"My great grandfather, Daniel, went to Acadia without a sou and built a new world out of swamp land. You children have heard this a million times, I'm sorry." He grimaced ruefully and paused but then his voice rose. "But he represents the true meaning of what it is to be an Acadian. I have come to think Oliver is right. Yes, this is *our* destiny, just as Acadia was for Daniel."

Agnes squeezed his hand. The old Jambo LeBlanc was back. For the first time in months, years, he had found his voice again, and instantly, despite her half-hearted argument moments before to make the best of their woeful predicament, she knew where her destiny lay.

He continued, "We have to accept that we can never return to our homeland, but do we have to accept the tyranny, indifference, and injustice of France? My belief in God has been shaken, maybe lost forever, but I do believe in Acadia, what it meant, and what it can mean again. I believe in the the spirit of us Acadians, our traditions, what our very being stands for. Why have we fought to stay alive for so long? To go home—yes—but since that is impossible, what we can do is rouse that old idealism one last time to resurrect our country again in this Louisiana."

"It will be our last adventure," said Pierre.

The pulse and shades of the fire outlined their silhouettes against the empty white walls, throwing each face into focus as if urging their answer. A log slipped, sending the embers flaring, catching the dog, which yelped in surprise.

From his place near the door, Jean-Baptiste, said, "Father, I am sorry to say this, but this is not the time. In fact, I do not believe there ever will be a time that is right to leave. The moment has long passed. It's true that we pay too much in taxes, and yes, there are often troubles. Discrimination—all that. But it amounts to little when you weigh it with the advantages and the changes that are coming. When you talk to the locals—and not just the laborers or the poor folk who can't find work, but the honest merchants, people like my boss at the pottery—you understand there is no *them and us* any more.

"Mark my words, there will be revolution soon which will see the lazy swells who own the country and the devious crooks who flatter themselves that they govern it brought low.

"There will be equality for all men with no division between rich and poor, local or immigrant. Some say the king and his deadbeat bootlickers. not to mention his whore of a queen, will be driven out, and a republic put in his place. The country will be transformed. We should be looking forward to being part of the changes here, not recreating a long-lost way of life in a strange country.

"We must put aside the accident of our births, and make sure we are part of a community where people will no longer hear our names and say, '*Ah—LeBlanc, Hebert, Richard—Acadian parasites But welcome, citizens of France*'. Look at us, Osite and I. Father, mother, you said it yourselves—just like those first settlers in Acadia, we too arrived here empty-handed, and now we have made it a home. Yes, I do have a good job. I stand a good chance of being made overseer in a year or two's time, so why would I risk everything for another futile adventure in some tropical outpost? No, this is not for me."

"Surely," said Osite, stumbling in her reluctance to distress her father, who was looking at her with an expression so intense it was almost like longing. "Surely my brother is right. I too have read many letters from our cousins in Louisiana, Oliver. Probably more than you have, and yes, they have roofs over their heads and spades and livestock, but they complain of the heat and the mosquito-infested swamps.

"The Spanish might say we are welcome, but as Pierre said, they are bound to have their own selfish motives, and the old French population who still live there do not accept us. Then look who is just over the border—the British colonials."

"They like us less than their old masters used to," said Pierre.

Osite continued with quiet assurance, "You say we want to work as true Acadians, but I am told that the farming along the Mississippi is completely different from the old country. What do we know of cotton and coffee? The settlers that I correspond with do not think they have found a new Acadia, no. For them it is just another place to scratch a living. Isn't that what we have done all our lives? I can understand why you would want to return to your—*our*—homeland, whatever is left of it, but not to this place."

"The truth is, I cannot remember Acadia," interrupted her brother. "I do remember the prison. It was where I grew up. And father, I was so proud of you. You were a hero to me and to all of us in that bleak place.

"I can still see you standing in the middle of the warehouse, smell the condensation, that peculiar dank odor of rotten wood, and feel the slimy flagstones under my feet——well, we didn't often have shoes to wear, did we? It's all so vivid. How tall and noble you were, a beacon of strength in the ghetto's permanent twilight, exhorting our comrades not to give up, to fight on. To be resolute."

The old man looked at him, astonished. It was the first time his son had spoken in that way, had shown any emotion, had displayed his love. He was humbled.

The young man had not finished. "And mother. A shadow smiling." He gulped. "You tried to stop me seeing her on her deathbed, but I sneaked in behind the canvas awning that you had put up to hide her."

He swallowed and rubbed a hand over his face. "I hardly recognized her, she was so tortured by the disease, but she looked straight at him with those odd eyes the other children used to tease me about. She smiled at me.

"I will never forget that moment or those terrible days but that was another time. Father, we are here now. It is 1785. Our world is in France."

Osite left her husband's side and put her arms around her brother.

"I do not have even that memory to carry with me," she said, her voice breaking. "Acadia means little to me either," she said. "And I certainly do not want to travel to a strange place where we might be struck down by smallpox or cholera, or drown at sea getting there. Why would I want to take the risk of further torments when, like all of us in this room, my life has been measured out in funeral processions?"

She burst into tears, moved across the room to her father and wrapped her arms around him shoulders before kneeling in front of him. "I'm sorry. Father, mother. I cannot come with you. You must know that. I am proud to be born an Acadian, of course I am, but my future lies here with Jean, and I believe yours does too. We have to think of ourselves as French citizens. For you Acadia is a long, lost dream but for me it is not enough."

For years Jambo had been fighting the despair of disillusion, and stayed strong in the hope that their banishment would some time, some how, be ended. He had wavered, he had almost broken in the ghetto when Marguerite died, but he had never wept. He had acted strong. He had stayed strong. That had been the key to his self-respect, but in her rejection of their homeland, Osite had turned away from him.

To the carpenter, she had always represented the bridge between the old life and whatever the new might be, but she did not want that role. She was the living embodiment of Marguerite, but now she was to be lost to him. For the first time since the night in St. Charles Church, 30 years before when he had sworn that he would never let anyone see him weep, the carpenter broke down.

It was an acceptance that the argument was won. And lost.

"We shall go," said Pierre. This time there was no opposition.

Oliver scuttled from the room and returned immediately with passports and permits, which he had already prepared and brought with him in his hold-all. "I knew you would see sense," he said. "You must be at the dockside near Nantes on May 9th."

"Let's celebrate," said Charles and he reached for his lute. "A new l-l-life." But he saw the grey, old face of his younger brother, bleak with misery, and stopped.

A few weeks later the family gathered awkwardly outside the cottage where a wagon was stacked with their few possessions. At a loss for words, Jambo made a fuss of making sure everything was secure; that they all had what they wanted to take with them. That they were ready for this last journey – for that's what it would be for him.

He remembered how he and Marguerite had paused in the house in Grand-Pré that last morning thirty years ago before they had been marched off, and how they had committed everything to memory. The smell of the morning's new bread, and the cauldron with the remains of their last stew came back to him.

The red ribbons waiting to be worn at Evangeline's wedding.

This time he did not give the house that they lived in for 13 years a second glance. It had never been a home. They stood in silence. He kissed Osite on her brow, and shook his oldest son by the hand, then he held them in fierce embrace.

The young man, who had worked as hard at being as contained as his father had determined to be strong, broke away from him with an outburst of sobbing, only recovering himself to stand back from his father with his handkerchief pressed to his face.

Osite was calm. "Farewell father. Please, forgive me."

He was helping Marie-Francoise on to the cart when she suddenly pushed him to one side and jumped awkwardly to the ground.

"Wait," she said and grabbed Osite by one hand, and their father by another. "This is not right."

She was 22, and while she had inherited the luminous beauty of her mother's steady grey eyes, her forehead still bulged, and her damaged body was a confusion of awkward shoulders and spindly legs.

'No one will marry her,' her father had lamented.

'But so many love her,' Agnes always rebutted.

She was tremulous. "We cannot break up our little family. Osite, my darling sister, and Jean-Baptiste, it is your *duty* to stay with us and make this journey. We owe everything to father and mother. Look what they have done for us when they had nothing. If we were burdens, they never let us know.

"I have seen mama go without food so that we could eat one meal every day, and father worked all hours in the face of hatred and humiliation to provide for us. Now we should show our thanks by staying together. We should all go to Louisiana—not because that is what our parents want, but because that is what we LeBlancs should want.

"Osite should bring her skill as a teacher to this new frontier. Jean will find work on the river—it is one of the longest waterways in the world after all—and Jean-Baptiste, you are so smart you will flourish anywhere. You will have your own factory within a few years.

"After everything we have been through, we cannot surrender our identity now. We are LeBlancs before we are anything—before we are Acadian. Everything about us has been forged in the years of exile and now, for the sake of the family, for me, for you Osite and Jean-Baptiste, for us all, even for Charles who was taken from us so early, we must be together, because this new Acadia is just a place which will mean nothing without people. Without us."

She paused, her concave chest heaving, and burst into tears. There was a silence. It was if Jambo could hear the blossom falling from the hedgerows, and the wind rushing through the wings of the swallows as they dived and soared. In the distance was the comical call of a cuckoo. The carpenter scarcely dared to breathe. For a moment he thought the girl had prevailed.

Jean reached out a hand and held Osite by the arm. Jambo saw that it was meant as a comfort, not a restraint or warning, but his wife took an involuntary step back to be near him, and in that moment the carpenter knew she was lost to him. The hollow coo-coo sounded again, mocking him.

Osite wiped the tears from her face. "Marie-Francoise, so much of what you say is true. Of course it is, but there has to be a moment when we find a new way, and this is it. The world is changing and I am changing with it.

"My life is here. With my husband. We are the most important people in this saga, not a country that no longer exists"

Marie-Francoise cried, "No, no. It must be with us. You cannot desert us. Osite, my sister. No."

The older woman held her hand. "Listen, my sweet little sister, father, mother, I have been thinking. There is one symbol of our love that can help us rise above this pain and unite us even as we go our different ways.

"My real mother, the Marguerite some of us never knew, is, as Jean-Baptiste said the other day, like some sweet specter to me, but I do know, father, that you have grieved for her, and been have heartbroken not to be able to stand by her graveside and share your memories. She is buried alone in that that distant cemetery in a cold and hostile city, like so many of our family.

"They are lost to us but what I promise is that I will look after little Charles's grave. Jean and I, and Jean-Baptiste too." Her brother gave a disapproving grimace, as if he did not want to be included in such a promise, but recovered in time to nod. "We will visit twice, three times a year, and when I place flowers on it I will do so for him, and *all* our dear ones who are missing. I shall buy a new stone, and have our names inscribed on it. It will become our family memorial—a meeting place for generations of LeBlancs to come where our names will never die."

Agnes was weeping helplessly.

How well Osite is able to talk about momentous matters without being dramatic or showy, thought the old carpenter. Despite the anguish she knew she had caused, the young woman had stayed serene. Her inner clarity had spoken through with that quiet force that had made him understand that, though she had escaped the cage—the invisible bars that had held them in for thirty years—she had achieved it without compromising her love for him, and without diminishing the admiration she had for his heroism and for all those years of his sacrifice.

They could think of nothing else to say that could ease their anguish.

"God be with you," Jambo said. They held each other again, and then with one hand on his stick and the other looped around the bridle of the horse, he limped off through the lanes of Brittany to the port without a backward look.

As Oliver had promised the ship was waiting for them. Le Bon Papa, *a friendly name,* he thought, suggested perhaps by a proud daughter. They stood patiently on the quayside with 36 families, some they hadn't seen since Grand-Pré, some since the days in the bay off Virginia, some who had not even been born when the Great Expulsion took place.

"Jambo? It's you."

He peered at a man who had thick white hair, and a beard that concealed all but a pair of rheumy eyes. He did not recognize him.

"It's Charles Landry. A carpenter, like you. From Grand Pré. Surely you remember my brother, Pierre. He owned the mill. He was slain in that crazy escape from the ships."

"Charles. Yes of course." He still didn't recognize him. In fact, he had hardly known him. Had he been at his brother's funeral? He could not even remember that.

"I haven't seen you since we stood by the graveside," said Landry. He gave a few reflective nods as if to acknowledge that long-ago tragedy. He scratched his beard. "Forgive me, but you look a lot older."

They laughed at the absurdity of his comment.

"Only thirty years or so," said Jambo.

"Well, we are still alive. I've got seven children here somewhere." He peered into the milling crowd.

"I have my six," said Jambo. "No," He corrected himself and frowned as if he was trying to clear his mind. "Just the four."

"Our new world awaits," said Landry.

He was about to ask him his story, but did not bother. All their accounts amounted to the same extraordinary fact that though they all knew someone who had perished since the summons to St. Charles almost thirty years before, they were still alive.

Jambo murmured, "Happy and peaceable."

The other man looked at him enquiringly, but before he could explain a Spanish official called him forward. "Next. Name?"

"Le Blanc. Joseph 'dit Jambo' Le Blanc."

"Spell it."

"L E—"

"Age?"

"54. No, er 56."

"Never mind. Get on board. God be with you."

He tripped on the gangplank but stopped himself from falling by hooking his damaged hand over the rail, and limped up the steps.

THIRTY-TWO

New Orleans, Louisiana

July 29, 1785.

The Beginning

He was gripped by the lethargy of approaching death. He had seen his face in the cracked mirror when he had shaved in preparation for this day, and had been taken aback by the shrunken, careworn appearance of the man who looked back at him with creases so deep they made shadows in his skin. His hair was white and thin, though Agnes reassured him that it was as thick as the day they first kissed. He had shut his eyes tight as if he no longer wanted to confront his memories.

Eighty days the voyage had taken, but this time when the winds rose and the waves battered the hull, they hung on and laughed for joy. It had felt like a holiday. Of the 156 on board there had been only one death, a child—the last martyr of their years of torment, the last time tears were shed.

He held onto Agnes, and put an arm around Marie-Francoise, while the other children followed. He flapped distractedly at the mosquitoes and flies that whirred up from the wharf as he shuffled along the deck toward the gangplank. Despite the suffocating intensity of the mid-day sun, he was still wearing the same woolen clothes that he had worn when he set sail from France, and was so soaked by sweat that he was actually shivering. His hands trembled as he and the children clung to the ship's rail and gazed down at the tumult of shouting dockhands and riotous sailors, their babble of French, Spanish, and Carib competing with the concatenation of accordions, pipes, and lutes pulsating from the taverns that lined the wharf.

How many times he had stood on a ship's deck and watched a port come into focus, not knowing what his fate would be?

Busy shipping clerks weaved through the crowd while their wealthy merchant masters were carried in sedan chairs to oversee the unloading of barrels of rum, the stacking of timber, the piling of peppers and fruit. Slaves pulled carts laden with jars of molasses. The sickly smell brought back the memory of the transports, the way the sweetness had caught at the back of his throat and mingled horribly with the ash of their smoldering homes. He swallowed heavily to stop from vomiting.

The slaves were as crushed as always, but who were those coffee-colored dandies who were free to parade the quayside with their vividly painted women decked out in spectacular, outlandish, costumes of lace and silk?

The dog barked at them.

"Harlots," hissed his wife, and looked surprised when he laughed.

Beyond the wharf he could see the wide sweep of a levee along the river that curved off into the distance and behind, the tantalizing glimpses of tall white buildings with elegant porticoes, and broad balconies surrounded by flower-filled parks of palm trees and bougainvillea.

He looked across at his old companions. Oliver had told him that of all the survivors on the seven ships only fifty, maybe one or two more, had survived the journey from Boudrot Point to Virginia, to England, and on to the painful disillusion of France. Some had lost their wives or husbands, mothers and fathers, some their children, and all had cause for sorrow, but he and this handful of flotsam and jetsam were still standing.

Why us? he wondered.

Oliver was cleaning his glasses, peering glumly at the sight before him. The money he had been promised by the Coudrenière character had never materialized. It was back to cobbling for him.

"Shouldn't have been so greedy," said Francois, who had shrunk bad temperedly into enfeebled old age. Only his scar, stark against the red rawness of his face, was a reminder of his firebrand days. At 72 he would not be plowing any more fields. Pierre stood gravely surveying the scene, hand in hand with Francoise.

Good man to have with you in a new country, thought Jambo.

Would Charles be there to greet him as he had at Morlaix almost twenty years before? Probably not. His ship had been delayed, waiting for the last of the passengers to arrive when Le Bon Papa set sail. They would have a party when he did arrive though, he was sure of that.

Every day he had tried to put aside the grief he felt at losing Jean-Baptiste and Osite, but he could not. He would never see them again.

And Marguerite. That sweet face disfigured as she lay dying, blood dribbling from her mouth, gasping, gasping for breath. He knew it would soon be over for him too, and that intensified the feelings he had for those he had lost, and those that were still with him on this last voyage. He had been lucky. He had been loved. His name would live on. He pulled the children and Agnes close. He blew his nose and wiped his eyes. "It's the heat," he said to his wife when she looked at him questioningly.

At the foot of the gangplank, in the midst of all the exuberance, a caucus of dignitaries, incongruously formal in their frock coats, waited to greet the 234 passengers.

"Bienvenido a la colonia española de Luisiana," said one of the officials, reaching to steady the man who stumbled as he took the first step onto the quayside. "Welcome to New Orleans." Then in heavily accented French said, "You Caydjuns are welcome to our country."

"Acadians," said Jambo.

"Sí, Cajuns. Bienvenido."

THE END

POSTSCRIPT

Joseph 'dit Jambo' LeBlanc, Agnes and the four children were settled in a parish that came to be called the Manchac Coast on the east side of the Mississippi River, between St. Gabriel and the Spanish settlement of Galveztown.

The records are unclear, but he died either later the same year or the next. He had lived 30 years—more than half his life—in exile.

The memorial to the family in a Chantenay graveyard was cleared in 1851 to make way for the new railway.

CPSIA information can be obtained at www.ICGtesting.com
Printed in the USA
LVOW100212120613

338071LV00018B/1152/P